Spare Change: The Wyattsville S...
AF CRO   17

Midvale Community Library

SPARE CHANGE

The Wyattsville Series – Book One

BETTE LEE CROSBY

D0556177

SPARE CHANGE

Copyright © 2011 by Bette Lee Crosby

Cover design: Damonza.com
Interior formatting by Author E.M.S.

All rights reserved. No part of this publication may be reproduced or transmitted in any form by any means, electronic or mechanical, including photocopy, recording or information storage and retrieval system without permission in writing from the author, except by reviewers who may quote brief passages for a review to be printed in a newspaper, magazine, journal or review blog.

This is a work of fiction. While as in all fiction, the literary perceptions and insights are based on life experiences and conclusions drawn from research. All names, characters, places and specific instances are products of the author's imagination and used fictitiously. No actual reference to any real person, living or dead, is intended or inferred.

ISBN-13: 978-0-983887-91-1

BENT PINE PUBLISHING
Port St. Lucie, FL

Published in the United States of America

For Mom…

Who inspired my love of Southern Storytelling

and taught me to look at life

with a sense of humor.

SPARE CHANGE

The Wyattsville Series – Book One

OLIVIA ANN WESTERLY

I *don't suppose there's a person walking the earth who doesn't now and again think, "If I had the chance to live my life over, I'd sure as hell do it differently." When you get to a certain age and realize how much time you've wasted on pure foolishness, you're bound to smack yourself in the head and ask, What in the world was I thinking? Everybody's got regrets—myself included.*

Some people go to their grave without ever getting a chance to climb out of that ditch they've dug for themselves; others get lucky. Of course, the thing about luck is that you've got to recognize it when it walks up and says hello, the way Charlie Doyle did. But that's a long story, and to understand it you've got to start at the beginning.

COMING OF AGE

At an age when most of her friends had settled into routines of knitting sweaters and booties for grandchildren, Olivia Ann Westerly got married for the first time— to a man ten years her senior. "Are you out of your mind?" Maggie Spence shouted when she heard the news. "You're fifty-eight years old!"

Of course doing the unexpected was something that could be expected of Olivia. In 1923 when she was barely twenty-five years old, she went off on her own even though her father insisted it was scandalous for a single woman to be living alone. "What will people think?" he'd moaned as she tossed her clothes into a cardboard suitcase. But that didn't stop Olivia. She got herself a two-room flat in the heart of downtown Richmond and a job working at the switchboard of the Southern Atlantic Telephone Company. "That's *shift* work!" her father said. "Some of those girls come and go in the dark of night!"

"So what?" Olivia answered. Then she volunteered for the night shift, because it paid an extra sixty cents per day. Long after any respectable woman would have been snuggled beneath a down comforter, she'd paint her mouth with red lipstick, pull on a cloche hat, and trot off to the telephone company.

"Have you never heard of Jack the Ripper?" her friend, Francine Burnam, asked. "Have you never heard stories of women alone being accosted?" Married before her sixteenth birthday, Francine already had three children who clung to her like bananas on a stalk and a husband insistent about supper being served at six-thirty on the dot.

3

"That girl will be the ruination of our family!" Mister Westerly told his wife, but Olivia still stuck her nose in the air and went about her business. A year later when she was given a three-dollar raise and appointed supervisor of the night shift, her father disowned her altogether. The last thing he said was, "I want nothing to do with a girl who carries on as you do. A respectable daughter would be settling down with a husband and babies!"

"I've plenty of time for that," Olivia answered, but by then her father had turned away and refused to look back.

"How much time do you think you have, dear?" her mother asked. "You're twenty-six years old. What man would want to marry a woman of such an age?"

Olivia knew better. With her green eyes and a swirl of honey blond hair curled around her face, she had no shortage of boyfriends. Herbert Flannery, district manager for Southern Atlantic Telephone, had on three different occasions proposed marriage, the last time in the spring of 1929. That particular proposal followed on the heels of the worst winter Richmond had ever seen—months and months of ice crusted to windowpanes, and milk frozen before you could fetch it from the doorstep. In late December Olivia crocheted herself a wool scarf so oversized she could circle it around her throat three times and tuck her nose inside. Although she'd bundle herself in layers of sweaters, boots, and that scarf, she'd come in from the cold with her nose glowing like a stoplight and her feet near frozen. That winter there were few parties and people did very little socializing, so Olivia spent most of her evenings at home swaddled in a chenille bathrobe as she tried to stay warm.

In March, a month when she expected the crocuses to pop up from the ground, there was a six-inch snowfall and the wind rattled the windowpanes so loudly that sleep became impossible. When it seemed that spring would never arrive, Olivia began to question the emptiness of her life. Three weeks later Herbert went down on one knee and offered out a small velvet box. She nodded and allowed him to slip the diamond ring on her finger.

Olivia was genuinely fond of Herbert, and when she promised to marry him it was with the utmost sincerity. But that was before they started to discuss the aspects of their forthcoming life together. "Won't it be wonderful?" she said. "We can walk to work together every day."

Herbert circled his arm around her waist and pulled her to him in a way that tugged her blouse loose from the band of her skirt. "Umm," he hummed in her ear, making the same sound as a bee when it drains the nectar from a flower. "We'll do just that," he cooed, "until you've a bun in the oven."

"Bun in the oven?" she repeated.

Herbert grinned and affectionately patted her stomach. "A baby," he said, giving her a sly wink. "You know, a little tyke. A Herbert Junior."

"I know what it means," she replied testily, "but aren't you rushing things just a bit?"

It was impossible not to notice the downturn of her mouth so Herbert smoothed the situation over by claiming he was, of course, referring to such a time as they were ready for the thought of raising a family. He kissed Olivia, but when she closed her eyes there in back of her eyelids was the image of a woman with the look of hopelessness on her face and a bunch of babies clinging to her skirt. Olivia's eyes popped open, and she snapped her head back. "What if I don't want babies?" she asked rebelliously. "What about my job? There's a good chance I'll be promoted to the central office."

"Babies are something every woman wants," Herbert said. "It's the natural way of life. Men work and women have babies." He gathered her into his arms and held her close. "Don't worry, sweetheart," he whispered. "When the time comes you'll be itching to grab hold of a baby just like every other woman."

Although she let it go at that a feeling of uneasiness started to settle in, and Olivia couldn't dismiss it. Three days later she telephoned both of her older sisters and asked if such a thing was true. Yes, indeed, they'd each answered. She then telephoned her mother and asked the same question. "Of course it's true, sugar," her mother said. "As a young girl I used to imagine that someday I'd be singing at the Opera House in London, England. But after I married your daddy I got the itch, and then along came Robert. The following year it was Albert, and after him Bernice."

"But, Mama," Olivia interrupted, "didn't you think you'd missed out on something you truly wanted?"

"Think?" Her mother laughed. "With eight little tykes hanging on to me, I didn't have time to think!"

It seemed that no matter who she asked it was the same story. "Bounce a baby on your knee, and you'll forget about everything else," Sara Sue said.

"But," Olivia questioned, "weren't you planning to be a newspaper reporter?"

"At one time, maybe," her friend said. "But once Willie came along…"

As the days went by Olivia started to imagine a heavy weight tugging at the hem of her skirt, and at night when she closed her eyes and waited to drift off to sleep she could hear a baby crying. One night she dreamt of sitting at the switchboard with a stomach so large and round that, try as she may, she could not reach across the tandem board far enough to connect a call.

The following Saturday Francine Burnam stopped in for a visit. Eight months ago she had added another one to her litter, and she was accompanied, of course, by all four children, the youngest of them howling like a banshee. "He's teething," Francine apologized and jiggled the baby from one shoulder to the other. Olivia was about to suggest that Alma Porter used a piece of ice to soothe her baby's gums, but before the words were out of her mouth Francine, who already looked like a woman on the edge of a nervous breakdown, started to wail. "Oh, Lord!" She flopped down onto the sofa. "What have I let myself get into?"

"The baby crying has probably gotten you a bit frazzled," Olivia suggested. "Once his tooth comes in, everything will be just fine."

"Fine?" Francine exclaimed. "Fine?! Maybe for you! You've got a job where you're appreciated! Try taking care of four kids, and then see how you feel!"

Olivia was taken aback by the outburst. "But surely Joe helps?" she said.

"Oh, yeah," Francine answered. "He helps—helps himself to a piece of pie and tells the kids to shut up because the noise is giving him a headache. He's got a headache. Ha, that's a joke! He's concerned about his headache, never mind that I'm the one who listens to their carrying on every hour of every day."

"But…"

"That's not even the worst of it! Now that he's got me knocked up with a fifth kid, I find out he's carrying on with some redhead who works in his office. He bought that little whore a fur coat," she moaned. "Imagine that! A fur coat, when I'm wearing dresses older than the kids."

"If I were you, I'd divorce him," Olivia growled.

Francine started to cry even harder. "Oh, yeah," she sobbed, "and just what am I supposed to do with all these kids?" Just then Joe Junior, the eldest of the bunch, punched his brother in the face, and a new level of wailing ensued.

Suddenly Olivia could see the bars of an invisible cage, and she told herself that this was the truth of what happened. First came the itch, then the babies, then a woman was forever locked into a lifetime of drudgery. It happened to Francine, a woman who'd once worn chiffon dresses and polished pink fingernails, a woman who'd read poetry and loved music. It happened because Francine allowed it to happen. She'd donned a white satin gown and pranced down the aisle like a happy cow unknowingly headed for the slaughter house. If it happened to Francine, it could happen to anybody.

Two weeks later Olivia slipped the diamond ring from her finger and returned it to Herbert. She claimed that although she cared for him, marriage was simply out of the question.

"But, sweetheart," he said bewilderedly, "have I offended you? Have I done something to cause such a change of heart?"

"No," she answered. "I've simply come to the realization that marriage and children are not for me." She then kissed poor Herbert and escorted him to the door, saying it was her hope they could remain friends.

"Friends?" Herbert replied, but by then she'd closed the door.

OLIVIA ANN WESTERLY

I told people the thought of being tied down to a man who expected a clean shirt every morning and dinner on the table at the dot of six was something I simply couldn't face. But the real truth of the matter is that I've grown petrified of babies. They look all cute and cuddly in their little pink and blue buntings, but I've seen what they do to women.

Just look at poor Francine, and Alma, and Sara Sue, even my mama. Every single one of them left without dreams, without hopes, bent like apple trees heavy with fruit and yet still expected to bear more. The thought of such a life gives me hives and makes me itch from head to toe. Why on earth, *I ask myself,* would any woman want babies stuck to her like so many leeches.

But even with feeling as I do, I miss Herbert something terrible. Many a lonely evening I've lifted the telephone from its hook when I was on the verge of asking him to come back. Then I remember poor Francine with those five kids hanging onto her. After that I put the telephone back and find myself a book to read. A year after we'd said our goodbyes Herbert married Polly Dobelink. When that happened, I cried for weeks on end.

NEVER TOO OLD

In the years that followed, Olivia had her fair share of suitors. But whenever the issue of marriage came up she'd disappear, leaving them flat as a run-over nickel. That is, until the spring of 1956 when she met Charlie Doyle, a man with silver hair and a powder blue Chevrolet convertible.

Charlie had eyes the color of spring blueberries that were twice as tempting. "Now wouldn't I just love to have *him* slip into my bed on a cold night?" the women of the Wyattsville Social Club whispered to one another. Women who had been married for forty years would start thinking of divorce when they looked at Charlie. Widows showered him with baskets of homemade cookies, then giggled like school girls when he planted a kiss on their cheeks. Some were out-and-out flamboyant in vying for his attention. The Widow Mulligan on more than one occasion indicated that she would be willing to add his name to her sizable savings account were he to ask a certain question. And Gussie Bernhoff, daring as ever-you-please, invited him to spend the night at her apartment. Yes, you could easily say Charlie had everything a man could wish for in Wyattsville. And he probably would not have gone over to Richmond, were it not for his pal Herbert Flannery's retirement party.

As he and Herbert were sipping martinis and reminiscing, Olivia swished by in a rustle of green silk. "Who's that?" Charlie whispered into Herbert's ear.

"Her?" Herbert replied. "Forget her. She's a career woman with no interest whatsoever in men."

"We'll see," Charlie said. Then he marched over and introduced himself. From afar he had believed her to be a woman in her thirties, but close up he could see the cluster of lines crinkling the corners of her green eyes. Of course by then it was already too late. He'd been captured by a smile that made him feel younger than the powder blue convertible did.

Suddenly Charlie developed an overwhelming need for the excitement of Richmond. He began driving to town three times a week, even though it was seventy-seven miles each way. He'd start out thinking he'd go to the museum, or shopping for a new suit, or any of a dozen other destinations, but he'd always end up standing in front of the Southern Atlantic Telephone Company office at the very moment Olivia walked out. "Have you seen the new movie at the Strand?" he'd ask nonchalantly. If she'd already seen the movie, he'd suggest the ballet at the Civic Center or a concert over at the Music Hall. They'd start with dinner, then stroll across the park so engrossed in each other that they took no notice of time. On numerous occasions they missed both the coming attractions and the newsreel, and on one particularly starry evening they missed the entire first act of the ballet.

Olivia was as taken with Charlie as he was with her. A full hour before quitting time, she'd begin to powder her nose and smooth back her hair. She'd get to wondering whether he'd be there and then miss a meeting or forget to post a report that was scheduled to be sent off in the day's mail. In the midst of dictating a letter about employee benefits or training programs, she'd drift off to picturing his smile and the way he'd stroke her face with his fingers. Day after day she walked around with a goofy-looking grin curling the corners of her mouth and her heart beating three times faster than usual. "It must be love," the office clericals whispered to one another. Oblivious to their gossip, Olivia simply continued to float around, looking happy as a Fourth of July parade.

This continued for three months until one night in late July. After a particularly romantic evening at the Starlight Lounge Charlie, lost in the green of her eyes, blurted out a proposal. "Marry me," he said at the very moment she was about to swallow a chocolate truffle.

Olivia gasped with such a huge intake of air that the chocolate became lodged in her throat. "Well?" Charlie said as she sat there turning red-faced. When the chocolate melted to the size of a penny and slid down her throat, she told him that she was a bit shaken and needed to go home.

"But what about marrying me?" Charlie asked.

"We'll talk about it next time," she answered ruefully.

Looking square into the face of possible rejection, Charlie was flabbergasted. He sputtered, "You mean to say you're undecided?"

Olivia wished she didn't have to say anything. She wished they could go on day after day, week after week, year after year, never asking any more of each other, never mentioning the one thing that ruined every relationship. She found it virtually impossible to look into his eyes with what she had to say, so she fixed her gaze fixed on a single truffle—a truffle that had fallen from the edge of the plate, a truffle that stood as alone as she herself. "I'm sorry, Charlie," she mumbled tearfully. "If I were going to marry anyone it would be you. But I'm simply not a marrying woman."

As the words fell from her mouth she could feel her heart breaking, shattering into a hundred million pieces, each smaller than even a grain of sand. She loved Charlie more than she'd ever loved any man before. *Why?* her heart was screaming. *Why does falling in love always have to end this way?*

"Not a marrying woman?" Charlie repeated. "What's that supposed to mean?"

"I've never been one to fit the mold. Cooking, cleaning, babies—it's just too much dependency. It smothers a woman and takes the fullness of life from her."

"Babies?" Charlie echoed. "Who said anything about babies?"

Her answer was one she had stored away in her head. It hadn't been called upon for years. It had grown old and dusty and obsolete. But she hauled it out nonetheless. "I realize that, given your age, babies might not be a thing of foremost concern, but," she sighed, "who knows what might happen in the future?"

"I'm sixty-eight! Why, it would be *impossible* for me to father a baby! Besides, I wouldn't want one—not even if it came in a solid gold wrapper!"

Olivia blinked, brought to the reality of what Charlie was saying. "You're certain?"

"I only want you. I want us to sleep in the same bed and make love. If you don't want to cook, we'll eat in restaurants. If you don't want to clean, we'll sweep the dirt under the rug and get on with our life."

"No children?"

"Children? Absolutely not! I've got one, and he's no bargain."

"You've got a little boy?"

"He's hardly a boy. Benjamin's thirty-seven—old enough to know he ought to visit his dad now and then—but he doesn't. I haven't seen him for over fifteen years."

"Grandchildren?" she asked, her eyes lovingly locked onto his face.

"Benjamin and Susanna have a son," Charlie answered wistfully. "The lad's name is Ethan Allen, but I've never even met him."

❦

The following Friday Charlie slipped a diamond ring on Olivia's finger, and much to everyone's surprise it stayed there. And as if that weren't enough of a shocker, Olivia then announced she was going to give up her job of thirty years and move to Wyattsville. "I've heard tell it's a wonderful community," she told her friends, "and Charlie has an apartment on the seventh floor of a building that does not allow children."

The announcement generated an endless amount of gossip among Olivia's friends and co-workers. The girls in the typing pool suggested he might be after her money or, worse yet, be planning to take out a sizeable insurance policy then do her in. "What do we know about him?" they'd ask each other, but the answer was generally nothing more than a furrowed brow and a shrug of the shoulders.

Herbert Flannery, dumbfounded by the turn of events, went out and bought himself a powder blue convertible, then took to coloring his hair shoe-polish black.

Mabel Cunningham, a woman who had known Olivia since high school, claimed she'd heard rumors of Charlie being a philanderer.

"Not likely," Francine Burnam said as she stuck a pacifier into her grandbaby's mouth. Her daughter had recently divorced a ne'er-do-well husband and returned home to Mama with the infant and two toddlers. "Olivia's too smart to be taken in by someone like that," Francine sighed wistfully.

Even the boy who bagged groceries at the A & P seemed to be boggled by the sight of her new diamond ring. "*You're* engaged?" he said. Then he stood there staring at her while a ripe cantaloupe rolled off the end of the counter and splattered on the floor.

None of this bothered Olivia as she strolled around town shopping for a trousseau and looking every bit the prospective bride. She never noticed how shopkeepers would cover their mouth and giggle when she asked to see bridal veils and blue garters. She paid no attention when Alma suggested rethinking retirement, and she laughed out loud when Mabel said she ought to have Charlie investigated by a private detective.

❦

On the third Saturday in October Olivia Ann Westerly knew what sort of day it was long before she opened her eyes. She'd imagined the sound of wedding bells in a dream that ended far too soon, and she'd caught the fragrance of jasmine even though it was long past the season for such a flower to be blooming. It was a morning that dawned with a sun warm enough for anyone to believe it mid-August—a morning when crows had the sound of songbirds and flowerbeds overflowed with blooms. A morning, no doubt, that was an omen of good things to come.

Olivia had always been a person given to superstition, and by the time she turned twelve she had learned to understand omens—both good and bad. She avoided stepping on sidewalk cracks, covered her eyes if she saw a black cat, and never, ever, planned anything important on the eleventh day of the month. Experience had taught her that if anything bad was going to happen, it was going to happen on the eleventh. She'd kept that in mind when they selected a date for the wedding. Now, on this most glorious of all mornings, she had not a care in the world—the eleventh of October had already come and gone, and it would be almost a full month before she'd have to face another one.

While the coffee perked, she hummed "Here Comes the Bride" and painted her toenails pink. They'd be honeymooning in Miami Beach, and as she frolicked barefoot in the sand she hoped Charlie would take notice. Once they were back in their bedroom suite overlooking the ocean, she could imagine him kissing her toes one by one. "My bride," he'd whisper. "Angel of my dreams." A shiver ran along her spine as Olivia thought back on how she'd foolishly wasted all those years avoiding marriage; in actuality it was something that made a person feel truly wonderful. *Thank goodness I've come to my senses,* she told herself.

As Olivia sat before the mirror and applied her make-up, she could

13

swear years had disappeared from her face. The wrinkles that had come to be all too familiar were strangely enough missing, as were a few dark splotches and the droop of her cheeks. Her eyes were greener than she had ever known them to be: blazingly brilliant, the color of a blade of grass on the first day of spring. Quite obviously marriage was something that agreed with a woman of any age.

When the knock she had been waiting for came, Olivia whooshed open the door with such enthusiasm that she toppled over the potted philodendron that had been standing in the very same spot for almost twenty years. "Hi," she whispered breathlessly. She then slipped her hand into the crook of Charlie's arm and strolled out the door, leaving the shattered pot and a pile of dirt strewn across the floor.

⊱─✦─⊰

At Christ the Lord Church throngs of well-wishers filled the pews and spilled out into the vestibule. Francine Burnam had arrived late due to a babysitting problem, but she was standing outside the door dressed in a flowered hat and billowing voile dress. "Warm, isn't it?" she commented as the man alongside of her mopped his brow. Inside the church, ladies were fanning themselves and men were discreetly loosening their ties. The day had been forecasted to be in the mid-seventies, but before noon the temperature soared to eighty-six degrees. Olivia hardly noticed the heat. Yes, she felt the beads of perspiration settling on the back of her neck but attributed it to the anxiety of a first-time bride. As other women blew tiny puffs of breath downward to cool their bosoms, she clasped a bouquet of scarlet roses and marched down the aisle alongside Charlie.

The first clattering boom came just as Pastor Perkins asked if anyone knew of a reason why these two people should not be joined in holy matrimony. *Oh dear,* Olivia thought, *I hope it's not going to rain.* Any other time she might have considered it an omen, but on this particular day with nothing but thoughts of love floating through her head such a notion was nonexistent.

"I now pronounce you husband and wife," Pastor Perkins said. Just then a second roll of thunder erupted, one so loud it rattled the church windows and set the steeple bell to chiming. "You may now kiss the bride," the pastor told Charlie, but before the couple could lock themselves in an embrace a barrage of hail began pelting the building. As the scattering of people who'd been standing outside to escape the heat pushed into the vestibule, a ball of ice came barreling through the stained glass window and shattered a scene depicting the birth of Baby Jesus.

"You don't suppose…," a wide-eyed Olivia asked. Charlie smiled, shook his head, then went right ahead and kissed her.

"Hail's caused by hot air rising up and colliding with cold air," he whispered as they turned and walked back down the aisle. "It's a natural phenomenon, nothing to worry about." He gave a reassuring smile and tightened his hand around hers.

Despite Charlie's seemingly logical explanation, Olivia checked both their wristwatches to make certain the window hadn't shattered during some lingering minute of the eleventh hour. Luckily, it was twenty-five minutes past twelve. She breathed a sigh of relief and slipped back into the euphoric feeling of a woman in love.

After a reception of champagne and wedding cake they went back to Olivia's apartment, loaded the last few cartons of her belongings into the back seat of the blue convertible, and headed for Wyattsville.

Olivia Ann Doyle

*W*hen people start prattling on about how marrying a man with Charlie Doyle's reputation is opening myself up to heartache, I feel like laughing in their face. Heartache? A lot they know! Heartache would be seeing him walk away. I don't give a navy bean about the fact that he's had dozens of other women. All that's done with now.

I've done my own share of dating, but let me tell you, there's never been a man who makes me feel the way Charlie does. I can say flat out I am crazy in love with him. Charlie heats up such a fire in me I get red-cheeked just thinking how he stretches a line of kisses down the back of my neck.

Still, such talk can make any woman wonder whether or not she's doing the right thing. So two weeks before the wedding I went and had my fortune told.

I'm about to marry Mister Doyle, *I said to the gypsy,* and need to know if he's a man who will love me forever. *Keeping that question in mind, she had me pull a card from the deck, and then she laid a crisscross of other cards alongside of it. Right off she said the cards showed I had a terrible dislike of anything having to do with the number eleven. Well, I was about to explain it was with good reason, but before I got a word out she pointed to the card with a picture of eleven cups and said one was tilted to the sky, which meant the number eleven would someday bring a blessing. Not likely, I thought. But still, there was something about the woman—the way her eyes looked right past me and focused in on things from another time. It's said that only gypsies have the true gift of looking at a person and seeing their future, so I was happy as a red hen when she said a man named Doyle would be loving me for the whole of my life and then some.*

Could a woman ask for any more than that?

A DINNER TO DIE FOR

Charlie's apartment had the look and feel of a bachelor's place. *Esquire* magazines stacked high on the end table. Pipes scattered about a wooden rack meant to contain them. Overstuffed chairs with the indentation of his behind still in them. Despite all of this, Olivia began to think of the place as home the minute she entered. She hung her dresses in the closet, set her perfume bottles on the bureau, and placed her toothbrush in the bathroom holder alongside Charlie's.

"Don't bother doing that stuff right now," Charlie said. He circled his arms around her, playfully tugged her blouse loose from the waistband of her skirt, and slid his hands across the bare skin of her back. "First things first," he whispered and pressed her tight to his chest.

Olivia felt the thumping of his heart. It was synchronized to precisely match the beat of hers. Love you, the hearts drummed. Love you, love you, love you. Charlie eased open the row of buttons on her blouse and kissed her neck. He continued for a good long while, and then led her to the bedroom. Twining themselves together they climbed into bed, and he kissed her in every spot imaginable. Then in the bright of day, with the sun shining in on them, they made love. While other husbands were watching the final innings of a baseball game and housewives were basting a roasted chicken, they fell deeper and deeper in love.

This was a day more special than anything Olivia had ever dreamed. It was a day to be forever held in memory, a day that she would keep for all the years of her life. Trying to hold onto the moment she took the bedside clock, turned it face down, and buried it in the bottom of a drawer.

But hiding time is not a thing that will slow it. Moment by moment the sun slid behind the horizon as a dusky twilight settled into the sky. When the sky was black as a raven's eye and only minutes of their wedding day remained, Olivia suggested they jump into the blue convertible and start for Miami Beach that very night. But as fate would have it, Charlie's friends had arranged a round of parties in their honor. "When they've gone to all this trouble," he explained, "it would downright rude for us to not attend." She agreed, although somewhat reluctantly.

For the next five days Charlie squired a smiling Olivia from place to place, introducing her to the ladies of the Wyattsville Social Club. "It broke our hearts when an outsider stole our Charlie away," Emily Carter whispered jokingly. Barbara MacIntyre made a similar comment. The Widow Mulligan latched on to Olivia's arm and started asking about the secret for capturing such an eligible bachelor.

"Secret?" Olivia asked. "There's no secret. I simply fell in love with him."

"Love?" Widow Mulligan replied. "At your age?"

Six days after the wedding Charlie carted four suitcases downstairs and packed them into the trunk of his blue convertible. He tucked a road map into the glove compartment and slid behind the wheel. Then he and Olivia headed for Miami Beach, Florida. "We'll take our time," he told her. "Drive seven hours or so, and then stop for the night. By Monday we'll be sunning ourselves on the beach."

Olivia, a bit nervous about travelling such a distance in a convertible, counted up the number of days they'd be on the road: three. *Fine,* she thought, figuring that would bring them to the ninth day of their marriage. By the eleventh day they would have arrived safely in Miami Beach. She smiled and snuggled closer to Charlie, contemplating the three overnight stays at quaint little roadside inns.

The first night they stopped in Fayetteville, North Carolina. They'd driven the full length of the road looking for a place to stay—a Cozy Inn or Honeymoon Haven—but the only spot with a room available was Sleep Planet, a motel fashioned after a space ship. "It's not what I'd imagined," Olivia said, her lower lip quivering.

Charlie took hold of her and kissed her in such a way that the lopsided bed seemed somehow to level itself, and the worn spot on the carpet became nearly invisible. "Once we get to Miami Beach," he whispered, "we'll spend fourteen days at the Fontainebleau. Now *there's* a place you're gonna love."

Love? Olivia didn't need another thing to love—she had Charlie. What more could a woman ask? He was a man who watched out for her, did things to please her, saw to her needs. Finding a man such as Charlie was the reason that she, a person who had never relied on a soul other than herself, had fallen head over heels in love. "A woman doesn't need to love the place she sleeps," she said as they climbed into bed, "when she's so in love with the man sleeping alongside of her."

The second night they stopped in Georgia. The next day the car began overheating, and they had to make numerous stops. At the end of the third day, they'd only gone as far as Jacksonville. Even though they'd crossed into Florida, it was another three hundred miles to reach their destination. No longer fussy about where they bedded down, Olivia said, "If you're weary of driving, we can honeymoon right here."

"Nonsense," he answered. "I promised you two weeks in Miami Beach, and that's what you're going to get."

"If you're sure…" She noticed a bit of weariness around his eyes.

When they finally arrived at the Fontainebleau on Tuesday, the tenth day of their marriage, the spasm knotting Olivia's back relaxed a bit. "See?" Charlie said. "I told you there was nothing to worry about."

Olivia knew better. Tomorrow would be the eleventh day. Regardless of what the gypsy had said anything could happen. One of them could drown in the swimming pool or get a severe sunburn or possibly be mugged by some drunken sailor. "I don't know about you," she told Charlie, "but I am thoroughly exhausted. Let's just stay in bed all day tomorrow. We'll order room service and enjoy the view from our window."

"Yes, indeed," he said with the slyest of winks. "That sounds good to me."

So on the eleventh day of their marriage they did just that. In the morning they ordered up a tray of bacon and eggs. At noon they called down for sandwiches, and in the evening the tuxedoed waiter delivered a cart with chilled champagne and candles. After drinking such a sizeable amount of champagne, Olivia could barely open her eyes the next morning. But when she did, the first thing that came to mind was that the eleventh day of their marriage had come and gone without disaster. She bounded out of bed, ready, she claimed, for a dip in the pool.

Day after day they swam in the pool, warmed their toes in the sand, and walked along the beach. They dressed in their finest clothes and dined in restaurants with crystal candlesticks and starched tablecloths. Every evening they drank glasses of dark red burgundy and toasted their love. "Here's to us," they'd say, reminding themselves how fortuitous it was that they'd found each other.

On their eleventh day in Miami, Olivia suggested they play it safe—avoid the swimming pool with its ten feet of water where a person could drown, skip the beach where sand crabs and jelly fish could attach themselves to a person's skin, stay out of the sun that could quickly blister any spot not slathered with sunscreen. Charlie could almost swear there was a bucket of salt water sloshing around in his left ear and agreed. So they held hands, strolled along Collins Avenue, and shopped the boutiques. Olivia bought tee shirts in every imaginable color, sunglasses circled with rhinestone trim, three ceramic flamingos, and a conch shell with a dolphin painted on the side of it. On the way back to the hotel she spied another souvenir stand and claimed that she had to stop for some postcards to send to the girls at the Southern Atlantic Telephone Company.

Charlie had had enough of looking at such bric-a-brac and claimed he'd prefer to wait outside. While standing in the shade of a green awning fanned out across the front of the True Love Jewelry Shoppe, he noticed a display of necklaces hanging in the window and in he went. Twenty minutes later, when Olivia came out with two ashtrays and a handful of postcards, he was holding a small white bag in his hand.

"What's that?" she asked.

"You'll find out soon enough," he said with a grin.

That evening after he'd zipped the back of her dress, Charlie told Olivia to close her eyes. When she did, he fastened the pendant he'd bought around her neck. He placed her in front of the mirror and then said, "Okay, now you can look."

With her untold number of superstitions, Olivia gave a gasp of horror when she saw the pendant. "It's an *opal!*" she said. "Opals bring bad luck. Last year a woman wearing an opal ring was found dead in a ditch."

"Nonsense," Charlie said. "That was just a coincidence."

"Oh, really? What about Kathleen Riley? She bought a pair of opal earrings, and her house burned to the ground the very next day!"

"Things like that happen."

Were it not for the fact that Charlie had hung the pendant around her neck with the most genuine look of love in his eyes, Olivia would have ripped it off and dropped in right into the wastebasket. Were it not for the fact that they were on their honeymoon, she would have hidden the treacherous piece of jewelry in the darkest corner of some cupboard. But as fate would have it, she obligingly wore the pendant to dinner.

Halfway through the lobster bisque, Charlie said he felt a touch of indigestion coming on. Without another word he collapsed and fell forward into the bowl of soup.

SUSANNA DOYLE

*W*hen *I married Benjamin I never figured to live the life of Riley, but I did believe we'd move to New York City so I could make something of myself. It ain't like I lied about my ambition. Right off I told him,* I got singing talent but I need to be in New York where there's opportunities. *I was working in the shipyard then, making real good money. But Benjamin, who can be a real charmer when he wants to, says for me to quit my job because we're gonna get married and he's gonna take care of me. He didn't say word one about moving off to some God-forsaken farm where there ain't nobody but chickens and pigs to hear me sing.*

I know I got a real good voice. Everybody says so. At least, everybody who's ever heard me sing. But stuck in this backwoods dump, I got no chance of being discovered. Benjamin, *I keep saying,* if I ever hope to have a singing career, I have got to get to New York City! *I suppose I could talk 'til the moon turns blue, but the only thing that ever comes of it is me and Benjamin having the same old fight.*

ON THE EASTERN SHORE OF VIRGINIA

In a place where irrigation canals snake across flat stretches of farmland and a scream can drift for miles before anyone hears it, Susanna Doyle told Benjamin she was leaving him. It wasn't the first time she'd said such a thing, nor was it the first time he'd answered, "Like hell you are!"

Theirs was a fight that had gone on for years. It was raging long before Ethan Allen was born. It began three days after she stood in front of a Justice of the Peace in Bethlehem, Pennsylvania and swore that she'd love, honor, and obey Benjamin for the rest of her natural life. She did none of the three. The ink on their marriage certificate was not yet dry when Susanna took to saying she thought she'd made a mistake. "I thought we was gonna move to New York City," she'd moan. "I thought we was gonna live in a place where a singer has opportunities!"

Benjamin was so crazy in love with the curve of her body and the shank of dark hair tumbling down her back that he deafened his ears to such talk. The first time she threatened to leave, he placated her with a fancy dress he special ordered from Sears. After that it was an imitation sapphire ring. Then it was some perfume and lacy lingerie. When he came home with a ruby-colored satin nightgown, she threw it back into his face. "I don't want this crap!" she screamed. "I want to go to New York City!"

Had she asked for a simple thing such as the moon or all the stars in the heavens, Benjamin would have turned himself inside out to get it for her. But as for going to New York, such a thing was not possible. Susanna was a woman who would be blinded by the bright lights of Broadway. She would be drawn away from him just as a moth is drawn from the safety of darkness to the brilliance of a flame. She'd spend her days tromping from audition to audition, allowing men with fat cigars and hairy hands to paw her beautiful body. In time her face would take on the tawdriness of the city, and the song in her throat would sound bitter as the croaking of a frog.

It seemed to Benjamin that Susanna should understand the pitfalls of such a life, but instead of being grateful for the way he looked after her she screamed at him, threw tantrums, heaved heavy glass pitchers at his head, and set her lips into a pout. "I'm suffocating out here!" she'd shout. "There's no excitement, nothing to do but watch those damned soybeans grow!"

When she finally turned her back on him in bed and curled herself into a ball so he couldn't touch her breasts or find his way inside of her body, he agreed to take her to New York City. "Just for a vacation," he said. "After the winter harvest, we'll go for a three-week vacation."

Throughout that entire fall Susanna danced from room to room singing songs into the bowl of a wooden spoon. She'd stand on the front porch and belt out "Boogie-woogie Bugle Boy" to an audience of sunflowers or climb atop the kitchen table and take bow after bow. "I'm good as any of those Andrews Sisters," she'd say. "I just need to get discovered!" In the middle of planting a row of soy beans Benjamin would come to the house for a drink of water, and there she'd be wriggling through the living room in a brassiere and panties. "You think Maxine Andrews can do this?" she'd ask. Then she'd shake and shimmy until every inch of flesh on her body was quivering. She'd start in a standing position, but before she was done she'd be down on her knees with her back arched in a way that caused her bosoms to bust loose of the brassiere. Afterward she'd throw her arms around Benjamin's neck and kiss him with such passion that it brought about love-making.

Mid-morning on a Wednesday in early November Benjamin got to thinking about Susanna in her red lace brassiere, so he stopped working on the tractor and went looking for her. Instead of singing into a spoon she was in the bathroom with her head hanging over the toilet. "Those pork chops we had last night must've been spoiled," she groaned.

Benjamin dipped a washcloth in cold water and held it to her head. "I don't see how that's possible," he said. "I ate a plateful and I'm feeling fine. Matter of fact, I was thinking you might want to slip on that lacy brassiere—"

"Asshole!" she said, and then went back to puking in the toilet bowl.

By afternoon Susanna was feeling fine, so she raised the window and hollered for Benjamin to come back into the house. When he walked through the door there she was, atop the kitchen table, wearing a pair of red high heel pumps and a little bitty apron tied around her waist—and not another stitch. "You still in the mood?" she asked, then slid down and wrapped her legs around his neck.

That's how it was with her. Benjamin never knew from minute to minute whether she'd be crawling up the leg of his pants or jumping down his throat. Why, just the thought of such a woman in New York City scared him to pieces. Anything could happen there. He could fall asleep thinking everything was just as it should be and then wake to find she'd run off with some agent or songwriter. He could go out for a newspaper, return, and discover her in bed with the elevator man. Even worse, she could disappear without a trace. Trot off into some dark alley and never be heard from again. Benjamin began to think going to New York, even if it was only for a vacation, was definitely a bad idea.

That evening when they sat down to a supper of fried chicken and dumplings, he told her he'd changed his mind about New York City. "I'll take you to Norfolk or Virginia Beach," he said. "Those are fine vacation spots."

"Virginia Beach!" Susanna screamed. "In the dead of winter?"

"Okay, we'll go to Norfolk. Shop, eat in fancy restaurants, see a show."

"See a show? Watch another woman who got discovered? Some vacation that would be!" She pleaded for Benjamin to change his mind. "I've got talent," she sobbed. "I could be somebody."

"You are somebody," he answered. "You're my wife. It seems like that ought to be enough for a woman."

"Well, it's not!" Susanna shouted. Then she overturned the bowl of dumplings into his lap and ran crying to the bedroom. Benjamin followed after her, but she'd slammed the door and twisted the lock. That's when he decided that if he was to hold on to his wife, he'd have to trick her into staying there on the Eastern Shore of Virginia.

The next morning Susanna was sick again. "See what you've done," she said. "All that talk of canceling our vacation has upset my system."

With his eyes averted from her face Benjamin answered, "I didn't say we'd never go, I just said this wasn't the right time."

Susanna's face brightened.

He watched her from the corner of his eye. "New York winters are bitter cold," he said. "I've heard tell the temperature drops below zero, and the wind can freeze a person's tongue if they open their mouth long enough to ask directions. You think any talent scouts are gonna be out in weather like that?"

She sat down alongside him and slid her hand onto his thigh. "Can we go to New York in the spring?" she asked.

"Late spring, early summer—depends on what needs doing around here." He tugged loose the strap of her nightgown. "And whether or not you're being a good girl." He gathered a rough handful of her breast, but before he could slide himself into her Susanna became sick again and went running to the bathroom.

Three weeks later when Doctor Kelly told her she was pregnant with a baby due to be born the third week of May, Susanna flew into a rage of crying and hollering the likes of which the nurses had never seen. Barbara Ann Taylor, who had snow white hair and thirty years nursing experience, tried to calm her by saying how a wonderful little baby was well worth all the pain and suffering of childbirth. That's when Susanna heaved a tray full of sterilized instruments across the room. "You think a baby's so wonderful," she told Barbara Ann, "then you can have it!" Susanna begged and pleaded with Doctor Kelly to do something to get rid of the baby, but of course he said such a thing was against the law. "They do it all the time in China," she sobbed.

Benjamin was delighted with the news. Not because he was wishing for a baby, but because it seemed to be just the thing to prevent Susanna from running off to New York. "No talent scout's gonna be looking for singers the size of a milk cow," he'd said. Then he ducked when she hurled a pitcher of orange juice in his direction. Susanna was always quick to show her anger, and that winter was worse than most. She broke the kitchen window three different times, smashed an entire set of dishes, and flushed her wedding ring down the toilet.

In February she started to retain water and her feet swelled up to the size of melons and throbbed if she dared to stand for longer than a half-hour, which meant she had to quit her job at the furniture store. Although she'd sold only one maple sofa and three lamps in eighteen months the manager, who it was rumored had a weakness for attractive women, had given her five raises. Once she was no longer working in town, Susanna grew more foul-tempered and quicker than ever to fly off the handle. "What kind of a career can a singer expect to have with a kid hanging onto her?" she'd scream.

The baby was ten days late in coming, and when it finally arrived it was with a tearing and ripping apart of her flesh. Susanna kicked at the doctors and screamed profanities that bruised the nurses' ears. "I can't stand it anymore!" she cried. "Get this fucking thing out of me!"

Even after Doctor Kelly announced that she had delivered a fine healthy boy, Susanna continued to call the baby "it." "Start it on formula," she said. "I'm not about to have my tits look like a litter of pups has been sucking them dry!" She was in the hospital for three days, and not once did she cross over to the nursery to see the baby.

As she was getting dressed to come home, a nurse came into the room and handed her a copy of the birth certificate. "How can he have a birth certificate?" Benjamin asked. "He's not even been named."

"He's got a name," the nurse answered.

"He has?" Benjamin picked up the birth certificate and read it. "Shit, almighty!" he growled, after reading the boy's name. "You named the kid after that fucking furniture store?!"

Susanna laughed like a person satisfied with the results of a practical joke. "Maybe I can sell him," she said. "Like that maple sofa."

That's how it was the boy came to be called Ethan Allen. Once Susanna came home from the hospital, she ignored the child altogether and spent her days crying. She'd wake in the morning, then slide right back under the bedcover and pick up where she'd left off the night before. "Why me?" she'd howl. "Why me?"

For the first three months of his life, Ethan Allen screamed longer and harder than did Susanna. It seemed he was always hungry or wet or at times crying for no apparent reason. Despite his rough hands and lack of tolerance, Benjamin was the one who heated the bottles of formula and changed diapers. Once the baby had been fed and dried, Benjamin would drop him into his crib and hurry off to a bunch of soy beans that needed planting. "We're never going to New York if you don't get your ass out of bed and see to this baby," he'd tell Susanna, and then he'd beat it out the door before she let go of a string of profanities.

The first time she held the baby was one morning in late September. An early frost had covered the ground, and Benjamin, fearing the worst, rushed off without feeding the boy. Ethan Allen howled like a tomcat for three hours until Susanna finally went to him. "You gonna keep squalling forever?" she said, lifting the baby into her arms. The crying stopped immediately. "Ornery little cuss. Hell bent on getting your way, ain't you?" She grinned. "Just like your mama." After that Susanna found she could tolerate the baby and, at times, even love him. "You got eyes like Mama," she'd coo, then drop him into the crib and head off to the beauty parlor in town.

Benjamin had hoped having a baby would settle Susanna down, make her forget the nonsense about a singing career. Of course, it didn't. "When are we gonna take that trip to New York?" she'd ask. "I've heard tell Radio City Music Hall is hiring some new Rockettes." Once a thought like that got into her head, she'd work on her singing for days on end. Ethan Allen would be wanting his oatmeal, but she'd be dancing atop the coffee table in her panties and a lace brassiere.

"You gonna feed this kid?" Benjamin would ask, but she'd keep right on singing into the bowl of a wooden spoon and gyrating like there was an eggbeater caught inside of her. "Some kind of mother you are!" he'd growl and turn off in disgust. Still, when the darkness of night rolled around he'd feel the same old fire of wanting in his belly. "Come on over here," he'd say. "Make Daddy happy."

The first year Benjamin held off going to New York by claiming she'd have to get back in shape if she was to attract a talent scout. "Those Rockettes don't have an ounce of fat on them," he told her. That whole summer Susanna ate nothing but spinach and lettuce. She'd spy a Hershey bar and a line of drool would drizzle down onto her chin, but she stuck to the spinach and lettuce. She grew to be so thin that her eyes sunk back into her face until they appeared to be sitting on a ledge of cheekbone, and her arms became smaller around than those of Ethan Allen. Finally, when Susanna was too weak for lovemaking, Benjamin said he thought she'd taken the dieting a bit too far and suggested they postpone the trip until she got some meat back on her bones. The second year he insisted the boy was still too young to travel. The third year there was a problem with the crops. The fourth he had something else worrying his mind. Year after year he found an excuse to cancel the trip to New York, which was, of course, the reason for most of their arguments.

"I'm suffocating out here!" she'd wail. "I want more than just you and this kid."

Benjamin would answer, "You got a fine house, a kid, and a man who loves you! What more does a woman need?" Before the evening was out she'd be hurling cook pots at him or screaming profanities that caught hold of the wind and traveled far beyond the neighboring farms. Sometimes, in a town miles down the road, men would swear the voice had been that of their wife who was washing dishes in the next room.

Ethan Allen grew up with such sounds taking root in the canals of his ears. Before his first birthday he'd become so accustomed to the arguments that in the midst of a free-for-all he could nap peacefully. He'd sit there in the floor and not twitch a muscle when a piece of crockery sailed by and splattered against the wall. The first word the boy ever spoke was "damn" and the second was "hungry." While he was still small enough to be suckling milk from a bottle, he'd toddle along behind Susanna saying, "Damn kid hungry, Mama."

"See what you've done," Benjamin would moan. "The kid thinks that's his name."

"Oh, and I suppose you're not to fault!" she'd answer.

By the time the boy was three he'd learned to fix his own peanut butter and jelly sandwiches. He'd also learned that when the breadbox was empty he could drag a stepstool across the kitchen, scramble up onto the counter, and reach into the cupboard for a box of dry cereal. "That's my little man," Susanna would say and plant a kiss on his forehead as she headed off to town. At an age when most children are cautioned against playing with matches, Ethan Allen would light the stove and fry up an egg.

Susanna considered the boy's ability to fend for himself an admirable trait. "You ought to be more like Ethan Allen," she'd tell Benjamin. "You don't see *him* counting on me for every little thing!"

"A woman's supposed to do for her husband," Benjamin would answer in return, which inevitably led to the screaming of insults back and forth. They'd fight about almost anything they found at hand— things as inconsequential as a missing button or unmade bed. The arguments most always ended with Benjamin leading her off to the bedroom and closing the door behind him. "Slip into that lacy brassiere," he'd say, and she'd do it. Once she could feel the heat of his breath curling into her ear, feel the hunger of his hands groping her body, Susanna would elicit yet another promise of a trip to New York.

The year Ethan Allen turned eight everything changed. The promises wore thin, and Susanna began to doubt that she would ever see New York City. Despite her husband's objections she got a job working in the cosmetic department of Woolworth's. Every morning she'd pull on a skirt that was way too short and head into town. Benjamin would see neither hide nor hair of her until six hours after the store had closed for the evening. "Where the hell have you been?" he'd scream. "What about dinner?"

"Oh, please!" Susanna would groan, then turn her back to him and start fussing with some stray hair that had fallen out of place. "Ethan's got the good sense to fix up something when he's hungry," she'd sigh. "Seems like you could do the same."

"It's not my place!" he'd storm. "A wife's got responsibilities! You ought to be seeing to the needs of me and this boy!" Benjamin would gesture to a chair that, as it turned out, was empty, and then he'd wonder aloud where in the hell the boy had gone to.

Ethan Allen knew when trouble was coming. He knew that when his mama's car came rolling up the drive long after dark there'd be hell to pay. Given his daddy's shortness of temper, there'd for sure be name calling and screaming. If his mama wanted to she could sweet-talk her way out of anything. But if she was in the mood to start heaving dishes across the room there could be fisticuffs—the kind that sometimes ended with her having a black eye and Benjamin sleeping on the sofa. Nights such as that Ethan Allen hung around, tried to smooth things over. "Here, Daddy," he'd say, "I made you a sandwich. Cheese with mayonnaise, like you like." After that he'd sidle up to Susanna and whisper something about how Benjamin's bad temper was his way of worrying. "Daddy don't mean nothing by it," he'd say. "He loves you, Mama, he surely does." On a good day his parents could end up laughing and tickling each other. On a bad day there was no telling what would happen. Those nights the only thing the boy could do was sneak out with a flashlight and a Captain Marvel comic book, wait until things quieted down, then tiptoe back through the kitchen door.

Some nights it never quieted down, and when the sun came up they'd still be screaming insults at each other. Other nights he'd find the back door locked and have to sleep on the porch curled up alongside Dog, a stray that Susanna had lugged home one night when she'd claimed to have car trouble and stayed out until almost dawn. "Here, sweetie," she'd said and handed the dog to Ethan Allen. "This cute little fella's your birthday present."

The dog was as far from cute as possible. He was wobbly-legged and bad tempered with most everybody. "What's his name?" Ethan Allen asked.

"Dog," Susanna answered laughingly. Then minutes later all hell broke loose because Benjamin claimed he didn't believe for one second that she'd had car trouble.

"You think I'm stupid?" he screamed. "You think I got no idea of what you're up to?"

With never knowing which way the wind was gonna blow Ethan Allen figured he ought to have a hideout, a place to go on nights when there was no appeasing anybody. That's when he starting building the fort. First a hammer disappeared from the tool chest; then a good-sized sheet of aluminum and some wood Benjamin was planning to use for repairs. After that the large black tarpaulin used to cover the tractor vanished with not a trace, and then it was a shag rug that for years had been right there in the hallway. Cans of food began to be missing, a whole pound of weenies, blankets, a pillow, even the portable radio Benjamin claimed was nowhere to be found.

"Ethan Allen, you know anything about this?" Susanna asked.

"Me?" he said. "I'm just a kid, why you asking me?"

Susanna hitched her mouth up on one side and glared at him in a most suspicious manner. "Seems to me you know something," she said.

Just then Ethan Allen remembered his chores and scooted through the back door but, coincidentally, the disappearing of things suddenly came to an end. "I know you're up to something, boy," Benjamin said several times. Yet he never noticed that less than fifty yards from the house behind a stand of Douglas Firs was a lean-to covered with a black tarpaulin. He never noticed that late at night when the only sound he should have heard was the chirping of crickets, he could listen carefully and hear the sound of a baseball game being played at Memorial Stadium in Baltimore.

ETHAN ALLEN DOYLE

*M*ama is easier to love than Daddy. He's got a real serious nature and yells a lot. But Mama, she'll carry on and act a fool 'til we're laughing so hard our sides are likely to split open. Daddy usually starts cussing up a storm when she does that, because he figures she's making fun at his expense.

That's how Mama is. She's always getting into some kind of trouble. Mama needs somebody to stick up for her, and who else is there but me?

One time I asked Mama if Daddy was mad at her because of me; you know, because of how I don't mind so good. But she said Daddy's trouble was that he was just born in a pissed-off mood. The way I figure it, if he ain't mad cause of me then it's probably because Mama's so pretty.

This one time Daddy and Mama was fighting so hard, I thought they was gonna kill each other. I told Mama I was scared of that, but she just laughed. She said such a thing wouldn't ever happen. Maybe not, but I hope if it does Mama's the one who kills Daddy, 'cause then maybe we could have fun without always worrying about how we're gonna get in trouble.

PASSION FOR PIE

If Susanna hadn't been born with a fire inside of her, she might have eventually grown tired of traipsing around. She might have lived to be an old and settled woman, content with her life and with watching her son grow to a man. But she simply wasn't a person to slip into the rut of sameness, so with each passing year she became more restless. In the springtime she developed an itch that made her want to shed her skin. Then when winter came, her insides burned like the belly of a furnace. "I can't stand the boredom of this life," she said over and over again. When she got to feeling she'd scream if she watched another teenage girl breeze by the cosmetic counter and slip a tube of Tangee lipstick into her pocket without paying, she quit the job at Woolworth's. The news at first pleased Benjamin, and then she told him she'd now be waitressing at the all-night diner.

"Feeding dinner to other folks when you don't bother to so much as cook an egg at home?" he said, his words sharp as a butcher knife.

"I cook when I've a mind to," she snapped back.

"When you've a mind to ain't all that often."

"Yeah, well, maybe I got more incentive at the diner! You ever heard of tips?" Susanna said sarcastically. "With my way of pleasing folks I'll likely end up making two, maybe three times more than I was making at Woolworth's,"

"You'll be gone the whole night long!"

Susanna wrapped her arms around Benjamin's neck and wriggled her body up against his. "Don't think about me being gone all night," she cooed. "Think about what's gonna happen when I get home in the morning. You'll wake up, and I'll be standing at the foot of the bed." She edged her tongue along the back of his ear, "Wearing one of those lacy brassieres you're so crazy about."

The first three nights she worked at the diner, she did indeed come home with a glint in her eye and ready for love-making. But on the fourth she claimed he could just forget about such doings seeing as how she'd been on her feet eight hours and was dog-tired. "But you said..." Benjamin moaned. Susanna didn't bother to answer, just flopped her head down on the pillow.

All that summer Ethan Allen sat across the kitchen table from his father and ate warmed-up cans of spaghetti. Afterward, when his daddy settled down to read the newspaper or watch television, the boy would bicycle five miles into town and head for the diner. "Hi, Mama," he'd say with a broad-faced grin, and then she'd sit him down with an oversized slice of peach pie or a bowl of butterscotch pudding.

"Sweetie, this here is Scooter Cobb," Susanna said, cozily edging herself alongside the pudgy-faced man who was round as a pregnant cow. "He owns the place. Ain't he just the cutest thing you ever did see?"

"Pleased to meet you, Mister Scooter," Ethan Allen replied, chomping down on another bite of strawberry rhubarb pie. Although anyone watching would have thought the boy was one-hundred-percent focused on scooping up that chunk of rhubarb, the truth was he'd seen Scooter's hand slide down Susanna's back and come to rest on the round of her butt. "Mama," he asked days later, "do you like Mister Scooter more than Daddy?"

"Good Lord, Ethan," she answered, "what's got into you? If your daddy got wind of you asking a thing like that, there'd sure enough be hell to pay!"

"I didn't mean nothin' by it, I swear."

"I know you didn't, baby." Susanna playfully tousled Ethan Allen's hair and promised that if he'd keep such thoughts to himself, she'd make sure to have enough spare change for the movies.

"Candy too?" he asked.

She grinned. "Yeah, candy too."

After that Ethan Allen had only to mention Scooter's name, and he'd find himself jingling nickels and dimes in his pocket. He found he could go into the diner any time, night or day, whether his mama was behind the counter or not, and have all a boy wanted of pies and puddings. He'd order up a bowl of tapioca or two balls of chocolate ice cream, then tell the person scooping it up they ought to add some whipped cream and a cherry. "Ain't he something?" Susanna would grin. "Chip off his mama's block, that's what this boy is!"

When Susanna said something like that, Scooter would smack his hand up against her behind and start chuckling. "He sure is," he'd laugh. "He sure is."

Even a blind man could see there was something going on between the two of them. A blind man maybe, but not Benjamin. He was too busy counting up the dimes and quarters Susanna was dropping into the cookie jar every day. Each time that jar got heavy he'd empty it out and cart the money off to the bank in town where he'd opened up an account in his own name, claiming it would keep the money safe from robbers.

"What robber is gonna come way out here?" Susanna said, but he reminded her of all the things that had gone missing.

"What about the rug? What about the portable radio?"

It was true that any number of things had simply up and disappeared. So, even though she enjoyed counting up stack after stack of coins, she agreed the money might actually be better off in the bank. "Just you keep track of what's mine," she said. "Because when I got enough, I'm taking you and Ethan Allen on a vacation to New York City!"

"You *still* harping on that?" Benjamin asked. "Shit, you passed the age of being a Rockette ten years ago."

"Maybe so, but I still got a real good singing voice." If she wasn't afraid he'd come after her with a butcher knife, Susanna would have told him that men still whistled when she walked by. That they'd sometimes follow her for blocks just to watch the swing of her hips and the toss of her head. Benjamin might think she was no longer capable of making men stop dead in their tracks, but she knew better. She knew that a man such as Scooter Cobb would give most anything for her favors. Why, she already had a genuine gold necklace and a pearl ring hidden in the glove compartment of her car.

In the fall of the year, when you would expect a boy in the fifth grade to be slouched over the kitchen table doing his homework instead of bicycling into town for a free piece of pie, Ethan Allen showed up at the diner. "Where's my mama?" he asked Bertha, the waitress who'd been working nights for the past fifteen years.

"Ain't you supposed to be home doing your schoolwork?" she said, her mouth twisted off to one side. "Your mama told me you had arithmetic enough to keep you busy for a week or more."

"I finished," Ethan Allen said, even though he hadn't cracked open the book.

"You did no such thing," Bertha sneered. "With five kids of my own, I can tell right off when a boy's lying!"

"Well, it might be I've got a bit more to do, but I figured a piece of pumpkin pie would get my mind working."

"After you get a slice of pie, you'll get on home and take care of that arithmetic?"

"Yes, ma'am," Ethan said with a smile. "I'd get to it faster even if that pie had a fair bit of whipped cream atop it."

Bertha raised an eyebrow like she thought she was being had, but she handed over the pumpkin pie mounded with whipped cream. He started in on it and then asked again, "Where'd you say Mama went to?"

"I didn't say."

"Daddy told me she was working tonight."

"She is." Bertha stood there, her arms folded across her chest, and watched him eat the pie. As he swallowed the last bite, she scooped the plate off the counter. "You're finished up," she said. "Now get on home."

Ethan Allen went whistling out the door, but instead of heading straight home he circled around to the back of the diner figuring to scout up a few soda bottles and turn them in for the deposit. He'd expected to find some Pepsi bottles, maybe even a beer bottle or two, but he never expected to come across his mama's butt buck naked and bouncing around like a ping pong ball in the back seat of Scooter Cobb's big white Cadillac. "Well, shit my drawers!" he exclaimed.

"Damnation!" Scooter hollered when he heard the sound of the boy's voice.

Susanna bounced herself over and started tugging down the skirt of her pink uniform. "What in God's name are you doing here?!" she shouted. "You're supposed to be home with your daddy. I know you got homework to do!"

"I was hungry. I needed to get a slice of pie."

"I'll pie your ass! You get on home. Tomorrow morning we're gonna have us a nice long talk about this!"

"What? I didn't do nothing."

"Get home, I said!"

"Okay, okay." He climbed onto his bicycle and rode off, figuring there would no doubt be hell to pay. His mama would claim he'd been sneaking around, spying on her. She'd likely threaten that if he didn't mend his ways, he'd be shipped off to reform school. But once the fussing was over and done, knowledge such as this would be good for at least a dollar. When he got home Benjamin, who had now taken to drinking beer after beer as he stared glassy-eyed at the television, called out, "That you, boy?"

"Yeah, Pa."

"Didn't your mama say you had homework to do?"

"It's finished," Ethan Allen answered. He grabbed a bag of pretzels, slipped out the back door, and headed for the fort. He and Dog settled in for the night, something they'd done any number of times before. Sleeping in the fort was a far better alternative when his mama was on the warpath. He switched on the radio and listened as Hoot Evers came to bat. It was the bottom of the eighth, and the Orioles were down by three runs. "Looks like the birds are in trouble," said Chuck Thompson, the voice of the Orioles.

"In trouble?" Ethan Allen answered back. "They plain out stink!" It was a discouraging thing to root for a team that always lost. He'd already decided if his mama ever did haul ass for New York City, he'd start rooting for the Yankees. He rolled over on his side and curled up with Dog. They were both fast asleep when Brooks Robinson hit a bases-loaded homer in the ninth inning and won the game.

It was close to dawn when Susanna came home, and she was rip-roaring mad. "I'm gonna kill that kid," she mumbled as she crept through the house, calling his name in a whispered voice. "Ethan Allen! You'd better come out from wherever you're hiding right now!" she threatened. "Or else when I get hold of you…"

"Susanna, that you?" Benjamin hollered out from the bedroom.

"Yeah, it's me," she answered.

"Who you talking to?"

"I'm not talking to nobody!"

"Well, then, quit making such a racket. You'll wake the boy."

"That sorry little shit will *wish* I'd woken him when I finally get hold of his ass!" Susanna murmured as she trudged off to the bedroom.

In the morning Ethan Allen ate a handful of pretzels for breakfast, then bicycled off to school wearing the same shirt and pants as the day before. After school he went back to the fort and waited until he saw Susanna's car leaving, then he returned to the house. He followed the same routine for two days before she finally caught up to him.

"No, you don't," she said, grabbing at the back of his shirt as he tried to make off with a package of honey buns. "We've got some talking to do!"

"Why? I didn't do nothing!"

"You're supposed to be home on a school night. You're supposed to be studying, not jackassing yourself into town for free pie!"

"I was hungry."

"I don't give a crap if your stomach was turned inside out, you got no business—"

"You're just yelling at me cause I seen you waving your naked butt around!"

"Don't give me none of your sass!"

"I ain't to blame. You was the one."

"Ethan Allen, I'm warning you!"

"If Daddy was to know you showed your bare butt to Mister Scooter—"

"Shut up!" Susanna raised her hand and whacked it across the boy's face. "You don't never talk about such a thing!"

"I ain't afraid of you!"

"You might not be afraid of me, but you'd better be afraid of Scooter Cobb! His son's a policeman who'll toss your skinny little ass in jail."

"For what?"

"For telling lies on people, that's what!"

"It ain't no lie. I did see—"

"You're a kid, nobody's gonna believe you! If that policeman says you're telling lies on his daddy, then everybody's gonna believe you're telling lies!"

"They don't lock people up for telling lies."

"Oh, no?" Susanna said looking square into the boy's face. "Shows what you know. They might not put boys your age in jail, but they put them in reform school and keep them locked up until they've grown a long white beard."

"But I didn't do nothing!"

"I know that and you know that, but everybody else is gonna think different." Susanna let the corners of her mouth curl slightly. "That's why," she said, "it's important for you not to say anything about this."

"I won't, Mama, I swear I won't." He crisscrossed his heart. "Hope to die."

"Okay, then. This'll be our secret," she said with a smile. "Now get your butt over here and give your mama a big hug."

That afternoon Susanna fixed macaroni with cheese for Ethan Allen's lunch and gave him two dollars to buy the new basket he'd been needing for his bicycle. And for weeks afterward it seemed she always had enough spare change for him to go to the movies or buy some trinket that had caught hold of his eye. Their relationship suddenly turned noticeably better. First she came home with a new collar for Dog, and then it was three brand new Superman comic books. After that it was a bicycle horn, something Ethan had been wanting for the longest time. "You're spoiling him," Benjamin grumbled. "He skips doing homework and you reward him with presents. What kind of way is that to raise a kid?"

"He's just a boy," Susanna answered, and then she gave Ethan Allen a sly wink. Although she had put her foot down about him showing up at the diner all hours of the night, up until nine o'clock he was still allowed to come for free pies and cakes. "Not one minute later," she'd said with a no-nonsense tone to her voice.

Ethan Allen started coming in right after school, ordering hamburgers, barbecue sandwiches with extra sauce, grilled cheese platters, milk shakes, and, on two different occasions, banana splits. He'd pass by the house and stay just long enough to lift Dog into the new basket hooked onto the handlebar of his bicycle, then off he'd pedal, thinking of what new thing he was gonna order up that day. He'd climb onto a stool at the end of the counter and tell Scooter he had a hankering for some God-awful thing such as chocolate cream pie with a double scoop of ice cream on the side. Minutes later it would be sitting in front of him. When he'd eaten as much as he could hold, he'd want meat scraps for Dog. Although Scooter Cobb gave the boy everything he asked for and more, Ethan Allen had a genuine disliking for the man. He hated the look of Scooter's fat fingers, hated the laugh that rippled first one fold of chin and then the other, but most of all he hated the thought of his mama stretching her arms around that great paunch of stomach.

Once, just days after he'd seen Scooter grab hold of his mama's butt in full view of everyone, Ethan Allen asked, "Mama, are you gonna leave us for Mister Scooter?"

She was sitting on the porch at the time, giving her toenails a second coat of Cherry Blossom Pink. "Dear Lord," she sighed and set the nail polish bottle aside. "Come on over here." She pulled Ethan Allen up onto her lap as if he was still a baby. "I know there's times when I'm not a real good mama," she said, "but, honey, I love you and your daddy. Why, I'd never run off from you. Never ever, not long as you live."

Ethan Allen squeezed himself a bit closer. Susanna smiled and tightened her arms around him. At times his way of thinking seemed so grown up that it was possible for her to forget he was still a boy who needed his mama's hugs. "Honey," she said, "you simply got to understand, this business with Mister Cobb don't mean nothing. He's my boss, and I butter him up a bit so he'll take a liking to me."

"But, Mama..."

"Unh-unh," she put her finger to his lips. "No buts. Mama knows what she's doing, and me working for Scooter Cobb is what's gonna get us to New York City."

Ethan Allen gave her a wide smile. He'd been listening to stories of New York City for as long as he could remember and never tired of hearing them. He never grew bored of watching his mama's eyes sparkle as she talked about how the Rockettes at Radio City Music Hall could kick their legs higher than a man's head. While other toddlers were listening to stories of Peter Rabbit, he heard about how the women in New York were paid hundreds of dollars every week just for singing and dancing.

"You're gonna love New York," Susanna said. "It's like nothing you've ever seen before. More lights than a downtown Christmas tree, and the partying—why, it goes on all night long." She smiled and waited for him to ask the question he always asked. It was a game they played. She wove tales of fame and fortune and he urged her on, hoping to prolong those moments of intimacy.

"Are we *really* gonna move to New York?" he said with a grin.

"You betcha boots! Mama's gonna get a job singing, maybe even on the radio. Then we're gonna move into a fine apartment building with an elevator that carries people up and down anytime of the day or night they've a mind to go."

"What about Dog?"

"He'll come with us. We'll get him a fancy rhinestone collar and let him poop right out in the middle of Fifth Avenue."

For a few minutes Ethan Allen was laughing like a kid, and then the overly mature look of worry slipped back onto his face. "Is Mister Scooter going with us?"

Susanna shook her head. "Of course not," she answered. "It's gonna be just the three of us—you, me, and your daddy."

"Good!"

"Good?"

"Yeah, I don't like Mister Scooter. He's too fat, and he grabs hold of your boobies in front of everybody."

"He don't mean nothing by that. It's his way of acting a fool. He's been real good to you, Ethan, and he's good to me too. Why, he's paying me twice as much money as they did at the five-and-dime." She started to tickle his belly. "Besides," she said, "I get lots of tips, and you get all that free pie!"

"I wouldn't care if I didn't get no more free pie," he answered.

"Well, I'd care if I didn't get that tip money!" She smiled proudly. "Do you know I've got almost one thousand dollars saved up already? Come summer, we're off to New York City—and, that, my little man, is a promise!"

SUSANNA DOYLE

*T*here are times when I can say with absolute honesty I hate
*Benjamin Doyle. Because of him I got no life whatsoever. If I
didn't have my waitressing job I'd probably go stark raving
mad. At least with working I got a reason to get out of the house, but let
me come home the teeniest bit late and he starts carrying on like I been
dancing naked in the town square.*

*It's true enough that I got a good body, the kind that attracts men.
But if Benjamin would've taken me to New York like he said he was
gonna, I likely as not wouldn't be looking for other means of
entertainment.*

*Our kid, Ethan Allen, he's sort of like me. He knows how to make the
best of situations. He thinks I don't know he steals money out of the
cookie jar, but I do. I figure a kid's gotta have some fun, and there sure
as hell ain't no fun out here on this rat trap farm. One of these days I'm
gonna get loose of this place, and when I do. I'm taking the kid with me.
He deserves at least that.*

SUMMER OF RAGE

The year Ethan Allen became eleven was when things between Benjamin and Susanna turned rancid as a week-old pork chop. It had been a summer of one-hundred-degree days with hardly a drop of rain. Morning after morning the sun came up hotter than a fireball, threatening to blister any foolhardy soul who dared venture outside. Housewives kept their window shades pulled down and refused to fetch laundry that had been hanging on the clothesline for weeks. Men accustomed to spending their days in the field stood in front of their refrigerators gasping bits of cool air. "Why bother?" they'd tell their wives. "The corn's too puny to bring to market."

There was not a single person on all of the Eastern Shore who was not irritable and out of sorts, but Benjamin was by far the worst. Not only was he dealing with a crop of soy beans that wouldn't take root, but the tractor had suddenly taken to acting temperamental. He was in the barn replacing a rubber belt that had become drier than a dinosaur bone when Susanna walked in and announced it was time for them to start thinking about that trip to New York City. "Don't bother me with such nonsense," he answered. "You see I've got problems with the tractor."

Certain she'd never get to New York if she took into account every negative thing Benjamin had to say, Susanna continued. "I'm thinking maybe late August, early September."

"Well, I'm thinking a year or two down the road," he growled back.

"I ain't waiting no year or two! I got enough money saved to go now."

"When are you gonna give this up, Susanna?" Benjamin dropped the wrench he'd been holding and glared at her in the most hateful way imaginable. "You're a grown woman now. It's high time you forgot about such foolishness."

"Foolishness?" she answered. "Thinking I can be somebody is foolish? In case you haven't noticed, I got a real good singing voice. Everybody says so. 'Susanna,' they say, 'you ought to be singing on the radio.' But no," she rambled on, "you want to keep me stuck on this farm, where I ain't got the chance of a snowball in hell of being discovered."

"You know what you got? Big tits." He picked up the wrench and turned back to the tractor. "Big tits and not a speck of talent. I ain't interested in going to New York to watch you parade around and make a jackass out of yourself."

"You think you're so smart don't you, Benjamin? Well, you're not. You're stupider than me. Stupid and blind. If you wasn't so blind, you'd see my singing is a way for us to get a better life, have more money, and live in an apartment building that ain't run over with ground hogs and crickets!"

Benjamin twisted loose a bolt he'd been working on and said nothing.

"Well, I'm going to New York! Me and Ethan Allen. We're going to New York, and I don't give a rat's ass whether or not you come!" Susanna whirled on her heel and tromped out of the barn. She didn't hear Benjamin mumble that such a thing would only happen over his dead body.

The very next day Susanna began making plans for the trip. "You start getting ready," she told Ethan Allen, "because we're leaving here the first week of September." Every morning when she got home from work, hours before the sun came up hot enough to burn a hole in a person's head, she'd wake the boy and they'd swish back and forth on the porch swing talking about what they were going to do in New York City.

"Can we climb to the top of the Statue of Liberty?" Ethan Allen would ask. "Ride the subway? Maybe go to Yankee Stadium?"

"We'll do all those things and more!" Susanna answered gleefully. "Of course, I'll have to get some auditions first. But once I get a singing job, we'll go hog wild—paint the town from one end to the other, do whatever we want!"

"You think maybe I could get Mickey Mantle's autograph?"

"Sweetie, I'd bet on it!"

Such talk infuriated Benjamin, and he turned nastier than ever. When the tractor broke down for the ninth time and refused to budge regardless of how many parts he replaced, it certainly didn't help matters. Three weeks before they were to leave, on the very same day Susanna came home with the sequined dress she was planning to wear for auditions, he discovered the tiller was rusted through. "That's it!" he screamed and kicked over the toolbox. Although it was well before noon, he marched himself into the house and sat down at the kitchen table with a full glass of whiskey.

"Ain't it a bit early?" Susanna asked, eyeing the glass.

Benjamin glared at her like a man thinking of murder and poured himself another.

"Even if you could get the tractor fixed," she said, "this heat's already burnt those soy beans to a crisp."

He drained the whiskey glass and then refilled it.

"Just give it up and come to New York with me and Ethan," Susanna said, not noticing the way Benjamin's left eye was twitching. "We're gonna have the time of our lives! And once I've got a singing job—"

Without a word of warning Benjamin's hand flew up and whacked Susanna across the face so hard she tumbled to the floor.

"No, Daddy!" Ethan Allen shouted and grabbed hold of his daddy's arm.

"You thinking you can stop me, boy?" Benjamin growled as he shook his arm free. "Try it, and I'll split your head open."

"I didn't mean nothin' by it, Daddy. Mama didn't neither. She was just hoping you'd come to New York with us."

"Ain't nobody going to New York—not me, not you, and most of all, not your mama!" Benjamin turned and stomped out the door.

Susanna got to her feet and slid her arm across Ethan's shoulder. "Don't worry," she said with a nervous smile. "When the time comes, we'll slip off without him knowing."

After that incident they avoided any outward talk of New York. Susanna whispered bits and pieces in Ethan Allen's ear every so often and he kept imagining himself at Yankee Stadium, but other than that very little was said. Benjamin remained in a foul mood for a week because of the broken tractor, and then he finally went out and bought a brand new John Deere with four times the horsepower of his old tractor.

"This baby can do twice the work in half the time," he told Susanna. "Next year I'll be able to put in an extra field of soy beans. Maybe even a crop of radishes."

"Seems a man who can afford a new tractor ought to be able to take his family to New York City," she commented sarcastically, and then she went back to thinking about whether she should buy a pair of silver shoes to wear with her sequined audition dress.

⊶——⊷

Scooter Cobb slipped a fifty dollar bill into her brassiere the week before she planned to leave for New York, claiming that Susanna was one woman who deserved a nice vacation. "Baby, you have yourself one helluva fling," he said. "Then get your butt back here, 'cause I'm gonna be missing you something fierce!"

In the past year Scooter had come to feel about Susanna as he did his arms and legs: he couldn't do without a single one of them. When she smiled his heart started doing jumping jacks, and when she pressed her body up against his he could no longer remember his wife's name, or, for that matter, the names of his children. If Susanna were willing, he would have walked off and left everything—his wife of thirty years, a house that no longer had a mortgage, even the diner. One nod from her and halfway through frying up an omelet he would have thrown down his apron and followed along, leaving the egg to turn black on the griddle.

"Oh, sweetie," Susanna sighed, "you know how crazy I am about you, but I've got Ethan Allen to think about. Maybe when we get back from this vacation…" Not once did she mention she'd be looking for a singing job in New York or that she'd be staying there forever if things worked out.

The Friday before they planned to leave Susanna drove into town to withdraw her trip money from the bank. So far things were moving along without a hitch. Benjamin had grown so preoccupied with his new tractor he'd stopped watching her every move and switched to thoughts of planting some winter squash. He never once noticed the valise of travelling clothes pushed under the bed, nor did he think to ask why Susanna had all of a sudden decided on having her hair permed. He paid no attention to the way she'd dance around the house belting out song after song, and when she drove off Monday morning to register Ethan Allen for the new school term he wouldn't think to question it. Susanna figured by the time he discovered they were gone she and Ethan Allen would be halfway to New York, having their lunch served by a Pullman Porter in the dining car. She had only two more nights of working in the diner. *Then,* she told herself, *that's the end of that!* Of course, she'd miss Scooter. He was a man who truly appreciated the things she had to offer, but... Susanna parked in back of the Eastern Virginia Savings Bank and all but skipped in.

Bernice Wilson was the teller on duty. Bernice had been working at the bank for eighteen years and took pride in her ability to remember every customer and the most minute details of their account. But when Susanna said she wanted to withdraw eleven hundred dollars from her savings account, Bernice stood there with a blank look plastered across her face. "Excuse me?" she finally said, and Susanna repeated the request. Without any change of expression, Bernice slid open her customer card file and one by one flipped through the cards. When she got to the end of the drawer, she scrunched her nose and reversed direction. Going back to front she rechecked every card in the drawer. After a good fifteen minutes she looked up and said, "You don't have an account with us."

Susanna laughed a nervous little twitter that sounded somewhat like a gasp. "Of course I do," she said. "It's a joint account with my husband Benjamin."

"Oh, Benjamin Doyle's account!"

Susanna breathed a sigh of relief.

"He closed that out, a week ago last Tuesday."

"Impossible."

"I waited on him myself. Mister Doyle withdrew the money and said he didn't see any reason for holding onto an empty account, so I closed it." She pushed a small card beneath the bars of the teller window. "See, right there, that's his signature." The face of the card was stamped with bold black letters that read Account closed.

"But..." Susanna's eyes welled with tears.

"He took the money in cash," Bernice called out as Susanna fled through the door.

For a long while Susanna sat in the car and cried. After all those nights of working, every cent of her tip money was gone. There would be no New York. No New York and no singing career. For the rest of her life there would be nothing but soy beans and the dry dust of summer. She could picture her heart being torn from its rightful place and shoved into a graveyard of dreams; a place where singers were impaled on the shards of broken records, and the only sound to be heard was that of sobbing. It was one thing for Benjamin to grab hold of her breast and pinch until a purple spot in the shape of his thumb appeared, but it was quite another to rip away the flesh of her hopes, piece by painful piece. After almost two hours Susanna dried her eyes and drove to the diner.

As soon he caught sight of her face, Scooter said, "What's wrong?"

By that time her eyes had puffed to the shape and color of an overripe tomato. "Did you mean what you said?" she asked. "About us running off together?" Without waiting to hear his answer, she hurled herself up against his body and stretched her arms around his waist for as far as they could reach.

"'Course I did, sugar," Scooter answered. "There ain't nothing I wouldn't do for you, I done told you that."

"What if I was to ask you to take me to New York City?" Susanna pushed her mouth into the folds of his neck and suckled them. "Would you do that?" she asked in a breathy whisper.

"I suppose," he answered a bit hesitantly. "You mean for a vacation?"

"Unh-unh," She slid her hand along the mound of his stomach and reached for the bulge in his crotch. "I'm talking about forever," she whispered. "You and me, pleasuring each other, night after night after night."

Scooter had fought hand-to-hand combat in the war and came away unscathed, but he was no match for Susanna. Once she ran her tongue along the edge of his ear, he forgot he had a wife at home. He no longer cared about the customers who would line up at the diner door looking for their morning coffee, and he never gave Benjamin a thought. Susanna could do that to a man. "When?" he asked.

"Tomorrow morning," she answered, edging her hand toward his crotch. "I'll come to work tonight like nothing's wrong. Then tomorrow morning we'll drive over to Norfolk and catch the ten-thirty train. Ethan Allen can meet us here."

"The boy? He's coming?"

"Well, sure. You can't expect me to leave him on the farm with Benjamin."

For a fleeting moment Scooter remembered his own son who would indeed be left behind, but when Susanna pushed her tongue inside his mouth the thought was quickly forgotten.

BENJAMIN DOYLE

I suppose I always knew a woman like Susanna could be trouble, but there wasn't a damn thing I could do to hold back from falling for her.

She's a woman who drives a man crazy with that body of hers. She can please you in ways other women ain't even dreamt of. The first time I laid with Susanna, I knew right then I'd be craving her 'til the day I died. Maybe I should've realized such a woman wouldn't ever settle down, but I figured once we was married and had a kid things would change. They did. They got worse.

The kid, Ethan Allen, he's a lot like her. They figure I'm blind but I see them, whispering secrets back and forth, and I know damn good and well what they're up to.

Susanna keeps filling the kid's head with a lot of bullshit about going to New York when the truth is nobody's going nowhere. She's got no talent, and I got no money. How's that for a shit-sorry life?

No Hell Like Home

When Susanna arrived back at the house, Ethan Allen was out in the field shooting at the groundhogs that had been digging up what was left of the soybeans. Benjamin was in the yard hosing a splatter of dirt from his new tractor. "Where you been?" he asked.

"At the bank," she answered, her voice cold and sharp as a razor.

Benjamin gave her an icy cold look but stayed with the hosing.

"I wanted to withdraw my money."

"For what?" he asked sarcastically. "A trip to New York?"

"It was *my* money! You had no right!"

"I got every right!" he shouted. "I'm your husband. I say what money gets spent on! This tractor's more important than some jerkwater notion of you becoming a singer!"

Susanna scooped a rock from the ground and hurled it at Benjamin's head. He ducked and the rock cracked hard against the side of the tractor. "Jesus Christ!" he shouted, then came running across the yard and grabbed hold of her hair. He dragged Susanna back to where the tractor was standing. "See what you've done!" he shouted and shoved her nose into the dent.

"You think I give a fuck about this tractor?" she answered defiantly. "That thing's a worthless piece of shit far as I'm concerned!"

"Worthless? You call a tractor that cost more'n a thousand dollars worthless?"

"I'd call anything *you* got an interest in worthless!"

"I had enough of your mouth," Benjamin said. He raised his hand and whacked Susanna hard enough to send her sprawling across the yard.

Ethan Allen saw it happen as he was walking back from the field. He took off running and came at Benjamin. "No, Daddy, no!" he shouted.

"Keep outta this!" Benjamin roared. He yanked the shotgun from the boy's grip and smacked him to the ground. "You dare raise a hand to me, you'll get worse than she got!" With a disgusted sneer he turned and strode off.

After Susanna had gathered herself from the ground she went to the boy and said, "Don't worry, we're still going to New York City." She told Ethan Allen he was to stay clear of his daddy until after dark, then slip off to the diner and meet her. "Scooter's going with us," she confided. "He's gonna see to it we got everything we want. He's even gonna take you to see that Yankee game you been itching to see."

"Does Daddy know?"

"Shit, no," Susanna answered. "That's why it's real important for you to keep clear of him. One wrong word and the cat's out of the bag."

Ethan Allen nodded.

"And don't you pack no clothes. That's a dead giveaway."

"I gotta bring my mitt!"

"Okay, the mitt—nothing else!"

"What about Dog?"

Susanna gave him a look of disbelief. "No Dog," she said.

"But, Mama..."

"No buts."

"I can't leave Dog here with Daddy," Ethan Allen whined. "He'll shoot him in the heart soon as he finds out we're gone."

Susanna knew such a thing was true, for Benjamin always claimed the dog was a reminder of her whoring night. "Okay," she relented, "you can bring Dog, but not another thing. Not a toothbrush or even a stick of gum."

"I swear," Ethan Allen promised, making the sign of the cross over his heart. He breezed through the kitchen, latched onto a wrapper of bologna and a half loaf of bread, then disappeared out the back door.

Throughout the afternoon as the sound of dishes breaking and pots clattering against the wall echoed through the trees Ethan hunkered down in the fort, the fielder's mitt in his lap and Dog by his side. He listened to a barrage of angry words fly back and forth. It was the same as always. He'd heard it a thousand times before. After a while they'd tire of the name calling and go off to the bedroom together, and then it would quiet down. On this day, however, such a thing never happened. The voices continued to grow louder and angrier, which is why Ethan Allen took to keeping his eye on the house. After a particularly violent exchange of words, Susanna ran from the house with a valise tucked under her arm. Her audition dresses were the only thing she couldn't stand to leave behind.

Benjamin followed her out shouting, "Get your ass back in this house!"

"Like hell I will!" she answered. "I had enough of you and your bullshit! I'm going to New York, and nothing on earth can stop me!" She tossed the valise into the back of the car, but before she could slide behind the wheel Benjamin's fist came up beneath her chin with such force that it lifted her from her feet. When Susanna dropped to the ground, there was a loud cracking of bone and she made no effort to move.

Benjamin stood looking down at her for what seemed to be the longest time, and then he said, "Okay, enough pretending, now get up!" He nudged her with the toe of his shoe, but still she did not move.

Peering through the lower limb of a Douglas fir, Ethan Allen whispered, "Come on, Mama, please get up."

Twice more Benjamin poked her with his foot. "Okay, bitch, stay there! See if I care!" he shouted and stomped back into the house. Moments later he came back with a folded towel and tucked it beneath her head. "I'm sorry," he mumbled tearfully. "I didn't mean to do this." He lifted Susanna into his arms and carried her inside, promising over and over again that such a thing would never happen again.

Afterward there was no more arguing to be heard. Figuring Susanna would be a while smoothing things over with Benjamin, Ethan Allen went back to the fort to wait. Dog, having eaten most of the bologna, rolled over onto his side. Caught up in his thoughts of going to New York Ethan Allen didn't feel much like sleeping, so he turned on the radio and listened as the Orioles battled the Boston Red Sox. When Brooks Robinson drove home two runs with a double in the top of the ninth, the Orioles got hold of the lead. "Looks like our birds are just three outs from getting a big win here at Fenway," Chuck Thompson said, but Ethan paid little attention.

Ordinarily in such a situation the boy's ear would have been pinned to the radio, but on this particular day he was listening for something else. He was waiting to hear the sound of his mama slamming out the door and tearing off down the drive, but so far there hadn't been anything other than the deep-throated sobbing that every so often stopped and started.

In the bottom of the ninth Zuverink struck out Jensen, then Klaus, and the win seemed a sure thing, so Ethan Allen left the game and slipped out of the fort. He crept through the stand of trees and inched closer to the house, wondering if maybe he'd missed the sound of Susanna leaving. But, no, her car was still parked in the driveway with the front door hanging open. "Shitfire, Mama," he mumbled, "get a move on." It was one thing to be late for work on any other night, but not *this* night! If Benjamin had stomped off to the barn as he usually did, Ethan could have gone inside and told Susanna, who at times was damned irresponsible, to get hurrying. But Benjamin was still inside the house.

Ethan moved closer and crouched behind the stump of an oak tree. He tilted his ear every which way but still could not catch wind of what was happening. Susanna had told him to stay clear of Benjamin but it was late in the afternoon, a time when she ought to be playing the radio and snapping on some lamps. The house was still dark with no sign of anyone moving about. He circled around the far end of the barn and came up on the side of the house where he'd be able to see into her bedroom. Stretching his neck, Ethan saw his mama lying on the bed still wearing the same shorts and halter she had on earlier, not even starting to ready herself for work. "Shitfire!" he grumbled, figuring this to be another of those situations when she'd promise to do something and then forget about it. He stood and turned to walk away, and then he spotted Benjamin sitting at the foot of the bed hunched over and slobbering a string of words about how he was sorrier than he'd ever been in his whole entire life.

For as long as he could remember Ethan Allan had known his parents to do battle—scream and yell until a person in the next county could hear them; cuss each other up one side and down the other; hurl heavy pots the full length of the room. But *never* in all that time had he seen a situation such as this. Something was terribly wrong. He crept closer and closer to the house until finally his nose was pressed up against the bedroom window. He saw Susanna's head lolled off to the side like a broken arm. "Mama," he cried and went running into the house.

"Get the hell out of here!" Benjamin snarled.

"No!" Ethan Allen answered defiantly. "Something's wrong with Mama!"

"She's sleeping. Nothing's wrong."

"You blind, Daddy? She's bleeding!"

"A bonk on the head, that's all. Now get."

"It ain't no bonk on the head, she's bad hurt. Can't you see?"

"Enough!" Benjamin grabbed hold of Ethan's arm and dragged him across the living room to the door. "You're gonna be hurting a lot worse than your mama if you don't get the hell out of here!" He pushed the boy out the doorway with a shove that propelled him halfway to the gate.

"Shithead!" Ethan Allen screamed as the door slammed shut. He scrambled to his feet and headed back to the bedroom window, but by the time he got there the shade had been pulled tight against the sill and it was impossible to see a thing. "Damn you, Daddy!" he yelled. "Damn you anyway!"

Ethan Allen turned and walked back through the trees. He couldn't shake the image of Susanna from his mind. She wasn't sleeping; he was almost sure she wasn't. Her eyes were wide open. He tried telling himself everything was okay, but it didn't feel okay. It was true enough that Benjamin had a mean streak wide as the Chesapeake Bay, but Ethan knew his mama was tough and could take care of herself. She'd done it before and she'd do it again. He thought back to the time she stayed gone for two whole days. Then when she finally did get home, she ended up with a broken arm. And there was another time when Benjamin blackened her eye for coming home stinking of whiskey. Even after she'd been knocked flat on her back, Mama always got up. She'd say she was real sorry for carrying on in such a manner, and then things were all right. Mama had that way about her. No matter how mad a person might get, they'd end up forgiving her and laughing like they couldn't ever remember being mad.

Edging through the open corner of the tarpaulin, Ethan Allen crawled back inside his fort. Dog was still asleep. The game was over and Wild Joe Bonomo was telling listeners that Jimmy Piersall's ninth inning home run had been a lousy break for the birds. Ethan snapped off the radio. He didn't much care if the Orioles lost another game. "The hell with you," he grumbled and curled up alongside Dog. Although he would have sworn he wasn't the least bit sleepy, Ethan's eyelids drifted shut. Before long they were at Yankee Stadium, him and Susanna, Mickey Mantle at the plate. With a count of two and two, Mickey swung and sent a home run ball rocketing into the stands. Just as it was about to land in Ethan's fielder's mitt, he woke to the sound of a car. Still half-asleep, his first thought was that his mama had got to feeling better and headed off to the diner.

Ethan pushed back the tarpaulin and saw a flash of light in the distance. With his hand latched onto Dog's collar, he slipped through the trees for a look. The house was still dark as a coal mine, but in the whiteness of a full moon he could see Susanna's car right where it had been earlier, the door still hanging open. Only now there was a big white Cadillac pulled up behind it, a car exactly like the one that belonged to Scooter Cobb. Given his daddy's already foul mood, Ethan felt sure this was gonna mean more trouble.

Scooter Cobb climbed from the car. There was no mistaking him. He was a man the size of a standing grizzly. "Susanna!" he shouted. "Susanna, you in there?" He walked to the front of the house and began pounding a fist against the door.

A low growl rumbled in Dog's throat, but the boy quickly put his finger to his mouth and made a shushing sound. They silently worked their way from the edge of the tree line to a spot behind the wisteria. After several minutes the porch light came on, and Benjamin cracked open the door. "Susanna's sick," he said, sticking his nose through the narrow slit. "She ain't coming to work."

"Sick?" Cobb repeated dubiously.

"Yeah, sick!"

Cobb slapped his huge paw against the door and pushed it open. "Funny," he said, "she was feeling fine this afternoon."

"She ain't now."

"Suppose you let *her* tell me."

"She's sleeping."

"How about I see for myself?" Scooter Cobb pushed Benjamin aside, left the front door hanging open, and tromped into the house. He switched on the living room lamp, then continued through to the bedroom like a man familiar with where he was headed. In the darkness it first appeared Susanna was sleeping, but when Scooter went to her he saw the pool of blood beneath her head. With him not being a terribly quick-witted man, it took the better part of a minute before he came to understand she was dead. Once he knew that the woman who brought his blood to a boil and caused the hair on his neck to rise up was lost to him forever, he let out such an agonizing cry that it rattled the walls and made the floors tremble. He turned back to the living room and grabbed hold of Benjamin's shoulders. "What have you done?" he screamed. "What in God's name have you done?"

"Not me," Benjamin stuttered as he was lifted from the floor. "It wasn't my fault. She made me—"

"You killed her, you stupid son of a bitch! You killed her!" Scooter shook Benjamin so violently that his head ping-ponged back and forth, and a spurt of blood shot from his nose. Over and over again he moaned, "You killed her, you killed her."

Benjamin began crying and pleading like a man afraid for his life. "It wasn't my fault," he sobbed, "it was her…she was the one…always saying she was gonna leave…always talking about how she was going to New York."

Perhaps it was the mention of New York. Perhaps it was knowing that Susanna was leaving to spend the rest of her life with him. There's no telling what finally caused Scooter to snap, but he suddenly lifted Susanna's husband into the air and hurled him through the plate glass window. Not even the sight of Benjamin lying on the front lawn, a spear of glass rammed through his shoulder and his face covered in blood, was enough to quell Scooter's rage. He stormed outside like an angry bull and stomped on the man's head time and time and time again until the left side of Benjamin's skull cracked open and his face was no longer recognizable. Scooter Cobb then got into his white Cadillac and drove off.

Ethan saw it all. He heard the screams and cries. He tasted blood trickling down his own throat, the same as his daddy. He felt a stream of urine run down his leg. Yet through it all he stood there too petrified to move. Ethan wanted to make himself small, so small he could burrow into the ground like an ant or a beetle bug, small enough that Scooter Cobb would forget he ever existed. He curled himself into a ball, rolled under the wisteria, and stayed there for hours after the white Cadillac's headlights had faded from view.

OLIVIA ANN DOYLE

*S*ome people think superstitions are pure nonsense, but I say they give a person fair warning. If you choose to pay them no heed, then stand back because all hell is likely to break loose. I know in my heart if I'd taken that opal necklace and thrown it into the ocean the very second Charlie gave it to me, he'd still be alive today.

I suppose happiness can make you blind to reality. That's what happened to me. I was so busy focusing on my blessings that I glossed right over the significance of our being in Miami for eleven days. Me—a woman who has lifelong knowledge of the tragedies hovering around the eleventh of anything. I still remember when I turned eleven. In that one year I had whooping cough, measles, mumps and the chicken pox. Then I was left back to spend another year in the sixth grade, which resulted in my being the tallest, gangliest girl in Miss Munroe's class. Being called Wall-Tall-Westerly leaves its mark on you! It makes you have a keen eye for avoiding any sort of eleven. Why, I'd no more eat eleven jelly beans than take off flying, yet I wasn't all that watchful of poor Charlie on the eleventh day of our Miami Beach honeymoon.

Letting down my guard as I did, I suppose I could say I deserve what I got. But the thing is it happened to Charlie, not me. I'd have been better off if it had happened to me. Being dead all over is far better than walking around with just a dead heart inside of you.

SPARE CHANGE

Olivia, a blushing bride just twenty-two days ago, was now a widow. Not just a widow, but a widow stranded more than a thousand miles from home. And as if that weren't bad enough, there was also the problem of transporting the powder blue convertible and Charlie's body back to Virginia.

Olivia did the only thing she could think of at the moment: she had Charlie cremated so that he'd be a somewhat smaller package, and she locked herself in the room at the Fontainebleau and cried for five days straight. She cried until her heart was as hollowed out as a jack-o-lantern and her arms too heavy to lift, and still she kept right on sobbing. She'd close her eyes to sleep, but there on the inside of her eyelids was the picture of Charlie face down in the lobster bisque. Dead before he landed, according to a doctor who'd left his wife on the dance floor and rushed over. No matter what she tried to concentrate on, she couldn't erase that image.

Olivia felt certain Charlie's untimely death was her fault. She had a number of jinxes that followed her around, attached themselves like fleas to a dog, and then when it was least expected jumped over to take a chomp out of someone close by. It wasn't just the number eleven that was unlucky, it was any multiple or divisor of eleven. She'd been on the lookout for trouble on the eleventh day of their marriage, but she'd slacked off on her watchfulness when they'd been in Miami for eleven days. Then there was the matter of the opal. Lord knows she should have expected the worst from a thing such as that!

The hotel manager told Olivia there'd be no charge for her room and she could stay for long as need be, but he began to show concern when day after day went by and she didn't so much as stick her nose out into the hallway. He sent pots of tea and platters of croissants to her room, but the trays remained outside the door, untouched. On the third day Olivia's sobbing became so loud that a couple at the far end of the hall asked to be moved to another floor. When on the fifth day Charlie's ashes arrived from the crematorium the manager feared the worst, and justifiably so. That night Olivia's sobbing was louder than it had ever been before. She held his remains in her arms and howled like the wind of a hurricane. Throughout the night she remained in front of the window watching a black and stormy ocean.

When morning came she packed her bags and left. "This is no place for us," she said. "We're going home." She placed the silver urn alongside of her in the front seat of the convertible and drove off. On the first day of her trip home she had to stop thirty-seven times to wipe the blur of tears from her eyes, because every time she thought of Charlie bottled up as he was she'd start crying all over again.

The next nine days went along pretty much the same way. When Olivia finally crossed the border into Georgia, she figured it to be a milestone and decided at two o'clock in the afternoon to stop for the night.

"Welcome to Hopeful, Georgia—Pop. 387" the sign at the edge of town read. After she'd driven past numerous peanut farms, Olivia came upon the town. She was hoping for something such as a Howard Johnson Motel, a place with air conditioning and room service, a place where she could throw herself onto an overstuffed mattress and cry for as long as she wished. Of course, there was nothing of the sort in Hopeful. The town was barely two blocks long. There were no restaurants, no movie theatre, and most certainly no Howard Johnson's. The only place to offer a person an overnight accommodation was the Main Street Motel. Given the state of her weariness, Olivia parked the convertible in front of the weathered building, slipped the bottled-up Charlie into her overnight tote, and walked inside.

There was no one behind the counter, so Olivia rang the bell and waited. She stood there a good five minutes and when still no one came she then tapped the bell a second time. "I'm coming, I'm coming," a voice hollered out. Minutes later a woman bent from the waist and leaning heavily on a walking stick poked her head out from behind a calico curtain. "Sorry," she said. "I was tending to business in the johnny."

Olivia had expected a young man wearing a uniform or at the very least a badge with his name spelled out in bold letters. This woman was wearing a flowered housecoat. She was little more than a skeleton with a top knot of snow white hair and a coverlet of loose skin. How, Olivia wondered, could they expect a person such as this to carry bags in?

"Need a room, sugar?" the woman said, introducing herself as Canasta Jones.

Olivia nodded.

"Just you?"

"I've got my husband…"

"Oh. Then you'll be wanting a double bed. All I've got is three singles."

"A single's okay."

"Sweetie," the woman said apologetically, "much as I need your business, there's no possible way two full grown people could squeeze into one of them beds. Why, they're narrow as a cat's whisker." She gave a wink that made her seem far younger than her years. "Honeymooners maybe could, nobody else."

Olivia was going to mention that she was indeed a honeymooner, but the thought of being a honeymooner without a husband brought tears to her eyes. She'd planned on waiting until she could throw herself onto a mattress and weep the night away, but all of a sudden there she was squatted down on a bench sobbing hysterically.

"I say something wrong?" Canasta asked.

Olivia took the hem of her skirt and swiped the droplet hanging from her nose. "Not you," she snuffled. "Charlie."

"Charlie?"

"He was a man who was truly in love with me," Olivia sobbed. "We could've been happy for a thousand years."

The old woman scooted down alongside Olivia and leaned in closer. "Your husband run him off?" she asked.

"He *was* my husband."

"Was?"

"I killed him. Oh, the opal pendant may have been partly to blame, but I think it was mostly the jinx. He died twenty-one days after we were married, so on the twenty-second day I became a widow." Olivia saw the puzzlement on the old woman's face and explained, "Twenty-two—that's two elevens!"

"What's eleven got to do with anything?"

Olivia gave an exasperated sigh. "It's only the unluckiest number in the universe," she said. "If anything horrible is going to happen, guaranteed it will happen on the eleventh of something!"

Canasta scrunched her face, adding a few more wrinkles. "Who told you such hogwash?" she asked.

"Nobody told me. I learned from experience. I'm a person who's jinxed!"

"Hogwash!" the old woman repeated. "Nobody's jinxed. Specially not by no number eleven."

"A lot you know," Olivia growled. "I could name dozens of bad things tied in to some sort of eleven."

"Yeah, well, I could name some good things!" Canasta shot back.

"Such as?"

"Me. I was brought into this world on November eleventh, and year after year I get a slew of presents on the eleventh day of the eleventh month. I'm ninety-nine years old, and that's nine elevens. I got me eleven grandkids, and Lord knows how many great grandbabies, every one of them sweet as pie."

"You're lucky; you missed out on the jinx."

"There is no jinx!" Canasta said with an air of impatience. "You're just reasoning a way to feel sorry for yourself."

"What about Charlie—a perfectly healthy man one day and dead the next! That's not jinxed? That's not a true misfortune?"

"It's a true enough tragedy but not a jinx," Canasta answered wistfully. "Nobody knows better than me the pain of losing a husband. I buried four and cried a bucket of tears for each and every one."

"Four?" Olivia repeated. She stopped sobbing and turned to the old woman.

Canasta nodded. "The last one was Elmer. He died a month ago."

"I'd no idea," Olivia stuttered. "You seem to be getting along just fine."

"What's a body to do? Caskets ain't sized for two people."

"Huh?"

Canasta slowly shook her head side to side. "No matter how much feeling you got for your man, there's no way to keep him on earth when the Lord decides it's his time to go. Once they close that casket lid, he's gone. You can't go with him. Only thing you can do is keep on with living."

"What's left to live for?" Olivia moaned tearfully.

"Sugar," Canasta sighed, "there's always something to live for." She reached across and placed her bony hand on Olivia's knee. "Why, a young woman like you—"

"Young? I'm fifty eight!"

"Prime of life!" Canasta snapped back. "You got years of loving yet to do."

"A woman my age?"

"Yes, indeed. I married my dear sweet Elmer when I was eighty-two."

"Fine for you, but me…" Olivia looked down at the floor and shook her head side to side, "Unh-unh," she sighed pitifully. "Without Charlie, there's nothing."

"Oh, I get it," Canasta turned and fixed her eyes square on Olivia's face. "You're wanting sympathy. You're looking for somebody to say how bad off you are. Well, it ain't gonna be me! Everybody gets to feeling low at times, but—"

"Of course, you, a woman who's had four husbands, wouldn't understand what it feels like to be lonely!"

"I understand aplenty. Lord knows I've done my share of grieving and crying. But no matter how you love somebody, there comes a time when you got to let them go. See, sugar," Canasta took Olivia's hand in hers, "having a man crazy in love with you is like having your pocket full of money. When you got it you feel like a rich woman, but when you ain't got it you start feeling poor as a church mouse."

"That's surely true," Olivia nodded.

"Thing is, you ain't."

"I'm not?"

"Shoot, no. Making people think they can't scrape up enough to buy a dime's worth of happiness is the Devil's doing. It's his way of handing out heartaches. The Good Lord don't do things that way. When he sees a person's flat out of hope and feeling dead broke, He slips a bit of spare change into the bottom of their pocket. Not a lot maybe, but enough for them to get by."

Leaning into the words, Olivia crooked her neck to the same angle as Canasta's.

"Well, now," the old woman said with a smile, "the same thing's true of the feelings inside a body's heart. The Devil wants you to believe you're emptied out, but trust in the Lord, sugar. He'll see a fair share of love comes your way."

"Oh, I doubt that," Olivia replied. "I'm not one who's lucky in love."

"Maybe you ain't been trusting in the Lord."

"I go to church."

"Regular?"

Olivia had to admit that more often than not there was some other matter that held her back from attending services—a brunch with friends, a book that had to be read, laundry that needed washing.

"Seems you ain't on real close terms with the Lord," Canasta said. "And if that's the case, you ought to seek out an ear willing to listen."

"Listen to what?"

"Your troubles."

"Oh, I don't need—"

Canasta spread her mouth in a wide open grin. "Course you do," she said. "Ain't a soul on earth who don't." She linked her arm through Olivia's and led the way into a tiny apartment situated behind the calico curtain.

They sat together at a small wooden table and drank black tea, tea so strong that it loosened Olivia's tongue and prompted her to tell of things that for thirty-two years had been picking at her mind. She told of beaus who had knocked on her door and been turned away. She told of how the sorry sight of Francine Burnam weighted down by five children had dissuaded her from following along on such a pathway. "Many a night I was so lonely, I'd cry myself to sleep," Olivia said, "but then I'd remember the look of Francine and figure being lonely was better than being chained to a flock of kids that weigh a woman down worse than a sack of stones."

"Most every woman's got stones of some sort or another," Canasta replied. "Some troubles are way heavier than babies."

Olivia conceded in certain instances such a thing was true.

"Christine Flannigan," she said. "Now there's a case in point." She then went on to tell of the poor unfortunate telephone operator who'd suffered a nervous breakdown while she was sitting at the tandem board and ultimately had to be institutionalized. But the moment Olivia finished the story, she jumped back to how she'd met Charlie and fallen in love. "Head over heels," she said. "The very first time he kissed me, I knew he was the one I'd been waiting for!"

Long about dark Canasta set a pot of okra soup on to warm, then served up steaming bowls of it and continued to listen.

After Olivia had finished telling most every story that came to mind, she gave a breathy sigh and said, "My Charlie, he was sure a wonderful man."

"No doubt," Canasta answered. "He don't sound like a body who'd want you weeping and wailing over spilt milk."

"Charlie? No indeed." Olivia swallowed the last of her soup and asked if she might have another bowl. Without any realization of what was happening, a strange feeling settled on Olivia as she sat there and gulped down bowl after bowl of okra soup. First she began to feel lighter. Then her feet seemed to be rising up from her shoes and wiggling around like they were wanting to dance. Then it was her arms and hands, and before she toddled off to bed her brain was floaty as a feather.

When she got to her room, Olivia set Charlie atop the dresser and climbed into bed. "Goodnight, sweetheart," she whispered. Then she switched off the light and closed her eyes. For the first time in two weeks she didn't picture Charlie lying face down in a bowl of lobster bisque. Instead, she dreamt of him as he was on their wedding day. She could picture him laughing, chucking her beneath the chin, and teasing her for being the worrisome person she'd become. When she woke the next morning Olivia realized she could hear the trill of a bird and catch the scent of jasmine, both things she'd been unable to do since Charlie's death. *It must be due to some sort of flavoring in the soup,* she thought. Then in the shower she caught herself singing—something that was totally out of character. She pulled on a pair of pedal pushers and hurried over to Canasta's door. "You suppose I could have a bit more soup for breakfast?" she asked.

The old woman had on several other occasions seen her okra soup have the very same effect and smiled. "You most certainly can," she said and opened wide the door.

For the next five days Olivia had okra soup for breakfast, lunch, and dinner. "There's something in the soup," she insisted, "something that causes a person to taste happiness." Such a possibility certainly appeared to be the case, for day by day she grew a bit brighter. It began with the hearing of song and the smelling of fragrance. Then she started feeling the warmth of sunshine and the softness of a down comforter. After that it was the sight of flowers abloom with color such as she had never before seen. When she discovered the right side of her mouth curling into a smile of its own volition, Olivia went to Canasta and begged to have the recipe. "Please," she said, "tell me the secret ingredient."

"It's the having of a friend to listen," the old woman insisted. Still Olivia continued to harangue her for the secret of the soup. Finally when Canasta's ears had grown sore from the sound of the pleas, she told Olivia her secret was the seed of a vine that grew deep in the woods.

"Take me to it," Olivia begged.

"Impossible," Canasta claimed, saying she was far too old to go tromping through a thicket of briars. "Anyway," she said, "no seed is gonna help a person who ain't regular about visiting with the Lord." Of course Olivia swore she'd seen the light and would be attending church every Sunday from now on.

Seven days after she arrived in Hopeful, Olivia happily tucked a packet of seeds into her purse then loaded Charlie into the trunk of the car and drove off. "I know you'd want me to get on with my life," she'd whispered apologetically as she wedged the silver urn back behind a carton of souvenirs.

With her gold tooth sparkling in the sunlight, Canasta waved goodbye from the front step of the Main Street Motel. She knew sooner or later Olivia, like all the others, would realize the seeds were nothing more than green peppercorns. Hopefully by then she'd be on speaking terms with the Lord and would have no need for such foolishness.

OLIVIA ANN DOYLE

*S*ome folks say once a person's departed this earth they've got no connection to the poor souls left behind, but I don't believe such a thing is true. I know without a whisker of doubt Charlie Doyle was responsible for my landing in Hopeful. He more than likely caught sight of me looking like a person turned inside out and figured I could use a bit of uplifting.

I truly do miss Charlie. You might wonder how a woman married just twenty-one days could come to be so dependent on her husband—I wonder it too—but the truth is it happened. That night at the Fontainebleau, I felt my own heart dying right along with Charlie's. When he stopped breathing, my lungs suffered from the lack of air. And when they told me Charlie was gone, I could almost feel my soul slipping out of my body and marching up to heaven right alongside of him.

I know Charlie wouldn't want me to go on being miserable forever, so I'm trying to see the brighter side of things. The seeds Canasta gave me help a lot. But to be on the safe side, I've thrown nickels and dimes into the pockets of every outfit I own. That way I'll remember about God providing the spare change to get me through. I'm hoping this pain inside of me will someday ease a bit. But right now, Lord oh Lord, how my heart does ache.

GOING HOME

With Charlie in the trunk, driving became a bit easier. Olivia set the radio to a station that played mostly country music and she sang along with Patsy Cline through to the top end of Georgia. In South Carolina she switched over to Elvis and pressed her foot down on the accelerator. By late afternoon she was nearing Raleigh, which is when the convertible took to sputtering. "Oh, dear," she sighed and eased off to the side of the road. Once the car had rolled to a stop, she climbed from behind the wheel to look the situation over. A flat tire she would have recognized right off, but smoke billowing out from beneath the hood was something else entirely. She pulled the owner's manual from the glove compartment and read it cover to cover, finding page after page of information about the horses beneath the hood but not a word on sputtering engines.

Furious with Charlie for stranding her in a situation such as this, Olivia was contemplating the thought of gulping down the seeds Canasta had given her when a trailer tractor pulled up behind her. A bearded man with what she'd call a troublesome glint in his eye stepped down from the truck and asked, "Need help?"

She hesitated recalling how this was the sort of situation where a woman travelling alone got robbed and murdered, left by the roadside for buzzards to pick apart.

Ignoring the fact that she hadn't answered, he said, "Your engine's probably overheated," and came walking toward her.

Another woman may have had other options. Olivia did not. She tried to force a smile, but the result was a look of paralysis with the whites of her eyes showing the full way around and the left corner of her mouth tilted at an odd angle. "It'll be okay in a minute or two," she eventually mumbled.

He popped open the hood. "Let's take a look." A cloud of steam rose from the engine when the hood was lifted. "Not good," he announced and took to fingering his chin. He waited a bit for the car to cool down and then started poking around. "Ah-ha," he finally exclaimed and directed her attention to a black hose that had split apart. "There's the culprit! Looks like you're gonna need a tow." He gave a sympathetic smile, which, despite the beard, made him seem somewhat less menacing. "I can give you a lift into Claymore," he said. "You'll find a mechanic there."

It was late in the afternoon. In an hour or two it would be pitch black. She could stand here hoping things would take a turn for the better, or she could risk a ride with the stranger. "Okay," she answered, then opened her purse, took out one of the green peppercorns and swallowed it. A month ago Olivia would not have thought it possible that she'd hike up her skirt and climb into the truck of a man she'd known for less than fifteen minutes. But there she was riding shotgun for a load of cantaloupes and headed for a town smack in the middle of nowhere. The truck swung back onto the highway, and she watched in the side view mirror as the blue convertible got smaller and smaller then finally disappeared.

"Peter O'Ryan," the man said. He let go of the right side of the steering wheel and shoved his hand across the cab. "You?"

In an effort to seem less a woman travelling alone she answered, "Missus Charles Doyle." She noticed the photograph of a round-faced woman and five little girls stuck to Peter's dashboard, then added, "Olivia." When she learned Peter was a church-going man who'd been married for sixteen years and taught Bible studies on Sunday mornings, she let down her guard. "If you ever pass through Hopeful," she said, "you ought to stop and visit Canasta Jones." Peter claimed he was generally pretty anxious to get home to his family but promised to keep the thought in mind.

Claymore was twenty-three miles from where Olivia had abandoned the convertible and had two gas stations, but only one was equipped to repair automobiles. And, as fate would have it, their mechanic was off on vacation for the remainder of the week. "But," Olivia moaned, "surely there's someone else?"

"Not 'til Monday," the clerk repeated.

Olivia's eyes welled with tears as she turned and walked out into the street. It seemed things were going from horrible to even worse, helpings of bad luck stacking up like dirty dishes. Whatever had she gotten herself into? When she got to the corner, Olivia turned. Whether it had been right or left, she'd be hard pressed to say because by then she was without direction. The sky turned dusky as she tromped aimlessly up one street and down another. She passed by a Boy Scout who rattled a tin can in her face and called out that it was time to help the poor. "I'm the one who's poor," Olivia mumbled and continued to move one foot in front of the other. She took no notice of anything until she found herself standing in front of a brightly-lit Ford showroom. Right there in the window was the answer to her prayers: a shiny new black sedan. That was the kind of car a woman of her nature should have. Something solid and dependable, something with a roof that didn't fold up like a hankie, something *black*, not a frivolous shade of powder blue. Without a second thought, she walked in.

"Do you take trade-ins?" she asked the young man standing behind the counter.

"Yes, indeed."

"Even if the car's got a broken hose?"

"No problem."

"How about if it's stuck out on the highway?"

"Hmm," the young man twitched his mouth to the right in a mannerism quite like Charlie's, which immediately gave Olivia a good feeling. "We could send a tow truck, but that's an extra charge."

"An extra charge?" Olivia repeated. She was about to ask how much that charge would be when the salesman held up his hand.

"Okay, okay," he groaned playfully, "you've twisted my arm. No extra charge if we do the deal right now."

"Right now? But I still have my things in the trunk." It was not like Olivia to go about blabbing her business so she felt no need to explain Charlie's death, but she did nonetheless feel ashamed about including him under the heading of "things."

"No problem," the salesman said. "We'll have your old car towed back here. You can take whatever you want."

Two days later Olivia arrived back in Wyattsville driving a Ford Fairlane equipped with air conditioning, a static-free radio, and customized floor mats. "Where's Charlie?" the neighbors asked. "What have you done with his lovely convertible?"

When Olivia explained how Charlie died of a massive heart attack and had to be brought home bottled up inside a silver urn, everyone raised an eyebrow.

"Charlie was never sick a day!" Clara Bowman said.

"A day?" Maggie Cooper sneered. "Why, not even five minutes!"

"And what about his convertible?" Henry Myerson asked. "Charlie loved that car. Are we supposed to believe *that* died too?"

"It did," Olivia answered. "Not died exactly, but boiled over in such a way I thought it was going to explode." She was about to explain how she found herself stranded at the side of the road in North Carolina and had no choice other than to trade Charlie's car in for a more practical replacement, but by then all the neighbors had turned and walked away. "I'm sorry," she said tearfully, but no one was listening.

Olivia pulled the luggage from the car and tugged it through the lobby of the building. She heaved and pushed to maneuver the things into the elevator and then one by one dragged the suitcases and cartons of souvenirs to the far end of the seventh-floor hallway. Not a single person came to help. Husbands who suggested that lending a hand would be the neighborly thing to do were quickly shushed by their wives. "Help that hussy?" they snarled. "The woman who murdered Charlie?"

Once the last of the bags had been carted into the apartment, Olivia closed and bolted the door behind her. She fell upon the bed—the same bed where Charlie had kissed her mouth and made love to her, the same bed where he'd promised to love her for a thousand years. How, she wailed, could he have misled her with such a foolish promise when in truth he had less than a thousand heartbeats to offer? And how could *she,* a woman with such a practical nature, have given up everything and waltzed off like a love-crazed schoolgirl? Now here she was, all alone in an unfamiliar place, with neighbors who banded themselves together and turned against her as they would a person carrying the plague.

By morning Olivia had decided the boundary of her new world

would extend no further than the threshold of Charlie's apartment. For almost three weeks she cracked the door open early in the morning, stuck her arm out far enough to retrieve the daily newspaper, then locked herself inside. She used an outdated carton of powdered milk for her coffee, ate tins of Spam and baked beans for supper, and, once she'd finished the only can of orange juice in the freezer, simply did without fruit. With her life turned topsy-turvy as it had been, the balancing of five basic food groups seemed of little concern.

Three weeks to the day after Olivia arrived back in Wyattsville there was a knock on the apartment door. "Who is it?" she called out.

"Clara Bowman," the voice answered.

Olivia slid back the bolt, opened the door, and without saying a word stood there looking Clara square in the eye.

"I hate to intrude," Clara said frostily, "but I believe I left my yellow sweater in Charlie's closet, and with the weather turning somewhat cool..."

Olivia swung the door open and motioned Clara inside.

"Thanks." Clara strolled over to the hall closet, rummaged through a jumble of hangers, and tugged loose the sweater. "This is it," she said tucking it under her arm. With one foot already out the door, Clara turned back to Olivia and asked, "Are you all right?"

It was a fair enough question, for Olivia had developed the look of a ghost. Where there had once been a fullness of face, she had turned gaunt. Her eyes were rimmed with red, and a grey ash of sadness had settled upon her. "I'm fine," Olivia answered politely.

"But, you don't look..." Before she could carry on with the thought, the door swung shut. Clara, a woman known for her keen observations, was not about to let a question go unanswered. She rang the bell for a second time and then pounced forward when Olivia opened the door. "You don't look good!" she said, pushing her way back into the apartment.

"Excuse me?" Olivia stammered in a somewhat indignant fashion.

"You look sick," Clara replied and tromped through to the kitchen. "Like a person who's not been eating." She yanked open cupboard after cupboard and glared at the almost-empty shelves. "No wonder," she snarled. "Look at this—not a crumb of food fit to eat!"

"It so happens I like canned soup."

"You like getting scurvy? Because that's what people who don't have fresh fruits and vegetables get!" Clara was shorter than Olivia but almost twice as wide and built like a fireplug. She charged from the kitchen into the living room. "Why, this place is a mess," she exclaimed. "There's a month's worth of newspapers that need throwing out!"

"I'm not finished reading them," Olivia answered.

"You're finished!" Clara scooped up a huge armful of papers and stomped out the door, grumbling how it was shameful the way Olivia had been treated when she was so obviously distraught over the loss of her husband. "It's Maggie Cooper's fault," she huffed. "Maggie *never* sees the good in people." With that Clara disappeared down the hallway but five minutes later she was back, bing-bonging the doorbell for a third time. She was carrying a laundry basket full of food. "You locked me out," she said when Olivia opened the door.

"I thought you were gone."

"Gone? I'm not even half finished." She reached into the basket and hauled out an orange. "Eat this," she said, pushing the fruit into Olivia's hand. Without another word Clara marched herself into the kitchen and set about making a chicken casserole. "It's a good thing I got here when I did," she said, "otherwise you never know…"

"Nonsense. Feeling down about Charlie's death is the only thing wrong with me."

"Oh, really? Do you think a person's skin is *supposed* to be grey? You think eyes are *supposed* to be red as a beefsteak?"

Olivia had to admit she'd been unaware such was the case. She then settled in alongside of Clara and lent a hand to the peeling of onions. By the time the casserole was ready to take from the oven she'd gone through the full tale of Charlie's death, including the part about the unlucky opal.

"You poor thing," Clara said sympathetically. She dished up two plates of chicken and set them on the table. Sliding into the chair opposite Olivia she leaned forward, waiting to hear the rest of the story.

"There I was," Olivia said when she got to the part about the convertible breaking down, "stranded by the side of the road, miles from civilization, no way to get home."

"You did the right thing, honey. Getting yourself a good serviceable car is exactly what Charlie would have wanted you to do!"

Strangely enough, sitting there and talking openly as she was, Olivia started to feel a bit lighter. Not quite as floaty as she'd felt from

Canasta's okra soup but close. "Is there some sort of secret ingredient in this casserole?" she asked.

"Heavy cream," Clara answered and shoveled a forkful into her mouth.

When Clara left what she now considered Olivia's apartment she went directly to Maggie Cooper's and told Maggie they'd been all wrong about Olivia. "Why, the woman is devastated!" she said. "We owe it to poor Charlie to take care of his wife."

Next Clara rapped on Henry Myerson's door and gave him the same message. She then stopped off at Barbara Jean Conklin's, Fred Magenheimer's, Tillie Rae's, and Susan Latimer's, setting everyone straight as to what they should and shouldn't do about the widow Olivia Doyle.

Before noon of the next day Olivia had received eight condolence calls, six casseroles, three fruit baskets, and a spray of red gladiolas so large the delivery man had to turn sideways to squeeze through the apartment door. She'd also been invited to a Fuller Brush party, a gin rummy luncheon, and Friday night Bingo. When Olivia suggested she was not yet up to socializing, Gertrude Plumber turned a deaf ear and rambled on about how the group desperately needed someone to co-host the monthly pot luck dinner. "We can't possibly ask Louise to do it again," she told Olivia, "so you've simply *got* to say yes."

Although nothing could replace the sweetness of Charlie's kisses, the sudden onslaught of friends and neighbors helped to brighten Olivia's days. Her skin gradually regained its color, and the redness left her eyes. Every once in a while, mostly when she was with Clara who soon became her closest friend, Olivia would feel a strange tugging at the corners of her mouth and before there was time to wonder what was happening she'd find her face crinkled into a smile.

ETHAN ALLEN DOYLE

*P*eople think a kid's got no brains, but I was smarter than Mama. Leastwise I knew not to go sassing when Daddy was on the warpath. Mama, she didn't care. She'd sass anyway. Go shit in your hat, she'd tell him, even when she knew it meant a punch in the face. Seems she would've learned, but, no sir, not Mama!

Daddy never even thought twice about punching people, but then he was mean enough to shoot the eye out of a bird for singing the wrong song. I ain't one bit like my daddy. He used to say I got Mama's foul mouth and sneaky ways, but Mama said what I got was her love of living. I liked when she said that.

Me and Mama both knew Daddy would throw a shit-fit about us going to New York, but seeing as how she could unruffle his feathers anytime she'd a mind to I figured she'd smooth things over when we got back home. I sure as hell never figured the fighting to get bad as it did.

Daddy should've just let Mama have her fling. Then she'd have been done with it and we would have come home. Course, I was wishing we'd see a real live Yankee game before we did. Now that Yankee game's gone to hell, along with everything else.

TRUTH AND CONSEQUENCES

It was one thing to hate your daddy so much that you sometimes wished him dead but quite another to see his head split open like a rotted pumpkin. Ethan Allen huddled beneath the wisteria, afraid to move, trying with all his might to twist his brain around to believing that any minute Susanna and Benjamin would get up and stumble to the bedroom together. There had been plenty of fights before and nobody had ever ended up dead. But then Scooter Cobb, a mountain of a man with fists the size of ham hocks, had never before gotten involved. Much as Ethan wanted to go see about his mama, he couldn't force himself to leave his hiding place. When he tried to stand his knees buckled under. When he tried to crawl his arms stayed locked in place, and if he even thought about crying out for help his heart took to jumping around as if it would explode. There was no telling what would happen if Scooter came back.

He might have stayed hidden forever, but as a splinter of light edged its way into the sky three black crows zoomed down from nowhere and began picking at Benjamin. Suddenly Ethan Allen was no longer held prisoner by the thought of Scooter's return. He let go of Dog and bolted from beneath the bush, hollering at the top of his voice and flapping his arms about wildly. He'd figured Benjamin to be in pretty rough shape, probably feeling meaner than he'd ever before felt, but when the boy saw his daddy's faceless body sprawled across the yard a sickness slithered from his stomach into his throat. A spew of thick yellow bile suddenly erupted from his mouth. It was more bitter than anything he had ever tasted. He wanted to scream and cry out for his mama to come but there was no sound inside of him, just the mean yellow bitterness rising time and again.

Once, years ago, he'd come across the bloody carcass of an animal torn apart by something bigger and stronger. A lone rat was chewing the last bit of gristle from what had once been a leg. For weeks on end the sight of such a thing haunted his dreams. Sometimes the animal appeared as a fox, sometimes a dog, sometimes even a newborn calf skinned to the bone. But no matter what form it took, the cry was always the same. It was a sound so pitiful it woke him from his sleep night after night. All that summer he heard it. When the wind blew he heard it. When the night was still he heard it. Right now he heard it louder than ever before. Ethan clapped his hands over his ears, then finally let go of the call for his mama. He wasn't a boy given to fear, yet he stood frozen in the spot screaming for Susanna. "Mama," he cried over and over again. Then, when no one came, he turned and stumbled toward the house.

She was still lying on the bed. "Wake up, Mama!" he shouted, grabbing onto her arm. Susanna's skin, skin that always seemed silky soft, was cold to his touch, her arm incredibly heavy with the weight of a crowbar attached to it. He held on to her for a moment then tried to pull his hand back, but he couldn't. His fingers simply refused to let go. One by one he had to pry them loose. Once he had released his hold on her, Susanna's arm dropped to the side of the bed.

Ethan Allen had seen dead things before. Not people, but calves, chickens, and, worst of all, the mare that died giving birth to a foal. He knew when a living thing stopped breathing that was the end of it. You either buried it in the ground or carved it up for eating. Although he could see Susanna had the same blank-eyed stare as the mare, he raised his fist and brought it down hard against her chest. "God-dammit, Mama," he shouted, "wake up!" He pounded his fist against her chest again and again until his arm ached and his hand swelled to the size of one that had been bee-stung. "Wake up!" he screamed. "Wake up, God damn you, wake up!"

Susanna never moved. "Son-of-a-bitch!" Ethan finally screamed and started kicking at the sideboard of the bed, then the dresser, after that the chifferobe. He whacked a table lamp to the floor and then heaved the wedding photo of Susanna and Benjamin across the room with such force that it gouged a chunk of plaster from the far wall. "Lousy, son-of-a-bitch, bastard!" he screamed as loud as he could. Then he connected a string of obscenities and shouted them over and over again. It was the way he came back at the unfairness of life; he cussed and screamed until he couldn't cuss or scream anymore, until the words grew dry and bitter-tasting in his throat.

It's said that a single tear falls with more weight than a boulder, so when Ethan Allen lowered his head to Susanna's bosom and sobbed, "Why, Mama, why?" it was possible that a passerby at the far edge of the field might have heard the boy's heart crack open. He stayed there for a long time and cried tears enough to soak her halter through, but nothing changed. Nothing ever changed. Life was what it was—shit, lousy, awful. When he finally gave up on crying, the sun was high in the sky. "Son-of-a-bitch," he said. The crack in his heart pushed itself shut, and his face once again took on that rock hard look of resignation. He picked up the lamp, set it back on the nightstand, then stumbled to the telephone and asked the operator to ring up the sheriff.

"Does your mama know you're bothering the sheriff?" asked Carolyn Stiles, one of the switchboard operators who knew Susanna from the diner.

"My mama's dead."

"Don't you go smart-mouthing me, Ethan Allen."

"I ain't," he answered, his voice black and heavy as an iron skillet. "It's the truth. Mama got killed."

Given the sorrowful sound of his words, Carolyn quickly realized this was not another of Ethan Allen's pranks. "Lord God Almighty!" she gasped. "What happened? Where's your daddy? Is he there with you?"

"Daddy's dead too," Ethan mumbled through another choke of words.

"Your mama and daddy's both dead?" she gasped. "What happened, honey? Are you okay? You hurt?"

Ethan didn't answer any of her questions. He just stood there, holding the telephone to his ear and listening as Carolyn called out for someone to have the sheriff's office send a man out to the Doyle place on the double 'cause there'd been some kind of tragedy.

"What happened to your mama and daddy, honey? You can tell me," Carolyn said. "Was it an accident? A burglar? I got a deputy on his way, but, sweetie, you can go right ahead and tell me what happened."

When grown-ups started asking questions in such a way, Ethan Allen knew from experience, they were after something he'd be better off claiming to know nothing about. "I got no idea," he finally answered. "It must've happened while I was asleep."

"Asleep? This late in the day?"

"I might've been up a while, but…"

"Well, how exactly did your mama and daddy die?"

"I don't know. They was dead when I found them."

"Where'd you find them?"

"Right where they died." It went on like that, question after question, meaningless answer after meaningless answer until he heard the police car screeching to a stop in the front yard. Ethan Allen hung up the telephone, then watched from behind the screen door as two policemen climbed from the car. Jack Mahoney, the short light-haired detective, he'd seen at the diner. But the other one, the one wearing a blue uniform with a silver badge shined up brighter than an automobile headlight—the one nearly the size of Scooter Cobb—he was someone Ethan Allen had never before seen. Not at the diner and not around town.

"Boy," the big one called out, "you know what happened here?"

"No, sir," Ethan answered, stepping outside the door. "I must've been sleeping." He'd swallowed down the last word because he'd looked up and read the policeman's badge. Samuel Cobb. Scooter's boy—the policeman his mother said would claim he was telling lies on people and quick as a wink toss him into reform school for a thousand years. "I sleep real sound," Ethan added. "Mama used to say a shotgun blast couldn't wake me."

"Is that so?" Cobb answered. "I suppose, then, you didn't hear a bit of whatever scuffle took place in this here yard?"

"No, sir. Not me. Not last night. I was sound asleep 'fore my head hit the pillow."

Officer Cobb took note of how the boy kept his eyes to the ground and shifted his weight from one foot to the other. "Asleep, huh?"

Ethan Allen nodded.

"A fight such as this, and you didn't hear nothing? No hollering? No breaking glass?" Cobb gave a dubious frown.

Susanna always claimed she knew when a boy was lying, and now Ethan Allen began to worry Scooter's son was gifted with the same ability. The boy nervously shook his head side to side, his eyes turned away. He was afraid to look up. One wrong move and Cobb might see straight through to where the truth was hidden. Ethan felt something dreadful wriggling along his back. It was probably what his mama always said would happen: a lying snake had come to call on its kin.

"Seems when that window broke you would've heard it," Cobb said.

"I done told you, I didn't hear nothing." Ethan was suddenly starting to feel sicker than ever. Cobb knew he was lying, he was certain of it.

"You sure you're telling me the truth?"

"Me? Yes, sir." Ethan wiped a line of sweat from his forehead.

"Good. Because if I thought you was lying, I'd have to arrest you. Not telling what you know is concealing evidence."

"I ain't lying! You keep asking me all these questions but I done told you, I don't know nothing. I was asleep. I swear."

"Oh, really? And exactly what time did you go to bed?"

"Before dark. Seven, seven-thirty, maybe."

Until that moment Mahoney had been busy securing the ground area around Benjamin's body and calling for a unit of crime scene investigation detectives to be sent out. As he heard Ethan's reply he said, "Ain't that a bit early? Most nights you're hanging around the diner until ten or eleven."

"Yeah, but my mama wasn't working last night."

"How come? Don't she usually work on Friday?"

Ethan Allen shrugged. "She stayed home 'cause I was feeling sick."

"I thought you said you went to bed early last night."

"Yeah." Ethan Allen's fingers suddenly got so fidgety he had to stuff his hands into his pockets. "But it was 'cause I didn't feel good."

"So you just went to bed and slept through what must've been one hell of a commotion going on out here?"

"I told you. I didn't hear nothing, I didn't see nothing. I was asleep."

"Let's take a look at where you were sleeping so soundly," Cobb said. He followed Ethan into a small alcove adjacent to the living room. "This is where you were doing all that sleeping?" he asked, eyeing a bed with several empty cartons and a stack of towels piled on top of it.

"Yes, sir."

"Close as this is, you didn't hear a thing?"

"No, sir."

"No arguing? No fighting?"

The boy shook his head side to side, but his heart was thumping so hard he thought for sure Cobb would hear it. "I done told you," he said.

"Ten times I told you, I didn't hear nothing and for certain didn't see nothing!"

"That's what you told me," Cobb replied, pushing the cartons aside and folding back the coverlet, "but I got a hunch it ain't the full and honest truth. The way this stuff is piled up here makes me wonder if this bed's even been slept in."

Ethan Allen just stood there staring down at his feet.

"Leave the boy be," Mahoney finally said. "He don't know nothing."

"I ain't so sure," Cobb replied as he turned toward the back bedroom.

When the crime scene detectives arrived they tromped back and forth through the house checking every piece of overturned furniture, marking spots where the tiniest droplet of blood had fallen, looking in every crack and corner for some smidgen of evidence as to what had taken place and taking picture after picture. Mahoney and Cobb continued to question Ethan Allen. "Your mama or daddy have enemies?" Mahoney asked. "Anybody who might want to do them harm?"

"Your daddy owe anybody money?" added Cobb, who was himself itching to make detective. "How about your mama?"

"Why you asking me?" Ethan Allen said. "I'm a kid. I don't know nothing!"

"That new tractor, where'd your daddy get the money for such an expensive thing?"

"How about your mama and daddy, did they get along?"

As they pummeled him with question after question, Ethan Allen's resolve grew stronger. His answers switched over to nothing more than a shrug or shake of the head. The boy knew how it would go: one whisper of what Scooter Cobb had done, then *he'd* be the one punished. Lies, they'd say, made up stories, and off he'd go to reform school. No, sir, that wasn't gonna happen. They could drag him from the house, strip him buck naked, and hang him up by his thumbs, but he'd never admit he knew the truth of what went on.

Late in the afternoon as he stood on the front porch and watched the two men from the coroner's office carry off his mama, Ethan Allen felt the crack in his heart pushing open again. Never before had anything hurt as much as this—not all the forgotten birthdays in the world, not a bushel basket of broken promises, not even his daddy smacking him clear across the room. At least then he had somebody. Now he was alone, more alone than anybody else on earth. A string of tears rolled down the boy's face as he watched the truck disappear down the driveway. "You just had to tell him, didn't you, Mama?" he sobbed. "You just *had* to tell Daddy we was going to New York."

"What's that about New York?" asked Mahoney, who had come up behind the boy.

"It ain't nothing," Ethan answered. "Mama and me was gonna go there on vacation, but I guess we ain't gonna go now."

"You got folks in New York?"

"Nope. We was just going for vacation."

"What about relatives? Is there somebody who can take you in?"

Ethan Allen shook his head. For nearly four hours he'd managed to say almost nothing at all, certainly nothing of any significance. He wasn't about to start blabbing now. The less they knew the better. Start talking and they'd try to worm the truth out of you. He was wise to that game. "Don't let the cat out of the bag," was one of the last things Susanna had said, and it was advice to live by.

"Nobody?" Mahoney said solemnly.

"I don't need nobody."

"You'll have to go somewhere."

"I'm staying here."

Mahoney wrapped his arm around the boy's shoulder. "I'm afraid we can't let you do that, son. You've got to be in the care of an adult."

Ethan Allen didn't answer right away. He just stood there watching the road, like he expected his mama to come walking back. "I got a grandpa," he finally said. "He'll come stay with me."

"I thought you said you didn't have any kin."

"I meant any kin other than Grandpa." He was starting to sweat again.

Mahoney had raised five youngsters of his own and gave a knowing smile. "Why don't you give me your grandpa's telephone number?" he said. "That way I can give him a call and make sure he's coming."

"Grandpa don't talk to no strangers."

"Oh, he don't, huh? Well, that's too bad, because you can't stay here unless I'm certain you got somebody to look after you. The law don't allow little kids to be living alone."

"You don't believe me?" Ethan Allen challenged. "You think I'm lying?"

"Hard to say. Anyway, it's against the law for me to leave you out here without somebody to watch over you. So if you don't give me your grandpa's telephone number, I've got no choice but to take you out to the children's home until we can locate a relative." Mahoney draped a kindly arm around Ethan's shoulder and smiled in an easy sort of way. "That's not what either of us want, son, so how about helping out here?"

The truth was Ethan didn't have a telephone number. The only thing he'd ever known of his grandfather was the name and return address he'd seen written on the back of an envelope. Every year he'd receive a birthday card with a dollar bill folded inside. No message other than the words "Love, Grandpa." A number of times the boy had asked Susanna why a grandpa who bothered to send a dollar didn't come to visit. "It's the fault of your daddy," she'd answered with no further explanation. Apparently words couldn't account for why Benjamin's own kin wanted nothing to do with him.

For a brief moment Ethan Allen considered telling Detective Mahoney that Charles Doyle was his grandpa's name, but luckily he remembered how truth-giving could backfire on you and he kept his lips locked. Ethan knew that the littlest things could spin out of control. His mama was proof of it. She'd still be alive if she hadn't flared up and told Benjamin the truth about going to New York. *Unh-unh,* he thought. *The less said the better.*

After a considerable amount of arguing the two officers bundled the boy into the patrol car leaving behind the dog, who'd been impossible to catch. Cobb drove; Mahoney sat in the passenger seat. Ethan Allen was alone in the back seat, his heart dangerously close to cracking open again, but his mind fixed on holding back the tears.

When they were a mile or so from the house, Cobb eyed the boy in the rearview mirror and asked, "You hungry, kid?"

"No," Ethan Allen answered, snuffling the word back into his nose.

"I sure am," Mahoney said, turning to smile at the boy. "What say we stop at the diner and get ourselves a sandwich? Maybe even some pie?"

"I told you, I ain't the least hungry." The thought of coming face-to-face with Scooter set Ethan Allen's lower lip to trembling, and regardless of his intention a stream of tears let loose down his face. Ethan figured Sam Cobb was already suspicious. The next thing would be for him to tell his daddy. Scooter wasn't a man to go easy on someone, not even a kid. One word from Policeman Sam, and Scooter would come back to finish the job. Ethan remembered how time after time he'd taken a heaped-high plate of pie from the same hands that left his daddy's head looking like a scrambled-up egg. He felt a swell rising in his throat. "You better pull over," he said. "I think I gotta puke."

"You're probably hungry," Mahoney said in a kindly way. "You'd feel a lot better if you had something in your stomach."

"I ain't eating no damn pie!" Ethan shouted angrily. "It's made outta shit and maggots! I ain't never eating it never again. Never!"

Cobb turned with an angry glare. "Watch your mouth!" he growled.

Mahoney broke in. "Leave him be," he said. "The boy's scared, and he's got a right. Ain't that so, Ethan Allen?" He glanced back and saw the boy swiping at the tears overflowing his eyes. "Still," Mahoney said, "you ought to eat. A bowl of soup, maybe? Or a dish of ice cream?"

Ethan Allen shook his head.

"I'll tell you what," Mahoney said, a gentle note of concern in his voice. "When we get to the diner, you order anything you think you *might* want. If you feel up to eating it, fine. If you're still not hungry, we'll get Bertha to pack it up for you."

"Why do I gotta go in?"

"Officer Cobb and me have been working all day. We need to get some supper, and we can't just leave you sitting in the car now, can we?"

"Why not?"

"If you was to up and run off, we'd be the ones held responsible."

Although precisely such a thought had already crossed his mind, Ethan Allen said, "I'm just a kid. Where's a kid gonna go?"

Mahoney gave the boy a knowing grin.

By the time they pulled into the diner parking lot, Ethan's heart was about ready to explode. He could feel it already stretched out to three times the normal size. "I ain't feeling too good," he moaned. "If I was to eat one bite of anything, I'd for sure puke." Mahoney clamped a firm hand onto his shoulder and hustled him inside.

Scooter Cobb was hanging over the counter with a sizeable piece of jelly donut crammed into his mouth and a lump of what could have been raspberry jelly or could have been a part of Benjamin's face sliding down his right thumb. Ethan Allen, figuring it to be the latter, felt a rise of vomit in his throat. Scooter looked bigger than ever: his head round as a basketball, his body mounded to the size of a mountain, and his hands—

big, thick, massive hands that could squash a boy's head with hardly trying. Ethan wanted to look away. He wanted not to see the hands. He wanted to turn his eyes from the heavy-lidded face. But instead he stood there and whimpered. It was a tiny sound that simply slid from his mouth, a dead giveaway of his fear. If Scooter hadn't known before, he surely knew now.

Scooter Cobb lumbered from behind the counter and grabbed hold of the boy. "Poor kid," he moaned, pressing Ethan Allen into the thick of his stomach. "It's an awful thing what happened to your mama."

There was no noticeable mention of his daddy.

For what seemed to Ethan an eternity Scooter hugged and squeezed, at times pressing the boy's nose so deep into the greasy apron he could barely breathe. When Scooter finally let go Ethan swallowed a gasp of air to clear away the smell of fried hamburgers and meanness.

Mahoney moved to the far end of the diner. He eased Ethan Allen into a booth and then slid in alongside of him. Sam Cobb sat on the opposite side; Scooter next to him.

A short while later Bertha, a woman with her own share of troubles, dropped four menus on the table. Bertha's husband had lost four jobs in the last two months, her oldest boy was about to be sent off to reform school, and the bunion on her right foot throbbed from morning until night, but still she mustered up a sad-eyed smile. "Sweetie," she said to Ethan Allen, "your mama was a well-meaning person, and she sure deserved better than she got. I'm real sorry about what happened." She told the boy she'd be saying a prayer, then switched over to asking what he wanted to eat.

"Nothing," Ethan answered, locking his eyes onto a speckle of yellow mustard at the far end of the tabletop. "I ain't one bit hungry."

"Even so," Bertha winced a bit as she shifted her weight to the left leg, "you ought to eat something. How about I bring you some cherry pie with ice cream on top?"

Without looking up Ethan Allen shook his head

"Fix him a grilled cheese," Scooter said, "with home fries, and a slice of blueberry pie. Matter of fact, bring two slices. I'm gonna have one too."

Mahoney and Sam Cobb gave their orders, then Bertha limped off. As soon as she out of earshot, Scooter started in with a barrage of questions about what had taken place at the Doyle farm. "You got any suspicions as to who it was?" he asked eagerly. "What about clues? Eye witnesses?" When Bertha set the food down in front of them, Scooter ignored the pie and gulped down the black coffee as he leaned in to hear every last detail of how the investigation was progressing. When it seemed there was no more to be told he asked, "What about the boy? What's gonna happen to him?"

"I don't know," Mahoney said. "Right now we don't know of any relatives. Ethan claims there's a grandpa, but he doesn't know the phone number."

"The kid's lying up one side and down the other," said Sam Cobb, who had a sharp-tongued manner. "He knows plenty of stuff he ain't telling."

Ethan felt his heart explode with the force of an overblown balloon, and a rush of air whooshed from his mouth. He started coughing so furiously his face went blue as the pie.

Mahoney reached over and thumped a heavy hand against the boy's back, giving Sam Cobb a look of disgust at the same time. "Back off," he said. "The kid's got enough troubles. So what if he can't recall his grandpa's phone number right off? Tomorrow we'll try again, huh, Ethan?" He slid his arm around the boy's shoulder. "For now we're gonna let him bunk in over at the stationhouse."

"He's just a kid," Scooter said. "Kids ought not be sleeping in the jailhouse."

"It's too late to make any other arrangements tonight," Mahoney said. "Tomorrow we'll try to locate the grandpa, but if nothing turns up—"

"If nothing turns up?" Scooter repeated in an angry voice. "What? You'll have him live in the jailhouse, like some sort of criminal?"

"Of course not. He'll probably go to Holy Trinity." Mahoney shifted uncomfortably in his seat, trying to look away from the boy as he spoke. "Nobody wants such a thing to happen, but we don't have a choice."

"Holy Trinity?" Scooter sputtered. "You'd cart Susanna's boy off to the orphanage?"

"There's no choice," Mahoney mumbled apologetically. "It's the law."

"Well, that ain't gonna happen!" Scooter slammed his fist down so hard the butter dish bounced from the table and fell to the floor. "There's no way in hell I'd allow Susanna's boy to be sent off to an orphanage!"

"Pop!" Sam Cobb stammered.

"Don't Pop me! We got plenty of room at our house. Emma won't mind caring for another boy. She misses having a youngster around."

Ethan looked up. His eyes had popped out like giant blueberries. "Oh, no," he said. "Mama would never want that! She *always* told me not to be a bother to people." The thought of being bundled off to an orphanage wasn't half bad. A boy could survive at an orphanage. He could wait it out until there was a chance to escape. But getting turned over to Scooter—Ethan gave a quick glance at the man's hands and knew beyond a smidgen of doubt that in such a situation, he was good as dead.

"You ain't no bother."

"But I wanna spend the night at the jailhouse. Ain't nobody I know ever done an exciting thing like that!"

"Ain't nothing exciting about sleeping on a rock-hard cot," Mahoney said with a smile tugging at the corner of his mouth. "You'd be a lot better off at the Cobbs'."

"But—"

"No buts," Scooter said. "I owe your mama. Susanna would want me to make sure you're taken care of."

Ethan could feel himself being boxed in. His right eye started twitching something fierce, and beads of sweat rose up on his forehead. It was obvious what Scooter's plan was. He'd make it appear he was being real friendly, then when nobody expected it—pounce! Ethan had to find a way out. First he considered the possibility of sneaking out through the back door, but that wasn't much of a plan because Mahoney would never allow him to go wandering off by himself. Then there was the chance he could break and run, but the probability was even if he ran faster than he'd ever run before he'd not make it to the door.

Mahoney, who'd right off accepted Scooter's offer, suggested they could drop the boy off on their way back to the station if Emma wouldn't mind.

"You needn't bother," Scooter replied. "Leave him here. I'll be heading home in a few hours. He can ride with me."

The boy's heart came to a dead stop. He knew for certain he wouldn't make it to the house once Scooter got hold of him. "He just up and disappeared," Scooter would claim as he served up a plateful of suspicious-looking meatloaf. Nope, if he wanted to go on living Ethan had to make a move right now! Mustering up every bit of acting ability he had he nonchalantly stretched his arms in the air and yawned, then started telling how tired he was. "I'd surely appreciate it," he sighed, "if I could get to bed early 'stead of waiting around."

"Well, now," Mahoney replied, "I think we can take care of that." He hooked his arm over the boy's shoulder and headed for the door.

At the last minute Ethan turned and looked back. "Bye, Mister Scooter," he called. "See you later."

ETHAN ALLEN

I am the most unluckiest kid on earth. I got a dead mama, a dead daddy, and the meanest man on earth wanting to kill me. Being dead might be better than having no place to go, 'cept I seen how Scooter Cobb kills people and that sure ain't for me.

Mama's mostly to blame for this problem I got. If she'd kept her mouth shut we could've snuck off and Daddy wouldn't have been any the wiser. But, no, she had to have the last word. That's how Mama was. You'd love her one day and hate her the next. She'd smear kisses across your face and tell how much fun you was gonna have together. Then just when you was believing such a thing would really happen, she'd forget you was alive. That's when you'd wind up hating her. Right now I hate her. If she was here right now I'd sure let her know how much I hate her. Or maybe I'd just be glad she was here and forget about the hating.

Mister Cobb says on account of his feelings for Mama, he's gonna see to taking care of me. Ha! I say what he's gonna see to is me being dead. If I ain't looking to be dead, I gotta get my ass outta here.

I got no choice but to take a chance on that grandpa I ain't never seen. He probably won't be none too happy about Daddy's kid wanting to come live with him, but so what? I'm blood kin. Everybody knows you ain't supposed to turn away blood kin.

NO GOODBYE

Emma Cobb was no more than a head taller than Ethan but nearly as wide as Scooter. She had a pleasant smile and a mother's warm-hearted way of telling the boy to brush his teeth before he got into bed. If things were different, if Ethan didn't have to act quickly, he could have easily succumbed to having a woman such as this fuss over him, serve warm cocoa, and ask if he was feeling a bit better. But as it was he simply said he was dog-tired and needed to go right to bed.

"You ought to at least have a peanut butter and jelly sandwich," Emma suggested. "And maybe some milk?"

Ethan hadn't eaten all day, and he was feeling his belly button rub against his backbone. Not that such a thing bothered him, for he'd gone without eating plenty of times before. Still, at this particular moment a peanut butter and jelly sandwich seemed the answer to at least one of his problems. Besides, the making and eating of such a sandwich wouldn't use up more than a half minute. "Okay," he answered, licking at his lips. He gulped down three such sandwiches and two glasses of milk, then hurried off to bed.

Ethan had at first figured the Cobb house would be somewhat like his own, a pancake sort of structure with windows nose-high from the ground. Instead he'd come up against a narrow two-story building with attic rooms rising up in peaks. With his luck already on a downslide, it came as no surprise when he was led up two flights of stairs to a top-floor bedroom with sloped ceilings and a single window.

"This used to be Sammy's room," Emma said, "when he was a boy just about your age." She folded back a worn coverlet and plumped the pillow, then handed Ethan a pair of frayed pajamas and a toothbrush. Brushing a kiss across his forehead, she whispered, "Sleep tight," then left, closing the door behind her.

Ethan hurriedly pressed his ear to the door. He heard her footsteps on the stair and listened for the click of the light switch on the landing. When it came he waited for what seemed to be a million heartbeats, then, certain she was gone, crossed over to the window. It was a tiny window far too narrow for a full-size person to squeeze through but big enough for an eleven-year-old boy who was small for his age to begin with. Ethan pushed at the sash but it was stuck, cemented in place by layer after layer of paint. "Figures," he moaned, then pulled a pen knife from his pocket and began chipping away. It took the better part of an hour before he could pry the window open—time he couldn't afford to lose. At first he'd thought only of breaking loose and running, but while he was poking loose the paint he'd come to realize he needed a plan.

At the bottom of the closet Ethan found a carton of clothes—jeans, flannel shirts, and the like. It was the time of year when days were warmed by the sun, but once darkness came a chilling dampness settled into people's bones. Ethan grabbed hold of a dark blue sweater and pulled it over his head, then mounded the remaining clothes in the center of the bed. He shaped a figure the size of himself and pulled up the coverlet. *There,* he thought with satisfaction. *That ought to give me 'til morning.*

On a night when the air smelled of coming rain and dark clouds drifted back and forth across the moon, Ethan crawled out the attic window and eased it shut behind him. Once outside he began looking for a way down. With barely enough light for him to see the toe ends of his sneakers and a roof pitched at a preposterously steep angle, he lost his footing on the very first step. It happened quicker than a hiccup. A shingle popped loose and his foot slid from beneath him.

The only thing he could do was drop to his belly and pray he'd catch hold. "Please, Jesus," he gasped, "help me." Apparently the Lord didn't hold a grudge over the fact that Ethan had been to church only three times in his entire life—his christening day counting as one of them—because he suddenly stopped. For several minutes he didn't move a muscle, just suckered himself to the roof, telling the Lord how appreciative he was for the help and swearing to show up at Sunday service.

A few moments later the clouds passed by and the moon was bright as a streetlight. Ethan glanced down to get a feel for exactly where he was, but looking at the ground from such a height caused something inside his head to start spinning. "Stay with me, Lord," he whispered. After a moment the dizziness left him, and by then he knew he was on the northwest side of the house somewhat close to the back. Remaining on his hands and knees, he began crabbing his way toward the place where a back porch ought to be.

He moved slowly until he finally spotted a drainpipe. It was a stretch—two feet, maybe more—but it was the only way he could get down. He flattened himself out and inched past a darkened window, praying that no one was inside the room and no one would spot him. On the far edge of the roof he eased his right foot onto the gutter of the drainpipe and got ready for the leap. There would be a thump when he landed, of that he was certain, but all he could do was pray nobody heard it. "I believe in you, Jesus," he mumbled, "so help me out here." He swung his legs across and latched onto the pipe. Ever so slowly he shimmied down, as concerned about not making noise as he was about making progress. But the moment his foot touched the ground, he took off running like a jack rabbit.

It was almost midnight when Scooter Cobb came through the door. Emma was quite used to the irregularity of his hours and was sitting in the living room working on a piece of embroidery she hoped to have finished for Christmas. "I put the boy in Sammy's old room," she said without looking up.

"Good," Scooter grunted. "He asleep?"

Emma nodded. "Has been for hours." She knotted the thread she'd been working with and set the embroidery aside. "I feel real sorry for the boy," she said quietly. "Imagine the grief of losing both a mama and daddy as he did."

"That daddy of his was no loss. The man was a rotten son-of-a-bitch."

"Hush such talk."

"I'm speaking the truth! He's the one to blame for the boy being wild as he is. Susanna used to say…"

Even a stranger who was blind in one eye would have noticed the look on Scooter's face when he spoke Susanna's name.

"Do you think I don't know?" Emma asked, an ocean of hurt brimming her eyes.

"Know what?" Scooter replied apprehensively.

"Know what's been going on between you and Susanna Doyle."

Figuring the boy had told, he shot back, "You believe a kid like that?"

"I believe what my heart tells me."

"What kind of bullshit is that supposed to be?"

"For months I've known you were carrying on. I could tell by the way you'd splash on a half-bottle of cologne to go fry hamburgers, then stay out the biggest part of the night. You think a wife don't notice when her husband keeps to the far side of the bed?" Scooter opened his mouth as if to answer, but she continued. "I figured a man who's been married for thirty years is bound to have an occasional itch or two, but I told myself, 'Just wait, give it time.' I thought this thing with Susanna would eventually burn itself out, but," she moaned, "it obviously didn't."

"It wasn't what you think," Scooter said defensively. "I was simply being kind to the woman, listening to her problems—"

Emma gave him a hard glare and went on. "That's not the end of it. Today when I started to launder that shirt you wore last night I found blood all over it. Not little specks, such as you'd get from a splash of meat, but a sizable amount. It didn't make much sense 'til Jack Mahoney brought the boy to the house and told me the story of how Susanna had been killed and her husband beaten to a pulp. 'It had to be a monster of a man,' Jack said. 'A monster of a man.'"

"You can't think it was me?"

"I don't think. I know."

"Good God, Emma! After all the years we been together, you ought to realize I'd never do such a thing."

"Really? You're practically a stranger to me now. At one time I might have known if you would do or not do a thing. But now I can't begin to imagine the ungodly deeds you're capable of!"

"That's great!" he exclaimed. "Really great! You think I murdered the woman I was supposedly having an affair with?"

"No," she answered coolly. "But I wouldn't doubt you had something to do with the beating of her husband."

Scooter looked visibly shaken. "Is that what you told Jack Mahoney?" he asked.

"No." She allowed the word to hang in the air a long time before she spoke again. "But if you *ever* so much as glance at another woman again, I will." She turned and picked up her embroidery.

"You're crazy, Emma!" Scooter shouted. "Crazy as a loon to think you can threaten me with a thing such as that!"

"Perhaps..." she drawled, slipping a thread of blue yarn through the eye of the needle, "I forgot to mention that I never did get around to washing the shirt."

Scooter narrowed his black eyes and glared at Emma, but seeing the iron set look of determination on her face he bit down on his lip and wisely said nothing. When she went back to her embroidery, he turned away and stomped up the stairs.

"Don't you dare wake the boy," she called out before he was halfway to the landing. Then she circled the thread around her needle and eased a lovers knot into place. "He's already been through more than any child should have to endure."

Mumbling some belligerent under-his-breath answer, Scooter continued.

"I'm warning you," she said.

Although he was not generally a man to be ordered around, he knew better than to cross Emma. Maybe given some time she'd simmer down and he'd find a way to convince her that such suspicions were pure nonsense, but for now he wasn't going to stick a single toe over the line. Of course, if the boy was still awake... He tiptoed up the stairs and cracked open the door to what was now Ethan's room, but the boy appeared to be huddled under the comforter, sound asleep.

Scooter returned to the second floor and climbed into bed, making sure to position himself smack in the middle of the mattress. He was still awake when Emma came to bed and for several hours afterward. Finally, just minutes before the first ray of sun lit the horizon, he dropped into an exhaustive sleep.

⚓

It took Ethan almost two hours to walk from the Cobb place back to his own house. It was a forty-five minute drive, but that was following the road that circled around half the farms on the Eastern Shore. Ethan boosted himself up and over the chain link fence at the far edge of the Kramer farm. Then he traveled as the crow flies, tromping through pitch black cornfields and row after row of soybeans. He stayed back from the houses and moved silently as a shadow. With any luck he'd get what he needed and be long gone before Scooter Cobb discovered him missing.

In the woods south of Miller's pond Ethan heard the growl of something in the underbrush and took off running. It was rumored that rabid wolves had been spotted in the area and any other time Ethan would have turned back or gone off in another direction, but on this night there was no time to waste. He'd seen what Scooter Cobb could do and it was a hell of a lot worse than any wolf, rabid or not. He zigzagged his way through the Morgans' overgrown orchard, then cut through a field of cabbages that had been left to rot. Two minutes later he arrived at the place that for the whole of his life had been home. The front door of Susanna's car was hanging open, although Ethan Allen could swear he'd seen the policeman close it.

"Mama," he shouted and darted across the yard. For a split second he'd slipped back to yesterday or the day before or possibly some time weeks ago and imagined she'd be there sitting behind the wheel, ready to twist the key in the ignition and head off to work. Then that moment of thought disappeared, and he remembered how the men from the coroner's office had carried Susanna away in a black plastic bag. Ethan Allen didn't want to cry. He didn't have time to cry, but that didn't stop the tears from coming. He slid into the driver's seat of his mama's car, then leaned forward and dropped his head against the steering wheel. Sitting there and remembering back on how Susanna had said she'd drive all the way to New York City if she had to, he came up with the idea for a new plan.

Ethan knew how to drive. At least, he sort of knew how. He'd done it sitting in Susanna's lap a dozen times, maybe more. Okay, there was the problem of his feet falling short of the pedals, but if he scooted forward far enough, well then... The new plan was formulating itself inside his head. He'd headed home with every intention of putting Dog in his bicycle basket and pedaling all the way to Wyattsville, but driving *would* make considerably more sense. For one thing, it was faster. Before sunup he could be clear to the ferry, maybe even to Norfolk. By noon he could be in Wyattsville. On the other hand there was the chance he'd run into some policeman who'd arrest him for being too young to drive a car. Ethan sat there for five minutes wrinkling his brow, scratching his head, and twisting his mouth first to one side and then the other. Finally he stiffened his back, jutted his chin forward in a way that made him look remarkably like his mama, and came to a decision. Of course, before he went anywhere there were things he had to get hold of: the cookie jar money, Mister Charles Doyle's address, and the ignition key.

As the boy started toward the house, the dog suddenly trotted out of the woods and followed along at his heels. "Good thing you came back," Ethan said, "else, I'd leave you behind." Despite his words Ethan knew he had no intention of doing such a thing. Dog was all he had. Dog and a grandpa he hadn't heard from in over a year. A grandpa who apparently figured a boy of eleven didn't need a dollar, because this year he hadn't sent a card for Ethan's birthday. A grandpa who according to Susanna had no use for his own son. A grandpa who Ethan hoped would feel more kindly about having a grandson.

A police order telling people to keep out was posted on the door of the house, the same door Ethan had banged in and out of millions of times. "Like hell," he grumbled. He took hold of the knob and tried to turn it, but the door was locked tight. And the key his mama kept under the geranium pot for just such an occasion was gone. He gave the door an angry kick then stomped around to the back. That door was also locked. "Damn," he moaned. He then tried window after window, but every one of them was locked.

Luckily the sky had remained cloudless, and a white moon was shinning down brighter than ever. Ethan supposed it could be midnight, perhaps later, but he was running out of time. In a few hours they'd discover he was gone and come looking for him. Likely as not it would be Officer Cobb, possibly even Scooter. A trickle of sweat rolled down his back as he thought, *Maybe they already know.* Maybe they'd checked the bed and found nothing but a rolled up bunch of clothes. Maybe they were right now rounding the bend at Klausner's Corner. Maybe they'd be *here* in a matter of minutes!

Ethan scooped up a rock and hurled it through his bedroom window. The sound of breaking glass crashed through the night, louder than he figured possible, loud enough to maybe be heard for miles. For the third time that evening he began calling for the Lord to lend a hand. "Please, God," he prayed, "let me get gone before Scooter comes." He didn't allow the praying to slow him down as he climbed onto the sill and went through the window feet first. The sweater he'd taken from Sam Cobb's closet caught on the jagged edges of glass, but Ethan slid out of it and kept moving.

With the moon bright as it was, there was no need to switch on a light. Still, he moved slowly and stuck close to the walls, just in case somebody was watching. Twice he thought he heard the sound of pounding at the door, but it turned out to be only the thumping of his heart. He took the cookie jar from the top shelf of the china closet and emptied it onto the table: nine dollars and sixty-six cents. He crammed the money into his right pocket, then moved on to Susanna's room.

His mama had two sets of car keys; Ethan knew that for a fact. She was a person given to locking her keys in the car, then calling home for somebody to come rescue her. Three times Ethan himself had bicycled down to the diner with her car keys jingling in his pocket. He could remember the last time. "Ethan Allen," she'd cooed across the telephone line, "be a sweetie and bring me my other set of car keys." He could hear the sugary sound of her voice but with the way she was always switching hiding spots to keep Benjamin from finding her secret stuff, he plain out couldn't fix his memory on where that last place had been.

Ethan lifted the lid of the jewelry box, but before he could do any searching music began bing-bonging like a brass band. He instantly slammed the lid closed. She'd never hide the keys there anyway; too obvious. Still trying to recall his mama's words, the boy rummaged through drawer after drawer with no luck. He fished under the bed far as he could reach. Still nothing. He squeezed his fingers into the toe of every shoe, checked the zipper pouch of an old grey pocketbook, and shook eight lacy brassieres hoping the keys would fall out. He was on the verge of tears when his mama's voice came to him. "Sugar, get my car keys, and bring them to me," she'd said. "They're hidden in the pocket of my blue audition dress."

Ethan went tearing out the front door. Her audition dress was one thing Susanna would never leave without. Sure enough, in the back seat of the car was her suitcase. He snapped it open and right there on top was the blue sequined dress, a set of car keys in the pocket. He needed just one more thing and knew exactly where it was.

For years he'd saved those cards, envelope and all. It seemed nice somehow to think he had a grandpa. Ethan would carry the folded dollar bill in his pocket for months on end without spending it. With the dollar bill in his pocket, he could imagine a grandpa who might one Christmas Eve show up with an armload of presents or a pony. Sometimes he could even imagine a grandma who roasted turkeys and smelled of chocolate chip cookies. Ethan dug down to the bottom of his baseball card box and hauled up the greeting cards signed, "Love Grandpa." On the back flap of every envelope was a carefully written return address. No telephone number, but he didn't need one. He stuffed the cards into his left pocket and walked out the door, leaving it to swing open behind him.

Ethan lifted the dog into his mama's car, then slid behind the wheel. He sat for a moment, then stuck the key in the ignition. Inching forward in the seat, he stretched his toe toward the clutch pedal. He could barely reach it. The other times he'd driven Susanna had been behind him. He'd leaned his back against her and easily enough reached the pedals. He scooted up to the front edge of the seat where he could lay his foot flat on the pedal. At first it seemed to work but the car had a heavy clutch that had to be pressed clear to the floor before the transmission would slide from one gear to the next, so when he tried to push down on the clutch he slid back to his original position. Three times he gave it a go. Then he got out of the car, took hold of Susanna's valise, and wedged it up against the back of the driver's seat. It was a boxy thing that didn't leave a whole lot of room for his body, but once he'd squeezed behind the wheel he knew for sure he wouldn't be sliding back. He tried again. With a grunt he pushed the pedal to the floor, turned the key, and, mumbling, "Thanks, Mama," shifted into reverse.

Once Ethan was out of the driveway, he slid the gearshift into first, then second, then third and was on his way—him, his mama's suitcase, and Dog. With the moon bright as it was, he could see well enough to drive without lights, which meant there was less likelihood of someone spotting the slow-moving car as it crossed over the back roads and headed toward the old towpath. It was a dirt road that ran alongside the canal and stretched clear to the end of the island. Best of all no one ever used it, so he wasn't gonna encounter some wise-ass policeman asking if he wasn't a tad young to be driving a car.

Ethan thumped down the Millers' tractor run for almost two miles; then he spotted the towpath and turned onto it. The towpath ran behind a stretch of farms; farms where people might be on the lookout for an escaped kid, Ethan figured, so he continued to drive without lights. He sat small behind the wheel and had to stretch his nose to keep an eye on where he was headed, but he was moving, putting distance between himself and Scooter Cobb. After several hours, once he believed himself to be out of the county and far enough away to be safe, he began feeling hungry and took to wishing he'd brought along a snack. A sandwich maybe, and some dog food. Probably even his third baseman's mitt. "Shitfire!" Ethan grumbled, thinking back on all the things he'd stupidly left behind.

A short while before sunup when there were streaks of red poking splinters into the sky but still no daylight, the car sputtered to a stop. "What the hell?" Ethan groaned. He tried starting the car again. The engine coughed once, then settled into a hollow whine. Susanna had taught Ethan to drive—start the engine, shift gears, stop and go—but she'd not bothered with the necessity of gas-buying. The boy twisted the ignition key numerous times, then finally gave up. He took hold of Dog's rope and stepped out onto the road. "You hunk of junk," he said, giving the fender one last kick before they began walking south along the towpath, him kicking at the dirt, the dog panting as if he was thirsting for a drink of water. "Forget it," Ethan moaned. "We ain't got none." Once the light of morning broke they turned east in search of a main road, some food and water, and hopefully someone who could give them a ride to Wyattsville.

ETHAN ALLEN

We'd've been in Norfolk by now if that stupid ass car didn't give out. Mama would be real proud of me, driving off in her car and escaping as I did. She says I'm free-spirited like her. She says her and me has got a God-given gift for seeing past bad times and fixing our eye on some bright spot in the future. I ain't figuring on no bright spots coming up anytime soon, but leastwise I ain't getting my ass pounded to a pulp by Scooter Cobb.

I'm glad I'm like Mama, even if she is dead. Leastwise I'll be having myself some fun instead of grumping all the time, like Daddy. This grandpa I'm headed for, he's from Daddy's side of the family, but I sure hope he ain't nothing like Daddy, 'cause if he is I got myself one hell of a problem.

One time I asked Mama where her side of the family was, but she said there wasn't none. She said she never had no mama or papa. She just one day crawled out from under a rosebush, full grown and singing like a lark. That was Mama, always making up stuff and acting a fool. Daddy used to think she was poking fun at him, but Mama poked fun at everybody, even herself. Daddy never did see that.

HELP AT HAND

"Welcome to Exmore" the sign said, but for as far ahead as Ethan could see there was nothing but dirt road. He'd been walking for what seemed to be hours. He was tired, thirsty, and damn sorry he hadn't brought his bicycle. *If I had it,* he thought, *I would have been clear to the ferry by now, instead of dragging my sorry ass through a bunch of back roads.* Almost an hour after he passed the sign Ethan came to the first inkling of civilization: a gas station. Standing alongside the pump was a man wearing a uniform that read *Go ESSO.* "You got water for a dog?" Ethan asked.

"Around back," the man answered. "There's a spigot and pan."

"You sell food? Sandwiches, maybe?"

"Just soda pop and snacks."

Ethan led Dog around to the back of the station and waited as he lapped up two full pans of water. Then he trudged inside the garage where a rack of cupcakes and candies sat next to a red cooler. Ethan took hold of two Moon Pies, then lifted the lid of the cooler. A bunch of pop bottles were bobbing around in a tub of lukewarm water. "Hey," he shouted, "this pop ain't cold!"

"It's all I got," the man answered.

"Figures," Ethan groaned. He pulled out a bottle of Yoo-Hoo, then slid a pack of gum into his pocket on his way out the door. "How much for two Moon Pies and a pop?" he breezily asked the attendant.

"Fifteen cents for the pies and ten for the pop, two cents deposit if you're taking that bottle with you." The man, willowy as a reed and, according to neighborhood boys, suspicious by nature, raised an eyebrow. "And," he drawled, "that gum in your pocket's an extra six cents."

Ethan had a knack for sliding things into his pocket smoothly and had never before been caught in the act. He turned red-faced. "Oh, yeah, the gum," he stammered. "I almost forgot about that." He fished in his pocket and counted out thirty-one cents. "I ain't gonna take the bottle," he said.

Ethan squatted on the curb and peeled back a Moon Pie wrapper. He took a bite, then broke off a piece and fed it to the dog, took another bite and fed the dog another piece. The attendant watched as this continued until the first Moon Pie was finished, but when the boy unwrapped the second one and started doing the same thing he called out, "You ought not be giving that dog chocolate, it'll kill him."

Ethan turned. "Huh?"

"Dogs," the man said. "They can't eat chocolate the way people can. Speeds their heart up, causes them to fall over dead, that's what it does."

"You pulling my leg, mister?"

"I sure ain't. I got eight dogs. I'd feed any one of them gun powder 'fore I'd give them chocolate." The man walked over to the curb and sat down alongside Dog. "Bet you love this dog, don't you?"

Ethan nodded.

"Can't say I blame you. He's a mighty fine animal. Yep, a body sure wouldn't want to harm a fine animal like him."

"No, sir," Ethan answered. "I wouldn't."

The ESSO man smiled. "What's your name, boy?"

Ethan swallowed hard then spit out the first name that came to mind. "Jack," he answered. "Jack Mahoney."

"Well, Jack Mahoney, my name's Tom. Tom Behrens." Tom reached over and scratched the back of Dog's neck. "Yes, sir, you got a mighty fine animal there. You two ain't from around here, huh?"

Ethan nervously shook his head.

"I'd know if you was," Tom said, "because I'd remember such a fine animal. Where you headed?"

"Wyattsville," Ethan answered. No one was looking for a Jack Mahoney, and a truthful answer might help him learn what way to be travelling.

"Wyattsville? Why, that's way past Richmond!"

"Could be. My mama gave me a note saying how I was to get there, but I done lost it. Can you point me in the right direction?"

"Well, it's over on the mainland, but that's a mighty far distance for a boy your age to be travelling alone. Your mama ought to be taking you."

"Oh, she would, Mister Behrens, but she's flat on her back. At death's door, the doctor said. She likely won't make it through the week. That's why she sent me to fetch my grandpa." Ethan sniffled as though he was fighting back a tear.

"Good grief," Tom Behrens said, shaking his head side to side. "That's a lot of worry for a little fella like you to be carting around." Tom stood and walked into the garage. Minutes later he was back with a map of Virginia. "Okay now," he said, unfolding fold after fold. "Let's find out exactly where Wyattsville is." It took almost ten minutes, but he finally plopped his finger down on a tiny speck and said, "Here!"

Ethan stretched his neck and looked, but not having any map-reading experience he wasn't all that sure of what he was actually looking at.

"It's about fifty miles northwest of Richmond," Tom said, "and Richmond's one hundred-and-fifty miles from here, give or take."

"Whew! Further than I figured."

"Was you planning on walking the whole way?"

Ethan lowered his eyes and nodded solemnly.

"You'd be an old man by time you got there. You got to catch a ride." Tom started fingering his chin. "Let's see," he hummed, "with it being Sunday, there's less folks likely to be headed over to Richmond. So we got to figure who'd have cause." He sat there for what seemed to Ethan an awfully long time. Then he said, "Kenny Wilkes! Kenny harvested a slew of soy beans last week, and he's probably going to market today."

When Tom went to call Kenny Ethan picked up the map and started studying it, tracing his finger from town to town, wondering if he would ever make it to Wyattsville. And what if he did? Maybe this grandpa he'd never even seen would simply slam the door in his face and tell him to go on back home. *What then?* he wondered. By the time Tom returned, there were tears rimming Ethan's eyes.

"What's this?" Tom asked and offered out a greasy handkerchief.

Ethan set his mouth in a perfectly straight line and said, "Nothing. A cinder might've blew in my eye."

Tom shrugged. He knew damn good and well the boy was lying, but sometimes it was a kinder thing to believe a lie than probe for the truth. "Kenny took the beans over last week," Tom said, "but he fixed it for you to ride with a friend of his, name of Butch Wheeler. Thing is, Butch's working on a tight schedule, so you got to meet him at the truck stop over on Route Thirteen at one o'clock, on the button."

Ethan glanced at the clock outside the garage. "I'll never make it," he said with the corners of his mouth turned down. "It's twelve-thirty now."

Tom smiled. "You will if I drive you." As they climbed into the truck, he handed the boy a pack of Twinkies and a stick of beef jerky. "On the house," he said, "but don't you go giving the dog any of the cupcake."

Tom whirled into the Lucky 13 Truck Depot with almost two full minutes to spare. Butch Wheeler was already there. He was standing outside the cab of a flatbed loaded with crates of squawking chickens. The sight of him, back turned, caused Ethan to shudder, for if ever Scooter Cobb had a twin, it was surely Butch Wheeler. He had the same massive build, taller even than Scooter, certainly wider. As it turned out, there were two differences: Butch Wheeler was blacker than a night sky, and he had a robust laugh such as Ethan had never heard. "Well, boy, I sure hope you ain't allergic to chickens," he growled, then he laughed so loud it sounded like thunder.

"No, sir," Ethan mumbled, still taking measure of the man's size. "I ain't afraid of nothing, leastwise chickens."

Butch Wheeler laughed louder than ever, so loud in fact that Dog's tail drooped to the ground. Not given to the same level of joviality as Butch Tom cracked a bit of a smile, then told Ethan allergic was when a thing caused you to itch or sneeze. One minute later on the dot of one o'clock, the flatbed pulled out carrying a very large man, a boy, a dog, and seventeen crates of live chickens.

Just before Ethan climbed up into the truck, Tom had pressed a dollar bill into his palm and whispered, "Take care of yourself, Jack, and get to Wyattsville safely. I'll be praying for you and that sick mama of yours." After that he'd given Ethan a real friendly hug and sent him on his way, expecting nothing in return.

Several miles later as Ethan sat watching the road signs whiz by, he thought back to the incident and started hoping this grandpa he was going to see had the goodness of Tom Behrens. *Maybe,* he thought, *Grandpa will feel real bad about me losing my mama and buy me a new bicycle.* After that Ethan started wondering whether it would be better to ask for the bicycle right off or start with a third baseman's mitt.

"Whatcha thinking about, Jack?" Butch asked. "Jack? Jack?"

OLIVIA

I know the people here at the Wyattsville Arms apartment building mean well. At first they were real standoffish, but now they treat me as kindly as they would one of their own. Someone is always telephoning to ask if I've an interest in going shopping or joining up for some social event, and I make an effort to be sociable right back. But still, there isn't a day that passes when I don't wake up and wonder how I can possibly struggle through another twenty-four hours. I look at that chair, and instead of seeing a plumped up pillow I see a hole where Charlie ought to be sitting. A single day hangs onto me like a week and a week—why, that seems longer than a lifetime.

Sometimes I wish I could stop thinking about Charlie for just a few minutes of the day, but I can't. I suppose it's only fair I suffer this way, because sure as the sun rises I'm the one who caused his death. I was so caught up in the way he was doting on me I let him hang that opal pendant around my neck without giving thought to what the consequences might be. I might just as well have poured a cup of arsenic into his soup.

Most every night I kneel down alongside the bed and pray for God to come and take me too. What good is a life like this? *I ask him.* What earthly good?

WAY OF A WIDOW

Olivia thought of Charlie every day. Sometimes he'd seem real as life, so real that she could believe he'd come walking through the door at any minute. Other days, try as she might, she'd be unable to picture his smile or the tilt of his head. Such a thing usually happened when the wind howled and sheets of rain cascaded down the windowpane, or when a fog thick as oatmeal rolled in from the river. On days like that she'd turn against herself and swear he'd been a figment of her imagination, a fantasy lover who never truly existed. Moments later she'd open a closet door and see his jacket, or reach for a salt shaker and slide her hand across his eyeglasses; then it would slowly come back. Bits and pieces at first—the crook of his nose, a single dimple on the left side of his face, a callous on his index finger—until eventually she'd see the whole of him. When she recalled the way he held her hand, whispered in her ear, or cupped her breast, a heavy wedge of sorrow would press against her heart and she would wonder whether such a brief interlude of happiness was worth the heartache that followed.

Olivia's marriage had come and gone like a tornado. She had everything for a moment; then there was nothing but loneliness. "What have I done?" she would ask herself, picturing the brass nameplate that for thirty years sat atop her desk at the Southern Atlantic Telephone Company District Office. For more than five decades she'd been Olivia Ann Westerly and regardless of the circumstances couldn't settle into the wearing of any other name. Once when the Parcel Post deliveryman asked for Missus Doyle Olivia said, "Are you sure you don't mean

Boyle? There's an Althea *Boyle* downstairs on the third floor." The puzzled driver indicated the nameplate on her door read Doyle, but she simply sighed and said, "Ah, *that* Doyle. That was dear, sweet Charlie."

Olivia could not get used to living in the Wyattsville apartment. She was burdened with the identity of a person passing through, a visitor with no right to clear away Charlie's clothes or discard the yellowing toothbrush. Even after she'd been there for months she'd crawl into bed, her clothes on and shoes within reach, always ready to leave at a moment's notice. Most nights she'd lie awake for hours counting stars, watching as the moon rose and then faded into nothingness. Not until daylight threaded a ribbon of pink across the sky would she drift off to sleep, and then she'd dream of being back in her own apartment. She'd see the pink wallpaper and the polka dot towels in the bathroom, the geranium on the kitchen window sill, the blue silk bedspread. When she woke up she'd wonder how she came to be in an altogether different place—a bedroom where there was a large brown ashtray on the night table and a pair of men's slippers poking out from beneath the bed. Once she remembered she'd cover her head and slide back under the blanket, hoping another hour or two of sleep would remedy the sorry state of affairs.

Charlie's apartment was nothing more than a temporary stopover, Olivia told herself, a place to stay until she could move back to Richmond where she had friends to visit and things to do. Of course, she no longer had her wonderful job, which was of considerable concern, but surely she could come up with something else. With that as a plan, her suitcase remained packed and sitting alongside the front door week after week. She bought only enough groceries to last a day, two at the most. She passed right by the four-roll packages of toilet paper and tomatoes that would have to sit on the windowsill for a day to ripen. "Who knows where I'll be by then?" she'd say and opt for an overripe avocado instead.

When Clara Bowman brought a dish garden for the kitchen windowsill, Olivia refused to accept it. "I honestly don't think I'll be staying," she said.

Forgetting the urn on the living room mantle, Clara replied, "Why, Charlie Doyle would turn over in his grave if he heard such a thing!"

Still, Olivia felt she belonged somewhere else. Richmond, she reasoned. It had to be Richmond. Twice she went to visit the building where she'd lived; where, if she'd had any sense, she'd still be living. The first time she'd gone as far as the front walk and then stood there for almost an hour, remembering how it felt to reach into her handbag, take out the key, unlock the door, and walk in. Two days later she came back again, this time venturing into the vestibule.

It was all wrong. The walls, which for as long as she could remember had been a glossy white, were now painted flamingo pink. Gone was the serviceable gray carpet, in its place a flowered thing already marked with scuffs of dirt. Olivia sighed and flopped down on the lobby chair, which had been re-covered in a hideous shade of rose.

Unfortunately at that moment, along came Helene Kapuski, a woman with a tongue rumored to be so loose it flapped at both ends. "I certainly hope you're not thinking of moving back," Helene said, "because your apartment's been rented to a charming young couple from Atlanta. He's a stockbroker. Charlene, his wife, she's a decorator."

The words stung Olivia like a swarm of angry hornets.

"Charlene was the one who did the lobby," Helene beamed. "And your old apartment—why you wouldn't even recognize it!" When she started telling how they'd painted the walls apple green Olivia walked off, so despondent she cried the entire way home.

Afterwards she abandoned all hope of returning to her old apartment and started to think that perhaps Richmond was no longer the place for her. Two days later she dug the road maps from the trunk of her car and began to consider the alternatives. For days on end she traced her finger along the various highways—North, South, East, West—until finally she colored bright yellow stars on top of Norfolk, Virginia and Charleston, South Carolina. *A seaport town,* Olivia thought, *now that's the sort of place for a woman starting over.* She promised herself that once the weather turned a bit warmer, she'd drive over to Norfolk and look around.

But in February everything changed. It started when Clara announced, "I'm going to need a new dress for the Valentine's Day party." She then suggested Olivia ought to have one also.

"Me?" Olivia answered. "Why, I've no need of a new dress."

"Oh no?" Clara took hold of Olivia's arm and tugged her over to the full-length mirror. "Look at that!"

Olivia was taken aback by the reflection of a sorrowful looking woman dressed head to toe in black. "This isn't me," she said.

"It is you!" Clara snapped. "You're a woman who's forgotten how to live."

"I've done no such thing," Olivia answered indignantly.

"Oh? What then? You *choose* to look like a lump of sackcloth and ashes?"

"Well, no," Olivia said, "but with my being here so temporary…"

The next thing Olivia knew she'd been bundled out the door and was on her way to Baumhauser's, which was supposedly the finest department store in downtown Wyattsville. "We'll have lunch at the Cocky Rooster," Clara said, tugging Olivia along, "then we'll spend the afternoon shopping."

"All afternoon?" Olivia moaned.

Were it not for the two glasses of burgundy Clara foisted upon her, Olivia would not have given the red tulle dress a second glance. She certainly would not have lugged it into the dressing room and slid it over her head. She was a woman of practical tastes, a woman who appreciated the reserved sophistication of black shantung, yet somehow she allowed herself to be talked into buying a flouncy-skirted thing that teetered on the brink of making her appear promiscuous.

"Whatever was I thinking?" Olivia wondered aloud as she hung the dress on the inside of her closet door. "Me, a woman in mourning." She shook her head in what appeared to be disbelief. "How could I?" For three days she avoided looking at the dress. "I'll not allow myself to be coerced into attending some silly party," she'd grumble, then quickly snap shut the closet door. And when Clara brought over a pair of heart-shaped earrings, Olivia begrudgingly tossed them onto her dressing table.

Now if the morning of February fourteenth had been drizzling rain or blustery cold things might have happened differently, but the dawn broke with such an unseasonable burst of sunshine that the residents of Wyattsville woke up believing spring had arrived. Windows were suddenly flung open and radios turned up so loud that merchants downtown figured it had to be some sort of a parade. Maggie Cooper forgot about the arthritis plaguing her knee and began tangoing across her living room. Walter Krause, a man who had not danced in twenty-seven years, pulled his tuxedo from the closet and shook the dust from it. Although she had not for one second considered going to the Valentine's Day party, Olivia took a look at the dress hanging on her closet door and gasped, "What shoes am I going to wear?" She hurriedly dressed and headed downtown where she was fortunate enough to find a pair of red satin pumps a scant half-size smaller than she preferred.

That evening when Olivia slipped into the red dress she immediately felt ten years younger, and after she'd clipped the rhinestone hearts to her ears a rainbow of sparkles began dancing across her skin. She painted her mouth the exact same shade of red as her dress, then twice checked her reflection, as if she feared the glow that had settled upon her might up and disappear the way Charlie had.

She had no sooner situated herself in a chair when Fred McGinty strolled over and asked if Olivia would come and sit at his table. Moments later Frank Casper did the same, and after him it was Wayne Dolby. Although she thanked them all, she remained in the seat alongside Clara. "I came with Clara," she told Fred, giving him the most flirtatious of smiles, "so I'm sure you understand."

Fred gave her shoulder a squeeze. "You're forgiven," he said, "but only if you promise to let me take you to the Saint Patrick's Corned Beef Dinner."

By the end of the evening Olivia also had agreed to partner with Wayne for the Tuesday Bridge Club, accompany Harry Hornsby to Bingo, and co-chair the spring dance along with Barbara Jean Conklin who, she now realized, was far less snooty than originally thought. She'd danced seventeen waltzes, a dozen fox trots, and a tango without once remembering the soreness of her bunion. That night Olivia realized the red tulle dress was unfit for any sort of sleeping. She opened her suitcase and took out a pair of cotton plisse pajamas. She then folded back the coverlet and curled up beneath the blanket where by the oddest circumstance she found a spot in the mattress that molded itself to precisely the size and shape of her body.

The following morning, rationalizing the damp air of a seaport town would more than likely aggravate a person's sinuses, Olivia went to Piggly Wiggly and shopped until her grocery cart was filled to the brim. In addition to the dozens of other things she bought a super-sized box of laundry detergent, four green-as-grass bananas, and a fifteen-pound sack of Idaho potatoes. The grocery order was so large that it overflowed the trunk of her car and left a canned ham and twelve bottles of ginger ale to ride in the back seat. "Oh, dear," she said, momentarily considering the possibility she'd gone a bit overboard. Of course such a thought flew by quickly enough, for on the way home she stopped at the florist and bought six potted plants including a hyacinth without so much as a single bud. "That won't flower until April," the florist warned, but Olivia plopped it into the basket anyway.

Once home Olivia set about filling what strangely enough had become *her* kitchen cupboards with the store of foodstuffs. She placed three different kinds of cereal and a row of spices on the first shelf, then stacked cans of mushrooms, corn, and peas on the second. She lined up row after row of Campbell's Soup atop the next shelf, then wedged in packages of macaroni and cheese. After she'd squeezed the final box of beans into place, Olivia threw open the cupboard doors and admired the look of what she saw. The cabinets, which for months had been empty as a broken heart, were now chock full, and by some odd coincidence there was not a vacant spot on a single one of the shelves. "Providence," Olivia murmured happily, and then she began to wonder why she hadn't realized from the start this was where she was destined to be. *It's so obvious,* she thought, *why, even a blind person would have seen it right off.*

When Clara stopped by early in the afternoon, Olivia was already at work unpacking. "What's this?" Clara asked, her voice registering a note of surprise. She had come to expect an air of gloominess but instead there was Olivia, humming a rather pleasant tune and pulling clothes from her suitcase.

Olivia dropped her blue blouse atop a pile of things to be laundered. "I've come to my senses," she said. "A woman alone needs to live in a place where she's got friends, where she can put down roots and feel she belongs!"

"I don't get it..." Clara stammered. "What exactly are you saying?"

"It's simple." Olivia hesitated long enough to consider a pair of brown shoes she'd pulled from the suitcase. She wrinkled her nose, set them aside, and continued. "Last night I got to remembering something Canasta told me when I was looking to find my way back home. 'Honey,' she said, 'people don't find a home, they gotta make one. Sometimes sad folks hurry off to some new place, and then when they get there they say, Why this ain't home at all. Thing is, you got to give it time. You got to set growing things on the window sill, say howdy to your neighbors, and write little notes on the wall calendar. Then one day you get a whiff of your own stew simmering, and it hits like a brick dropped square onto your head: you're right where God intended you to be.'"

"I still don't get it," Clara said. "You trying to tell me you made a stew?"

"Actually, I made a meatloaf. But that's not what's important. See, the stew was simply Canasta's way of meaning a person had settled in."

"So," Clara said, still looking a bit confused, "does this mean you're staying?"

"Absolutely!"

Although Clara claimed she had already defrosted a stewing chicken, she stayed for supper and declared the meatloaf to be one of the best she'd ever tasted. "It should be," Olivia said wistfully, for in it she'd used the very last of the seeds given to her by Canasta Jones. Once the meatloaf was gone, she'd be on her own.

After Clara had gone home Olivia finished unpacking her suitcase. With a lengthy stretch of dresses, skirts, and blouses lined up across the sofa, she went in search of hangers and found three. Even those she'd had to pry loose from a closet still crowded with Charlie's clothes. She searched again and twice thought she'd come upon an empty hanger, but as it turned out both had trousers hanging across the bar.

It seemed highly impractical for a man to have so many clothes, particularly since he'd been deceased for several months and no longer had need of them. Initially Olivia removed only the plaid suits, thinking they were somewhat outdated anyway, but that gave her just four more hangers. She then did away with all of the suits: grey, blue, green, and one that was the color of day-old buttermilk. "Why, he wouldn't be caught dead in this thing," she mumbled without thinking.

After the suits were gone it seemed rather senseless to hang on to a collection of ties, sport jackets, and slacks, so one by one Olivia removed the things from their hangers and folded them neatly. "I'm sorry," she whispered into the lapel of his grey blazer. "I never wanted it to be this way." When she caught the whiff of cologne that lingered on his blue cardigan, she cried for a good half-hour. "Please try to understand," she sobbed. "I've got to get on with life." When she pulled his shoes from the closet floor, Olivia slid her feet into them and drifted back to the time when he had waltzed her across the dance floor as if there was a carpet of rose petals beneath them.

But it was his bathrobe—the bathrobe that still carried the odor of not cologne, but *him*—which caused Olivia to fall upon the bed and weep through most of the night. By morning, she knew what she had to do.

As soon as the sun came up, Olivia telephoned Clara. "If you're not too busy, I was hoping you could come for a visit," she moaned soulfully.

"Visit? At seven o'clock in the morning?" Clara growled. Then she plopped down the telephone. She rolled over to go back to sleep but the sound of Olivia's voice stayed with her, the echo of neediness squeezed in between words. Moments later Clara stormed into Olivia's apartment looking like a bulldog in yellow pajamas. "Okay now," she said, thumping her hands onto her hips. "What's the problem?"

Olivia explained how she'd suffered through the night and finally come to the conclusion that she needed a bit of help, advice maybe, or someone to lend a hand. "I know it's what needs to be done, but I can't bring myself to get rid of Charlie's things," she sniffled. "One minute I'm thinking about painting the bathroom or getting new curtains for the kitchen, then some little belonging of his grabs hold of me and I switch right back to crying." Olivia stopped to blow her nose and wipe a well of water from her eyes. "See that," she moaned, "it happens every time. I take a jacket or shirt out of the closet and whoosh—I end up with a picture of him wearing it. I go into the bathroom and run head on into his decrepit old toothbrush waiting for him to come back. And his bathrobe! One glance at that, and I start wishing I was buried alongside of him."

Any of the other residents would have noticed the way Clara's head was cocked to one side, the corner of her mouth curled, and one eye flickering like a firefly. But Olivia was a relative newcomer, unaware that such actions along with the tapping of Clara's right foot were lifelong habits that clicked on whenever there was any heavy thinking. "What you need is breakfast," Clara finally decreed. "Meet me in the lobby in a half-hour. We're going to the Pancake House."

"Pancake House?" Olivia echoed, thinking a stack of pancakes didn't seem to be much of a solution. She would have preferred an offer of help or maybe the name of a charity in need of men's clothing.

Of course, Clara made no mention of how in the span of ten minutes she could line up a crew of neighbors to clear out every last trace of Charlie Doyle. Not that anyone intentionally wanted to do such a thing, because Charlie was certainly well liked, but once a man was dead, he was dead. And dead men simply didn't come back. That was one thing Clara understood only too well, for she'd spent almost six years mourning the loss of her Henry. Were it not for Martha Cunningham taking matters into her own hands, Clara herself might still be in the same sorrowful situation.

The first call was to Peggy Mendel. "Yep," Peggy answered. "I've got a storage room full of cartons, but my tape is all dried out."

Donna Swift had five perfectly good rolls of tape and a hand truck suitable for hauling the cartons off to another spot.

Norma Ryan knew a man who lived in the building across the street and was somewhat down on his luck. "He's about the same size as Charlie, and Heaven knows he could use some nice clothes," she said. After that she segued into telling how on the coldest day imaginable she'd witnessed the poor man shivering in a threadbare sweater. Halfway through the story Clara interrupted and told her to save it for later.

"Now, you understand what's to be done?" Clara asked Maggie Cooper, who'd agreed to take charge of the operation. "The key is under the mat, so the minute we leave you girls go in and pack up Charlie's suits, jackets, trousers, shoes, slippers, pipes, ashtrays, underwear, and don't forget the toothbrush. Everything—get rid of everything."

"Even the ashes?" Maggie asked. "Get rid of the ashes?"

"Lord God, no!" Clara gasped. Charlie Doyle had been a friend, someone she'd dated and on a few occasions allowed certain familiarities. It was one thing to clear away his belongings, but quite another to dispose of the man himself. That was something Olivia was going to have to deal with herself, like it or not.

At ten minutes before eight the two women met in the lobby and started for the Pancake House. Clara had to stretch out the period of time they'd be gone, so she turned to Olivia and said, "It's a lovely morning. Let's walk."

"Walk?" Olivia answered. "The whole two miles?" She eyed the grey clouds hovering overhead and wondered if perhaps Clara, well-meaning as she might be, was suffering from a lapse in judgment.

"Fresh air gives a person a healthier state of mind."

Olivia doubted such a claim was true, but once Clara set her mind to something there was no arguing. She gave a shrug and fell into step.

With window shopping in first one place then another, it took almost two hours to reach the Pancake House. And when they finally got there, Clara told the hostess they were in no particular hurry and would wait for an available booth.

"I've a table right now," the hostess said.

Clara shook her head. "We'll wait," she replied. Then she stood there eyeing the overhead clock and rat-tat-tatting her foot like a jackhammer.

Twenty minutes later the hostess said she had a booth ready for them. "Not there," Clara replied wriggling her finger toward the back of the room. "That booth is way too close to the kitchen. We'll wait for the next one."

"But..." Olivia stammered.

"Trust me," Clara insisted and waved the hostess away.

With the subsequent refusal of two more unsuitably situated booths, they didn't even glance at a menu until eleven o'clock, and when they finally did Clara flip-flopped for fifteen minutes, deciding whether to have pancakes with blueberry syrup or strawberries and whipped cream.

"Either sounds good to me," Olivia said.

Clara finally settled on the strawberries. When the pancakes were set in front of her she cut them into tiny pieces and ate so slowly you could have believed she'd fallen asleep between bites. Halfway through she indicated that maybe the blueberry syrup would have been better after all, so she ordered a stack of those and did exactly the same thing. When she finished the blueberry pancakes, she ordered coffee and sipped it so slowly it became ice cold, so she ordered another cup. In all that time she never mentioned a word about Charlie or the disposal of his belongings.

"Well," Olivia said, growing restless. "I suppose we should start home."

Clara delayed for yet another half-hour, saying she'd probably have to visit the ladies lounge momentarily, and then on the walk home she slowed her steps to a snail's pace.

"Is something wrong?" Olivia asked.

Clara hesitated for a long time then stopped dead in her tracks, her head cocked and her foot twitching. "How would you feel if you walked back into the apartment and found all of Charlie's things gone?" she asked apprehensively.

"I don't know," Olivia said after a minute. "The bits and pieces of Charlie are like a bouquet of roses. I look at them and see a world of sweetness and beauty, but when I try to hold onto them the thorns rip me to pieces."

"I went through the very same heartache after Henry died."

"Henry?" Olivia never pictured Clara as a widow. She was someone who wore bright-colored dresses and laughed at most anything, a person who could turn the simplest get together into a party. "Henry?" Olivia repeated quizzically. "He was your husband?"

Clara nodded. "Yes, indeed, of twenty-eight years." She began walking again, this time at bit faster pace.

Olivia slipped into the same stride. "I never would have guessed," she said. "I mean, now you seem to be so happy, so settled in your life. When did he…"

"Six years ago."

"Oh my." Olivia could feel the pain of separation twisting in her heart. "How," she asked, "did you handle such a loss?"

"Pretty much the same as you. I hid in my apartment and cried 'til my eyes were so swollen I couldn't see straight. I quit eating and got so skinny I looked like—"

"Skinny? You?"

"Yeah," Clara laughed. "Hard to believe, huh?"

"It's just that now, you're so…"

"You'd better not say fat," Clara warned.

"No," Olivia answered, "not fat, but robust and full of life."

"It's because of Martha Cunningham. She's the one I have to thank. I was just like you; maybe sorrier even than you. I used to go to bed and sleep with a pair of Henry's pajamas stretched out alongside of me, pretending, I suppose, he was still in them. But one day after I'd gone to work—I was still working at the insurance company then—dear, sweet Martha came into my apartment and cleared out every last trace of Henry. All except the pictures of course. She knew I'd want to keep those."

"Were you furious with her?"

"At first I was, but given a bit of time I started to realize that although I'd loved Henry in life I wasn't doing him a bit of good wherever he'd gone to. And I was doing myself an awful lot of harm. Once I came to that understanding, my life changed."

"But," Olivia said haltingly, "she just threw Henry's belongings in the trash can?"

Clara laughed, and a soft look of remembering settled around her eyes. "At first that's what she told me. But once I got over the hurting she confessed there were eleven boxes stored in the basement, and I could do with them as I wanted."

"Eleven?" Olivia gasped, figuring the story would now take a hateful turn with the unluckiness of such a number.

"Eleven," Clara nodded. "I loaded them into my car and took them over to the Old Sailors Home. Let me tell you, those men were truly glad to have such nice things. Why, they thanked me seven ways 'til Sunday."

"Eleven, huh?" Olivia mumbled as Clara turned to open the lobby door. "And nothing bad happened?"

"Just the opposite. Once I quit tormenting myself with those sorrowful memories, I started enjoying life again. Oh, I still did plenty of thinking about Henry, but I'd think about the good times we had instead of wallowing in my misery and wishing I was dead too."

"You *sure* it was eleven cartons?"

"Yes, eleven. But never mind about the number of cartons, there's a more important reason for me telling you this story." Olivia unlocked the apartment door as Clara continued to speak. "I never forgot what Martha did for me, and I hope you'll feel the same about what we've done here today."

"What we've done today?" Olivia repeated with a bewildered expression.

"Not me and you," Clara explained. "It was the girls—Maggie Cooper, Peggy, Norma, Donna—they're a bunch of women who want to be your friends. We're anxious to see you get on with your life."

"What..." As soon as Olivia stepped into the living room she noticed a different smell. Not the odor of stale tobacco, but lavender or lilacs. Hyacinth maybe. Her clothes were gone from the sofa. The club chair with a seat cushion squished into the shape of Charlie's behind was also missing. The pipes, ashtrays, stacks and stacks of magazines—gone. Uncertain of whether to scream, cry, or double over in a fit of hysterics, she walked through to the kitchen. Gone was the wall calendar with pictures of scantily-clad girls pumping gasoline, and in its place hung a brand new calendar with February featuring a bouquet of red roses.

Clara followed along worrying that maybe Olivia, who still hadn't said word one, had slipped into shock. "Believe me, it's for the best," Clara mumbled when Olivia opened the closet door and found nothing but her own things. Dresses, skirts, blouses, lined up one after another, extra hangers spaced out in between, her pink flowered bathrobe looped over the hook that once held Charlie's.

A tear slid down Olivia's cheek. The complete disappearance of

Charlie seemed so sad, and yet in some strange way it was peaceful. She was reminded of a balloon held back from heaven until an earthbound soul let go of the string. After a long while of saying nothing, she whispered, "Goodbye, Charlie." Then she turned and circled her arms about Clara.

Two weeks later with Olivia at the wheel, five women from the Wyattsville Social Club drove over to the Old Sailors Home and donated nine cartons of perfectly good clothing. They stayed for lunch and watched as the men happily divvied up jackets, suits, sweaters, and so forth. Olivia had to admit the bearded man who won out for Charlie's powder blue suit looked strikingly handsome. All in all, she had never before witnessed quite so much smiling in a single afternoon.

The club chair was far too cumbersome to transport any distance and was given to Herman Hopmeyer, a man who lived three doors down and had the same roundness of behind as did Charlie.

In the weeks that followed Olivia transformed the apartment bit by bit. She bought a Queen Anne slipper chair to replace the one given away, painted the bathroom a rose petal pink, hung new curtains in the kitchen, and set row after row of potted plants on every windowsill. She also had the name "Westerly—Doyle" etched in brass and affixed it to the front door.

One night in early April, shortly after the hyacinth burst open in a profusion of purple, Olivia had a dream. She was walking through the park holding tight to the string of a powder blue balloon when suddenly the string slipped from her hand. As it floated upward she saw the sky filled with brightly colored balloons, all of them rising higher and higher until at the very top of the heavens they became part of a rainbow. Although the people around her seemed to be singing a truly joyous song, Olivia started to sob. "Why are you crying?" a boy asked.

"Because I've lost my balloon," she answered.

"Lost? It's not lost. Look." The boy lifted his hand and pointed a finger toward a brilliant speck of blue dancing on the edge of the rainbow.

"But," Olivia sobbed, "when the rainbow is gone—"

"It's never gone," the boy said. "It's always there if you go looking." The child eased his hand into hers and looked up with eyes blue as the balloon.

The next morning Olivia awoke with the strangest peace of mind.

Thus began a new life. Olivia had gone through a thousand heartaches and passed by countless milestones, but at long last she had arrived at the place where she could spend her days enjoying the simple life of warm-hearted friends, pot roast dinners, and neighborly parties—a life free of complex relationships.

ETHAN ALLEN

It was a real nice thing, Mister Behrens fixing me a ride to Wyattsville. But I gotta say the closer I get to Grandpa Doyle's house, the more I'm worrying he ain't gonna be too pleased with the sight of me.

Mama said he didn't want nothing to do with Daddy. Could be he's got no use for kids. 'Course, I don't know if Grandpa didn't want nothing to do with Daddy when he was a kid or just after he got growed-up and mean. I'm hoping it was the growed-up part. Leastwise then I got a chance.

Daddy wasn't always mean. Mama said when they was first married he was sweet as honeysuckle. 'Course, you couldn't prove it by me. I only knowed him as mean.

Blood's thicker than water, according to Mama, so I'm trusting this grandpa's gonna let me stay. I'll say I take after Daddy when he was a kid. That ought to make Grandpa feel good. If it turns out Daddy was a mean kid, then I'll say I'm more like Mama. If I can't get this grandpa to take some sort of liking to me, I'm really shit outta luck.

THE CROSSING

When the flatbed of chickens pulled out of the Lucky 13 Truck Depot Ethan Allen had his eyes focused straight ahead, watching only where he was headed. Had the boy turned to look back he would have seen Tom Behrens, a man standing apart from the others, his hands jammed deep into the pockets of ESSO coveralls and his foot kicking at the dirt. Tom watched as the truck shrunk to the size of a toy, then disappeared altogether. If he was smart, he told himself, he'd walk away. Walk away and forget what he'd seen in the boy's face. Forget that it was the same look of hardness and hurt he'd seen in the mirror a thousand or more times. It had taken him twenty years to forget those days, and now in the span of a few short hours it was all back again.

"May the Lord God have mercy on you, Jack Mahoney," he mumbled, then turned and walked off.

❦

"You got dirt in your ears, boy?" Butch Wheeler shouted in a booming voice.

Lost in the thumping of tires against the road and thoughts of how to explain himself to this never-before-seen grandpa, Ethan Allen looked over. "Dirt in my ears?"

"Yeah. Four times I asked, whatcha thinking about Jack, but you sit there like you're deaf as a stone."

"Oh, sorry," Ethan said with a sheepish grin. Obviously, he was gonna have to keep an ear open for answering to the name of Jack Mahoney.

"No harm done." Butch Wheeler signaled for a left hand turn, then pulled into the line of cars waiting for the ferry to dock.

Ethan craned his neck, checking out the cars on both sides of the truck. He saw plenty of Fords, Plymouths, and Pontiacs, but, happily, no police cars. All he needed now was another hour or two of luck. Once he made it to the mainland Scooter would never find him. Never in a million years. Even if Cobb nosed around the truckers asking if they knew anything of Ethan Allen Doyle, they'd say no and shake their head. Good thing he'd thought to say his name was Jack Mahoney.

They sat there for another twenty minutes, the chickens squawking and the motor grumbling like it was in need of some oil. Finally the line of cars began to inch forward. They'd moved two, maybe three, car lengths when Ethan spotted a uniformed man up ahead. His heart came to a standstill—no beating, no pumping blood in one side and out the other, nothing. It could be they had his picture. If that was the case it wouldn't matter what name he was using. A faint heartbeat started up again and he slid closer to the door, looping his fingers around the handle. He could run if he had to, if his heart held out long enough, but maybe… He turned and in the high-pitched voice of a castrated canary said, "Okay if I squat down under the seat when that policeman gets here?"

"Policeman?" Butch roared. A cascade of laughter slid down his chins and set his belly to bouncing. "Why, that man's just a ticket taker!" He laughed again, then said, "But you…well, now, you got the look of a lad who's up to something."

Ethan's mouth flew open. "Not me," he stammered. "I ain't up to nothing!"

"Is that so?" Butch said, a chuckle still rumbling through his chins. "Could be you robbed a bank. You got the shifty eyes of a bank robber. Yes, sir, robbed a bank, or maybe stole that dog. You do either of those things, boy?"

"No, sir," Ethan Allen answered in earnest. "I never robbed no bank, and this here dog was a birthday present from my mama."

"That so?" Butch laughed again, then stuck his arm out the window and handed the uniformed man his ticket. Once the ferry was underway, he turned to the boy and asked, "You running away from home, Jack? Is that why you're so skittish about the police?"

Ethan Allen had now tuned his ear to listening for the name Jack and answered, "No, sir."

"Your mama, she knows where you're headed?"

"Yes, sir."

"And she allows for you to be hitching rides on chicken trucks?"

Ethan could make up stories quicker than you'd imagine possible, and he could tell them in a way that was most convincing. He also knew when he was skating too close to the edge of believability, and the look on Butch Wheeler's face indicated it was time for him to move back. "Truth is," Ethan said in a heavy-hearted voice, "my mama's dead. But when she was breathing her last, she told me to go live with Grandpa."

"Hmm."

"Honest! Look here." Ethan fished in his pocket and pulled out a card that read "Love, Grandpa." "See, this is who I'm supposed to go live with."

"Oh? And where exactly does this grandpa live?"

Ethan showed the back flap of the envelope with Charlie Doyle's return address.

"Doyle, huh? He your mama's daddy?"

Still tuned in to using the name Mahoney, Ethan nodded.

Butch handed the envelope back. "Where's your own daddy?"

"He got shot in the war and died." Ethan thought about adding that his daddy had been a hero with all kinds of medals, but he decided against it. Sometimes saying too much was what could get a fellow in trouble.

"That's sure enough a rotten break," Butch said, "but it don't explain you being so afraid of the law."

"If they get hold of me, they'll lock me up in an orphanage. This kid I know got sent to an orphanage, and he said it was God awful. They make you sleep on the floor and eat things that ain't fit for human consumption."

"It ain't quite that bad," Butch said with an easy smile, "but it sure enough ain't pleasant. Anyway, you got no worries. You got blood kin willing to claim you." He glanced over at the way one side of the boy's mouth was sloping toward his chin. "Your grandpa knows you're coming, don't he?"

Ethan forced a happy-looking smile onto his face and nodded.

After that things went along smooth as a pig's belly. Butch Wheeler unloaded the crates of chickens in Richmond, then turned west onto Route 33 and drove Ethan Allen all the way to Wyattsville, right to the front door of his grandpa's apartment building. "You want me to go in with you?" Butch asked, but the boy shook his head and hurried off.

◦━✦━◦

Ethan Allen ran his finger along the names printed on the mail slots—Parker, Cunningham, Ryan, Casper, Dolby—Doyle! Apartment 7D. He gave Dog's rope a tug, walked past the "No Pets Allowed" sign, stepped into the elevator, and pushed number seven. As the brass doors rattled shut, he started to sweat. It was one thing to say you were going to live with a grandpa who didn't know you from a knothole, but something else entirely to be standing there when the door opened. He spit into the palm of his hand and slicked his hair back. "He's my grandpa, he's gotta like me," Ethan told his reflection.

When the elevator doors opened, Ethan stepped into a hallway with carpeting that stretched from one wall to the other. There was not a soul in sight, and it was way too quiet for his liking. It didn't give off the sounds or smells of a place where people lived. He heard the far-away echo of people talking, but after the elevator doors rattled shut even that was gone. Using the smallest whisper possible, he tried to practice what he would say when Grandpa Doyle answered the door. "Hello," he squeaked. "I'm your grandson, Ethan Allen. I've come to live with you." The words flip-flopped in his throat and made him want to gag. They sounded stupid and shrill as a tin whistle. He started down the hallway and tried again. "Hi there, Grandpa Doyle," he said, this time mustering up a feigned gleefulness. It sounded worse than "Hello, I'm your grandson." One more try, and then he found himself face to face with apartment 7D. He gave the doorbell a quick glance, then decided he wasn't quite ready and shuffled off to the far end of the hall. "Grandpa Doyle," he repeated over and over again, trying for the sound of sincerity, the sound of a boy genuinely glad to be spending time with an old man. When he finally got it right, he started working on what would follow.

The better part of an hour had passed before he finally gathered himself together and went back to apartment 7D. He positioned himself square in front of the door with Dog partway behind, hopefully looking smaller than his actual size. "Hi, Grandpa. I come to thank you for all those dollars you been sending me," Ethan mumbled in one final run through. Then he straightened his back, forced a smile to his face, and pushed the doorbell. He waited for what seemed an awfully long time, then pressed his finger to the bell a second time. This time he heard the chiming, a muffled sound like the ringing of a steeple bell miles off, but once the sound of the bell died away there was nothing else. No shuffling of feet, no calling out just a minute, no sound whatsoever. He stood there a while longer, then went back to the lobby and checked the mail slots again.

There it was. Westerly-Doyle, 7D. No other Doyle in the building.

Figuring Westerly to maybe be Grandpa Charlie's real first name, Ethan Allen took the elevator back to the seventh floor and rang the bell again. Still no answer. With nowhere else to go, he had little choice but to wait.

OLIVIA

At one point I believed I would spend the rest of my life crying over Charlie but Clara, bless her heart, has helped me to get over it. At first I saw her kindness as meddling and wished she'd leave me alone. I certainly to God am glad she didn't.

At least I've got a life now. Not the real happy sort of life I had with Charlie, but it's a whole lot better than it was after his death. I keep busy, but I still think about him every day and I can't help but wonder if he's looking down on me.

If he is, I certainly do hope he's not put out about me getting rid of all his personal belongings. I doubt that he would be. Charlie's simply not the sort.

Sometimes I have dreams where we're back together again. They're so real I wake up expecting him to be there lying alongside of me. Whenever that happens I keep my eyes shut tight and stay in bed. I keep hoping I'll slide back into the dream, but of course I never do. If ever I do, I'm going to ask Charlie how he feels about me going to dances and parties.

Clara swears it's what he would want me to do, but me—I'm not so sure.

UNINVITED GUEST

When Olivia returned with Fred McGinty, who on this particular evening had escorted her to the movie theatre, they found the boy and his dog propped up against her apartment door. Both of them sat sound asleep. "Stand back," said Fred, who was forever trying to impress Olivia. "I'll handle this." He kneeled down with his face on the same plane as the boy's. "Wake up, son," he said and gave the lad a gentle shake.

Tuckered out from a full night's lack of sleep and hard to rouse under the best of circumstances, Ethan Allen tipped over onto the floor, still fast asleep. Dog, however, jumped up and started barking so furiously you'd wonder if his head might pop off. The barking finally woke Ethan. The first thing the boy saw was Fred McGinty's face, a face as round and happy looking as Santa Clause himself. "Grandpa Doyle," Ethan said, trying to rub the sleep from his eyes and remember the speech he had planned.

"Doyle?" Fred McGinty gasped. He stood up so fast he almost toppled over. "You think *I'm* Charlie Doyle?"

"You're not?"

Fred was as superstitious a man as ever lived and suddenly turned pale as paste. "What is this?" he asked angrily. "Some sort of sick joke?"

Ethan Allen clambered to his feet. "Joke?"

"How'd you get in here? Who the hell are you?"

"I'm your grandson, Ethan Allen Doyle."

Olivia's hand flew up to her mouth. She inhaled a gasp of air and then fainted dead away.

Still reeling from the thought of the boy mistaking him for a dead man, Fred caught Olivia half a heartbeat before she would have landed face down on the hallway floor. "Are you okay?" he asked, although her eyes were glazed over and her legs so rubbery they could barely keep her upright. "Are you okay?" he asked again but the answer was obvious, for she had the look of a woman who had seen a ghost. He pried the key from her hand, unlocked the door, and helped her inside. "You need to sit down," he said, gingerly guiding her to the sofa. "I'll get you some water."

Ethan Allen and his dog, both of whom had been forgotten, followed them inside the apartment. "I suppose I've come at a bad time," he mumbled meekly, but made no attempt to leave. He waited a few minutes then looked at Fred and said. "I'm sorry I surprised you, Grandpa, but—"

"Stop calling me that!" Fred shouted. "I'm not your grandpa! Charlie Doyle is—"

Olivia bolted upright. "That's enough, Fred! This boy's come here to see his grandpa, which, as you well know, is none of your concern!"

"Well, I think he ought—"

"Nobody cares what you think! Just go home. I'll handle this." Having made a miraculous recovery, Olivia crisscrossed her arms over her chest and fixed her eyes in a hard set glare, which ultimately caused Fred to stomp off in a huff. While the bang of the door was still echoing across the room, she turned to the boy and in a voice given over to sweetness said, "Honey, that man wasn't your grandpa, he was just a neighbor."

"Oh," Ethan replied, his expression more bewildered than ever.

Olivia gave a great sigh and lowered herself back down onto the sofa. "So," she said, "you're Ethan Allen Doyle."

"Yes, ma'am."

"And you've come to see your grandpa?"

"Yes, ma'am," Ethan answered. "Is he here?"

The boy had the same blue eyes as Charlie. The same look of earnestness. The same way of tearing at Olivia's heart. Obviously he knew nothing of what had happened. "Well, now…" she stammered, the popcorn she'd eaten at the movie theatre exploding all over again. Kernel after kernel burst open, hammering buttery little holes in her chest. "He's not here," she finally blurted out. "But you and I are, and we've got lots to talk about." She jumped up and began plumping some sofa pillows that weren't the least bit mussed. "Of course, before we get to all of that," she said nervously, "we ought to have ourselves a cup of cocoa and something to eat. You look like a boy who's been travelling, and I'll just bet your poor little tummy is practically turned inside out from hunger." Olivia headed into the kitchen and motioned for him to follow. Moving about in a fidgety sort of way, she flung open the refrigerator. "Let's see now," she rambled on. "I've got boiled ham, cheddar cheese, tuna fish salad, cherry pie—any of those things strike your fancy? I could warm up a bit of sweet potato casserole. How's that sound?"

Feeling a bit overwhelmed, Ethan Allen said, "You got peanut butter?"

"Peanut butter?" Olivia once again found herself wishing she and Charlie could exchange places. "Honey, I don't have any peanut butter. You could've asked for a dozen different things and I'd have had them, but I don't have peanut butter." She began another rundown of all the other things she did have.

Ethan watched as the woman flitted from one side of the kitchen to the other, opening cupboard after cupboard, fidgeting her hands, shuffling her feet, never settling in any one spot. Every time he looked at her, she'd glance off in some other direction. He'd decided on a ham sandwich, but she set three in front of him, along with a helping of potato salad and two cupcakes. Without anybody asking, she'd given Dog a bowl of water and some broken-up pieces of meatloaf. In Ethan's book people didn't go around doing stuff like that unless they were up to something. He eyed her suspiciously for a good long while, then asked, "Are you my grandma?"

"Me?" Olivia gasped. "Me?" With the look of a woman who couldn't fathom the carrying of another burden, she lowered herself into the chair directly across from Ethan. "Because of my being married to your grandpa, Charlie Doyle, I suppose I would legally be considered your grandma, but only in the most formal sense. See, grandparents and grandchildren have relationships that go way back in time. You and I, why, we've just met. We hardly know each other, and given such a circumstance you wouldn't actually regard me the same as you would a blood-relative grandma."

"Oh. Okay then. I suppose I could do with just having a grandpa."

Olivia looked at the boy's blue eyes and wanted to cry. *How many times can you lose somebody you love?* she wondered. *Do they just keep coming back, forever and ever and ever?* How long did she have to pay for having twenty-one days of happiness? She gave a sigh so deep it had the sound of something hauled up from the basement of her soul. "Ethan Allen," she moaned. "It truly breaks my heart to have to tell you this, but your dear sweet grandpa passed on months ago. It happened in Miami Beach, Florida, while we were still on our honeymoon."

"Grandpa's dead?"

"Yes, honey. I would have notified—"

"Aw, shit!"

"Shame on you, using such language! I know this is a shock, but—"

"You don't know the half of it. I got no place else to stay."

Misunderstanding the meaning of his statement Olivia said, "You can stay here tonight, and tomorrow I'll call your mama to come pick you up."

"You can't call Mama, 'less you got a telephone that reaches up to heaven."

"Excuse me?"

"Lady, my mama's dead!"

"Well, then, who brought you here? Your daddy?"

"Nobody brought me. I hitched."

"Well, then, I'm sure your daddy is quite worried about you."

"No, he ain't. It breaks my heart to have to tell you this," Ethan Allen said, sarcastically mimicking Olivia's words, "but my daddy's dead too."

Olivia clutched her chest in such a way you'd wonder if she was headed down the same pathway. "Who then," she gasped, "is taking care of you?"

"Nobody," he answered. "I was figuring to stay with Grandpa, but if he's dead I suppose I gotta find someplace else."

"Maybe another relative?" she asked hopefully.

Ethan Allen shook his head. "There ain't no other relatives."

It seemed to Olivia some days were simply too long and troublesome for their own good. When days like that happened along a person should give up and toddle off to bed, forget about that day, and start over again in the morning, which is precisely what she decided to do. She folded a bath towel for the dog to sleep on and fixed the boy a place on the sofa. She then poured herself a full glass of sherry and carried it to the bedroom.

Long about midnight the hooting of a night owl set the dog to barking loud enough to wake the people in downtown Wyattsville. Olivia, sound asleep by then, leaped from the bed in a panic and went running to the living room. "Shush," she shouted at the dog, in a voice louder than the barking. "There's no dogs allowed in this building! Don't you understand that? No dogs!" Olivia knew that having a pet was something the residents of the Wyattsville Arms apartment building would not tolerate. Why, just two months ago a man on the ninth floor had been sent packing because of his cat—a cat that mewed in a barely-audible voice and didn't poop outside on the lawn. She gave the boy's shoulder a shake and pleaded for him to get up and take control of the dog.

Unfortunately Ethan was not one to be easily woken so he cracked an eyelid, then rolled over and went back to sleep, leaving Olivia to deal with the situation as she would. "Go back to bed," she said, pointing a finger at the folded towel. The dog didn't budge, just sat there grumbling like he had a bark stuck in his throat. "Go on," Olivia repeated, trying to sound authoritative, but the dog, unimpressed, turned in the opposite direction and trotted over to the window. "Not there!" Olivia shouted, but before she could yank the dog back he began barking again.

After being bribed with two slices of ham, three shortbread cookies, and a bowl of warm milk, the dog finally curled up on the towel. Olivia waited for a full fifteen minutes to make certain he was going to stay there, then stumbled back to her own bed. Of course, sleep was nigh on to impossible, so she lay there staring up at the ceiling and picturing the eviction notice that was sure to be slid under her door before morning.

Although certain she wouldn't catch a single wink she did at some point doze off, and by the time she opened her eyes the sun was well into the sky. Pushing off a residue of drowsiness, she pulled on a bathrobe and hurried into the living room. Both boy and dog were gone. The blankets lay in a crumpled heap at one end of the sofa. The folded towel was still on the floor. She walked into the kitchen. The counter was exactly as she'd left it the night before, no dirty dishes, no used glasses.

The boy had obviously gone off without a bite in his stomach, without even a glass of milk to tide him over.

"Oh, dear," Olivia sighed, knowing that *she*, of all people, should understand the feeling of being alone and having no family to speak of. She thought back to the September morning when she walked out of her parents' house. She could still picture her father standing on the front porch, arms akimbo. *If you go, you're on your own,* he'd hollered, *don't come back here looking for help.* Then before she reached the end of the walkway, he'd turned back inside the house and slammed the door behind him. Of course, she was twenty-five years old at the time, a grown woman capable of making her own way in life. This poor boy looked to be eight or nine, maybe ten at the most. Olivia felt a lasso of guilt knotting itself around her heart. She'd always considered herself a Christian woman, yet last night she'd lain in bed wishing she'd never set eyes on either the boy or his dog.

With a sprig of regret taking root inside of her, Olivia returned to the living room and began folding the blankets. "He's Charlie's grandson," she muttered to herself. "His grandson! Whether or not I've any love of children, I should have seen to the lad having a place to go and some way to get there." Long about the time Olivia began believing Charlie's ghost would be back to haunt her, the doorbell chimed.

"Sorry," the boy said. "I forgot to leave the lock open."

"Oh," Olivia answered, already forgetting the guilt connected to him being Charlie's grandson. "I thought you'd gone."

"Gone where?" he asked as he tromped through to the kitchen, leaving a trail of dirty footprints behind. "I don't exactly have no place else to go."

"Oh, right." She poured a glass of milk and handed it to him. "Don't worry," she said, offering solace to herself as much as to the boy. "We'll work it out. There's got to be someone who'd be real anxious to have you come stay with them. A blood relative on your mama's side maybe."

Trying to remember her thoughts of being a bit more charitable to what was surely the last of Charlie's kin, Olivia turned to fixing breakfast. "What would you like to eat?" she asked, forcing herself to give off the sound of cheerfulness. "Eggs and bacon? Cereal? French toast maybe?"

"You got any potato chips?"

"Well, yes, but not for breakfast."

"Why not?" Ethan Allen asked.

"Because it's not proper breakfast food. Why, there's not an ounce of nutrition—"

"Mama says potato chips is a fine breakfast."

"I'm not your mama!" Olivia snapped. But before a half-second had passed she regretted making such a comment to the motherless boy. "Goodness gracious," she said in a voice sweet as sugar cane, "just listen to me, acting grumpy when I ought to be thinking about our breakfast. Let's see now, I could fix us a scrambled egg omelet with some potato chips alongside of it, how's that sound?"

"Okay," he shrugged. "But far as I'm concerned, you can skip the omelet."

By the time Olivia cooked up an omelet and set it in front of the boy, she was wishing she'd never married Charlie Doyle. Of course she could wish from now until doomsday, and it wouldn't change a thing. She simply had to focus on what it was she could do with this boy and his mangy-haired dog. Olivia knew for a fact Charlie had no brothers or sisters, and the woman who gave birth to his son had died some thirty years ago, which left only the maternal side of Ethan's family. She poured herself a cup of coffee and sat down across from him. "So," she said, "are you acquainted with any of your mama's relatives?"

The boy shook his head. "I don't know that she had any."

"Surely there were some. Sisters maybe, or brothers?"

Ethan, now busy slicing the omelet into pieces for Dog, simply shrugged unknowingly, then lowered his plate to the floor.

"Well, maybe if you tell me your mama's maiden name and where she came from, I could locate somebody."

"Mama?" he laughed. "Nobody knew where Mama came from. According to her way of telling it, she crawled out from under a rose bush."

"That's no way to talk about your mama!"

"It ain't me what said it! Shit, Mama's the one—"

"Stop that cussing!" Olivia commanded. "An eight-year-old using such language. Why, you ought to be ashamed of yourself!"

"I ain't eight."

"Well, excuse me! What are you then?" she asked flippantly. "Nine?"

"No," he answered, rolling his eyes like people do when they've heard something that's beyond believing. "I'm eleven."

"Eleven!" Olivia slumped back in her chair. "Eleven? You're eleven years old?"

"Yeah, and you can just save the wisecracks about being small for my age."

Before Olivia could start piecing together the loss of the boy's parents and the unlucky circumstance of him being eleven, Clara burst through the door. "Guess what?" she called out on her way through to the kitchen. "Somebody in this building has smuggled in a—" The statement was cut short when Dog came flying through the air and landed against her bosom. Being low to the ground and built with a substantial center of gravity, Clara wavered a bit but stayed upright and as soon as she'd regained her balance, she screamed, "Dog!"

Olivia could already picture all of her belongings set out onto the curb.

"How could you?" Clara shouted. "You know the rules!"

"It's not what you think," Olivia mumbled apologetically. "The dog isn't mine."

"Not yours? When it's standing right here in your kitchen?"

"The dog belongs to Ethan Allen Doyle, Charlie's grandson."

"Oh." Clara looked over at the boy, then lowered herself into a chair. "Still," she went on, "you know the rules. If the Committee gets wind of this…"

Olivia felt the need to talk and knew she had some explaining to do, so she suggested Ethan sneak the dog down the back stairwell and walk over to the building across the street. Pressing a dollar bill into his palm, she said, "You might even want to take a stroll down to the market. Pick up some peanut butter and a can or two of dog food."

Once Ethan was beyond earshot, Olivia told the entire story. How she'd found the boy on her doorstep, how he supposedly had no other family to turn to, and how the dog had come along as part of the package. "What was I to do?" she sobbed. "Toss the poor child out into the street?"

"But the Rules Committee has specifically stated—"

"It's not as if he'll be here forever," Olivia pleaded. "Just until I can work things out. It might be a day or two, a week at the most."

"Well," Clara hedged, "I suppose if the Committee didn't know…"

"I'd make sure the dog stays quiet."

"A few days, you say?"

"Maybe less."

"I guess I could speak to some of the neighbors."

OLIVIA

I can't help wondering if the turmoil of this life ever ends. Just when I start believing I have an existence to call my own Ethan Allen shows up at the door, claiming to be Charlie's grandson.

I can honestly say if it weren't for those blue eyes, which are exactly the same color and shape as Charlie's, I would have turned the boy away, figuring him to be an imposter. I probably should have done it anyway. I mean, what's a woman like me going to do with a child?

Worst of all, he's eleven! Why, I could barely handle my own year of being eleven.

I can't even venture a guess as to how this thing will turn out. More than likely I'll end up evicted. I'll be set out on the street with a handful of belongings and nowhere to go. No apartment, no friends.

I feel sorry for the child, but having him and that awful dog live with me is simply too much to ask. I'm willing to lend a hand and help the lad find his true family, but I don't think I can do much more than that. There has to be somewhere the boy can go—some family, someone who's accustomed to having children around and knows how to deal with them. Heaven knows that's way beyond the realm of my capabilities. I don't like making such a decision, but I can't think of any other alternative.

I'm not really the boy's grandma and I've got no obligation, but I still feel for the child. Everybody ought to have somebody who loves them

THE BEST KEPT SECRET

Who knows what might have happened had Clara not agreed that tossing Charlie's poor grandson out into the street would be quite unchristian. But after she'd spent two whole days going from door-to-door explaining the situation and telling folks they were beholden to help Olivia Doyle in her time of need, the Rules Committee had no chance. Even if they had brought in members of the Spanish Inquisition to ask about the rumored barking, residents would have simply shrugged their shoulders and claimed not to have noticed the clumps of dog hair on the seventh-floor carpet.

Clara reported this back to Olivia on Tuesday afternoon as she and Ethan Allen were sitting down to a dinner of macaroni and cheese, which the boy claimed was his favorite. "Does that mean I can stay here?" he asked when he heard the news.

"For a while," Olivia answered. "Until we can sort things out. I'm sure somewhere there are relatives who are worried sick over your whereabouts."

Ethan rolled his eyes, then swallowed a bite of macaroni.

Olivia was starting to picture herself hobbling through life with both the boy and the dog chained to her right leg. How could such a thing be happening? Especially now, when she'd pulled the remnants of her life together and started over? Hoping that maybe the boy had rushed to judgment in thinking there were no relatives, she tried again. "So, Ethan," she asked, "did your mama ever mention where she and your daddy met?"

"Nope."

"What about Christmas cards or birthday cards? She maybe get cards or letters from the folks back home?"

"You gotta be kidding!"

"I most certainly am not. Folks generally stay in touch, one way or another."

"Not Mama!"

"Well, what about friends or neighbors?"

"We didn't have no neighbors. The Pickens' farm was closest, but Mama claimed she wouldn't wipe her ass on that mealy-mouthed Missus Picken."

"I told you to stop using such language!"

"You said if I was eight—but I'm eleven!"

"That's still too young to be cussing."

"I ain't cussing," he replied sullenly. "I'm just repeatin' what Mama said."

"Well, repeat it without cuss words," Olivia snapped. She scooped up his dish and carried it over to the kitchen sink. She would have been angrier with him for bantering about foul language as he did, but obviously the boy had a bunch of hurts tearing at his insides. Anybody could see it in his eyes, in the way he'd look down at his shoes and mumble answers that had the sound of words pushed through a mouthful of marbles. It was a terrible thing to lose somebody you loved. *Nobody,* Olivia thought, *knows that more than I do.* She slipped back to thinking about the days that followed Charlie's passing—minutes weighted like hours, hours longer than a day, and an aching loneliness that rubbed her nerves raw. Caught up in the moment of remembering she turned to the boy and said, "I'm real sorry about your mama and daddy, Ethan."

"Yeah, well." He shrugged, then reached into his pocket and pulled out a Spalding rubber ball which had "accidentally" followed him home from the market. "I can't do nothing about that," he said, and started thunking the ball off the side of the cabinet. Bounce-thunk-bounce. Bounce-thunk-bounce. Bounce-thunk-bounce. It was a sound that could jangle a person's nerves real quick.

"I wasn't expecting you could do anything about it," Olivia answered, sounding unbelievably tolerant. "I was just offering up some sympathy."

Bounce-thunk-bounce.

She'd come across people like this before—clerks or telephone operators, singled out for some rinky-dink infraction of the rules—angry, but yet unwilling to defend themselves. You had to draw people like that out, ask question after question until you got them started talking. Then you might learn the truth of things. "Who was it that died first," Olivia asked, "your mama or daddy?"

Bounce-thunk-bounce.

"Ethan?"

"They was both killed," bounce-thunk-bounce, "the same time."

"Killed?"

He nodded but focused his concentration on smacking the ball.

"In a car accident? How?"

"Murdered," the boy answered, then whacked the Spalding with such force that it rebounded off the cabinet and went sailing through the kitchen window. Although she was certain everyone in the Wyattsville Arms building had heard the breaking of glass, Olivia went to the boy and in the most comforting way imaginable whispered, "It's okay, honey." She wrapped her arms around him and pulled his head to her bosom. "When you're ready, Ethan," she said, "then we'll talk about what's happened."

He pulled back and screamed, "I can't never talk about it! I didn't see nothing!"

"Okay," Olivia replied as if she'd accepted his answer and wanted nothing more. But she knew the explosion of words was hiding something terrible, and sooner or later the boy would let go of it. When he stomped off to the living room, she remained in the kitchen and finished doing the dishes.

Later on she followed him into the living room and found the dog sitting on her new silk chair. Ethan Allen was stretched out across the floor, his dirty sneakers tracking footprints up the side of the wall. "You got any playing cards?" he asked.

"I believe so." Olivia stepped over his legs and began looking through the desk drawer. After she'd rummaged through a number of boxes and packets, she came upon a worn deck of cards—cards that Charlie, who had a fondness for gambling, had no doubt spent many an evening with. "Here you are," she said and handed them to the boy.

Ethan shuffled the deck a number of times, then turned to her with a sly glimmer in his eyes. "You know how to play poker?" he asked.

"Not very well," Olivia answered.

"But good enough to maybe get by?"

"I suppose." She shooed the dog from her chair and sat down, ready for the start of "The Red Skelton Show." It was her very favorite hour of television, because his antics usually had her laughing so hard tears slid from her eyes. It was virtually impossible for a person to think sorrowful thoughts when they were watching Clem Kiddlehopper.

"How about we play a few hands?" the boy asked.

"Play cards? Now?"

"Yeah," he answered. "It'd keep me from dwelling on how I been orphaned."

Under any other circumstance Olivia would have flatly refused, but the boy seemed to be so needy that without complaining she walked over and snapped off the television set. "Okay," she sighed. "You want to deal?"

Ethan nodded, his grin stretched out wide as could be. "Penny a point?" he asked.

Olivia agreed, and before she could change her mind there were five cards lying in front of her. "Looks like you've played this game before," she said.

"I used to play with Mama. She was good as they come. Even if she was holding a royal flush, you couldn't know by the look on her face."

"Royal flush? What exactly is that?"

"How about we up it to two cents a point?"

Olivia shrugged. "Okay. *If* while we're playing, you tell me a bit about yourself."

"I reckon that's okay," he said begrudgingly, "but don't ask me no questions about Mama or Daddy's murder 'cause I done told you, I didn't see nothing."

"Not a word about that," she crisscrossed her heart.

After an hour of playing Ethan had won ninety-eight cents, but Olivia had learned almost nothing of any significance. Certainly nothing about his having any other relatives. What she did learn was that his mama had a fine voice and high hopes of one day becoming a Radio City Rockette. "You ever been to New York City?" he asked. When Olivia answered that she hadn't, he simply shrugged and said, "Me neither."

It didn't take a terribly astute person to see the boy was hiding something. He'd start out talking about one thing or another, rethink it, and stop in the middle of a sentence. He did that most every time Olivia hit upon questions about his mama and daddy's relationship. "Were they real happy together?" she'd asked, and for a moment it seemed he was on the verge of letting go of something. Then he smacked the cards down and snarled some comment about how he was tired of the game.

Olivia started wishing she'd held back a few of the peppercorns given to her by Canasta Jones. One or two of those in a bowl of okra soup, and Ethan Allen might get to feeling better.

⊙━━◆━━⊙

That night Olivia tossed and turned until the sheets were tangled into a knot and the blanket slid off the bed. Every time she closed her eyes and settled into a comfortable spot there it was: the image of Charlie walking hand-in-hand with this miniature look-alike. There was no wondering whether the boy was actually related. They both had eyes sloped down at the corner and colored the shade of blue that drifts across the sky just minutes before nightfall. Long about three o'clock in the morning Olivia, badgered by the voice of her conscience, decided that she owed it to Charlie to look out for the boy. Minutes later she bolted upright, wondering if she'd lost her mind entirely. For the remainder of the night she was haunted by a picture of herself looking like Francine Burnam, a dozen Ethan Allen look-alikes dangling from her arms and legs like the ornaments on a Christmas tree. Still, she kept telling herself, she owed it to Charlie to do something.

⊙━━◆━━⊙

By morning Olivia had come to a somewhat shaky decision. She would watch over the boy. Not forever but until she could find a place where he truly belonged. As soon as they'd finished breakfast, which was cereal for her and potato chips for him, she loaded both boy and dog into the car and headed for Clairmore, a town nine miles from Wyattsville. A town where there'd be less chance of being spotted by someone on the building's Rules Committee. "We need to get you some clothes," she told Ethan. "You can't go around wearing the same thing day in and day out."

"Why not?" he answered, then said he'd prefer to have a new ball seeing as how his Spalding had disappeared through the kitchen window.

"You shouldn't be playing ball inside the house," Olivia replied without taking her eyes from the road.

"It's not a house," he grumbled.

"Okay then, you shouldn't be playing ball inside the apartment."

"There's nothing else to do."

"There is too," Olivia said. But after watching television she was hard pressed to come up with a second suggestion, which is why she ended up purchasing five comic books, a set of checkers, a Monopoly game, and a jigsaw puzzle picturing the entire Baltimore Orioles Baseball Team in addition to the selection of underwear, tee-shirts, and dungarees. At first she'd thought the comic books, mostly about monsters and superheroes, were somewhat unnecessary, but then she remembered games required a partner's participation.

When the clerk finished tallying the cost of everything, which was more than Olivia had planned on spending, she turned and saw the boy balancing himself on a bright red Schwinn bicycle. "Now this," he said, "is something I could *really* use."

She took a peek at the price tag and shook her head.

"But," he reasoned, "if I had this bike, I'd be riding it morning 'til night. I'd *never* be inside dirtying up the house."

Although such a prospect was tempting, Olivia shook her head again. She led the boy out of the shop and across the street to the luncheonette. After lunch they made one last stop. At the pet shop she bought a small bag of dog food, some flea control shampoo, a leash, and a harness. "You could've saved your money," Ethan Allen said, "'cause he hates baths and *really* hates being tied down."

❦

Within days of his arrival the boy and his dog became the best kept secret at Wyattsville Arms. Everyone knew but no one uttered a whisper, lest the Rules Committee catch wind of it. Residents who spotted a shaggy-haired dog darting down the back staircase would hold the door open and signal when the coast was clear. People on the seventh floor began to discreetly pluck loose dog hair from the hall carpet and carefully dispose of it in their own waste baskets. Others began stopping by to bring some silly thing Olivia would never in a million years have need of. First it was Bessie Porter, who came trotting in with a sack of

Hershey bars that she supposedly brought just in case Olivia was to have a craving for sweets. Next Harry Hornsby dropped off a baseball mitt his grandson no longer used. Fred McGinty found it in his heart to forgive the boy for thinking of him as a dead man and brought over eight cans of dog food, then stayed for hours playing checkers with Ethan. "He's a fine lad," Fred whispered into Olivia's ear. "Why, anybody would enjoy having him around."

"Maybe so," Olivia said in a way that had a questioning undertone. "But remember, his being here is temporary. Once I've located his real family, he's sure to be moving on."

Fred shook his head. "That's unfortunate," he said, "losing a lad like this. What a shame." Olivia, however, remained blank-faced and voiced no opinion.

True, she'd noticed the way the boy had made an effort to cut back on his cussing and spoon up some cereal for breakfast, but that didn't change the fact that he was *eleven*! Not just eleven, but also attached to a scraggly looking dog that likely as not would get her evicted. Olivia could name a thousand reasons why it was better for the boy to move on, but although she never once mentioned it aloud the number one reason was the nightmare that kept recurring. It was a painful thing to imagine you could turn into Francine Burnam, and even worse when the thought haunted you all night long and caused you to wake up gasping for breath.

In an effort to speed up the finding of Ethan's true family, Olivia began spending more time with the boy. Night after night they'd sit together and play poker or work on fitting pieces into the picture puzzle he had spread across the dining room table. "This looks like Hoot Evers' ear," Ethan would say, and while he was fixing that piece in place Olivia would start asking about his mama and daddy.

"Did your mama ever mention wanting to go to some special place?" she asked. "Her hometown maybe?"

"New York City," Ethan Allen answered, as he rummaged through a pile of pieces in search of Brooks Robinson's nose.

"New York. Was that where your mama was from?"

"Unh-unh," he answered, shaking his head but focusing his concentration on the finding of a foot. "That's where she wanted to go."

"She ever mention any cousins? Distant cousins maybe?"

Although he'd eased off the snippiness of his answers Ethan Allen still claimed to have no knowledge whatsoever of any other relatives, which exasperated Olivia to no end. Finally, after running out of questions relating to the life of his mama, Olivia asked how exactly her death had come about. The boy turned red-faced and bolted from the chair like he'd been charged through with electricity. Before Olivia had time to think he swept his arm across the table and sent the pieces of the puzzle they'd been working on for almost a week flying to the floor. "Just leave it be!" he screamed. "I was sound asleep when it happened, and I don't know nothing! Nothing!" He turned on his heel and slammed out the door, leaving Dog behind.

TOM BEHRENS

I sure hope little Jack Mahoney got hold of his grandpa in time to get help for his mama. It's an awful thing seeing a boy small as him saddled with more worry than a grown man ought to have.

I can still remember back when my own mama died. I was the same as that kid. There wasn't a single soul to look out for me. Not even a grasshopper to care whether I lived or died. It ain't right for a boy to go through such a thing. It ain't even the littlest bit right.

Human beings ought to look out for one another. If I was a decent sort, I'd do something to help that boy out.

Maybe, by God, I will.

RIGHTING A WRONG

After Tom Behrens watched the boy ride off in the chicken truck, he returned to the ESSO station. That afternoon he swept the office floor five times without recalling he'd done it before. Then he opened up a second case of oil cans, figuring to stack them in a display rack that he'd already filled. Tom thought he had forgotten that summer when his life took such a terrible turn, but now here it was back again, haunting him with a slew of memories bitter as hardpan kale.

Even now some twenty-two years later, he regretted not running his daddy through with a pitchfork when he had the chance. Tom moved a stack of tires from one side of the doorway to the other, all the while wondering if he would have been able to do it. At the time he was taller and more filled out than this boy but still a kid. *Tommy,* his mama had said, wiping the tears from her eyes, *you're the man of the house now.* But such a responsibility should never have been shoved onto a kid's shoulders. What, he wondered, did she expect from a thirteen-year-old boy? What could he do? Nothing, that's what!

Tom Behrens turned to wiping down the front window of the station, oblivious to the sound of sloshing water and the squeak of the squeegee as it slid from the top of the glass to the bottom. The memories were pricking pins at his brain, and the only thing he could hear were the moans of his mama lying in bed day after day, her color growing pastier, her breath more shallow. When it got near the end, he'd have to lower his ear to her face to determine if she was breathing at all. "You want a pill,

Mama?" he'd ask nervously. Then he'd try to steady her trembling hands as she lifted the glass of water to swallow it down.

For several hours Tom fiddled around, moving things from one side of the station to the other, straightening storage cabinets and cleaning things that didn't need cleaning. Long about four o'clock his fingers began twitching like he had an itch to play the piano, so he hung a "Closed" sign on the door of the station and grabbed hold of his fishing pole.

Alongside of a creek with the sound of water splashing against rocks was the one place a person could go for clear-headed thinking. Tom Behrens knew that as well as anybody did. It had been his salvation even though it was also the very same spot his daddy had let loose of the fact he'd be leaving.

It was an August afternoon when the sun was a ball of fire that would blister your face if you turned to look at it, but still they'd gone fishing. Tom remembered his mama saying it was too hot for such a thing but nonetheless his daddy loaded him into the truck and headed for Donnigan's Creek, a place thick with weeping willows and cypress trees, a place so quiet you could hear the chipmunks breathing. They sat together on a rocky overhang, Tom lying on his back watching a family of squirrels scamper up and down the tree, his daddy drinking beer after beer. Without any conversation whatsoever his daddy stretched his legs toward the edge of the rock and dropped a line in the water, even though he knew it had been a summer when the fish were too lazy to bite. They sat there all afternoon without speaking a word to each other, but on the drive home his daddy grumbled, "You gotta understand, it ain't my way to stick around and watch what's happening to your mama."

At the time Tom gave the statement little attention, figuring it to be what his mama called "a man feeling sorry about his lot." But the very next morning when he got up there were two twenty-dollar bills on the kitchen table and his daddy was gone as gone could be. There was never even so much as a postcard after that.

In September when the other boys his age were lined up in Miss Brannigan's sixth-grade classroom Tom was missing. He was at home watching over his mama and fearing at any moment she would take her last breath, which didn't happen until the day before Christmas. He could still envision the look of sadness that settled in around his eyes that year, a look of worry far beyond what any boy should know. On the day they planted his mama in the ground, Tom caught a glimpse of himself as he passed by a mirror. Any resemblance to the boy he had been was gone. The person looking back was an old man; a man well-acquainted with misery.

Tom could still picture that reflection. It had a bitter, rock-hard look, the same sort of look he'd seen on the face of the boy, Jack Mahoney.

Tom fished for three days straight, leaving the door to the gas station locked tight and pushing aside thoughts of customers who'd be standing at the pump waiting to purchase fuel for their automobiles. He sat alongside the creek and dangled his line in the water, all the time remembering that summer when he'd been the most miserable boy on the face of the earth. Every so often a silvery bass swallowed the bait and started yanking on the line, but Tom was interested in thinking, not catching, so he'd cut the fish free and send it on its way. He kept reminding himself that he'd been just thirteen. What more could a boy of that age have done for a mama who was dying?

On the fourth day Tom returned to the gas station with a ball of resolve pushing up against his chest. As a boy he'd had no choice but to stand there and watch his mama slip away. But he wasn't a boy anymore. He was a man now, and he could sure as hell do something about the sorrowful condition of Jack Mahoney's mama.

Tom wished he had asked where the boy came from or what his mama's Christian name was, but he hadn't so that was that. All he knew about the boy was that his last name was Mahoney and he'd traveled south along the Eastern Shore headed for the mainland, which probably meant his mama lived somewhere on the island. Unfortunately nine different counties ran end to end along the narrow peninsula, and each one had their own telephone directory. Scooping up every loose dime in the cash register, Tom positioned himself at the pay telephone on the outside wall of the gas station.

The telephone stood alongside a rack of directories. He opened the first book—Flaubert County—dropped in a dime, and dialed the number listed for Albert Mahoney. Albert, who answered on the first ring, claimed he had no knowledge of a boy named Jack nor a Mahoney woman who might be lying on her deathbed. Tom thanked the man, hung up, and tracked his finger down to the next name. He dropped in another dime and dialed Allen Mahoney. After that it was Anna, then Charles, then Daniel, and he continued on until one by one he had called every Mahoney in Flaubert Country.

At eight-thirty, after a number of people had complained he'd interrupted their dinner, he stopped calling. He had gone through three counties, but so far no one knew anything about a boy named Jack Mahoney.

The next morning he was back at the telephone a full two hours before the gas station was scheduled to open. Eugenia Mahoney was the first call. She answered on the second ring, her voice registering the sound of a sob ready to follow. "Hello."

"Good morning," Tom said cheerfully. "I hate to be a bother, but I'm looking to find the mama of a boy named Jack Mahoney—"

"How dare you!" the woman angrily screamed into the receiver. "How dare you wake a sound asleep person and make them think somebody's died!"

"I'm real sorry," Tom mumbled. "I surely had no intention—"

"No intention? No intention?" Eugenia, it seemed, had a tendency to repeat herself, with the second go around being considerably louder than the first. "What else," she screamed, "is a person supposed to think when the telephone starts jangling off the hook in the middle of the night?"

"Actually, it's six-fifteen."

"Are you some sort of a wise guy? Is that it? Well," she snapped, "you're barking up the wrong tree, because I'll get the law down on you, that's what—"

Tom quietly slid the telephone receiver back into its cradle and ended the conversation. He'd be better off, he decided, waiting until eight or nine o'clock to resume his search. He walked back inside the station and set a pot of coffee to brew.

When Clifford Pence stopped by to fill his truck with gasoline, Tom asked if he knew anything of a boy. "Nine or ten, maybe," he said, "got himself a wiry-haired brown dog. You know anybody like that?"

Clifford fingered his chin for a moment, then shook his head. "Can't recall that I've seen such a lad," he said. "You checked the orphanage?"

Tom asked the same question of everyone who drove in and even of two people who were simply passing by on the sidewalk. Margaret Walters claimed she had a nephew in New Jersey who pretty much fit that description, but everyone else simply shook their head and went on about their business. At eight-forty-five, Tom started making telephone calls again.

By four o'clock he'd moved on to the ninth name in the sixth directory. He dropped a dime into the slot, dialed the number, and waited as the phone rang four, five, then six times. Just as he was ready to hang up, a man answered. "Hold on a second," he said, "let me close the door."

As soon as the voice came back on the line, Tom swung into his apology for interrupting the man's day and went to his questioning. "I'm looking to locate a woman who's bad sick. As I understand it she's the mama of a Jack Mahoney—"

"I'm Jack Mahoney, but—"

"Oh, I'm sure you ain't the same Jack Mahoney. The one I'm referring to is just a boy—a bit over four foot tall, blond hair, got a wiry-haired brown dog. You know anybody fits a description such as that?"

"I can think of one such boy," Jack replied, remembering Ethan Allen who was still among the missing, "but his name isn't Jack Mahoney."

"I doubt it's him. The boy I came across said his name was Jack Mahoney. I remember that for certain."

"When was it you met this boy?"

"Let's see now," Tom said, counting back the number of days. "Nine days ago," he finally answered. "Yep, a week back from last Sunday. That was it."

"He wearing a brown-and-yellow striped shirt, green pants?"

"Now that you make mention of it, I do believe he was."

"You remember the name of that animal he was traveling with?"

"Can't say I do," Tom replied. "I believe the lad just called him dog."

Mahoney, who for a solid week had been looking for Ethan Allen, said, "I know the boy you're looking for."

"Well, actually, I wasn't so much looking for the boy. He should be pretty well off with his grandpa. I'm looking to find his sick mama. I figured maybe I could offer up some help." Tom was on the verge of telling how his own mama's death had taken place under similar circumstances, but before he got the chance Mahoney interrupted.

"That boy was just playing on your sympathies. His name ain't Jack

Mahoney. It's Ethan Allen Doyle, and his mama's already dead."

"Shitfire!"

"He knew she was dead when he ran off. We had a place for the boy to live but—"

"Run off?"

"Yes, indeed. I personally dropped him off at the Cobbs' place and turned him over to Emma. She's one of the nicest people you could hope to meet. Emma's the mama of a patrolman in my station house, so we figured it would be a good place for the boy to stay. She fixed him a bite to eat and tucked him into bed. Next morning he was gone. There was nothing but a rolled-up mound of clothes under the blanket."

"Damnation!" Tom grumbled. "I been took for the fool I am! Listening to that boy, I would've sworn he was on the up and up."

They talked on and on for almost twenty minutes. Mahoney explained how he and Patrolman Cobb were the law officers called in when the boy's mama and daddy were murdered. "It happened right there in their own house," he said. "The boy's mama apparently died from a single blow to the head, but his daddy—that poor bastard looked like he'd gone through a meat grinder."

"Sweet Jesus."

"It's bad enough for a boy to lose both his parents," Mahoney said, his voice weighted with concern, "but we've also got a suspicion that Ethan Allen knows who did the killing. If that's the case, he could be in a considerable amount of danger."

"Sweet Jesus," Tom repeated, understanding now why the boy lied. Anybody who'd gone through such a thing would, of course, lie. Not just lie, but run like hell to get loose from the devil dogging his heels. A man could spend a lifetime trying to escape things from which there was no escaping. But Tom knew that sometimes all you got for your trouble was a bunch of bad memories.

"If you got any knowledge as to where he went..."

"Not right off," Tom answered. "But I know he was headed for his grandpa's place over on the mainland."

"That's like looking for a raindrop in a river," Mahoney sighed.

"It was one of those little towns west of Richmond," Tom said. "The address was written on an envelope." Tom closed his eyes and pictured the boy pulling the envelope from his pocket, but he couldn't focus in on the scribbled return address. "I remember helping the kid find it on the map—Wernersville, Waterboro, Wyattstown—it was someplace like that. Give me a day or so, and I'll have the name for you."

Eager for even the smallest bit of information, Mahoney quickly volunteered to drive down for a face-to-face talk with Tom. "I'll see you day after tomorrow," he said. After he hung up he called Sam Cobb. "I've got a line on the boy," he said, "and being you were in on the start of this I thought you might want to come along."

"Sure," Cobb replied, for he liked the prestige of working with a detective and didn't often get the chance. "'Course, I doubt he's gonna tell us what really happened."

"You never know," Mahoney answered. "You just never know."

OLIVIA

*S*ometimes when I look at Ethan Allen I can see Charlie looking back at me from inside those blue eyes. It's amazing how much the boy resembles his grandfather, yet there's a world of difference in their personalities. Charlie was open-hearted and full of fun, but this boy is the exact opposite. It might be because he's got so many hurts locked inside of him. But still, you'd think he'd be more receptive to my kindness. That's not the way it is. The more I try to get close to him, the harder he pulls to get away. I genuinely feel for the child, but I swear to God he's almost impossible to understand.

And that mouth of his—why, it's enough to make a sailor blush!

Despite what I might think Ethan Allen is Charlie's only grandchild, so I'm trying to do right by him. At first I figured us spending time together would encourage the boy to loosen up about his family, but getting him to talk is worse than trying to milk a stone. I'm sure he's got relatives somewhere, people who'd love to take both him and his dog. That would probably be for the best. An orphaned child belongs with blood relatives, not some stranger who happened to marry his grandfather. I'm no relation whatsoever. The boy deserves better than that.

THICKENING OF BLOOD

Olivia saw the look on the boy's face as he stomped out the front door and recognized it right off—how could she have not? It was the same wild-eyed frenzy she'd seen in her own mirror just after Charlie died. For a while she'd been tricked into believing it to be sorrow, so she cried buckets and buckets of tears. Then it masqueraded itself as anger, and she raged, hurling things against the walls and kicking at the furniture. Finally, on that stormy night when there was nothing left but the roar of the ocean and the agony of loneliness, she came to know it for what it really was: fear. The kind of fear that chewed holes in a person's heart; holes so cavernous every last drop of hope leaked out and left them believing they'd never again be safe, never again be loved. Olivia felt a thin line of perspiration sliding down her back. It was strange how when you thought yourself free of such memories, they could fly back and slap against your face like a sudden rainstorm.

After she'd picked up the pieces of the Baltimore Orioles puzzle he'd scattered across the floor, Olivia looked at the clock. It was almost nine-thirty. Ethan Allen had been gone two hours. He'd stormed off without a sweater or jacket, and this was the time of year when it turned downright cold once the sun had set. It would seem reasonable, she thought, that he'd have come home by now but of course reasonableness was the last thing a person concerned themselves with in situations such as this. A strange sort of regret began pressing down on Olivia's shoulders settling over her like a sack of stones. *I should have been more understanding,* she told herself. *I should have waited until he was ready to tell whatever he has to tell.*

For a good part of her life Olivia had swallowed down her own painful secrets. She'd choked back words that needed to be spoken and stepped aside as life rolled by. She'd bottled herself up like a person already cremated, which, in looking back, was a thing she wouldn't wish on anybody. Especially a child. Still, if the boy wasn't ready to let go of his troubles, it was downright mean to keep poking at him. The secrets hidden in a person's heart could be like a persimmon. Bite into it before it's ready to be plucked loose, and the bitterness will turn your mouth inside out. Olivia went to the window, parted the curtains, and stood watching for the boy to come home. Further down the street was dark, hidden by overhanging branches and shadows of buildings. But directly beneath the window was a watery circle of yellow illumination where she would be able to see him. *He has to come along this walkway,* she told herself as she watched and waited. She could already feel the chill of night air pressing up against the windowpane. "It's getting cold," she said worriedly. "He'll be back just as soon as his bones start rattling." *Maybe not,* the voice inside her head argued. *Maybe he'll never come back.*

While Olivia was still feeling miserable over thoughts of the boy huddled alongside a garbage can in some freezing alleyway, the telephone rang. In two long strides she crossed the room and jerked the receiver to her ear. "Ethan?" she asked.

"Ethan?" Clara echoed. "Isn't he in bed?"

"Oh," Olivia moaned. "It's you."

"Yeah, it's me! How come you asked if I was Ethan Allen?"

"I thought maybe it was him calling."

"Him calling? At twelve o'clock midnight? Why, a boy his age ought to be in bed! Why in the world would you let him—"

"I didn't *let* him. He got his dander up and went flying out the door."

"For no reason?"

"Well," Olivia stammered, "I might've pushed a bit too much in asking about his mama."

"You, of all people," Clara grumbled with an air of annoyance, "should realize that Ethan Allen ain't ready to talk about such a tragedy. Right now he just needs comforting, somebody to reach out..."

As the words settled on Olivia's ears, she could feel herself start to shrink. With every word she seemed to grow smaller and smaller. She was five feet tall, then four...

"You surely know how it feels to..."

She slipped down to three feet, the size of a toddler with a world that revolves around "me", and it somehow seemed appropriate considering her behavior.

"Have you no sense of compassion?" Clara chided. "Why, that poor motherless boy..."

By the time Clara finished Olivia envisioned herself only inches high, small enough to be swallowed up by the dog searching for his master. She inhaled deeply and said, "You're right."

Clara abruptly hung up the telephone and Olivia was left with her thoughts, thoughts of how she'd not been the least bit Christian in her treatment of the boy. Sure, she'd bought him some clothes and a few games, but the whole while she'd been wishing he'd hurry up and leave, taking his dog with him. "I'm so sorry, Ethan," she whispered into a flood of tears. "Please come home."

A stream of tears was still rolling down her face when the front door banged open, and in walked a gathering of neighbors. "We've gotta find that boy," announced Clara, who was apparently the person in charge. Fred McGinty nodded, but with his hair standing on end and his right eye partway closed he had the look of a man not fully roused from sleep. Harry Hornsby, although he'd had the presence of mind to grab hold of a flashlight, had missed the fact that a cuff of striped pajama was poking out from beneath the sleeve of his jacket. Barbara Conklin and Maggie both had a trail of nightgown hanging from the hems of their coats. With the exception of Clara, an acknowledged night owl, they were all red-eyed but anxious to join in the hunt for Ethan Allen.

"Which way was he headed?" asked Ed Vaughn, a man from the third floor.

Olivia brushed back a few last tears and shrugged.

Fred stepped forward and started organizing the operation. "Vaughn," he said, "you check down at the movie house. Paul," he pointed to a thin-faced man standing at the back of the crowd, a man Olivia had never before seen, "you check the all-night burger stand. Pete and me are gonna head over to the park."

"We ladies will search up and down the street," Clara volunteered. "Check the courtyards, behind buildings."

Maggie was a woman known for toting along her umbrella on even the sunniest of days; she wrinkled her brow. "Cold as it is," she said, "we gotta hope he's dressed warm."

"He isn't," Olivia stammered, her voice faltering and falling into another rush of tears. "He left here in shirtsleeves, no sweater or jacket."

"No jacket?" Clara screeched, but by then Olivia was sobbing so furiously it would have been unfair to expect an answer.

"Let's go," Fred commanded, thrusting his right arm forward. "We're gonna have to move fast." As the others started out the door, he turned back to Olivia. "Put a leash on that dog," he said. "Try and get him to sniff the boy out."

Olivia did as she was told. With a firm lock on the leash she trudged up one walkway and down the next, urging the dog to find his master. "Find Ethan," she begged. "Please find him. Find him and I'll buy you a gigantic steak bone."

The residents of Wyattsville Arms worked throughout the night, poking their heads down alleyways, crisscrossing the park behind narrow flashlight beams, and hollering out for Ethan Allen to come home. As the hours crept by, the call of his name grew more urgent and other people joined in the search. "Ethan Allen, can you hear me?" they'd shout, flashing a circle of light onto the wall behind a row of garbage cans or beneath the branches of an overgrown hedge. By morning a drizzle of rain started to fall. Not hard enough to send the searchers running for cover, but hard enough to dampen their clothes and set their teeth to chattering. They still had not found Ethan Allen.

"A boy as resourceful as he is could be miles from here by now," Olivia said, even though she doubted Ethan Allen had anyplace else to go. She mournfully suggested the searchers go home before they caught their death of cold. "I'll have to call the police station and report him missing," she sobbed. "What else can I do?" With her shoulders rounded and her chin drooping down into the collar of her coat, she and the dog walked through the front door of the apartment building.

Clara grabbed hold of her arm. "Olivia! Have you gone stark raving mad?" she said. "Do you want someone from the Rules Committee to see you with the dog?"

"What does it matter now?" Olivia answered. Then she stepped inside the elevator and pushed the button for the seventh floor.

"Don't worry," Clara said, following along with determination. "I'm not gonna leave your side 'til we've got some word of him."

Olivia shook her head. "I'd rather be alone." She turned into her own apartment and closed the door behind her, leaving Clara in the hallway. Olivia may have thought she wanted to be alone, but once she was the truth of the word settled heavily upon her. Alone was not at all the peace and quiet she envisioned it to be. It was a giant loneliness that draped itself across the ceiling and cascaded down the walls. Alone was cold and hungry and forgotten. Alone was so very…alone. She'd wanted the boy gone. So why was it she felt such a huge emptiness inside her heart? She tried to recall the reasons why she'd been opposed to his staying. She pictured muddy footprints running across the carpet, crusted bowls piled in the sink, dog hairs on the sofa, but those images faded as quickly as they came replaced by blue eyes like Charlie's and a grin that popped loose when he found a lost piece of puzzle. It was strange how such a troublesome boy could fill a place with his being.

"I'm letting my heart rule my head," she scolded herself as she bent down to unleash the dog, "and such a thing is foolish." The words were heavy as bricks tumbling from her mouth, and Olivia suddenly found a need to remind herself of why she'd always avoided entangling relationships. There was always the demanding husband and hanging-on children. She searched her memory for the snapshot of poor Francine Burnam, a woman with youngsters of every shape and size, a woman who couldn't take a sideways step without a little one underfoot. It took several seconds but she finally got hold of the image, which as it turned out wasn't at all the way she remembered it being. Olivia had seen Francine's babies as cumbersome things, bananas hanging onto a stalk and weighing her down with their presence, but suddenly she could see they weren't bananas after all. They were bright yellow sunflowers tilted toward the sun. Standing alongside them was Francine, an oak tree, straight and tall as anyone could ever hope to be.

"Good Lord," Olivia said and dropped down onto the sofa. "How could I have made such a mistake? How could I not have seen—" She reached for the telephone and dialed the number for the Wyattsville Police Station.

"Sergeant Grubber," a voice answered.

"I'd like to report—" The door clicked open, and Olivia screamed, "Ethan Allen!"

"Excuse me?" Sergeant Grubber said.

"Never mind." Olivia hung up the receiver, leaped across the room, and grabbed hold of the boy. "Thank heaven you're back—"

"I ain't back," he grumbled. "I just came to get Dog."

"But—"

He removed the new harness and tossed it to the floor. "Where's my rope?"

"But, Ethan, there's no need—"

"Look, lady, you got your ways and I got mine!"

"Maybe so," Olivia answered, knowing such a thing was indeed true. "But I'll wager we could find us a way to work it out."

"I ain't telling you nothing."

"I won't ask anymore."

"I'll bet," he said with a sneer. "Maybe not today, but—"

"I'll never ask again. When you're ready you'll—"

"What if I ain't never ready?"

"Then you'll never tell me," Olivia answered with what she hoped was a reassuring smile.

"Is this some kind of trick?"

"No trick." Olivia crisscrossed her heart.

Ethan Allen cocked his mouth to one side in an expression of doubt. "I don't know," he said. "I still think I ought to be moving on."

Olivia could see the determination in his eyes wavering. "To where?" she asked.

"I ain't got a specific place in mind, but—"

"Then how about staying here with me? At least until you've made up your mind about where you might be going."

"I can leave anytime I'm ready?"

Olivia nodded.

"And I don't have to answer no questions about what happened?"

She shook her head.

"Well—"

"I could sure use some help around here. I've been thinking of hiring a boy to help me with carrying up the groceries and other such chores."

"You pay anything for doing that?"

Olivia nodded. "Twenty-five cents a week."

"Hmm." Ethan Allen twisted his face into an expression that could make a person believe he was giving the offer serious study. "Okay," he finally said, "but if you start in with asking me more questions—"

"I won't," Olivia said. "Rest assured, I won't."

"Dog stays too, right?"

"Right." This, Olivia figured, was not the time to be worrying about the seven crotchety old farts who governed the Rules Committee. "Well," she said, relieved, "now that that's settled, how about some pancakes and sausage?"

"With potato chips?" Ethan asked, licking at his lips.

Olivia smiled and gave a nod. "I suppose," she said, then turned toward the kitchen. Before starting breakfast, she called Clara and whispered, "He's home."

"Ethan Allen?"

"Yes."

"Well, thank the Lord! I'll be right there."

"No," Olivia said. "Wait until this afternoon. We need to have some time alone."

⸻✦⸻

As soon as she set breakfast on the table, Ethan Allen dug in. He shoveled up mouthful after mouthful of syrupy pancakes while Olivia couldn't force down a single bite. "I'm really glad you decided to come back," she said. "When you left here and didn't come home all night, the most awful things ran through my mind. I couldn't imagine where you'd gone to, and I was worried blue that you might be shivering to death in some icy cold alleyway, no jacket, no sweater…"

"I wasn't even cold."

"Not cold? With the temperature dropped down to thirty degrees?"

"Unh-unh." He slipped a piece of sausage to the dog. "I wrapped up in a blanket."

"Where'd you get a blanket?"

"Mister Porter's storage bin. He's got a lot of good stuff."

"The storage bin? In the basement?"

Ethan nodded and passed down another piece of sausage. "He's got a hockey stick, and some shotguns, and—"

"You broke into Seth Porter's storage bin?"

"I didn't break in, I just pried the door open enough to squeeze through."

"You were hiding in there," Olivia said, perching her hands on her hips, "and didn't bother to answer when every last soul in this building was calling out your name?"

"I was asleep. I didn't hear nothing."

"Asleep? In the storage bin?"

Ethan nodded. "Mister Porter's got a whole bunch of furniture in his bin, and I figured he wouldn't mind none if I borrowed the sofa for a bit."

"You shouldn't be helping yourself to other people's belongings," Olivia said with an artificial air of disdain. Then she let go of the issue, happy that the boy had had enough sense to stay inside out of the cold.

THERE AND GONE

S am Cobb figured the kid was gone and that was that. Driving down to talk to Tom Behrens was probably a waste of time, but he jumped at the chance because it was an opportunity to work with a detective on a double murder, which was something that didn't come along every day. Sam was tired of patrolling a town with very few crimes other than the vandalism of run-amuck teenagers. He'd been looking for a way to prove himself for well over a year and now that chance was here. He was ready—more than ready—to make detective, to be assigned homicides on his own and not simply because he happened to be the patrolman on duty when the report of a double murder came in.

"We'd be better off questioning the neighbors," he said as if he were the voice of authority. "Chasing after that boy's a waste of time. If he wants to run off, I say let him go. The probability is a kid like that won't talk even if he does know something."

"Could be you're right, but I've got this feeling…" Mahoney said.

They arrived at the ESSO station shortly after lunch on Thursday. Mahoney stepped out of the patrol car and walked toward the attendant. "Tom?" he asked, extending his hand in a real friendly way.

"Yep," Tom answered, "and you gotta be Jack Mahoney."

After Mahoney introduced Patrolman Sam Cobb, the three men went inside the office and sat down. Tom poured the last of yesterday's coffee into paper cups and handed it to his guests. "Sorry," he said. "I'm fresh outta cream."

"Coffee's not much good without cream," Cobb replied, then took a sip of the coffee that was thick as mud and gave off the smell of burnt rubber. "Whew-ee," he grimaced. "You can't be expecting I'd drink this!"

Without a word Tom Behrens took the cup from Cobb's hand and set it to the side of the counter. After that there was an edgy bit of a silence until Mahoney started chit-chatting about how the weather this year seemed to be unseasonably cold. "Before you know it we'll be looking at frost," he said. "Frost, before the end of September, can you believe it? Newspaper claims we could get snow early as November!"

They hadn't yet gotten around to the issue of Ethan Allen when a farm truck pulled up to the pump. "I got a customer," Tom said and stepped outside.

As soon as he was beyond earshot Mahoney looked over at Cobb and growled, "What's with you? Are you deliberately trying to tick this guy off so he won't give us anything on where the kid went?"

"Of course not," Cobb answered, "but that was the worse coff—"

"You think I give a crap? If he comes back in here and hands you a cup of warm piss, you better drink it down with a smile on your face!"

Tom was a man unaccustomed to hurrying and left them sitting in the office for almost fifteen minutes. When he finally did return there was more chit-chat, another customer interruption, and a half-hour of telling bits and pieces of the tragedy that occurred at the Doyle house. Eventually Mahoney was able to ask, "The boy who came by here, you think you'd know his face were you to see it again?"

"Sure. We sat nose-to-nose right there." Tom waggled his finger toward a spot at the far end of the curb. "Talked for a good half hour. Then I closed up shop and drove him over to the truck depot on Route Thirteen."

Mahoney reached into his pocket and pulled out the photograph he had pried loose from the Doyle scrapbook shortly after Ethan Allen disappeared. It was a photograph taken two years ago, a photograph taken when they'd obviously had better times. Ethan Allen, Susanna, and Benjamin were all wearing smiles as they lined up along the front step of their house. Dog was on the far side of Ethan Allen. "Is this the boy?" Mahoney asked, passing the photograph across to Tom.

"The one who come by here could've been a mite older," Tom said, squinting at the picture, "but that dog is sure as hell the same one."

"The boy. You say you drove him to the truck depot?"

Tom hitched up the right side of his mouth and gave a nod. "Sure did. He had me believing every word that came outta his mouth. I felt right sorry for him with his having a sick mama and all." Tom hesitated a moment. Then, with the sound of sadness woven through his words he added, "Of course, nowadays the truth's so scarce a man probably ought to question his own name."

"And the boy told you he was headed to his grandpa's over on the mainland?"

Tom nodded again. "He had this way of saying things so truthful sounding you'd swear them words was coming from his heart. When he told me the story about his poor mama I could see the hurt leaking out of his skin. Some folks might be able to turn their backside to a sorrowful situation such as that, but I'm a man who remembers when my own mama was deathbed sick. If you ever been there, you *know* what it's like."

Mahoney had a way of making folks feel he was in complete agreement with whatever they were feeling and gave a sympathetic nod.

"Anyway," Tom said, "I took it on myself to help the boy. I never once figured his story was a bunch of bare-faced lies."

"So you got him a ride to the mainland?"

"Yep. Just call me a fool and stick a dunce cap on my head."

"And did he give you the address of where he was headed?"

"Nope. Just said his grandpa's."

"He mention the grandpa's name?"

"Unh-unh," Tom mumbled, shaking his head side to side. "The boy had it writ down on the back of a folded-up envelope, but I can't for the life of me picture what it was."

"Doyle?" Mahoney suggested. "Was the name Doyle?"

"Can't say it was or wasn't. But I do recollect the name of the town: Wyattsville. It's a little place maybe fifty miles northwest of Richmond."

Mahoney smiled. "Well, now, at least we've got somewhere to start."

"You're going after him?" Tom Behrens asked. "Way over there?" He wasn't usually a suspicious man, but it did seem somewhat strange for two police officers to be chasing a runaway boy clear across the state. "How come?"

"Mostly to make sure he's okay," Mahoney replied. "But we also have a suspicion that the night of the murders he saw something."

"Saw something? Like what?"

"Who knows," grumbled Cobb, who felt he'd been pushed aside on the questioning. "A kid like that ain't likely to tell you—"

"We're almost done here," Mahoney cut in. "Sam, why don't you wait in the car?"

Cobb stood so abruptly his chair almost tipped over; then he walked out shaking his head to show his disdain for such an obvious waste of time.

"I got an uneasy feeling about that fella," Tom said once Cobb had gone. "Ain't many I take a dislike to, but him…"

"Sometimes I dislike him myself," Mahoney said with a smile. "Now this fellow who gave the boy a ride to the mainland, you think he might—"

"His name's Wheeler. Butch Wheeler."

"Any idea where we can get hold of him?"

"Butch?" Tom shook his head. "He's one of the few who does a run on Sunday. Sundays and Tuesdays. He generally stops at the depot on Thirteen for a fill-up before heading over to Richmond. Other than that I got no idea."

"Sundays and Tuesdays, huh?" Mahoney got a description of Butch Wheeler, then reached over and shook Tom's hand. "Thanks," he said. "You've been a real help."

THE SURPRISE

On the Monday that happened along three days after Ethan Allen had gone missing all night, Olivia's doorbell rang. She could hear the crowd rustling about and whispering long before she reached the door. Thinking herself about to be evicted, she cracked it open barely wide enough for an eye to peer through. "Yes?" she said apprehensively when she saw the group of residents congregated outside the door. "Did you wish to speak to me?"

"Not actually," Clara said with a grin tugging at the corners of her mouth. "We're here to see Ethan Allen."

"Clara!" Olivia exclaimed, flinging the door open to its full width. "You, of all people! I thought you were my friend!"

"I *am* your friend!" Clara responded trying valiantly to hold onto a straight face, even though the corners of her mouth kept curling. "Now we would like to speak with Ethan Allen."

"You most certainly will not!" Olivia defiantly perched her hands on her hips. "He's my guest, and he's staying until he's good and ready to leave! If the Rules Committee has decided to evict me because I have a guest, then so be it! But I'll not allow you to harangue the boy. Have you no shame? Have you—"

By now Ethan had come to see what was causing the commotion. He popped his head out from behind Olivia. "Hi," he said.

All of a sudden the word "Surprise!" rang out with such force that Olivia jumped back clutching at her heart. She landed on Ethan's foot and almost tumbled to the floor. The group of people standing at the door split apart like an eggshell, and in the center where a person would expect to see the yolk was a brand new blue bicycle. "This here's for Ethan," the crowd said in unison, and the boy broke into a grin that stretched the full width of his face.

Everyone started to talk at the same time. "I know you had your heart set on red," Clara said, "but this one's got a horn!"

"And a basket," Fred added, "so you can fetch groceries for your grandma."

"We took a collection…" someone said.

"A boy needs a bicycle."

"Remember, the school's ten blocks away!"

"But I don't understand," Olivia stammered with tears of relief rolling down her face.

"It's simple," Clara answered. "We decided if Ethan's to live here, he ought to have a bicycle for errands and travelling to school."

"Live here? But the Rules Committee…"

"We met with them yesterday, and they've agreed to make an exception for Ethan and his dog. Seems," Clara said sheepishly, "they've known he was here all along."

"Do I get to have the bike now?" Ethan asked apprehensively. "Even if my birthday ain't 'til next month?"

"Next month?" Olivia repeated. "Your birthday is next month?"

He nodded. "But they said I could have the bike now."

"You mean," Olivia clarified, "that next month you'll be turning twelve?"

He nodded again. "On the fifteenth!"

"Well, now," Olivia said with a smile wider even than Ethan's. "I suppose being twelve years old is cause for a party." *Yes, indeed,* she thought, *a very big party!*

Detective Jack Mahoney

I pride myself in understanding people, but Sam—he's beyond understanding. I know he's looking to make detective, but damn, he jams his foot in his mouth every time he opens it. He might have a valid point in thinking the runaway kid's not worth chasing after. But the way he says it, sure as hell rankles me.

Besides, I saw something in that boy's face. It could be he's just registering the shock of finding his parents in such a state, but my gut tells me different.

WORKING THE LEAD

Mahoney didn't speak for the first twenty minutes of their drive home. Neither did Sam Cobb. There seemed to be little to say. Although they'd worked together twice before, the two of them were used to having disagreements. Most times those disagreements were about procedural things—how something should or should not be handled. True, Sam was generally short-tempered, but never before had he been so openly antagonistic.

"What's the problem?" Mahoney finally asked. "It seems like you're deliberately trying to sabotage any chance we've got of finding this kid."

"It ain't that," Sam grumbled. "But how am I ever to make detective if you hold me down every time we're working together?"

"Hold you down? Telling you not to insult people is holding you down?"

"Not letting me take charge of the questioning, that's what you do. I'm ready to take the lead on this case, and I'm plenty capable."

"I'm sure you are," answered Mahoney with his trademark patience. "But when it comes to seeing the boy's involvement in this case, you've got a blind spot."

"I can see the truth of things just as well as you can! But I know for a fact that we're just wasting our time trying to find a kid who wouldn't tell the truth if you held a red hot poker to his tongue."

"You don't know that."

"Yeah, I do. Pop told me the kid's a born liar. Lies even when the truth's in his favor. Pop said—"

"Oh, and your father's an expert?"

"No expert maybe, but he's had a lot of experience with this kid."

Mahoney gave Cobb a look of doubt and shook his head.

"It's the truth! One time the kid even made up a story about his mama carrying on with Pop. The kid said he'd spread it all over town if Pop didn't give him free pie."

Mahoney began chuckling. "That's a new one—a blackmailer demanding pie!"

"So laugh," Cobb sneered, "but I'm telling—"

"Was he?"

"Was who what?"

"Was your pop having a thing with Susanna Doyle?"

"Shit, no!"

"Face it, Sam, such a thing ain't beyond believing."

"He's my pop!"

"He's also got a reputation for chasing after women. Remember the problem with that woman from Portsmouth—"

"Forget it!" Sam growled. "Just forget I ever mentioned it."

"Okay, it's forgotten," Jack answered. But the truth was that such an idea had started him thinking.

On Tuesday Sam Cobb, who for over a week had claimed to be having problems with his digestive tract, woke up feeling under the weather. So Mahoney went in search of Butch Wheeler alone, even though he'd promised that Sam could take over most of the questioning. Mahoney arrived at the Route 13 truck stop shortly before ten, parked himself on a stool across from the plate glass window, then sat and drank cup after cup of coffee. After the fourth cup, the waitress suggested he ought to have a jelly donut or crumb bun to soak up some of the caffeine he'd been downing. "That stuff will scald your insides," she said jokingly. Without taking his eyes off of the parking lot, Mahoney smiled and told her that he was willing to take his chances. He said nothing about what he was really thinking. Jelly donuts meant sticky hands; sticky hands meant a trip to the washroom—no thanks.

It was close to one o'clock when the truck carrying a load of chickens pulled in. According to the description he'd been given

Mahoney figured the man would be about the size of Scooter Cobb, but Butch Wheeler was bigger—the same height maybe, but much wider.

Jack swiveled around, stepped down from the stool, and walked outside. "Excuse me," he called across the parking lot. "You Butch Wheeler?"

"Sure am." Butch saw the badge clipped to Mahoney's jacket and gave the kind of wide open grin only a man with a clear conscience is capable of. "Am I in trouble with the law?" he asked laughingly.

"Nah," Mahoney replied. "I'm looking for a runaway boy, and Tom Behrens over at the ESSO station thought you'd be able to help."

"I had a feeling," Wheeler said.

"Had a feeling?"

"Yep. Jack Mahoney, that wasn't the boy's name, was it?"

Mahoney shook his head. "No, sir," he said. "That's my name."

"You're Jack Mahoney?"

"Unh-huh."

"Whoo-ee. That kid has brass ones, stealing a policeman's name."

"I wouldn't say he stole it," Jack replied. "More like fell back on it so he'd have somebody to be. His real name's Ethan Allen Doyle. That ring any bells?"

Wheeler shook his head. "Can't say it does."

"Anyway, he was supposedly headed over to the mainland to find his grandpa. Do you recall where you dropped him off?"

"Right in front of the building. Even waited to make sure he got in safe."

"You remember the address?"

"Wyattsville. I can't recall the address..." Butch scrunched his forehead into a washboard of wrinkles. "But I could tell you how to get there."

"Good enough," Jack answered with a smile.

Once he had a fix on where Ethan Allen had gone Jack couldn't wait to get to Wyattsville. The more he thought about it, the more certain he became. The boy had a story to tell, a story that quite possibly could get told if Sam Cobb wasn't doing the asking. Still, a promise was a promise, and he'd promised Cobb that he could handle the interrogations. Of course, if Cobb happened to be unavailable...

Had Jack Mahoney not agreed to be sitting in the front row when his daughter performed in the school play that evening, he would have started for the mainland immediately. But he'd promised and he'd already broken too many such promises, so the trip would have to wait until the following day. Wednesday, he reasoned, was more often than not a slow day, and the likelihood was that Sam wouldn't get back to work before the end of the week.

Wednesday, a good hour before dawn, on the road running smack through the center of town, a gasoline truck headed north jackknifed turning itself into a fireball and setting five of the stores on the western side of the street ablaze. By the time Jack got to the station house, the duty officer was handing out assignments to officers not even scheduled for work that day.

Despite the hullabaloo Jack didn't slow down as he whizzed past the front desk. "I've got a solid lead on the Doyle boy," he told the captain who was standing at the water cooler swallowing down some aspirin. "So if you've no objections, I'm gonna shoot over to Wyattsville and check it out."

"Not today," the captain answered. "I need every man I've got."

For the next two days Jack was assigned to investigating a number of vandalisms that occurred around the business area where several stores were left wide open because their front windows had been knocked out by fire hoses. When he was finished with that, there was a mountain of paperwork to attend to, and he didn't get clearance for the trip to Wyattsville until four days later. By then Sam Cobb was back at work.

"I don't think this kid's gonna talk to you," Mahoney told Cobb as they sat waiting for the ferry to the mainland. "Maybe you ought to wait in the car and let me handle the questioning."

By now Cobb had a severe case of hemorrhoids and was in a worse than usual mood; he grumbled, "Bullshit!"

OLIVIA

*I*t's strange how a thought that's been cemented inside your head for a lifetime can all of a sudden disappear. I used to pity poor Francine Burnam, because of her having those five kids. With one of them always wanting something, she never seemed to have a minute to call her own. But thinking back I can remember how I'd be beside myself because the kids were romping around like a herd of wild buffalo, but she'd just sit there with the most contented smile on her face.

It's an unexplainable thing, but having a youngster around makes a person feel they've got a more purposeful life. You wake up in the morning and instead of thinking, "Here I am stuck with another day to muddle through" you pop out of bed and start frying up an egg. After Charlie died I worried about what would become of me, but now I'm more worried about that boy. He's downright foul-mouthed and skinny as a snake.

You've got to wonder what kind of parents would let a child grow up cussing the way he does. Not me, that's for sure! Every time he lets go of one of those words, I say, "Ethan Allen, watch your mouth."

THE YOUNGEST RESIDENT

Once the Rules Committee decreed that Ethan Allen could stay at Wyattsville Arms, he took to marching through the hallways like a man who was part-owner of the building. He rode the elevator up and down for the least little thing—a drink of water, a snack, a trip to the bathroom. Sometimes he rode up and down just for the pure fun of doing it, pushing buttons for floors where he had no intention of getting off. When Mister Capolinsky frowned and said he ought not to be doing such a thing, Ethan replied that the Rules Committee had made allowances for him.

"Just for living here," replied Mister Capolinsky, who was rather crotchety. "Not for destroying private property."

After that Ethan held back from pushing the buttons for all twelve floors, except times when he found himself alone in the elevator. He figured a thing that was as much fun as an elevator should be used for riding pleasure. He reasoned that if a person simply wanted to get in or out of the building, they'd use the back staircase like he'd been doing for the past two weeks.

On the very first afternoon of his being allowed Ethan Allen loaded both the bicycle and dog in the elevator, rode down to the lobby, and strolled leisurely out the front door, nodding to folks he'd never before seen as he passed by. Missus Willoughby, who'd not yet heard the news of the Rules Committee's decision, gasped aloud and wobbled as if she was about to fall into a faint. "It's okay," Ethan said proudly. "*I'm allowed!*"

He wheeled his new bicycle to the sidewalk, lifted Dog into the basket, and off he went. He rode round and round the building walkway for hours, so long in fact that residents started waving from their windows and counting the laps as he passed by. Afterward he rode over to the park and then to the playground, which was locked because of it being a school day. Finally, having run out of places to go and tired of circling the building, he parked his bike in the lobby and went upstairs. "You need anything from the store?" he asked Olivia. "Bread, maybe? Milk?"

"Well," she answered, "I suppose I could use a bit more peanut butter."

"Okay," he chirped cheerfully and was out the door before she had time to mention they were also running a bit low on potato chips.

When that errand was finished, he went by Clara's apartment and asked the same question. She, it seemed, was short of buttermilk, so Ethan peddled back to the Piggly Wiggly and fetched it for her. Clara, pleased she wouldn't have to make the trip herself, gave Ethan a nickel for his trouble. After that, Mister Edwards sent him for the new issue of Life Magazine. Then it was a bag of onions for Hanna Michaels, a tube of toothpaste for Barbara Conklin, some sugar for Elsie Kurtz, and a newspaper for Fred McGinty, who gave him a dime for fetching a newspaper that cost five cents. By suppertime Ethan couldn't make a move without hearing the sound of coins jingling in his pocket.

"Where'd you get all that money?" Olivia asked as they sat down to eat.

"Earned it," he answered, his face bright as a Christmas tree. "Doing errands."

Olivia couldn't help but notice the way the boy's mouth stretched into a smile, smaller but angled exactly like Charlie's. "You're not going around bothering folks, are you?" she asked, but that wasn't really what she was thinking.

Ethan shook his head and reluctantly chomped down on a forkful of string beans, which, along with a chunk of fatback, had simmered on Olivia's stove for hours. "These is real good," he said letting go of the smile. "They taste different than beans from a can." He shoveled in another bite.

Olivia smiled. She knew the taste of canned string beans only too well. She'd been eating them for more than thirty years. Canned string beans, a single pork chop, one leg of a chicken—that was the way a single woman had to cook. Anything more would have been wasteful. But after a lifetime of canned goods and ready-made foods from the downtown delicatessen, she was ready for some home cooking. She'd planned to do it for Charlie—not just planned, eagerly anticipated, even gathered up a whole collection of recipes, but then... Olivia gazed across the table at the boy with twilight blue eyes and a curled-up grin and saw him as a miniature of his grandfather. *Close enough,* she thought.

After supper, while Ethan Allen was sitting at the table counting up his money for the fourth time, Olivia brought up the subject of school. "You've got to go," she said, "or else the truant officer will come looking for you."

Ethan Allen felt quite comfortable with the amount of schooling he already had so he said, "How can he come looking for me when he don't even know I'm here?"

"The truant officer rides around town looking for kids who are out playing at times they ought to be in school."

"I ain't playing. I'm running errands!"

"All the same," she said, "you've got to go to school." That was her final word on the subject. "Tomorrow," she told him, "we'll get you registered, and you can start on Monday."

When she turned back to washing the dishes, Ethan thumbed his nose at her back.

On Monday morning Olivia was up at the first light of dawn. She set a skillet of sausages to sizzling and mixed up a bowl of pancake batter with fresh blueberries thrown in for good measure, and then she woke the boy. "Get up, Ethan," she whispered, giving his shoulder a gentle shake. "It's time to get ready for school."

"Do I have to?" he moaned, wrapping himself in a tighter ball of drowsiness.

"Yes." She tugged the blanket loose from his grip. Once he was up and headed for the bathroom, she returned to the kitchen and set about fixing chicken sandwiches to pack in the Superman lunch box. After a considerable amount of time he arrived at the breakfast table, looking more reluctant than ever. "What's wrong?" she asked.

"I don't have a good feeling about this," he mumbled.

"Nonsense." Olivia placed a plate of pancakes in front of him. "Now, hurry up and eat your breakfast," she said, trying to sound cheerful. "You're going to love school, I'm sure of it. You'll meet new friends—"

"I already got friends."

"Honey," Olivia knelt beside him, "I know you consider the folks in this building your friends, but we're a bunch of old fogeys. You need to meet some kids so you can play with boys your own age."

"No, I don't."

Olivia knew by the look of determination in his eyes she could argue the point until the moon settled on top of the mountain, and it wouldn't change his mind. She also knew that if he rode his bike to school he'd end up elsewhere, which is why she insisted on driving him that first day. Had he ridden the bike, he might have arrived home earlier. He might have already been off on an errand to the Piggly Wiggly or upstairs with his eyes glued to the television. But with the walk home taking considerably longer, he turned into the building walkway just as Sam Cobb stepped from the car.

"Holy shit!" the boy gasped, then took off running like a scared rabbit. He went around the building through the back entrance and up the stairwell. He burst through the apartment door a full minute before Mahoney and Cobb arrived. "Say I ain't here!" he screamed before Olivia could ask how his day at school had gone.

"What's wrong?" she asked, following him into the bedroom.

"Please," he begged. "Tell those policemen you ain't seen hide nor hair of me!" He rolled under the bed, and just then there was a knock at the door.

When Olivia opened the door, Mahoney said, "Afternoon, ma'am." He smiled, showed his badge, and then introduced both himself and Sam Cobb. "We'd like a word with Ethan Allen Doyle," he said rather pleasantly.

Olivia could feel a swell of conscience rising up into her throat. It might be excusable to tell a little white lie when you had cause, but to do what Ethan Allen asked was flat out lying to the law. Once she'd told an officer her speedometer read forty miles per hour when in truth it had been waggling somewhere between fifty-five and sixty. It didn't work out very well that time, and she was reluctant to try again. Olivia hesitated for a minute, then without perjuring herself as to whether the boy was there asked, "What business do you have with my grandson?"

"There are a few questions we'd like to ask," Mahoney replied.

"What kind of questions?"

"Has the boy told you what happened to his parents?"

Olivia nodded. "Somewhat," she said, hoping they wouldn't ask for further details.

"Well, we think he might have actually seen what happened the night of the murders."

"And if he did?" Olivia snorted. "What then? You'd have him relive that horrible experience? You'd ask the child to suffer through it all over again?"

"Our intent is nothing like that—"

"Regardless of your intent, I refuse to allow you to badger the boy!" she said, cutting Mahoney off. "There's no justification—"

"You've got no say in it!" stormed Cobb, although he had been forewarned to hold back on his temper. "We can do whatever we—"

"The devil you can!" Olivia snapped. She defiantly squared herself in the doorway to block any thought they might have of getting inside. "I'm Ethan Allen's grandmother, and I'm telling you right here and now if the child doesn't want to talk to you he doesn't have to!"

Still trying to win her over to their way of thinking, Mahoney said, "All we want to do is ask a few questions. We've no intention of pressuring him."

"I'm sorry," Olivia said, looking only at Mahoney. "But he doesn't want—"

Hell bent on being the lead interrogator, Cobb snarled, "Look, lady, you got nothing to say about it! The kid's a runaway. We'll get a warrant—"

"Just you try it!" Olivia slammed the door with such force that a screw holding the hinge in place popped loose and rolled across the carpet. Despite the boldness of her words, her heart was pounding like a Salvation Army kettle drum.

After several minutes of waiting for her nerves to settle down, Olivia sucked in a deep breath, threw her shoulders back, and marched into the bedroom calling out for Ethan Allen. At first there was no answer, not even the sound of his breathing. It was so quiet that she could have believed he had run off again, but when she stooped and peered beneath the bed she saw two wide open eyes looking back. "Come out from under there," she said. "We need to do some talking."

"Are they gone?" he asked.

"Yes," she answered, "but I believe they'll be back."

"I gotta get going," Ethan Allen said, cautiously wriggling out from under the bed. "If I'm here when they get back…"

Olivia found it surprising the boy would admit to being afraid of anything. He had a papery covering of bravado and a sassy mouth, but if you peeled away those things you'd find a scared little boy trying to act tough. Olivia knew all about such pretensions. She'd stuck her nose in the air and marched out of her daddy's house as if she weren't afraid of the devil himself, but she'd been trembling inside. Once the boy scooted partway from beneath the bed, she reached down and took hold of his hand. "Don't worry, Ethan," she said as she tugged him to his feet. "There's nothing to be afraid of."

"That's what you think," he answered.

"Police officers don't harm children," Olivia said in a voice meant to reassure the boy and do away with his unfounded fears. "They're probably just following up, checking to see you're okay and getting the proper care, that's all."

"That ain't all!" he shouted. "That policeman wants to slit my throat!"

"Why on earth would he want to do such a thing?"

"'Cause then I can't tell."

"Tell what?"

"Nothin'. Just trust me. I gotta get out of here before they get back."

Olivia took hold of the boy's shoulders and twisted him around so that he was facing her. "No, Ethan," she said, it's time *you* trusted *me*. You have got to tell me the truth about why you're so afraid of those policemen."

"You're better off not knowing," he warned. "Believe me, Miss Olivia, you're much better off not knowing."

"Miss Olivia?" she echoed solemnly. The name took her aback. It somehow seemed so formal, proper in every aspect and meant to please, but with no affection attached. Surely he'd made a mistake saying her name in such a way. Although she didn't remember him ever before referring to her in that manner, neither did she recall him using any other name. Now that she thought back, she could picture the way he would wait until she was facing him to speak. He'd never once used a name. "Ethan," she said, "don't you think you should be calling me Grandma?"

"But…you said…"

"I was wrong." She bent down and hugged the boy to her chest so hard he began wheezing. When she finally loosened her grip she lowered herself to the floor alongside of Ethan Allen and said, "Your grandpa was a wonderful man, a man who knew far more of life than I ever did. His heart was the size usually afforded to three men. And it was filled to the brim with love, way more than is needed for sharing." She brushed back a tear and took the boy's hand in hers. "I'm absolutely certain," she said, her voice soft as a fluff of cotton, "that he was the one who brought you here, Ethan. Having you is almost like having your dear sweet grandpa back again. You've got Charlie's smile, the same blue eyes…" She looked down at the boy and knew her ability to love was not dead. It simply needed a reason to live. "So, you see," Olivia said, her smile growing wider, "I believe your grandpa's intention was for us to be together—to take care of each other the way he'd take care of us if he was here. Who are we to argue with an intention such as that?"

Figuring this wasn't the time for explaining the only thing he knew of Grandpa Doyle was the dollar bill that arrived at Christmas and on his birthday, Ethan simply nodded and said, "Okay."

"Okay, Grandma," Olivia corrected. "I *am* your grandma, and I'd be real honored if you'd call me that."

"Okay…" He hesitated for what seemed to be a long moment, then finally spat out the word that somehow had gotten stuck sideways in his throat. "Grandma."

Olivia gave him an affectionate hug. Then she whipped right back into asking why he had such a fear of the two police officers. "You've got to tell me the honest-to-God truth," she said. "Whatever the problem is, we can deal with it together."

"You don't understand," he moaned. "If I was to tell, I'd be sent to reform school or stomped dead as a doornail." Ethan's eyes began to fill with water.

Flabbergasted by such a statement, Olivia asked, "By who?"

"That policeman and his daddy—Mister Cobb."

"Officer Cobb is an unpleasant person, no doubt about it," she said. "But that doesn't mean he'd harm you for telling the truth."

"You just don't get it," Ethan said, a look of skepticism on his face, a look that was way beyond his years. "Those Cobbs know I saw what happened that night, and no matter what I say they'll claim I'm lying.

Who do you suppose people are gonna believe?" he asked. "A policeman and his daddy or a kid?"

"If you tell the truth," Olivia answered, "I'd believe you."

"Yeah, and how you gonna know if what I'm saying is true?"

"I trust you," she said.

"That's it? You're just gonna go by trust?"

Olivia gave him a smile and a nod.

"Then what?" he asked.

"Then we'll figure out the best way to deal with whatever needs dealing with."

"You're not gonna hand me over to them?"

"Ethan," Olivia said, her voice clear and straightforward, "those policemen would have to shoot me dead before I'd let them take you away."

"Honest?"

"Honest." Olivia drew a crisscross over her heart.

A look of dread settled over Ethan's face when he began to speak. "I lied," he said solemnly. "I lied when I said I was asleep and didn't see nothing. I saw it all."

Olivia said nothing, just waited for him to continue.

"That day Mama and Daddy were fighting fierce. 'Ethan,' Mama told me real secret-like, 'you slip out back and stay there 'til I get away from your daddy. Soon as I do, we're going to New York City with Scooter.' I did just what she said. Me and Dog went out back of the woods and hid in my fort. I waited all afternoon. Then finally Mama came out and stuck her suitcase in the car. Daddy came running out right behind her, yelling how she wasn't going nowhere. He smacked her to the ground and she didn't get up. After a spell, he picked her up and carried her inside the house. I figured Mama must've been hurt, elsewise she'd've called him every name in the book."

"Who's Scooter?" Olivia asked.

"The policeman's daddy," Ethan answered, his eyes full of fear.

"Oh. Were he and your mama…"

The boy gave a knowing nod and continued. "Later on, I snuck around back and looked in the window. Mama was stretched out on the bed like maybe she was sleeping off a headache. They was always fighting, Mama and Daddy. Lots of times she went to bed for a while after so she'd feel better. When I saw she was sleeping, I figured she'd be along later."

He hesitated for a moment. Then with the saddest look imaginable he said, "Mama wasn't at all mean the way Daddy thought. She just had her heart set on going to New York City so she could be a singing star." After that he slid back into telling the story. "I was waiting in my fort when I saw Mister Scooter's car come up our drive. Then I snuck closer to see what was gonna happen. I figured for sure there'd be shit flying if Scooter started mouthing off about going to New York, 'cause Daddy wasn't in the mood for no foolishness. But Mister Scooter didn't say nothin' about New York, he just told Daddy he needed to talk to Susanna—that's Mama's name. He pushed his way inside the door, and in no time at all he was screaming to the top of his lungs about how Daddy had killed Mama…"

Ethan's eyes filled with tears, and he stopped to wipe them away. With sorrow latching onto his voice he said, "That's when Mister Scooter started beating up on Daddy. Believe me, Grandma, you don't never ever want to see a thing like that. It was really, really awful…"

The words eventually slowed to a stop and Olivia understood. Ethan Allen was looking back in time, rerunning his memory of the event as it had happened. "It wasn't a fair fight," he finally said, his voice thick with resentment. "Daddy didn't do nothing to defend his self, just stood there and let Mister Scooter beat on his head 'til it was split open. I was scared Mister Scooter would kill me too, so I stayed hid. Even after I peed my pants, I stayed hid. I could've done something to help my daddy, but I didn't even try."

"You're just a boy," Olivia said, her arm wrapped around his shoulders. "You couldn't have done anything. A man such as that would have killed you too!"

"Maybe."

"There's no maybe about it. He's a violent criminal. He belongs in jail."

"You think his policeman son is gonna put him there?"

"Somebody has to!"

"I know you've a mind to help, but Mama warned me if I tell tales on Mister Scooter, his policeman son will see I go to reform school."

"Nonsense," Olivia answered, although she knew it was a good probability that the son would not, in fact, acknowledge the crime of his father.

"The best thing," Ethan said, "is for me to be gone when they get back."

"No," she answered. "Absolutely not!"

"Ain't you listening? That policeman knows I saw and he's sure as hell gonna—"

"Stop your cussing. Nothing is going to happen."

"That's what you think! He's gonna—"

"He's not going to do anything, because I won't allow him near you."

"Have you noticed that he's three times your size?"

"Yes, I have. But we've got truth and justice on our side."

"Oh, great," Ethan moaned. "That ought to scare the shit outta him."

"Stop cussing," Olivia repeated.

Irreconcilable Differences

After Ethan Allen's grandmother slammed the door in their faces, the two police officers walked out of the Wyattsville Arms apartment building and climbed into the car without saying a word. Cobb turned his face to the window like a man obsessed with seeing scenery, and Mahoney grabbed hold of the steering wheel so ferociously that his knuckles were bloodless long before they reached Richmond.

They went without a single exchange of words for almost two hours, and then as they sat waiting for the ferry to transport them back to the Eastern Shore Mahoney grumbled, "This just isn't working."

"What isn't?" Cobb replied, even though he could see the set of Mahoney's jaw was rigid as a railroad spike.

"Us working this case together. You've got zero tolerance, whereas I believe in giving folks the benefit of doubt, letting them tell their side of a story before—"

Cobb gave Mahoney an angry glare. "What I do is put an end to the crap you're willing to take," he snorted. "In my mind, that's just good police work."

"Good police work? Last month you handcuffed a seven-year-old boy. Is that what you consider good police work?"

"The kid was a menace, kicking at me, trying to—"

"He was seven years old!"

"Okay, so maybe I could've handled that situation differently, but that's one instance."

"It's not the only one. What about last week when you took the woman in the five-and-dime—"

"Okay, okay. Maybe I got a short fuse at times, but—"

"You're a hothead, just like your pop."

"Screw you," Cobb answered and turned back to the window.

For the remainder of the ride they didn't speak again, not even after Mahoney parked in front of the station house and they both climbed from the car.

Unpleasant as it might have been, it wasn't the drive home that sent Mahoney looking for the captain. It was the look on Sam Cobb's face: a look of pure hatred.

Captain Rogers was in his office trying to focus on some paperwork when Mahoney walked in and closed the door. "I've got a problem with Cobb," he said.

"I've got worse problems than Cobb," the captain replied and continued leafing through the pile of pages. "The department's over budget, I've got a car out of commission, and we're short two patrolmen. You got something worse than that?"

Mahoney shrugged. "Depends on your view of worse," he said. He segued into how Cobb had become a problem in the Doyle murder investigation. "The grandmother didn't want to let us talk to the kid, so Cobb starts threatening her and she slams the door in our face. I'm telling you, Captain, you've got to get him off this case."

Captain Rogers sighed. "Didn't I just say we're short two men? Other than Cobb, nobody's available for back up."

"I'll handle it alone," Mahoney answered. "It's a routine investigation."

"Go ahead," answered the captain wearily, sick to death of listening to complaints. Turning back to the pile of paperwork, he grumbled how he would now have to listen to Cobb throw a shit-fit. "Solve one problem," he moaned, "and there's five more right behind." He wrote a reminder to himself: "Talk to Sam Cobb."

GRANDMA OLIVIA

*S*omebody else might be inclined to believe the boy a liar but not me. I saw the look on Ethan Allen's face and can say without question he's telling the truth. In all my life I've never felt as sorry for anyone as I did Ethan Allen. The poor child was scared out of his head.

As far as I'm concerned, those two policemen can stuff their questions up their backsides! Regardless of what they say or do, I have no intention of allowing them near that child. Ethan Allen has been through enough already; he doesn't need to have them scaring the wits out of him.

Personally, I doubt the big lummox can even get a warrant. I'm the boy's grandmother, and he's got the legal right to be living here. He's not breaking any law, so that warrant stuff is just a lot of hooey. The big policeman is an out-and-out bully. I've seen his type before. He's trying to scare us, but he's about to find out Olivia Ann Doyle doesn't scare that easily!

As for the boy knowing what Mister Cobb did, that's another problem. Right is right and while I'd prefer to see the man punished, the truth belongs to Ethan Allen and he's got to be the one to decide whether or not to let it loose. I can tell you one thing: whatever he decides I'm gonna be standing right beside him, and if any harm comes to that boy it will be over my dead body!

SEARCHING FOR HOPEFUL

Fairly certain she had not seen the last of the two police officers, Olivia set about finding a way to deal with the situation. First she telephoned Clara, a woman with no legal expertise whatsoever but an uncanny knack for finding a way around even the most difficult problems. Unfortunately, this time Clara could think of nothing other than removing Olivia's name from the mailbox and having the other residents swear she'd moved off and taken Ethan Allen with her. Although Olivia generally praised Clara's ingenuity, this time she simply shook her head. "That's not much of a solution," she sighed. Then she called Fred McGinty. He thought perhaps Olivia should marry him and the two of them adopt Ethan Allen, but Olivia told him right off that such an idea was ridiculous.

"Ridiculous?" he said. "I beg to differ! You think those policemen are gonna come looking for an Ethan Allen McGinty?"

"I'd sooner stick with Clara's plan," Olivia answered. Then she hung up and went on to calling a long list of other people. After she'd telephoned most everyone at Wyattsville Arms and several of her friends back in Richmond, she still did not have one valid suggestion for dealing with the situation. Olivia then hit upon another thought. She dialed the information operator and said, "I'm looking for the number of the Main Street Motel in Hopeful, Georgia."

Once she had the number, Olivia dialed and waited as the telephone rang. Four…five…six times. It seemed an eternity. Finally a voice answered. "Sorry for being so slow," the woman said. "I was tending to business in the johnny."

"Canasta? Canasta Jones?"

"Yes, ma'am," the woman answered.

Olivia gave an audible sigh of relief. "It's me," she said. "Olivia Doyle!"

"I know you?"

"Of course you know me. I was there last fall, stayed over a week. Remember?"

"Not right off the top of my head."

"My husband died. I was carrying him in an urn. Remember? I came in crying and feeling downright miserable. You fixed that wonderful okra soup. Remember that? When I left, you packed up some of those happiness seeds for me to take."

"Well, land sakes alive! Course I remember you, sugar. Sometimes this forgetful old thinker of mine just goes on the fritz. How you doing?"

"Thanks to you, I'm getting along just fine. That okra soup of yours really did the trick. I was about ready to give up on living when—"

Canasta began chuckling. "Okra soup don't do nothing but warm your insides," she said. "You got to feeling better 'cause you decided to get on with the business of living. Only thing what helped you, sugar, was the having of a friend's ear to listen."

"Oh, dear," Olivia sighed.

"Oh, dear?"

"I was hoping to get some more of those seeds, but—"

"I thought you said you was doing fine. A person doing fine don't need to lean on such foolishness."

"They weren't for me exactly. I was figuring to feed them to this detective so he'd see the truth of things and stop chasing after poor little Ethan Allen."

"Whoa there," Canasta said. "You done lost me."

"It's a long story," Olivia said sorrowfully. She launched into the full explanation of how Ethan Allen had witnessed the murder of his mama and daddy and then traveled halfway across the state in search of his Grandpa Charlie—the same Charlie she'd brought home in an urn. "That poor child has certainly gone through enough, but now he's being badgered by the police!"

Listening intently Canasta said, "How come the police is bothering an unfortunate little fella like him?"

"Because he saw the whole thing and knows the truth of what happened."

"If he knows, why don't he tell?" she asked.

"Because," Olivia said, "the person responsible for the murder is the policeman's daddy!"

"Well, if that don't beat all!" Canasta gasped. "Sugar, you and that boy are truly in one sorry state! A situation such as this ain't nothin' okra soup can fix."

"Oh," Olivia said, her voice sliding downhill. "I was hoping—"

"Hoping? Hoping ain't gonna get you nowhere. You got to take action. You got to get to telling the truth to somebody who'll do something about it."

"Such as?"

Canasta thought a long while before she spoke. "When a murder's been committed, you got to tell a police officer. There just ain't no getting around it. That said I surely wouldn't have it be the fella whose daddy did the killing. He might well be on the up and up, but with family blood thick between them I wouldn't chance it. No, indeed," she concluded. "You got to find yourself a well-intended, God-fearing, honest policeman."

"How am I supposed to do that?"

"Look in his eyes. The truth of a person's soul is in their eyes."

"Truth of their soul? How am I supposed to recognize a thing like that? It doesn't exactly stand out on a person's face like freckles or bushy brows might."

"The truth's a sight more recognizable than folks think. Fix yourself in place for a bit and study a man's eyes. You'll catch hold of what I mean. A man who's honest and got a well-intentioned heart, he's got the light of God inside his head. You look deep in his eyes and guaranteed you'll see a shiny little speck sent down from heaven. Sugar, a man like that, believe me, he's one you wanna trust."

"I don't know," Olivia moaned, buckling under the weight of uncertainty. "What if I make a mistake? What if I look into some policeman's eye and imagine I see the light of God when it's nothing more than the reflection of a light bulb?"

"Hmm." Canasta hesitated a moment, then said, "Most women's got a built-in ability for this, but if you got doubts practice up by looking in your pastor's eye. A man of God has most always got the light."

"Pastor?"

"Pastor, preacher, minister, whatever." Canasta waited for a bit. Then, hearing no response, she asked, "You been going to Sunday services, ain't you?"

"No," Olivia answered hesitantly. "I've had intentions, but—"

"Well, no wonder you got all these troubles. Land sakes, sugar, if you ain't on speaking terms with the Lord, what right you got to ask Him to help out?"

Olivia could see the merit in such thinking. It was the same as having a neighbor who snubs you, walks by week after week pretending you don't exist, acts like you're a person they have no cause to bother with. Then one day they knock on your door looking to borrow a shaker of salt. She'd never intended to snub God. In fact, she'd said a number of prayers in the past two days. Most were requests for Him to send help. She was by no means godless. It was simply a case of being so wound up in the everyday problems of life that she'd been too busy to pay Him a call. "I suppose you're right," she answered solemnly. "I've no right to expect an answer to my prayers, when—"

"I never said He wouldn't help out, but I'm fairly certain that church-going people get shuffled to the front of the line when He's passing out favors."

"Well, then, I'm just plain out of luck."

"No, you ain't," Canasta said. "But quick as you can get yourself to services and sit right up front in the first pew. When the choir gets to singing, you and that boy sing out loud as you can so the Lord's certain to take notice."

"You really think such a thing would work?"

"Sugar, I'd swear to it."

"Let's see," Olivia murmured, thinking out loud, "there's a Methodist Church on the corner, and a block down there's a Baptist. Then over on Grant Street, a Catholic Church...they're all reasonably close by. Which one do you think He's more likely to listen to?"

Canasta laughed out loud. "It don't make a bean of difference," she finally said. "The Lord listens in all those places. They're just different slices of the same pie."

Fortunately, the next three days were rather uneventful. Ethan rode his new bicycle back and forth to school, then came home and ran errands for the neighbors. At night he did his homework with no argument and then worked on piecing the Baltimore Orioles jigsaw puzzle back together. Olivia kept a close eye on him at all times. She had his arrival home from school timed to the minute and usually found some reason or another to be standing in the lobby or outside on the walkway to greet him. Wherever he went—whether it was the store, the playground, or circling the block on his bike—she stood at the window and watched. A fistful of fear had taken hold of her heart. It was the fear of Cobb grabbing the boy if she lost sight of him for even a moment.

On Sunday morning she woke Ethan early. "You've got to dress for church," she said and handed him the brand new suit she'd bought. Olivia was already dressed with white gloves and a yellow felt hat.

"But," Ethan moaned rubbing sleep from his eyes, "I ain't had no breakfast."

"We'll go to the Pancake Palace after we've finished praying," she answered.

Taking no chances, Olivia first took him to the eight o'clock mass at the Catholic Church where because they were a bit late they had to sit five rows back. With so much being said in Latin and not knowing exactly when to kneel, stand, or sit, she lost track of what was happening a few times, but once the hymnal was opened not only the Lord God but also half of Wyattsville could hear her voice. Afterwards they went to the ten o'clock service at the Baptist church where they were able to get a seat smack in the center of the first pew. Lastly, they hurried over to the Methodist Church, and although they arrived just moments before the eleven o'clock service started they were able to sit right up front. Olivia sang louder than any other member of the congregation, and Ethan, with a look of pure pleasure on his face, matched her note for note. By the time they arrived at the Pancake Palace, they'd worked up such an appetite that both of them ordered the fat boy special: ten pancakes, stacked alongside a pile of sausages, ham, and bacon.

"You sure you want the special?" the waitress asked Ethan. "It's an awful lot of food for a little fella like you."

"I'm sure, ma'am," he answered. "I been singing real loud!"

That afternoon Olivia felt somewhat less worried about Ethan and permitted him to take Dog to the park, which was a full five blocks away.

When he started out the door she warned him, "Don't stay longer than an hour, and be real careful." Later that afternoon he was also permitted to ride his bicycle to Liggett's Drug Store so he could fetch a bottle of cough medicine for Walter Krause.

By Monday morning a relative peacefulness had settled over the Doyle household. Olivia felt considerably less threatened now that she had the Lord on her side and hummed "What a Friend We Have in Jesus" as the milk cascaded over Ethan Allen's cereal. As she spread peanut butter on bread she switched to "Onward Christian Soldiers," and as she wrapped the sandwiches and put them in his lunchbox she finished up with a chorus of "Bringing in the Sheaves."

"You sure you ain't overdoing it?" Ethan asked.

"There's no such thing as overdoing your service to the Lord," she answered, then kissed his cheek and sent him off to school. As soon as he was out the door, Olivia began work on the project she was planning as a surprise for the boy. One by one, she carted the dining room chairs down to the basement storage room, and then she turned the dining room table on its side and unscrewed the legs. Seeing how it was too large for one person to lift, she simply shoved it against the living room wall and continued. She was halfway through giving the walls a coat of royal blue paint when the doorbell rang. If she hadn't been preoccupied with fixing up a bedroom for Ethan Allen, she might have been more on guard. She probably would have pressed her eye to the peephole, seen who it was, then refused to open the door. But with figuring the Lord had already taken care of the problem and having a head filled with thoughts of what color bedspread to buy the boy, she flung the door wide open without a moment's hesitation.

"Good morning," Mahoney said with a smile.

"You?" Olivia gasped in astonishment. "What are *you* doing here?" She glanced over at the wall clock—twelve-fifteen. Luckily she had three hours until Ethan was due home. Before Mahoney had time to answer her question, Olivia said, "He's not here. Your obnoxious friend frightened the child into running away. God only knows what—"

"Cobb? I can see why the boy would be frightened by him. I'm glad to say he's not working this case anymore. Anyway, what's this about Ethan Allen running off?"

With her guard now on full alert, Olivia answered, "Don't even think about asking where he went, because I assure you I don't know."

"Actually, I was hoping to maybe have a word with you."

Olivia would have preferred not to. She would have preferred to go back to her painting, or, better still, to have never even answered the door. But she knew if she refused, the detective would get suspicious. If he got the impression that she was hiding Ethan Allen, he'd keep coming back and eventually he'd find what he was looking for. It was probably better to deal with the issue now. After a few moments of hesitation she stepped to the side and said, "Okay, you can come in. But," she added, "I'm in the middle of redecorating, so you'll have to make it quick."

"I apologize for the way Officer Cobb acted last time we were here," Mahoney said as he followed her into the living room. "Given the way he acted, I don't blame you for slamming the door in our faces. A man who behaves like Cobb has it coming."

"Isn't that the God-honest truth," Olivia added. She motioned toward the sofa and suggested Mahoney have a seat. She sat in the club chair on the far side of the room. "Ethan Allen was scared to death of the man," she said, "and I know that's the reason the boy ran off." Olivia wanted to act weepy to add a measure of conviction to her story, but with being so concerned about time the most she could manage was fidgety.

"The poor kid—off on his own again." Mahoney shook his head in a way that seemed sincere. "With all he's been through, I was rather hoping he'd settle in and stay here with you. Anybody can tell you're the sort of grandma who'd watch out for the boy and see that he's taken care of."

"How could he stay here with you policemen hounding him?"

"Me?" Mahoney registered a look of surprise. "Not me. I had no intention of questioning him. If the lad doesn't want to tell what happened that night, then so be it." Mahoney had made detective long before most patrolmen simply because he put people at ease and threw them off guard so they'd willingly tell things no one else could beat out of them.

"Oh, sure, that's what *you* say, but Officer Cobb—"

"He won't be coming around. He's off the case."

"Altogether?"

Mahoney nodded. "He's on report. The captain—"

"Excuse my manners," Olivia interrupted. "I've forgotten to ask if you might like a cup of coffee or a cold glass of tea."

"Umm, coffee sounds real good."

When Olivia returned from the kitchen with two cups of coffee, she sat on the sofa alongside Mahoney. From across the room she'd thought she'd seen a speck of sparkle shinning in his right eye and wanted to check it out. She focused on that right eye and leaned forward into his face. "So," she said, her nose barely inches from his, "if you're not looking to question Ethan Allen, why *did* you come here?"

"Primarily to apologize, but I also wanted to let you and Ethan know that I'm gonna continue working the case. I'll do whatever I can to find the person responsible for the murder of his mama and daddy."

"That's it? You didn't come to arrest the boy, take him back for questioning?"

"I'd never do such a thing!" Mahoney said with an air of indignation.

Olivia leaned in a hair closer and became almost certain: there was indeed a sparkle in his right eye. "Never?" she asked.

"Of course not." With Olivia leaning into his face as she was, Jack Mahoney had to ask, "Is something wrong?"

"No," she answered, moving back. "I was just wondering if you go to church."

"Yes. My whole family does. We belong to the Methodist Church in Back Bay."

Now she was certain the light was there. "What if," she asked, giving him one last test, "the child told you that he saw the murder and the person responsible for the killing was your daddy—what then? Would you believe Ethan Allen, or jump to the conclusion he was lying?"

Mahoney chuckled. "My folks passed on a good number of years ago, but regardless of who the boy said was to blame for the killing I'd be duty bound to investigate the matter. I'm sworn to uphold the law, and there's no allowance for friends or family."

"Of course," Olivia said. "I was speaking of a purely hypothetical situation, because as I've already told you, the boy's gone. But," she added, "*if* he were to come back and *if* he decided to talk to you..."

"I'll leave you my telephone number," Mahoney said. "Then if he does come back and wants to help find the killer, you can give me a call."

"You're not coming back unless I call?"

"No reason to," Mahoney said. Then he thanked Olivia for her time and left.

Olivia smiled. Without a smidgen of doubt she knew: he had the light.

❦

When Ethan returned home from school, Olivia said, "I've got two surprises for you." First she led him into what that morning had been the dining room and was now a bedroom. "This is your room," she said proudly. "I had planned on having it finished by the time you got home, but I had a bit of an interruption this afternoon." She then told him about her conversation with Mahoney. "He's a well-intentioned, church-going Christian," she said, "and I'm certain he'd do right by us. He's definitely got the light."

"I don't know," Ethan Allen said, worry tugging at the corners of his mouth. "Suppose he says one thing and does another? Suppose it's just a trick?"

"I believe he's a man who can be trusted, but you'll have to be the one to decide whether or not you want to tell him the truth of what happened."

"Why me?"

"Because," Olivia answered, "the truth belongs to you. It's yours to hide away in your head or let loose so he can arrest the man responsible for your daddy's death."

"But...he said he wasn't coming back if we didn't call him. Couldn't we just—"

"Sure, we could hide out here and say nothing. But then Detective Mahoney might never find out Scooter Cobb was the one who killed your daddy. Figuring he could get away with murder any old time he wanted to Scooter might kill some other child's mama or daddy, and after that who knows where it would stop."

"Jeez," Ethan moaned, "you gotta put it *that* way?" After a considerable amount of back-and-forth conversation, he reluctantly agreed to talk to Jack Mahoney. "But," he said, "I gotta do it my way. I ain't telling him it was Scooter 'til I see the light, okay?"

"Okay," Olivia answered.

ETHAN ALLEN

I know Grandma Olivia means well, but I got serious concerns about this "light in the eye" business. If Scooter's policeman son would send me off to reform school for lying, what's he gonna do if I claim his daddy's the one what did the killing?

I seen the damage those Cobbs can do, and believe you me, I ain't none too anxious to tangle with either of them. Grandma Olivia says—I call her Grandma Olivia now 'cause she said that's what I'm supposed to call her—anyway, she says she ain't afraid. She says truth and honesty is on our side. Maybe so, but size and meanness sure is on their side.

Other than nagging me for using cuss words, Grandma Olivia's nice. She treats me good, like I was her true-born grandkid, and she's always going on about how I remind her of my handsome grandpa. She says I got his blue eyes and the cut of his chin. I gotta laugh when she says that, 'cause in the picture I seen he's an old man and his chin's hiding behind a bunch of whiskers.

TRUTH BE TOLD

I n the fall of the year when a carpet of leaves covered the ground and tree pollen was thick in the air, Jack Mahoney's allergies ran rampant. He swallowed down pills and sniffed inhalants, but still his eyes watered constantly. Sometimes he appeared almost glassy eyed, and at other times you could believe you were looking into a still water pond reflecting the sunlight. When he finally began sneezing with every other breath, he called in sick and did not return to the station house for five days. On Monday there was a message from Olivia Doyle waiting for him. All it said was—"Please call," but he knew what it meant.

Jack called Olivia and told her he would be right over.

"No," she answered, "I'd rather you wait until tomorrow afternoon. Be here at three o'clock."

Although preferring sooner to later, Jack agreed.

⊙━━◆━━⊙

When Ethan arrived home from school on Monday afternoon Olivia told him Detective Mahoney would be there the following day, and they set about making their plans. First off, they had to know for certain that Mahoney came alone, that Officer Cobb was not waiting outside in the car or lurking in the dark of the stairwell. Secondly, they had to be absolutely positive there was no chance Ethan might be taken back to the Eastern Shore. And lastly, the boy had to see the light in Mahoney's eyes for himself. If there was no light, Ethan Allen would not be telling what he'd seen.

Once Ethan and Olivia decided what they would tell and under what circumstances it would be told, Olivia began calling the neighbors for help. Fred McGinty volunteered for the curbside watch, Sam Bowman to patrol the staircase, Clara and Barbara Conklin as sofa-sitting witnesses, and Seth Porter planned to hide in the bedroom, his shotgun ready, in the event anybody tried strong-arm tactics. When the doorbell rang at three o'clock Tuesday afternoon, all the pieces were in place.

Olivia opened the door and Jack Mahoney said, "Afternoon, Missus Doyle."

She took one look at those eyes, glittery as a springtime river, and smiled. "Come in," she said pleasantly and motioned him into the living room. After Olivia had introduced Clara and Barbara, she sauntered over to the window and looked down at Fred. He gave the all clear signal, waving his right hand. Mahoney had been alone in the car. She spent the next five minutes chattering on about nothing of consequence, waiting until she heard the three loud clunks echo up the radiator pipe. All clear: no one was hiding in the stairwell. "So," she said, abruptly changing the subject, "I suppose we should get Ethan Allen out here."

In response to her call, the boy came from the bedroom. He walked with slow shuffling footsteps, his hands jammed deep into his pockets and his head bent toward the floor. "Afternoon, Detective Mahoney," he said without raising his eyes.

Seeing the dread pitched over the boy like a pup tent, Mahoney squatted down until they were face-to-face. "Son," he said, "you've no need to be afraid of me."

Ethan looked into the man's river water eyes.

"I'm on your side," Mahoney said in a most convincing manner. "The only thing I really want is to see the person responsible for killing your mama and daddy brought to justice."

"You ain't gonna try to take me back to Missus Cobb?"

"Absolutely not. The best place for you is right here with your grandma."

Ethan looked square into Mahoney's eyes and saw the light. It was bright as the noonday sun shimmering on a still pond. If such a thing was proof enough for Grandma, then it was proof enough for him. "I wasn't sleeping," he said. "I seen it all."

"Good Lord," Mahoney replied. "You actually saw what happened?"

Ethan Allen nodded.

"Did the attacker see you?"

"Unh-unh." Ethan Allen timidly shook his head side to side. "He didn't see me 'cause I stayed hid, way far back under the bushes."

"Did you recognize him?"

Ethan Allen nodded and opened his mouth, but the words felt so painful in his throat that instead of speaking the name as he had intended he began to cry. "Honey," Olivia said, wrapping her arm around the boy's shoulders, "you don't have to be afraid of telling the truth. The Lord himself is on the side of truth, and so is Detective Mahoney."

"That's right," Mahoney said. "The only thing anybody can ask of you is the truth of what happened that night."

Turning his face into Olivia's shoulder, Ethan mumbled, "Mister Cobb did it."

"Sam Cobb?" Mahoney said, shocked.

The boy shook his head, "Unh-unh, his daddy. Mister Scooter."

"Scooter Cobb was the man who killed your mama and daddy?" Mahoney echoed with an overwhelming gasp of astonishment.

"Not Mama, just Daddy."

"Did you see who killed your mama?"

"Daddy, I reckon," Ethan answered, "but I think it was an accident."

"Do you suppose," Mahoney asked, "that you could tell me the whole story of how things actually happened that day?"

Ethan looked up at Olivia, his eyes questioning such a move. Only after she gave him a reassuring nod did he start to speak. "We was gonna run off to New York," he said. "So Mama told me to hide out back 'til it was time to leave. She thought I might slip and say something, and then Daddy would know what we were up to."

"Just you and your mama were going to New York?" Mahoney asked.

Ethan shook his head. "No, Mister Scooter was going too. That's why Mama didn't want Daddy to know. First off just me and her were going. But after Daddy took all Mama's money and spent it on a tractor, she said Mister Scooter was gonna take us 'cause he had a lot of money. Thing is, Daddy must've caught wind of it, 'cause him and Mama got into a real big fight. Once the cat was out of the bag she threw her suitcase in the car and told him she didn't give a beaver's tit about what he wanted. We was still going to New York. That's when Daddy punched her and she fell down." Ethan suddenly stopped talking and turned his attention to picking at a loose thread on the pocket of his pants.

Seeing the tears in the boy's eyes, Mahoney waited a long while and then said sympathetically, "So I guess your mama got hurt pretty bad when she fell down, huh?"

Ethan nodded.

"What happened then?"

"Daddy picked her up and put her in bed."

"You know if she was still alive?"

Ethan shrugged and kept picking at the thread.

"Scooter Cobb, was he there?"

"Not then," Ethan said. "He came late at night."

"Were you in the house when he got there?"

"Unh-unh." Ethan shook his head. "I was out back in the woods."

"How'd you know it was Scooter?"

"I heard the car. At first I figured it was Mama. I thought she might've felt some better and was leaving, so I snuck close by the yard to see. But it wasn't Mama. It was Mister Scooter getting out of his car."

"You sure it was him?"

"I'm *real* sure." If Mahoney had looked close enough he might have been able to catch sight of the image flickering across the boy's eyes, a memory-movie of Scooter Cobb heaving a bloodied Benjamin across the yard. "It was him all right," Ethan said. "He was driving his big white car. I seen that car plenty of times. One time I even seen him and Mama parked out back of the diner in that car—"

"Ethan," Olivia warned with a raised eyebrow.

"After Scooter got there," Mahoney asked, "what happened?"

"He went in our house, then he started screaming that Mama was dead. He called Daddy all kinds of names and said he'd killed her. Then he beat him up."

"Scooter beat up your Daddy?"

"Yeah. Daddy didn't even fight back, he just stood there and let Mister Scooter pound on him. I wanted to go help Daddy, but I was too scared so I stayed hid."

"In a situation such as that, keeping yourself safe is usually the best thing."

"It didn't feel like the best thing," Ethan replied sorrowfully.

"But it is a lot safer to stay hidden," Mahoney said. "Besides, if it was Scooter Cobb, I doubt there's anything you could have done to save your daddy." He went on with a number of questions as to where exactly the fight had taken place then reiterated, "Now, Ethan Allen, you're *absolutely sure* it was Scooter Cobb, right?"

"I told you I was."

"You're sure you ain't just making up this story to get back at Mister Cobb for his taking advantage of your mama?"

"I didn't say none of Mama's other boyfriends did it."

"That's true," Mahoney replied, nervously pushing his fingertips back and forth across his forehead. "Okay, I'm gonna take you at your word."

"Now you'll arrest Scooter Cobb?" Olivia asked.

"We'll see," Mahoney replied.

"See?" A frown drifted across Olivia's face. "What is there to see?"

"Every accusation has to be investigated, proven meritorious." Mahoney pulled his handkerchief from his pocket and swabbed his eyes. "We've got procedures," he said. "We don't go around arresting every person rumored to have done something."

Olivia bent forward and studied his eyes. The light was gone. There was not even a trace of glimmer. They were dark and dry. She had mistaken faulty tear ducts for the light of God. How absolutely stupid. "Don't think for an instant that I'll allow you to take this boy back with you," she said in a manner concrete as the building cornerstone. "Do whatever investigating you need to do, but expect nothing more from either of us."

Sensing a heavy-duty argument hanging in the air, Ethan slipped behind Olivia. Clara and Barbara Conklin moved forward to the edge of the sofa. A click sounded from the bedroom where Seth Porter had cocked his rifle even though he had no bullets.

"Let's just calm down and take it easy," Mahoney said, holding up the palms of his hands. "I'm not here to take Ethan Allen back. He's where he belongs. There's simply some groundwork to be done before I arrest anybody. The law states a man's innocent until proven guilty. The proving, that's my job."

"How can you possibly suggest that Scooter Cobb might be innocent? Ethan Allen saw him do it!"

"If we have nothing but the boy's say so, it's simply one person's word against the other. That's why we've got to substantiate his claim with actual evidence."

When Mahoney finally took his leave, Olivia was not feeling one bit good about convincing Ethan to tell what he knew. In fact, she was considering taking Fred up on his offer of marriage and the three of them moving off to Baltimore, Maryland.

Mahoney was feeling no better about the situation. "Hell's afire," he moaned as he slid behind the wheel, wishing he didn't know what he knew. He was suddenly wishing that he'd simply left well enough alone and settled for having an unsolved murder on the books. If the boy didn't want to be found, what business did he or anybody else have in finding him? Long before the ferry docked on the Eastern Shore, Jack Mahoney decided to do a bit of behind-the-scene investigating before he said anything to anyone, especially Sam Cobb.

DETECTIVE JACK MAHONEY

I'd like to believe that the kid is lying, that he's concocted the entire story just to get even with Sam. It would make my life a whole lot easier if I could just chalk the kid's story up to a case of misdirected anger.

After all the boy's been through, it's logical to think he might be looking to get even, to pay Sam back for the way he treated his grandma.

It was dark and the kid had to be seventy or eighty yards away. How probable was it that he could actually see the face of the attacker? And then how likely was it that he'd stay hidden in the bushes and watch his daddy being murdered?

That bit about Scooter Cobb taking them to New York...I gotta question that. Scooter might be a man to chase around a bit, but the women have come and gone and he's always stayed married. Running off to New York? What about Emma? What about the diner?

If I start thinking Scooter Cobb might have done this thing, then I have to ask myself: does Sam know? Is that his reason for acting so belligerent toward the boy? Is that the real reason he felt a runaway kid wasn't worth chasing after?

Let me tell you, the last thing any detective wants to do is suspect a fellow officer of covering up a crime especially one as heinous as this. Much as I hate the thought of what I could be walking into, I can't get rid of the feeling that the kid is telling the truth.

We'll see.

EVIDENTIARY FACT

On Wednesday morning Mahoney walked into the criminal records office and asked to take another look at the file for the Doyle murders. Line by line he read through every detail of the findings. He studied the photographs of the shoe prints alongside Benjamin's body: a man's shoe, size thirteen, a heavy tread on the bottom, the sort of shoe a man standing on his feet all day might wear. The window broken from inside. It matched up with Ethan's story. Then there was the partial thumbprint on the bedroom doorknob—not enough for identification, but sure evidence of a large hand. Susanna Doyle killed by a single blow to the back of the head, her blood found on a large rock alongside the driveway, her body found lying in bed—everything was just as the boy told it. "Shit!" Mahoney said and closed the folder. He left the station house and headed for the diner.

He knew Scooter Cobb would be there standing behind the counter nursing a cold cup of coffee or standing at the griddle and frying up some hamburgers. Scooter was a man who stood twelve hours a day, seven days a week. He more than likely wore shoes with a heavy tread on the sole, a tread that could absorb the pressure of his weight. Of course, Mahoney reasoned, there was any number of people about whom you could say the same thing, but the boy had specifically named Scooter. There were days when Mahoney wished that he'd chosen another profession. Anything but this. Teacher maybe, or a Southern Electric Company meter reader with little to do but stroll from house to house recording the amount of electricity each family used.

Mahoney arrived at the diner shortly before eleven. The noonday rush had not yet started. Scooter was standing at the counter with a half-empty coffee cup and gave a nod when Mahoney walked in. "How's the investigation going?" he asked. He set a cup and saucer in front of Jack, then filled the cup with coffee.

"Slow," Mahoney answered. "A lot of standing around. My feet are killing me."

Scooter topped off his own cup. "Standing's tough duty," he said.

Mahoney nodded. "You ought to know, you're on your feet all day."

Scooter rolled his eyes. "That's for sure."

"What I should do," Mahoney said, "is get myself a pair of cushiony shoes. Shoes meant for standing. Something like you've got."

"These is a lifesaver. Cost thirty-nine dollars, but worth every cent."

"Mind if I take a look?"

"Be my guest." Scooter bent over, untied his right shoe, and handed it to Mahoney. "Stick your foot in," he said. "These are probably too big for you, but you'll get the feel."

Mahoney pulled off his own shoe and slid his foot into Scooter's. "You're right," he said casually. "These are way too big for me. What size foot you got?"

"Thirteen, extra wide."

Mahoney pulled the shoe off and turned it over in his hand. The tread was a narrow-wide, narrow-wide, zigzag pattern, exactly the same as the footprint found alongside Benjamin's body. Same size, same tread pattern. Not what he'd been hoping to find. "Long as I'm here," Mahoney said, handing the shoe back to its owner, "mind if I ask you a few questions about Susanna Doyle?"

"Susanna? She worked here, that was about it."

"Oh? There's talk of her having a lover. You know anything of that?"

Scooter shrugged. "News to me," he said. "Where'd you hear a thing like that?"

"We got it from her boy," Mahoney answered. "Ethan Allen claims he and Susanna were supposed to go to New York City with this man."

Scooter began nervously swiping at the countertop, which didn't have a speck of dirt on it. "That kid," he said, his voice sounding a register higher than it had earlier. "He's a born liar. You can't believe a thing he says. Poor Susanna had all kinds of problems with him."

"Kids." Mahoney shook his head but offered neither agreement nor disagreement as to Scooter's opinion of Ethan Allen.

"And Susanna," Scooter went on. "She was sure as hell no angel. I wouldn't doubt for a minute she had a lover. More than one, I'll wager. Plenty of times I seen her hanging over the counter, eyeballing it with some passing-through salesman."

"Didn't she work the late shift?" Mahoney asked.

Scooter nodded but didn't look up. He focused his eyes on the speckled countertop, stretched across, and gave it another swipe.

"You and her worked together nights, right?"

"Most times." Scooter turned away, emptied a half-pot of coffee down the drain, and started scrubbing the Brew Master for all he was worth.

"Did Sam or Emma know that you were having an affair with Susanna?" Mahoney asked.

"What the hell kind of question is that? I wasn't having no affair with nobody, least of all Susanna Doyle!"

Mahoney believed enough bait thrown into the water would bring to the surface the truth of a person's guilt or innocence and said, "Ethan Allen claims he saw you out at the farm on the night of the murders. He claims you're the one who beat up Benjamin."

"He's a liar! A shit-faced, mealy-mouthed liar. I wasn't nowhere near the Doyle place that night, and the kid knows it!"

"Where were you that night?" Mahoney asked.

"Right here. I worked 'til eleven-thirty, same as every night."

"Where'd you go after that?"

"Home! That's where I always go when I'm done working."

As Scooter turned back to the Brew Master Mahoney drained the last of his coffee. Then, using a napkin, he picked up the saucer and slid it into his pocket. As he stood to leave, he asked, "Did you and Susanna Doyle ever make love in that big white Cadillac of yours?"

"Screw you," Scooter answered.

As soon as Mahoney was out the door Scooter Cobb picked up the telephone and called his son, Sam. "What the fuck are you trying to pull?" he asked.

"Trying to pull?" Buckling beneath the sound of his father's anger, Sam stammered. "About what?"

"You know damn good and well what I'm talking about. Sending

Mahoney over here with that shit about me and Susanna having an affair."

"Me send Mahoney? He's a detective. I'm a street cop!"

"Yeah, but you're working the Doyle case with him."

"Not anymore," Sam said. "The captain needed me for another job."

"Well, you better find a way to get back on the Doyle case," Scooter growled. "'Cause that shit-faced kid of Susanna's is saying I was there the night of the murder."

"You? Why?"

"How the hell should I know? The kid's probably just out to get me. He told Mahoney I was having a thing with Susanna."

"There's no truth to that is there?"

"Of course not!" Scooter answered emphatically. "I might've grabbed onto her tit or pinched her ass a few times, but that's it. The problem is I don't want your mama getting hold of this, so you gotta talk to the kid, make him see this is all a big mistake."

"Yeah, sure, Pop," Sam said. But even as he hung up the telephone, Sam Cobb knew there was no way the captain was going to put him back on the case. Whatever he was going to do would have to be done on his own.

❦

After Mahoney left the diner, he went to see Emma Cobb. "Hello, Jack," she said with a broad smile, then swung the door wide open and invited him into the house. She sat him at the kitchen table, and before he'd had time to refuse she set out a tray of lemon cakes and turned the coffee pot to brew.

Emma was a genuinely likeable woman, which made what Mahoney had to do all the more difficult. "Emma, I'm real sorry, but I'm here on official business," he said in an apologetic tone of voice.

"Business?" she replied laughingly. "What business could the police department have with me?"

"Not you," he smiled. "But we're still investigating the Doyle murders and trying to verify the alibi of anyone who had a relationship with Benjamin or Susanna. Since Scooter worked with Susanna, I've got to ask: did he come home after work the night of the murders? There are witnesses to prove he was at the diner until almost midnight, but

Benjamin Doyle's murder occurred later than that. Do you recall what time Scooter actually got home?"

"I can't say with certainty, because I usually go to bed about ten. I stir a bit when he comes to bed, and I don't recall him being any later than usual that night."

"The next morning did he seem stressful? Nervous, maybe? Out of sorts?"

"Scooter's always a bit out of sorts when he gets up, but I can't say he was any worse than usual. Of course, he didn't find out about what happened to poor Susanna and her husband until late that afternoon."

"After he found out about the murders, what did he have to say?"

"He felt real bad. Said it was horrible that such a thing could happen. I knew he was thinking how much he was gonna miss Susanna. She'd been working at the diner for a couple of years and was his only late-night waitress."

"Did your husband know Benjamin Doyle?"

Emma shrugged. "He might have come into the diner. I can't say."

After Jack Mahoney left Emma took the rosary beads from her pocket and fingered them one by one as she knelt and prayed to the Virgin Mary. "Holy Mother," she whispered. "Pray for us sinners, now and at the hour of our death. Protect my husband," she pleaded, "and forgive the lies I speak on his behalf."

❦

When he left Emma Cobb, Mahoney went back to the station house and submitted the saucer he'd taken from the diner for a fingerprint analysis. "Check if the prints on this match the partial taken from the Doyle bedroom door," he told the crime scene laboratory detective. He walked out with his shoulders hunched over as if he already knew what the answer was going to be.

Even if the print was a match, Mahoney told himself, it simply verified that Sam's dad had been at the Doyle farm. It could have been days before the murder. Scooter might have been out there visiting Susanna one afternoon when her husband was working in the field. There was no forensic evidence that could say how long the prints had been on that brass doorknob. It could have been weeks. Maybe even months. It was obvious that the house hadn't been cleaned for a while. Scooter Cobb was well-known for his indiscretions, and although having an affair might not be too respectable it wasn't against the law. Maybe that's what this was all about. Maybe the boy knew they were having an affair and that was why he made up such a story. Maybe, maybe, maybe… After Jack Mahoney had racked his brain counting up all the maybes, there was still the size thirteen shoe print. And that was no maybe.

For two hours he studied the crime scene investigation reports. Then he closed the file folder and headed home. Tomorrow was another day. Tomorrow he would tell the captain of his findings and question Sam Cobb. "This is some shitty way to earn a living," Mahoney grumbled.

SAM COBB

*M*y brother, Tommy, he's the smart one. He left home nine years ago and hasn't dropped a postcard since. Who could blame him? With Pop, nothing's ever right. You can bust your ass trying to please him, but he won't even bother to say thanks. The only thing he's got to say is how let down he is 'cause you didn't perform to his standards. His standards; that's a joke. He's got no standards; they're just for other people.

I swear, this is it. I'll do this one last thing for him, then I'm gone.

So long, that's what I'm gonna say. So long, Pop. And, by the way, you can kiss my ass when it comes to any more favors.

THE CONFRONTATION

Sam Cobb left the station house shortly after two o'clock. He climbed into his car and drove south along Route 13. It wasn't what he wanted to do, but he could think of no other way. He figured by leaning heavy on the gas pedal he could get to Wyattsville, take care of what he had to do, then return to Norfolk in time for the last ferry, which left at midnight.

Sam rewound the conversation with his father and played it through his head over and over again. He attached weight and meaning to every word, to every phrase, even to the few pauses and stammers. Then he separated the syllables and listened to hear what hadn't been said. All of this in an effort to sort out the truth.

There had been trouble before. The woman from Laughton; the dancer from Virginia Beach; the red-headed cocktail waitress. All of them swore Scooter had taken advantage of them, and he swore he'd done no such thing. Sam, blinded by an eagerness to please, had always accepted Scooter's version of the story. So, dressed in his patrolman's uniform, he'd visited each of the women and handed over an envelope of money, authoritatively suggesting that they leave town.

Sam stopped for a red light and wearily lowered his head down onto the steering wheel. "Stupid," he rebuked himself. "Just plain stupid." If he sat there and thought about it for a moment longer, common sense might have told him to turn around and head home. But as it happened a heating oil truck pulled behind him, and the driver began beeping his horn the instant the light switched over to green.

Despite memories of the past, Cobb blood ran through Sam's veins and by the time he arrived in Wyattsville he had once again convinced himself of his father's innocence. *So what if Pop is a bit hot-headed?* Sam reasoned. *That's not a crime. He may be guilty of indiscretion, but murder? Never!*

❦

After Olivia realized she'd been mistaken about the light in Detective Mahoney's eyes, she decided a new level of diligence would be required for watching over Ethan Allen. She informed the boy that she would be driving him to school in the morning and back home in the afternoon and that she or one of the neighbors had to be sitting in the playground whenever he was there. "From now on," she said, "you're limited to a one-block radius for this errand-running business, and you'll have to check in after each trip." When Ethan Allen complained he was being treated like a child, Olivia apologized. "I'm only doing this for your own good," she explained and hugged him to her breast.

"But, jeez," he moaned and wriggled loose.

Of course, Ethan was still free to roam the hallways of the Wyattsville Arms apartment building, which he did. He played catch with Dog for the biggest part of the first afternoon. Then he batted a brand new Spalding from wall to wall for a while. After that he practiced turning summersaults and tried walking on his hands, but before long he was bored. He then came up with the idea of running errands within the building and started ringing one door bell after the other. "Need somebody to fetch your laundry from the basement?" he asked Emma Kline, who had a faulty hip and was forever complaining about it.

"I surely do," she answered and gave him ten cents for his trouble.

After that he branched out to hauling things back and forth from the storage room and emptying garbage pails down the incinerator chute. He was in the midst of delivering a broccoli-and-cheese casserole from Sara Parker to Mister Bailey, who lived three doors down from Olivia, when he heard the voice.

"Hey, kid!" yelled Sam Cobb, still wearing his uniform.

The casserole jumped out of Ethan's hands and smashed to the floor with a noise that could be heard throughout the building. "Grandma!" he screamed in a panicky cry of desperation, and then he went flying down the hallway.

This was not at all what Sam had expected. "Wait up," he yelled. "I just want a word with you." Instinctively, he took off chasing the boy but by then several of the Wyattsville Arms residents had opened their doors. One of them was Olivia.

She'd been expecting trouble. A nagging feeling had settled into her chest the moment she suspected the light in Jack Mahoney's eyes had been a mistake, which is why Ethan Allen's baseball bat was standing alongside the front door. Olivia grabbed it and charged into the hallway swinging. Ethan Allen, still screaming her name, darted through the open door just as Olivia whacked Sam Cobb in the knee. As Sam tumbled to the floor, Olivia scrambled back inside the apartment and double-locked the door.

By then Mister Bailey had telephoned for the police.

Sam Cobb was lying on the floor with a broken kneecap when the Wyattsville patrol car arrived minutes later. Were it merely Olivia's word against that of a fellow officer in uniform, the two policemen may have shown favor toward Sam. But with a broken casserole dish splattered across the floor and nine neighbors pointing a finger at Cobb, they had little choice but to haul him off to the Wyattsville Police Station.

"But I'm on assignment," Sam protested as they helped him to his feet and down to the squad car. "I'm investigating an eyewitness report on the Doyle murder case," he told them. "Eastern Shore Precinct. Go ahead, check it out." Without a doubt that was the worst thing he could have said, because Sergeant Gomez, the duty officer that evening, immediately put in a call to Captain Rogers.

"Cobb?" the captain said. "He's off that case. Detective Mahoney's working it."

Jack Mahoney was at home having his dinner when he got the call. "Holy shit!" he moaned when told of the situation. Jack reluctantly confirmed that although Sam had originally been assigned to the case, he no longer had reason to be involved.

"Well, then," Gomez said. "Have you any idea why he's here?"

There was a lengthy moment of hesitation before Jack said, "I believe he's got a personal connection to the lead suspect in the case."

"Oh? And that is?"

"His father. The kid Sam allegedly went after is an eye witness who claims Scooter Cobb, Sam's pop, is responsible for a murder. Now that's not what the kid originally said and we're still waiting for lab reports, so we don't know if his story's on the up and up."

Fifteen minutes later, Sam Cobb was booked on charges of assault and attempting to intimidate a witness in a capital crime. He was placed in a nine-foot square cell and locked down for the night.

Mahoney replaced the telephone receiver and returned to the dinner table, but he didn't eat another bite. In all the years he'd been a detective this was the first time he'd ever had to turn on one of his own. Jack could easily enough believe Scooter Cobb capable of the crime in question. He was a bad-tempered man with a reputation for trouble. But Sam? Sam had his share of faults. He was arrogant, aggressive, even belligerent when he didn't get the assignments he thought he deserved. But how likely was it he'd try to cover up a murder? Sam Cobb? A man who had his heart set on making detective?

ETHAN ALLEN

I figured I was good as dead with Sam Cobb coming after me. When I took off screaming a bunch of folks poked their heads out the door, but nobody did nothin' except Grandma Olivia.

Let me tell you, it was a sight when she came out swinging that baseball bat! I'd never've figured a person her size could beat back a Cobb. 'Course, she got the drop on him 'cause he wasn't expecting such a thing. Next time, you can bet your sweet ass he'll be ready for her.

Grandma says now that the police has got Scooter's boy in jail, he ain't gonna be hurting nobody. She says I got nothing more to worry about.

But me...well, I say she don't know those Cobbs! Them is the meanest men on earth, and if you ain't looking to get pulverized you'd best be prepared.

Taking No Chances

After the Wyattsville Police had carted Sam Cobb off, Olivia's nerves took hold. She shivered and trembled as if there was an earthquake happening inside of her. Icy cold beads of perspiration rose up on her forehead, and her knees buckled under.

"No wonder," Clara clucked. "Given what you've just gone through, it's a miracle you didn't pass out cold!" Clara brewed a pot of chamomile tea, saying it was just the thing to help a person relax. Because of the incident when she'd backed her husband's car into a telephone pole Barbara Conklin knew tea alone was too weak a remedy for a severe case of nerves, so she added a large shot of brandy to the cup. Fred McGinty swore by the super-strength sleeping pills in his medicine cabinet, dashed back to his apartment, brought back two, and plunked them into Olivia's tea.

"What she needs," he told the others, "is a good night's rest. What she needs is to put the entire episode behind her."

Before she'd finished even half the tea Olivia began to yawn; then she toddled off to the bedroom, claiming she'd stretch out across the bed for a few minutes to rest herself. When the sound of snores echoed through to the living room the neighbors left, telling Ethan Allen to be sure to double-bolt the door behind them.

"Okay," the boy answered, although that was not at all what he intended.

By midnight the building was so quiet that a passerby would believe every resident tucked beneath the covers and sound asleep, which they were—except for one small boy. While the rest of the residents slept, Ethan Allen was tiptoeing down the back stairs. He knew what he needed, and he knew just where to find it.

Three of them were in Mister Porter's storage bin. He'd seen them there, less than a week ago, squeezed in between a carton of books and a broken coat tree. Of course, there was no knowing whether they were in working order. Pushing the thought of such a disastrous possibility from his head, Ethan Allen shimmied across the partition holding Seth Porter's belongings back from those of Bessie Morgan. He landed with a hard thud, waited a handful of minutes to make sure the sound had gone undetected, then pulled a flashlight from his pocket and switched it on. At first it appeared the guns were gone, vanished from sight, but such wasn't the case. Once he pushed aside a carton of sweaters that had recently been added to the mix there they were, standing like a trio of soldiers lined up for battle: two Browning shotguns—one a single barrel, the other a side-by-side double—and a Winchester rifle.

Ethan Allen took hold of the Winchester. Any one of the three might have suited his need, but a rifle was something special. A rifle was way more powerful than a shotgun and ten million times more accurate than the scattergun he'd used to shoot groundhogs. A rifle could hit square in the heart of what a person was aiming at and kill it dead. The Winchester was a gun that meant business. He released the lever action and pushed down. The chamber was empty.

If Seth Porter had a perfectly good Winchester he had to have bullets, Ethan reasoned as he began rummaging through carton after carton of the man's belonging. He removed the books one by one, then took the time to flip open each cover and check for a supply of cartridges that might be hidden in a nest of hollowed out pages. When the books failed to produce anything, he began searching through boxes of games. After that it was cartons of kitchenware and numerous valises filled with clothing. Time after time he bypassed a lone carton marked "Melissa's things," dubiously shaking his head as he moved on to another carton with a more promising name. He rummaged through a barrel marked "Camping," then tore into a box marked "Sporting goods," but neither contained cartridges to fit the Winchester. In fact, they contained no cartridges at all.

As a last resort, he opened the carton of Melissa's things. With a yellowed wedding gown right on top, it started out pretty much as expected. He pulled the gown from the box and set it aside. By now Ethan Allen was feeling pretty discouraged. Having a Winchester with no bullets wouldn't be much help. It could maybe scare the poop out of some knucklehead, but the Cobbs weren't knuckleheads and they didn't scare easy. Matter of fact, they didn't scare at all! He hauled out a swatch of lace that had fallen from the gown, then a music box that tinkled a few notes and stopped.

Maybe, Ethan thought, he'd be better off disappearing. But if the Cobbs couldn't catch hold of him they might take it out on Olivia, seeing as how she was his grandma. No, he decided, he'd not run. "No more," he grumbled as he thought back to how he'd trembled like a scared rabbit when he watched Scooter beat his daddy to death. On sleepless nights he could still hear his daddy's screams. No, he decided, this time there wasn't gonna be any running off. He was gonna stay and fight.

He dug his way through a number of other dresses, a book of poetry, and a bald-headed doll baby, then found what he'd been searching for. Well, not exactly what he'd been searching for, but close enough. At the very bottom of Melissa's things was a full box of twenty gauge shotgun shells—way too big for the Winchester, but they'd fit the double-barreled Browning. The shotgun wasn't Ethan's first choice, because with several strips of black tape circling the butt end of the stock it seemed somewhat worse for the wear. But a worn-out shotgun with shells was a lot better than an empty Winchester.

He set the rifle back in place and took hold of the double-barreled Browning. Shoving the lever to the right, he cracked the gun open and checked the breech. It also was empty. Ethan removed two shells from the box, loaded them into position, and then put the remainder in his pocket.

He returned up the back stairs and slipped into the apartment with Olivia never having been any the wiser.

He'd expected to climb into bed and sleep the sleep of a man in control of things, a man who was well prepared for whatever might be headed his way. But instead he tossed and turned with worries mounding like anthills in his brain. First off, he reasoned, he wasn't all that prepared. He didn't even know for certain Seth Porter's relic of a shotgun would fire. Then there was always the chance that when he pulled the trigger, the gun would blow up in his face. Old guns were known to do that. Tommy Tristan's daddy was killed in just such a way.

He'd gone hunting one morning, promising to bring home a rabbit for stewing, and instead came home dead. An old shotgun, that's what did him in.

Ethan wished he'd had a chance to give the Browning a try, but there was no way. It was one thing to rummage through the basement with barely a sound and quite another to slam off a shot in the middle of the night. And it was a given if Grandma Olivia found out he had a shotgun stashed under his bed she'd surely take it away. She'd make him return the gun to Seth Porter along with a hangdog apology and a promise not to go pilfering the storage room ever again. Nope, trying the shotgun was not worth considering. He'd have to trust to luck, hope for the best, and pray to God no Cobbs showed up.

Once Ethan Allen settled his mind, he closed his eyes and tried again to sleep. He turned to the wall, then to the doorway, then flipped over on his back, but he was still wide awake—as awake as awake could be. He'd heard of people counting sheep in order to drift off to sleep, so he pictured a meadow. Then he fixed his thoughts on a stretched-out rail fence, but before the first of his sheep took a jump he remembered something else. Size. Both Cobbs were big men. Shotguns were made for killing small animals. What good was a scattering of buckshot gonna do when a mountain of a man was coming at you? Not much, he feared.

Once he started dwelling on the size of the Cobbs, sleep was nigh on to impossible. He tried thinking back on the names and batting averages for every member of the Baltimore Orioles. Then he moved on to the New York Yankees, who now he'd probably never get to see. After that he conjured up an imaginary baseball game, which worked better than most anything else because he could almost hear Chuck Thompson screaming that Brooks Robinson had rounded third and was looking like he'd score on an inside-the-park home run.

The first light of dawn was creasing the sky when Ethan fell asleep, and even then the only reason he did was because he'd set his mind to ease with a new plan: a plan to take his errand money and go buy a box of cartridges for the Winchester. Tomorrow morning, he'd told himself as he drifted off—tomorrow morning. Of course, he hadn't counted on the fact that he'd be so exhausted he'd sleep through until almost noon.

EMMA COBB

A lifetime of sorrow is what comes of marrying a man with a *smile that draws women like flies to a spill of syrup. Such a man comes wrapped in the love of himself.* Here I am, *he says.* Isn't that enough?

You might look at my husband and see a man who's old, fat, and mean-spirited. Well, he wasn't always. Thirty years ago he was handsome and knew how to charm. He was a man with money to spend and a successful business. Why, there was not a girl in town who didn't itch to wear my shoes. The minute Scooter Cobb crooked his finger in my direction I went running to him. Little did I dream that for most of our years together he would lie beside me with the scent of other women still fastened to his skin.

What a fool I have been to stand silently all these years and watch so selfish a man destroy my family. He has already driven one son from the house, and now he is determined to corrupt the other. This I cannot bear. Not now, when there is no love left and barely a shred of civility between us.

I swear to you, with God as my witness, I will never allow my Sam to follow in his daddy's footsteps—never!

THE SHIRT

Mahoney left the house claiming he needed to clear his head. He bypassed the car standing in his driveway and started to walk. He told himself he was headed to nowhere in particular and walked for almost two hours, but in the end he found himself standing at Emma Cobb's front door. When he lifted his arm to knock, it felt heavy as a lead weight. His heart felt even heavier.

"Jack," Emma said with her broad smile. "Come on in." She swung the door back and he followed her without a word. "I've some fresh-baked raspberry cake," she went on. "It's the end of the season, but right now the berries have the most delicious flavor. Or, if you'd rather, I've got—"

"Emma," Jack interrupted. "Let's sit down. There's something I've got to tell you."

She stopped and turned, her face suddenly white. "Is it Sam?" she asked. "He's not hurt, is he? Tell me he hasn't been shot, please."

"Sam hasn't been injured," Jack said, tenderly circling his arm around her shoulders. "He's not hurt, but he is in jail."

"Sam?" she gasped. "My Sam, in jail?"

Jack nodded.

"But it's a mistake, isn't it?" she asked, nervously tugging at a handkerchief she'd pulled from her pocket. "Sam being in jail? He's a police officer, what could he possibly—"

"It's a long story," Jack replied. He guided Emma over to the sofa, and when she sat down he positioned himself alongside of her. "Emma," he said, taking her hand into his, "I believe Sam has gotten himself in trouble by trying to protect his daddy."

"Scooter?"

Jack nodded and went on. "It has to do with Ethan Allen Doyle, the boy I brought over here to spend the night. Do you remember him?" She dipped her head ever so slightly and continued to listen. "Well," Jack said, "a few days ago, the boy accused Scooter of being the one who murdered his daddy."

"Scooter? Why would he murder a man he barely knew?"

"The boy said his mama was involved with Scooter. He claims they were planning to run off to New York together. Emma, I realize this is a real painful thing to hear but try to remember it's just an allegation. We don't even know for sure if the kid's telling the truth or making the whole story up." Jack stopped speaking for a moment and waited, thinking she might have questions about her husband being linked to another woman. But Emma didn't say a word. She just sat there looking as empty as a dried-up well.

Eventually, a pool of tears rose to her eyes, and without any reference to Scooter she moaned, "But what's that got to do with Sam? He'd never get involved in such a thing. He has a bit of his daddy's temper, but he'd never—"

"Apparently, Sam took it on himself to go over to Wyattsville—where Ethan Allen lives with his grandma—and according to the local police, he attacked the boy." In an effort to soften the sound of what happened Jack deliberately worked in hope-rendering words such as "apparently" and "according to."

"My Sam?" she gasped. "My sweet Sam tried to hurt that little boy?"

"We don't actually know what Sam's intention was. The grandmother stopped him before he got to the kid."

"So Sam didn't really do anything?" After thirty years of being married to Scooter, Emma was able to focus her eye on the one rose in a bush full of thorns.

Jack slowly shook his head. "No," he said. "But it appears he tried."

Through the years Emma had learned to live with Scooter Cobb's meanness, but to have her son grow into the same nature was more than she could bear. She covered her face with her hands and began to cry with great shuddering sobs. There was nothing Jack could do but sit silently beside her. He waited a long while and then asked, "Emma, do you know if Sam was aware of Scooter's involvement?"

She sat there for what seemed a very long time, her shoulders hunched, the round of her back shuddering like ground that was about to give way. A flow of tears streamed from her eyes; then she moaned and said, "I'm the one who ought to be in jail. Me. I suspected what Scooter had done, but I turned my face the other way. The truth was right there in front of me, but I kept telling myself such a thing couldn't possibly be. He's got faults, I know, but something bad as this—never. All this while I've been lying to myself. But how could I possibly open my mind to the truth when I knew it would destroy my family?"

"Emma," Mahoney stammered, "what is it you know?"

Without answering his question, she continued. "I thought my silence would save what was left of my family. Instead, it's pushed the situation from bad to worse. I sure never thought it would happen this way. I love my boys, Sam and Tommy both. Those boys have been the light of my life, and God knows I'd sooner carve out my own heart than do intentional harm to either one of them. I'm their mother. A mother suffers something fierce to bring her children into this world, and she'd do most anything to keep those children from misery. You understand that, don't you, Jack?"

He nodded.

"I know meaning well don't excuse what I did. If I'd've told right off, Sam wouldn't have been dragged into it. The law would've thrown Scooter's ass in jail, and that would've been the end of that. It's where he ought to be. A man like him don't deserve one ounce of consideration. Not an ounce. He was given two fine sons, boys who trusted he'd show them right from wrong, and what did he do? He pointed them down the road to damnation, that's what." Emma gave her nose a noisy blow, then took the balled-up handkerchief in her hand and swiped at a fresh stream of tears rolling down her face. "Sam's a victim," she said. "You understand that, don't you? He's a victim, not a criminal."

"Emma," Jack said, circling back to his original question. "What you're apparently saying is that Scooter *did* have a hand in this. But what exactly is it that you're hiding?"

"If I tell you've got to arrest Scooter and put him in jail. If he's not locked up, he'll come back here and kill me. I know that for sure."

"Once we've got a reasonable amount of evidence that he's

committed a crime he'll be arrested. That's something you don't have to worry about."

"Well, I *am* worried. Scooter's got a mean disposition, meaner than you might imagine, and he's got a God-awful temper. If he figures I've turned against him—"

"He's not going to know it was you."

"He'll know. He'll know because I'm the only one who's got proof of what he's done."

"I'll keep anything you say confidential."

"I'm still not gonna tell unless you promise to lock Scooter away from me and Sam. He's done enough harm to this family. It's gotta stop here and now."

"Emma, without knowing what you have to say, it's almost impossible for me to promise you such a thing. But if you tell me something that's not enough to justify an arrest, I promise not to mention a word of what you've told me to anyone else. That way, your husband will never learn of our conversation."

"I'm gonna trust you, Jack."

"I respect that," he said, giving her a nod of confidence.

Emma let go of a sigh weighted with all the heartaches she'd stored up—years and years of worry and regret, let loose in one sorrowful swoosh of air. "I know for certain Scooter killed that boy's daddy," she finally said. "Sam didn't have a thing to do with it. It was just Scooter. Nobody else." She nervously twisted the wet handkerchief in her hands.

"The night it happened I was in bed fast asleep by time Scooter came home, so we didn't catch sight of each other 'til morning. Even then I didn't see much of him 'cause he had to get to the diner. It was Sunday. I know 'cause I always sort the laundry on Sunday and start my washing on Monday. Anyway, as he's flying out the door I tell him, 'Be sure to leave your dirty shirt out.' He calls back that his shirt don't need washing and keeps going. I remember it perfectly clear. I heard what he said. But I was thinking, 'That'll be the day!' Scooter's a man who sweats buckets. If he wears a shirt for an hour it needs washing."

Emma hesitated for a long moment, as if remembering something too private to share, and then she continued. "After he was gone I went looking for that shirt and found it. He'd stuck it way back under the bed, so far back that I had to get down on my hands and knees to reach. I got hold of the shirt and pulled it out. That's when I saw it was covered with blood. Not little speckles like he gets from cutting up meat, but enough blood to make me wonder if he'd butchered a cow."

"And this shirt you found under the bed, you know it's Scooter's?"

"For a fact," she said. "Week after week, I washed that shirt. Then I'd stand there and iron the wrinkles from it. Yes, I *know* it's his shirt." She gave a sigh of weariness, then went on. "I saw all that blood and couldn't imagine what he'd been up to, so I set the shirt aside thinking I'd ask him about it that night. All this happened before I'd heard about the murders."

"The day you found this shirt with blood on it, was it the same Sunday I brought Ethan Allen Doyle over here to stay?"

"Yes, but earlier on. I already knew Scooter was carrying on with Susanna Doyle. They'd been going at it for six or eight months. But when you told me her and her husband was both murdered, I just couldn't believe Scooter had a part in it.

"Later on that night when I started asking about how he happened to come by all the blood on his shirt, he got bristly as a starved alley cat. Right then I knew. I knew sure as I was standing there, Benjamin Doyle's blood was what was all over Scooter's shirt. 'I know what you been up to,' I told him, and he gave me a look that felt like a razor slicing down my back. I believe he wanted to tear me apart right then and there. But I warned him that I'd put the shirt away for safekeeping and if he laid one finger on me, it was gonna make its way to the sheriff's office. He huffed and puffed for a few minutes, then he stomped off and that was the end of it."

"You've still got the shirt?"

She gave a slight nod of her head, barely any movement at all, mostly her eyes, looking up and then down. "I thought my holding on to it would force him to stop this sort of behavior," she said. "I figured maybe he'd start acting the way a man ought to act. I never dreamed he'd drag Sam into this mess or cause harm to that little boy."

"Where is the shirt?"

"Put away."

"Washed?"

"No," she answered. "But I'm not giving it up unless you promise to let Sam go free. I know my Sam, and I can swear he hasn't got his daddy's meanness. He'd never harm the boy. I'd stake my life on it. His daddy's the one who's got to be held accountable."

"I wish I could promise you such a thing, Emma, but it's not in my power. Sam's being held over in Wyattsville. Whether or not he's released is up to the district court in that area. But I'll sure see what I can do. I'll put in a word for him, let the arresting officer know the circumstances of his situation."

"He's all I've got, Jack."

"I know," Jack sighed. Then he wrapped his arm around Emma who, burdened by the weight of her words, had become smaller and quite pitiful.

After a long while of sitting in silence, Emma finally pushed herself to her feet and walked through to the back of the house. Jack remained where he was. He knew she'd be back and he knew when she returned she'd be carrying the shirt in her hand.

He was right.

⎯⎯✦⎯⎯

The following morning Mahoney was standing at the crime lab when the door opened. "I think the blood on this shirt might match one of the victims in the Doyle murders," he said and handed the detective an evidence pack.

"I'll get back to you this afternoon," the detective answered impatiently. He tucked the package beneath his arm and disappeared through the swinging door.

Mahoney then went to the Eastern Shore station house. He sat at his desk, drank a cup of coffee, and called Olivia Doyle. "I'm sorry for what happened with Officer Cobb," he said. "That was not a department-sanctioned visit. He came out there on his own."

"Sorry?" Olivia shouted back. "Sorry?! That's what you say when a policeman shows up and frightens a child witless?"

"If I'd known what he was planning, I'd have taken measures—"

"You said he was no longer on this case!"

"He's not. But I have reason to believe that Officer Cobb's father may have asked him to speak with Ethan."

"Oh? Now our lives are in danger? Is that it? We have to go into hiding like—"

With Olivia being on a tear as she was, Mahoney had to interrupt to squeeze in an answer. "That's not it at all," he said. "Officer Cobb's locked up in the Wyattsville jail, and there's a good possibility we'll be taking his daddy into custody sometime today. So neither you nor Ethan Allen have anything to worry about."

"That's easy enough for *you* to say!"

"Actually, I don't think Officer Cobb ever intended to harm the boy. Our understanding is that he came there to try to find out the truth of what happened, probably because his father has been identified as a suspect."

"He scared Ethan Allen half to death, is that not harm? Do you have any idea what might have happened if I hadn't had a baseball bat ready?" Once Olivia got wound up, there was little chance of stopping her. The words came in rapid fire succession. "I'll tell you what probably would have happened," she went on. "Ethan Allen and I would have been murdered stone cold dead! We'd have been lying here in a pool of blood on our own doorstep!"

"That's not true," Mahoney said. "If Officer Cobb intended to harm either of you, he would have been wearing his service revolver. Sergeant Gomez of the Wyattsville Police Department said he wasn't carrying a gun or any other type of weapon. And that's the truth. I checked Officer Cobb's locker here at the precinct. Both his gun and gun belt are in there."

"He was probably carrying some less obvious type of weapon. A wire or a nylon stocking for strangling."

"There was nothing. Officer Cobb was still lying in the hallway when he was arrested, and he underwent a thorough search before the doctor even tended to his broken knee."

"He has a broken knee?"

"Actually, they say it's shattered. He'll supposedly have a pretty pronounced limp once he's able to walk again."

Olivia paused for a moment, then went on in a slightly more conciliatory tone. "I'm sorry about that. My only intention was to stop him from coming after Ethan Allen. I had to protect the child; after all, he is my grandson."

"Missus Doyle," Mahoney said hesitantly, "I've still got a few questions as to what happened. If you've no objection, I'd like to come by and have a word with Ethan."

"Don't you come over here upsetting the child," she warned.

"I've no intention of upsetting him. But a report has to be filed, so I've got to ask about what happened."

"Are you coming alone?"

"Absolutely alone," he assured. Promising to be there in the afternoon, he hung up.

Before he left the office, Mahoney called the crime lab. "Any news yet?" he asked.

"It's been an hour since I saw you," the detective growled. "I *said* this afternoon!"

It was just after two o'clock when Mahoney arrived at the Doyle apartment. "I apologize for the intrusion," he said, making every possible effort to sound sincere.

Olivia, clinging to her wariness, invited Jack in and half-heartedly extended an offer for a cup of coffee. At times she imagined she could still see the light in his eyes, but a light that could pop in and out as this one did was surely cause for skepticism. "You do understand," she said, "I won't let you talk to Ethan Allen alone, right?"

"I wouldn't ask you to," Mahoney answered.

She called Ethan Allen into the room and positioned herself between the boy and Jack Mahoney in such a way that to speak face-to-face one of them had to lean forward. They sat on the sofa, Olivia in the middle, the boy on one end, Mahoney on the other.

"I'm sorry to bother you with these questions," Mahoney said, tipping himself forward. "But it can't be helped. There's certain information required to file a report. It's a real serious thing to charge an officer with trying to intimidate a witness." His voice slid down a bit lower. "Real serious. You understand that, right?"

"Yes, sir," Ethan stammered.

"But the truth is the truth, and that's all we're looking for here."

Olivia glared at Mahoney, her way of warning him not to start badgering the boy. "My grandson always tells the truth," she said emphatically. "Don't you, dear?"

Ethan swallowed hard on that one, but gifted with his mama's way of dancing around a thing he said, "I never once lied about Mister Cobb."

"See?" Olivia grinned triumphantly.

"That's a real honorable thing," Mahoney commented, even though the boy was rumored to be a tale-teller. "Real honorable." Jack pulled a pad and pencil from his pocket. "Okay, Ethan," he said. "Why don't you tell me the complete truth of what happened when Officer Cobb was here and I'll write it down—word for word?"

Ethan looked up at Olivia, and only after she'd given a nod of approval did he start to speak. "I was doing what Grandma said, not stepping foot outside of the building, when it happened. Missus Parker— she lives down on the second floor—said she'd pay five cents for me to bring a casserole up to Mister Bailey—he lives right down the hall. I said sure, five cents is a fair amount for delivering. The dish was real hot, so I was watching where my foot was stepping and I didn't see Policeman Cobb coming up on me. First thing I heard was him yelling how he wanted a word with me. That's when I let go of the dish and took off running."

"You dropped the dish because you were frightened?"

Ethan gave a wide-eyed blink and nodded.

"Then you started running?"

"Yes, sir."

"Did Officer Cobb grab hold of you?"

"No, sir. I ran off too fast."

"How far away was Officer Cobb?"

"He was down the far end of the hall."

"And when did he catch up with you?"

"He didn't ever catch up to me. Grandma Olivia came out and batted him in the knee, and I run in the house fast as I could."

"Did you think Officer Cobb was trying to hurt you?"

Ethan Allen shrugged. "I suppose so," he said.

"Did Officer Cobb threaten you? Did he say he was gonna hurt you, anything like that?"

"He was calling for me to wait up, that's all."

Mahoney turned to Olivia. "When you encountered Officer Cobb, where was he?"

"Three or four yards behind Ethan. I heard a huge commotion, and when I opened the door Ethan flew by like the devil was after him. I could tell he was in trouble, so I grabbed the baseball bat and went at the policeman."

"Officer Cobb wasn't trying to get into your apartment?"

"He didn't have the chance."

Mahoney thanked Olivia and the boy for their time and left. After that he went door to door asking the neighbors the same sort of questions. Tobias Wassermann, who'd been the first to open the door, said the policeman asked the boy to stop. "That policeman was calling out he just wanted a word with the boy," Tobias said, "but by then all hell had broke loose, so I doubt Olivia could hear him."

Mahoney collected nine statements in all. It would have been ten, but Matilda Grimes had her television turned up so loud that she didn't hear any of the commotion. When he left the apartment building Mahoney went down to the Wyattsville Police Station and asked to see Sam Cobb.

Sam was sitting in a cell with a cast that went from ankle to thigh on his right leg and a pair of crutches leaning against the wall. "Can you get me outta here?" he said when he saw Mahoney.

Jack shook his head as if the sight of a fellow officer behind bars was more than he cared to see. "I'll try," he said. "But you sure got yourself in one hell of a mess this time."

"You think I don't know that?"

"What on earth were you thinking? Going after some kid who's probably gonna testify against your daddy? Looks like you'd know better."

"I wasn't gonna—"

"It doesn't matter what you weren't gonna do! You know what this looks like? Witness intimidation, that's what!"

"I was just gonna ask—"

"You weren't assigned to the case, so you had no right to ask!" Mahoney growled. "Your daddy's a suspect in a double murder, and you go running down the one and only eye witness. You know what that is? Crazy, that's what. Downright stupid!"

"If you've got nothing but criticism, why'd you come?"

"Because of your mama, that's why!"

"Oh, shit! She knows?"

"Yeah, she knows," Jack replied. The hard set line of his mouth gave way a bit. "She's probably the only person on earth who'd go out on a limb to help a bad-tempered pain-in-the-ass like you. Your mama believes in you. She claims this whole affair is your daddy's doing. She says you're not the type to harm a kid—"

"I'm not," Sam cut in. "I was just trying to help Pop—"

"Don't go there! With your daddy the primary suspect in that murder investigation if you so much as look cross-eyed at Ethan Allen Doyle there'll be more trouble than you ever dreamed possible."

"Somebody's got to make him tell the truth! Pop wouldn't—"

"Stay out of it!"

"But—"

"No buts!"

Before leaving the station house Jack spoke with Pete Harmon, the arresting officer, and he had a long conversation with Sergeant Gomez. He told them of his interviews with the residents at the Wyattsville Arms and his conviction that Sam had no intention of harming the boy. "He's a good man," Jack said, "a good man who's done a dumb thing. He was looking to find out the truth of what happened, that's all. I know, you know, we all know, he shouldn't have been there. But there's not a man on earth who doesn't do stupid things some time or another."

Both Pete Harmon and Sergeant Gomez nodded reassuringly. Late in the afternoon Sam Cobb was released with a warning that he was expected to head straight back to the Eastern Shore and never again come within one hundred yards of Ethan Allen Doyle. "Next time," Gomez said, "we won't be so lenient."

SCOOTER COBB

I got problems—big problems! That fucking Mahoney is out to nail me, I know it. He started with that shit about needing shoes. Next thing I know he's claiming the kid told him me and Susanna was having a thing. I should've never gotten mixed up with her and her crazy ass husband. I can say that now, but eight months ago the only thing I could think about was the itch I had morning, noon, and night.

Mahoney says the kid told him I killed Benjamin, but it's probably more of his made-up bullshit. Nobody was there. Nobody. Not the kid, not nobody. You think I'm stupid enough not to know if somebody's standing there watching?

My boy Sam's gonna find out what the kid has to say. If it's a bunch of horseshit about me and Susanna getting it on, I ain't worried. Shit like that goes on all the time. No big deal. Sam will make sure I know what's happening. He's a good boy. Real loyal. Not smart as his brother, but real loyal.

Course, if it turns out the kid really did see something—well, then...

WHEN THE TIME COMES

Because of the cast on Sam's right leg, he had to leave his car parked in front of the Wyattsville Arms apartment building and hire a yellow taxicab to drive him the full way to the Norfolk Ferry Terminal. The trip was considerably more than he'd figured on and left him with barely enough to purchase a ferry ticket. Inside the terminal he hobbled to a telephone booth and placed a call to his father's diner. "Pop," he moaned, "I got a problem." Sam explained how he'd had his knee broken and was going to require a ride home from the ferry terminal.

"What about the kid?" Scooter asked impatiently.

Misunderstanding the question, Sam answered, "Oh, he's not hurt."

"Hurt?" Scooter repeated. "I don't give a rat's ass about whether or not he's hurt. I wanna know what he's got on me. What he had to say."

"Well, he didn't actually say much…"

"Anything about seeing me beat up his old man?"

"No, but…"

"But what?" Scooter snapped. "Say what you've got to say!"

Dreading this moment, Sam mumbled, "I didn't talk to the kid."

"What the hell? You was there, right?"

"Yeah, but the grandma hit me with a baseball bat and busted my knee before I had a chance to talk to the kid."

"So, go back and talk to him."

"I can't Pop."

"Can't?!" Scooter stormed. "What kind of shit are you giving me? When I say do something, you do it! Now get your ass back there and find out what the kid knows!"

"Look, Pop, I'm real sorry about your predicament, but there's no way I'm going back. First off, I couldn't get there even if I wanted to. I've got a cast on my leg and can't drive. My car's still over there in Wyattsville. Second off, I—"

"Your car's still at the kid's place?" Scooter asked, his voice suddenly sounding considerably more tolerant. "So somebody's gotta go pick it up?"

"Eventually," Sam answered. "Right now what I need is a ride from the ferry terminal."

"No problem," Scooter said. "You gonna be on the five-thirty?"

"Yeah," Sam answered, bewildered by this sudden change of attitude.

"Okay, I'll be there. Now, what's the address for the car? I'll have somebody get it."

"You don't need to bother about that right now, Pop."

"No bother! I owe you. Now where exactly is this place?"

"Wyattsville. Take Route thirteen south 'til you pass through Richmond, then swing over to Thirty-three and go west. It's the third exit, Bolder Street. My car's parked smack in front of the Wyattsville Arms. You can't miss it."

"Wyattsville Arms, huh? Okay."

"Pop? You *are* gonna meet me at the ferry terminal, right?"

"Yeah, sure."

Ten seconds after he'd hung up the phone Scooter Cobb was behind the wheel of his car headed south toward the ferry. He'd left the diner without a word to anyone, giving no indication of where he was going or when he'd be back.

He made it to the terminal in record time, whizzed right past the parking lot, and edged into a lane of cars driving onto the Norfolk-bound ferry.

⚬━◆━⚬

When Jack Mahoney arrived back at the station house, he had two messages waiting for him. The first was from his wife who had indicated it was urgent he call home as soon as possible; the second was from Detective Pratt at the laboratory. Seeing as how his wife had specified "soon as possible," he dialed her first.

"Jack," she said tearfully, "Boomer died. He was perfectly fine one moment, and then all of a sudden he just fell over dead."

"Well, Christine," Mahoney said sympathetically, "Boomer was well on in years. Most Saint Bernards don't live twelve years. Boomer was—"

"You've got to do something," she wailed.

"Do something? What can I do? When a dog's dead, he's—"

"Boomer's in the middle of the living room floor! The kids are curled up alongside that big furry body and crying their poor little hearts out. Just listen!" Christine extended her arm and turned the telephone receiver in the direction of the living room. "You hear that?" she asked.

"I hear it," Jack answered, "but what am I supposed to do?"

"Come home. Come home, and get this dog out of here!"

"I'm in the middle of a murder investigation!"

"I don't care what you're in the middle of! Your children are contracting germs by the millions hanging onto that dog's body! You know how much they loved Boomer! Right now they're crying hysterically and working themselves into an emotional state. Is it too much to ask that you give them some consideration?"

"No," Jack sighed, "it's not too much to ask. I'll be there shortly." He hung up the receiver and sat looking at the second message for a few moments. It was five-thirty. Chances were Pratt was already gone home. Lab people weren't ones to hang around after hours unless they were in the middle of some red hot investigation, and Jack could tell Pratt didn't consider this one a priority. Nonetheless, he picked up the receiver and dialed.

"Pratt," the detective answered.

"Glad I caught you," Mahoney replied. "Anything new on the shirt?"

"We got a match. Most of the bloodstains came from the male, Benjamin Doyle, but on the left arm there were trace amounts from the female, Susanna Doyle. I sent an analysis report. You should have it by morning."

"Thanks," Mahoney said and hung up. Now he no longer had a choice. Like it or not, he had to arrest Scooter Cobb. "Poor Emma," he sighed and pushed back from his desk.

Normally, Jack would have addressed the situation with Captain Rogers immediately. He would have requested another detective to accompany him and gone directly to the diner to arrest Scooter. But there was this situation with the dog. How long, he figured, could it take to haul the dog's carcass from the living room to the back woods? He'd be back within the hour, and then he could do what he had to do.

As it turned out the children, and Christine as well, insisted upon a proper burial for Boomer. They sang three rounds of "Jesus Loves Me" and went on with a eulogy, which consisted of each child's lengthy description of loving Boomer. After it ran on for twenty minutes Jack complained, but when Christine glared across the mound of dirt with a look that could kill he kept quiet for the remainder of the service. After Christine herded all three children into the car and drove off toward Tastee-Freeze, he returned to the station house. By that time it was quarter of nine.

When he got there Paul Puglisi was the only detective still in the station house. "Are you available to go on a pick-up with me?" Mahoney asked.

"Yeah," Puglisi answered. "Who you got?"

"Scooter Cobb."

Puglisi, who was nearly the size of Scooter but in better shape, raised an eyebrow. "Whoa, boy," he said. "We're gonna have our hands full on this one. What are you bringing him in for?"

"Murder. We've got blood evidence that ties him to the Doyle killings."

"Does Sam know?"

Mahoney shook his head sorrowfully and gave a shrug. "I sure as hell hope not," he said, "because he's already got a gigantic problem."

When Mahoney and Puglisi arrived at the diner, they were expecting trouble. Knowing Scooter Cobb they expected him to heave stacks of dishes at them, slam his fist into a coffee urn and send it flying in their direction, whack a heavy boot at their shins, then punch and cuss for all he was worth. What they didn't expect was for him not to be there. "You got any idea where he is?" Mahoney asked Bertha.

"Nope," she answered. "He flew out of here like his pants was on fire, and I ain't seen or heard from him since."

"What time was that?" Puglisi asked.

"About five o'clock. It was before the dinner rush. He got a phone call and then out he went. He didn't say one word about how I'm supposed to handle the cooking and serving when people are lined up waiting for dinner. I'm one person, how am I supposed to handle—"

"You know who was on the phone?" Mahoney asked.

"You think I got X-ray hearing?"

"Did he maybe mention a name? Or a place where he'd be going?"

"No. I got better things to do than eavesdrop on other people's fighting."

"So," Puglisi said, "he was arguing with somebody?"

"Might've been. He don't tell me his business."

With thoughts of Emma jumping to his mind, Mahoney told Puglisi, "Let's check his house," and they turned to leave.

"Hey," Bertha yelled, "what about me? I'm supposed to quit at ten, and there ain't nobody here to take over. What am I supposed to do?"

"Soon as I find him, I'll let you know," Mahoney called back.

"Well, make it fast, 'cause I been on my feet all day," she grumbled. But by then they were gone.

When the two detectives arrived at the Cobb house, Emma answered the door with red-rimmed eyes and a pasted-on smile. "Would you like some coffee? Cookies, maybe?" Her voice was hollow, thin as an eggshell.

"No, thanks, Emma," Jack said sympathetically. "We're looking for Scooter."

"He's not here," she answered, registering a look of surprise. "Have you checked the diner? He ought to be there. He usually works 'til after eleven."

Jack nodded. "Bertha said he left early this evening."

"Without telling her where he'd gone?"

"I'm afraid so," Jack answered.

Puglisi, already eyeballing the room, asked, "Mind if we take a look around?"

Mahoney glanced over at his partner and gave a slight shake of his head, but Puglisi was a by-the-book man and pursued the issue. "Of course, if you got something to hide…" he said, suspicion hanging all over his words.

"Look around if you want," Emma answered. By then Puglisi had already started trekking through the house. Once he was gone from earshot, she whispered to Jack, "He's not here, I swear he's not."

"I believe you, Emma. Puglisi, he's just following procedure."

"I'd tell you if he was. I'd tell you for sure. You're the only one I've got to look out for me and Sam. I swear, Jack, I'd tell you."

He didn't say anything right off but simply took her hand in his and patted it reassuringly soft and easy, the way he would have done for his own mother had she not been dead for some fifteen years. "Don't worry about Sam," he finally said. "Things have a way of working out for the best. I spoke to Sergeant Gomez over in Wyattsville. Sam's been released and should be home sometime this evening."

Emma registered the slightest trace of a smile. "Thank you, Jack," she whispered. "Thank you."

After Puglisi had thumbed through the house and satisfied himself that Scooter was nowhere about, they left Emma and headed for Sam's apartment. Jack figured with Sam being released that afternoon, he'd probably be home by now. A man with a full cast on his leg wasn't all that mobile, he reasoned.

Sam, as they soon found out, never made it home. What they didn't know was that he was still sitting in the Eastern Shore Ferry Terminal waiting for his daddy.

You might wonder why Sam who'd been sitting there for hours hadn't called the diner to ask if his daddy had left and when he'd be arriving. But Sam knew Scooter wasn't a man to question. He got there when he got there. Argue the point, and you'd wait twice as long.

OLIVIA

*I*f a year ago somebody had told me I'd be loving an eleven-year-old boy, I'd have figured them downright crazy. Me? I'd have said. Me? A woman with a deathly fear of anything eleven and no use whatsoever for children?

Now here I sit with Ethan Allen Doyle tucked under my wing like a newborn chick, which just goes to show how little folks actually know about themselves. I suppose Charlie would be pretty surprised at this turn of events. I sure am.

Of course, I'm also frightened about what could happen. Ethan Allen's right when he says the Cobbs are worth worrying about. I don't know the father, but the son sure is a mean one. God only knows where I got the courage to take a swing at a man that big and bad-tempered. I guess when I saw him coming after Ethan Allen I didn't stop to think, I just started swinging. Well, swinging and praying that I'd be able to get my boy inside before I fainted dead away.

My boy—it's pretty ironic to hear me saying such a thing after a lifetime of running away from such a thought. I should telephone Francine Burnam and tell her about this. She of all people would get the biggest kick out of it.

THE GREATER POWER

On the way to Wyattsville Scooter Cobb drove through three red lights without so much as slowing down. "There's no way," he said out loud, "no way I'm gonna let that little shit send me to jail!" He sifted several plans through his head but it seemed the best was to catch the boy playing in the street, then go straight at the kid with the gas pedal pushed flat to the floor. Hit-and-run accidents were simply things that happened, not a crime likely to be traced back to him. Scooter Cobb pictured how he'd drive off and leave Ethan Allen lying in the street with tire tracks emblazoned across the small of his back.

Of course, by the time he arrived in Wyattsville it was almost nine o'clock and pitch dark. So dark that he failed to see Sam's car parked in front of the apartment building and drove clear to the center of town before realizing the mistake. Having to turn around and backtrack caused his disposition to grow fouler. "Son-of-a-bitch," he grumbled over and over again. By then it was so late he doubted he'd find the boy outside in the street, which meant he'd have to go to the woman's apartment.

His best bet was to get the kid outside, Scooter reasoned. Get him outside and then figure how to get rid of him. That way he could claim he was simply having a talk with Ethan Allen when the kid up and ran off. Kids like him ran off all the time. Nobody was gonna worry about it. Without the kid Mahoney had nothing.

By nine o'clock most residents of the Wyattsville Arms apartment building had settled down to watch their favorite television show or thumb through the daily newspaper. No one expected trouble. Why would they? Trouble was not a thing that came calling on folks once they were snug in their own living room with the windows locked and the door bolted for the night.

Ethan Allen did not feel the same way. He knew trouble was *most* likely to show itself in the dark of night. It came when you least expected it. It came crashing through the door and grabbed you by the throat. Then you were good as dead. He tried not to dwell on such a possibility as he lay across his bed listening to the Orioles lose the last game of the season. He couldn't help wishing he'd been able to slip away long enough to buy cartridges for the Winchester. Okay, he still had the Browning under his bed, but having a loaded Winchester would have made him feel a lot better. Ethan tried to focus his concern on the fact that the Orioles had the worst batting average in the entire American League, but it simply didn't seem to matter all that much. In the top of the ninth with the Yankees leading nine to three, he snapped off the radio and turned to a Superman comic book he'd already read so many times the cover was torn loose.

Olivia was not reading nor was she watching television. She was busy at work preparing her favorite pineapple upside down cake. The Bingo Club was having their annual bake sale and she had volunteered to provide not one but two cakes, which seemed only right seeing as how everyone had been so forgiving about Ethan Allen living at the Wyattsville Arms. The first of these creations was already in the oven when she discovered she'd run short of brown sugar. Had it been an hour earlier she could have dashed down to the market and purchased a box, but now with everything closed she would have to try and borrow some. The first person she called was Clara. "Brown sugar?" Clara replied. "Why, I've not used that in years." She suggested Olivia try white sugar mixed in with a cup or two of maple syrup. "Now, I've got *plenty* of maple syrup," Clara said.

"No, thanks," Olivia answered, and then she set about calling a number of other people. As it turned out Barbara Conklin had a brand new box of brown sugar, one that was not yet opened. "Oh, would you mind?" Olivia asked.

"Not at all," Barbara answered. "I was just about to step into the tub.

Soon as I finish my bath and dry off, I'll bring it up."

Olivia would have happily run downstairs to fetch the sugar herself or sent Ethan Allen for it, but knowing Barbara Conklin to be a person insistent upon doing things in her own good time, she decided to wait. *She'll be here soon enough,* Olivia reasoned, as she set about mixing the batter. When the doorbell rang fifteen minutes later, she figured it to be Barbara and flung the door open without inquiring as to who was on the other side.

Standing there was a man half again the size of Sam Cobb; his face had a look of meanness too impossible to imagine. Olivia knew without asking: the man was Scooter Cobb. She instantly tried to bang shut the door, but such a thing was like trying to un-mix cake batter. What was done was done, and there was no undoing it.

"Where's the kid?" he growled.

Fear grabbed hold of Olivia and without thinking she fell back a step. Almost immediately she realized the move was a grave mistake, for now the baseball bat positioned alongside the door was beyond her reach. Scooter took advantage of the opportunity and pushed his way inside the apartment. He slammed the door behind him with such force it sent the hall table and potted plant flying.

Ethan Allen bolted upright when he heard the noise. An apprehensive growl was rumbling in Dog's throat, but the boy whispered, "Shh" and held a finger to his mouth. He then waited, listening to make certain he'd heard what he thought he heard.

"Where's the kid?" Scooter shouted this time, his voice booming so thunderously it rolled through to the living room and rattled the pictures on the wall.

"He's not here," Olivia answered, reaching for every ounce of courage she possessed. "He's gone, gone someplace safe."

Ethan Allen glanced over at the window. He could easily enough raise the sash, step out onto the fire escape, and disappear down the metal stairs. Scooter would never be any the wiser. Then what? With Scooter being the sort of man to take his frustration out on somebody, that somebody would be Grandma Olivia. Ethan's thoughts flashed back to the image of Benjamin being beaten and tossed about like a broken doll. That night he'd done nothing. He'd just let it happen. But this time would be different. With his heart thundering like a kettle drum, he climbed from the bed and reached for the Browning. As quietly as possible, he cracked it open and checked the two buckshot shells in the side by side chambers. He closed the gun and released the safety.

"Well, now," Scooter said to Olivia, "you're just gonna have to tell me where that place is, aren't you?" The sound of his voice was heavy and threatening.

"No," she answered, the word trembling through her throat. "The child is gone, and that's all there is to it."

Ethan Allen was more frightened than he'd thought humanly possible. He felt like his stomach could slide out his back end at any minute. Even so, he raised the Browning into position and wedged the butt of the shotgun tight against his shoulder. With his hands trembling and a line of perspiration sliding down his back, he took a step forward. If he'd had the Winchester he could've counted on felling Scooter Cobb with a single shot. That was a rifle meant for killing. But all the Browning would give off was a spray of buckshot, scattered about in every which direction. With the Browning he'd be lucky to kill a squirrel, but a man of that size, never. Yet if he didn't do something…

"Lady, you are *so* wrong," Scooter shouted angrily. "That's not all there is to it! You're gonna tell me where that kid is, or you're gonna get the shit kicked outta you!" He moved a step closer.

Olivia was hoping—no, praying—that Ethan Allen would not try something foolish, that he'd have the good sense to slip out the window and go for help. He had to have heard Scooter's voice by now. Surely that would drive him away. She prayed the boy would run, run fast enough to escape the ugliness that was coming. If she could hold Scooter Cobb back for a few minutes he'd have time enough to get away, time enough to find a place and hide. "Just go away," Olivia told Scooter. "Leave the boy alone. He's already had enough misery."

"You and him is both gonna learn something about *real* misery if you don't quick tell me where he's gone!"

"He ran off this morning. I have no idea where he is," Olivia answered. "Now leave here or I'm calling the police!"

Ethan pushed his bedroom door open and silently inched his way along the back side of the foyer wall. Maybe he'd be lucky. Maybe the Browning would stun Scooter enough that he and Olivia could get away. Hopefully the spray of buckshot wouldn't hit her. Hopefully the old shotgun wouldn't explode in his face.

Scooter gave a loud laugh. Not the chuckling sort you'd expect to hear when a thing is funny, but a laugh that was mean as mean can be. "You're gonna call the police on *me?!*" he shouted uproariously and then charged toward Olivia. He slapped a huge hand down on her shoulder before she had time to make a move. In one fleeting second—a second you would believe too short to have any thought, let alone one so profound—she suddenly knew why Ethan Allen was so deathly afraid of this man. With his right hand still clamped to her shoulder, Scooter balled his left into a fist and drew back. Olivia was too petrified to do anything. She tried to pull loose, but he had a firm grip. Nothing would stop him now. It was too late. Nothing could...

Like a lightning flash Dog came flying through the air, snarling, yapping, aiming himself at the attacker. Scooter didn't let go of Olivia's shoulder, but his grip loosened the slightest bit as he turned toward the sound. She stumbled backward. The heel of her shoe caught onto a bit of carpet and then over she went, the weight of her body jerking her loose from Scooter's grasp. Just as she slammed into the floor, Ethan Allen stepped from behind the wall and fired. For a moment Scooter Cobb stood there looking bewildered. Then he toppled over.

Ethan Allen's heart catapulted from its rightful spot and began spinning like a whirligig. He wobbled back and forth for a moment, then fell backward onto the floor.

As it turned out, he had simply fainted dead away when the sound of the explosion rocketed through his head. When he came to, Olivia was fanning her hand in front of his face and calling out his name. "Are you okay, Ethan?" she asked, but he was unsure of how to answer.

After a few moments it started to come back. He remembered shooting Scooter Cobb. He'd been scared—so scared he thought he'd die—'but he'd pulled the trigger anyway. He sat up to make sure of what he'd done. Sure enough there was Scooter Cobb, sprawled out across the foyer, with the biggest part of his chest blown away. A stream of tears began rolling down Ethan's face. "I did it, Grandma," he said proudly. "This time I wasn't no coward. I didn't run off and hide. I saved your life, didn't I, Grandma?"

Olivia saw a look of pride in the boy's eyes. He was reaching out for her love and giving more than she ever dreamed possible. The shell had cracked open and he was trusting her with what he'd held inside. "Yes, Ethan," she answered, "you surely did save my life." Then she tearfully hugged him to her chest.

When the sound of the shots echoed through the building, a fair number of the neighbors had been roused. Fred McGinty was frantically pounding on the door. "What's going on in there?" he shouted.

"Shush," Olivia hissed in Ethan Allen's ear. "Don't you say a word." She knew such a thing could be viewed as murder, even when the man was mean as Scooter Cobb, even if he deserved whatever he got. The circumstances didn't matter. They had a dead body on their hands. A dead body with a blown-apart hole in the middle of his chest. A man the size of Scooter Cobb wasn't something that could be swept under the rug or slid down the incinerator.

"Go away, Fred," Olivia called back. "We're okay."

Clara pushed past Fred and began her own fist-pounding. "You open up this door, Olivia Doyle!" she screamed. "Open it this minute!"

"Go home, Clara," Olivia answered.

"Don't you tell *me* go home! I heard gunshots! You'd better open this door!"

"*Please*," Olivia begged, "don't get involved. There's been an accident, but Ethan's not hurt. Both of us are all right."

"Accident?" Clara screamed and took to rattling the door so furiously that Olivia worried it might pop loose from its hinges.

"If you want to help," Olivia shouted, "go home and call for the police!"

Claiming that under no circumstances was she leaving, Clara sent Fred to place the call and stayed where she was, pressing her ear to the door. "I'm listening to what's going on in there," she called out, which caused Olivia to start speaking in a whisper.

"Ethan," she whispered, "you've got to do *exactly* as I say, and you've got to do it without one word of disagreement." She pulled the boy close enough to hear the hum of his heartbeat and said, "We've got to keep what happened here a secret. A secret that is just between the two of us."

"But, Grandma..." Ethan gave a sigh of disappointment.

"Believe me, sweetheart, I'm *real* proud of you. You saved my life, and you are without a doubt the bravest person I've ever known."

"So why can't we tell nobody?"

"Because if the police suspect you shot Scooter Cobb, it could lead to a whole mess of trouble. Even if you didn't get sent to jail you'd have a black mark against you, and that could last your whole life long."

"I don't care about no black marks."

"Not now maybe, but someday you will. I'm old. I've already done most everything I'm gonna do, so I've got less to risk. Besides, the police might say you shot Scooter Cobb because of what he did to your daddy, and they could consider that murder!"

Ethan sat there wide-eyed, taking in every word she spoke.

"Me," she said. "Well, now, I had no grudge against the man, so I can claim it was self defense. I'll say he tried to break into my apartment, and I had to shoot him. There it is, plain and simple!"

Ethan had to admit it did seem a better plan. "But," he said, "nobody's gonna know I saved your life."

"You know," she answered. "You know and I know. That's what really matters."

The boy gave her a smile that stretched the full width of his face.

Three times Olivia went over the way it would be told. She tried to think through any loose ends, tried to make sure there wasn't some detail that would jump out the minute she started explaining what happened. Once that was done, she wiped the Browning clean, took it in her hands, held it to her shoulder in position for shooting, and fingered both triggers. She pressed her fingers firm against the butt, then the barrel, and as she was doing so she asked, "Where'd you get this thing?"

"The storage bin in the basement," Ethan answered.

"Seth Porter's storage bin?"

He nodded.

"This is his gun?"

He nodded again.

"I told you not to go pilfering that stuff," Olivia said, even though inside her heart she was thankful the boy had taken the gun that saved both their lives.

Given the circumstances she had to alert Seth Porter. "I'm terribly sorry to involve you," Olivia explained over the telephone, "but I'll have to tell the police the gun is yours. I'll say I borrowed it, borrowed it because I was fearful for my life."

"What gun?" asked Seth Porter, a man deaf in one ear.

"The Browning shotgun that was in your storage bin. I'm ashamed to say I took it without asking, and I'd prefer to tell the police it was *borrowed*."

"That old Browning? What would you want with that thing? It's likely as not rusted through. If you're looking to borrow a gun, what you want is—"

"Thanks, Seth, but I've already made use of the Browning," Olivia sighed, then hung up.

When the Wyattsville police arrived Clara was still standing outside the apartment with her ear pressed to the door, but she'd been unable to hear a single word of what was going on. Once the door was finally opened there in the foyer was a mountainous hulk of a man, dead as dead could be, and spilling blood all over the carpet.

By then Ethan Allen was dressed in pajamas. His bedspread had been folded back and the pillow crumpled to match the shape of his head. Still wearing the dress splattered with Scooter's blood, Olivia was sitting on the sofa. She was trying valiantly to hold onto her composure although her fingers, having a mind of their own, were twitching and twiddling. "Clara," she said, "perhaps you should take Ethan Allen back to your place. This isn't something a boy of his age should see."

Clara grabbed hold of Ethan's hand, but before they were out the door the police sergeant said the boy had to stay until they'd heard his version of what happened. A rookie named Timothy Michaels was on his first full tour of duty that night, and he'd turned queasy at the sight of Scooter's body. Taking note of his condition, Clara asked, "Would you care for some Pepto-Bismol? Or tea maybe?"

Officer Michaels shook his head, and then with Clara leading the way he tromped off to ask if the neighbors had seen or heard anything. The questioning of Olivia was left for Sergeant Gomez to handle.

After having released Sam Cobb earlier in the day Gomez breathed a sigh of relief when he arrived at the Wyattsville Arms apartment building and discovered the attacker was Scooter Cobb, not Sam. Knowing Mahoney had identified the elder Cobb as a murder suspect, Gomez immediately put in a call to the Eastern Shore Precinct. For hours Mahoney had been bouncing from bar to bar in an effort to find Scooter. When he heard the news of what had happened, he turned the car around and headed for the mainland. He pulled onto the last ferry of the night with not a minute to spare.

Gomez was a man with a bushy black mustache. He was low to the ground and round as a pumpkin, as different from Charlie Doyle as a man could possibly be. But when he spoke Olivia could swear it was the voice of her dead husband. "There are questions I have to ask," he said, "but it's simply so that we can get an understanding of what happened here. It's nothing to worry about."

Already a nervous wreck, Olivia broke into tears.

"Now, now," Gomez said and patted her hand in the most comforting manner.

Olivia's sobbing grew louder.

"This is routine procedure," he assured her. "There's no reason—"

"I'm sorry," she sniffled, "it's just that you remind me of Charlie."

"Charlie?"

"My husband, Ethan's grandfather." She immediately segued into a lengthy tale of what happened—not an explanation of how Scooter Cobb was shot to death in her foyer, but the story of how Charlie had died of a heart attack while they were still on their honeymoon.

"That is a tragedy," Sergeant Gomez said sympathetically, "but let's get back to what happened here tonight."

"Well," Olivia said, "I was in the kitchen preparing pineapple upside down cakes for the bake sale…" She hesitated a moment and asked if he'd care to have a piece. When the sergeant shook his head, she continued. "That's when the doorbell rang. After Sam Cobb was here last night I borrowed a shotgun from Seth Porter, and I had it right here on the hallway table. When I opened the door and saw who it was, I grabbed hold of the gun."

"He was the one at the door," Gomez pointed to the body. "Right?"

She nodded.

"So why'd you open the door?"

"I thought it was my downstairs neighbor, Barbara Conklin, delivering the box of sugar I'd asked to borrow."

"You have a neighbor who looks like him?"

"Barbara doesn't look anything like him! I just didn't look."

"Do you normally do that—open the door before you check through the peephole to see who's standing there?"

"No!" she answered indignantly. "But I was busy in the kitchen, and I figured for sure it was Barbara. I'd spoken with her a few minutes earlier and she said she'd be up in a few minutes, so—"

"What did he say when you opened the door?"

"Say? He didn't say much of anything, just came charging at me."

"That's when you shot him?"

"Yes. If someone came charging at you, wouldn't you shoot them?"

Sergeant Gomez gave her a deadpan look and didn't answer.

The detective was wearing an expression that concerned Olivia. His mouth was stretched straight across and eyes narrowed. She began to worry that he might have seen some incriminating bit of evidence she'd missed, or maybe she'd said something that gave him cause to doubt the truth of her story. "He was nine times my size," she blurted out nervously. "If I hadn't shot him, he would have killed me—me and my grandson both! If it were you, would *you* stand there and let an intruder murder *your* family?"

"So you thought he was an intruder?" Gomez asked.

"Absolutely! The way that man charged at me, I knew he was here to do us harm. Look at this," Olivia slid back the shoulder of her blouse to show the mark of Scooter's hand, which was already turning purple. "I had to protect Ethan Allen. He's already lost his parents. I'm all he's got."

Gomez glanced over at the huge body, then back to Olivia. "How could you get to the shotgun and take aim with him standing so close?"

This was the question she'd been dreading, the make or break believing of her story. Olivia knew she had to watch every word. A line of perspiration was already rising up along her forehead, but her hands were colder than a chunk of ice. "It happened so quickly," she said. "I can't swear to the *exact* order of things. All I remember is that I reached for the shotgun the minute I saw him, and then he grabbed me by the shoulder—"

"Where was the gun?"

"On the hallway table."

"Isn't it a bit unusual to have a shotgun on the hallway table?"

"I wanted it there for our protection. Ethan Allen had been attacked once by this man's son, and I was afraid he'd come back here and—"

"Okay, okay. Then what happened?"

"I tried to get loose, but my shoe got caught in the carpet and I tripped. As I was falling down, I squeezed the trigger as hard as possible and the gun went off."

"Let's see if I got this right," Gomez said, a considerable amount of doubt mingled in with the words. "While you were falling you were able to fire both barrels?"

"Yes," she answered. "You see, I didn't fall straight back, I sort of stumbled, then fell. So the first time I pulled the trigger, I was still in the process of stumbling."

"Well, now," Gomez said shaking his head as if he'd heard something beyond believing. "That's truly amazing. You were off-balance and unfamiliar with the gun, yet you were able to pump two shotgun shells into your assailant."

"God must've been on my side," Olivia replied, figuring a mention of the Almighty would make her seem a bit less culpable.

"Where was the boy when all of this was happening?"

"In bed, sound asleep."

"The commotion didn't wake him?"

"The sound of the shots did. When he came to see what was going on, he told me this man was Scooter Cobb."

"Hmm," Gomez fingered his chin pensively. "And you say you've never before handled a shotgun? No target practice? No other shooting experience?"

"Not really," Olivia said. "but the Good Lord—"

"I know, was on your side," Gomez reiterated. "Well, what about the boy? Does he know how to use a gun? Has he maybe done some hunting?"

"He's eleven! An eleven-year-old boy has no business with a gun!"

"Maybe not in town, but on a farm—"

"The boy had nothing to do with this. It was me. I shot Scooter Cobb. Shot him because he was breaking into my house. That's all there is to it."

"Would you be willing to take a lie detector test?"

"I most certainly will not," she answered. "You have no right—"

"Whoa," Gomez said, "it was just a question. With a shooting like this, it's routine. It just helps us to determine the truth right off."

"I've already told you the truth!"

"The lie detector is just to confirm—"

"No!"

After he'd finished with Olivia Sergeant Gomez questioned Ethan, but the boy did just as he'd been instructed. He swore he was sound asleep and didn't hear a thing. "No doorbell ringing? No shouting?

Arguing maybe? You hear any of that?" Gomez asked, but Ethan shook his head repeatedly. The few things Ethan did make mention of matched what Olivia said, word for word.

The rookie returned long about the time Gomez gave up on questioning Olivia and Ethan Allen. "A few of the neighbors claim they heard gunshots," he said, "but nobody saw anything. Fred McGinty, the man who lives directly beneath this apartment, he's the one who called the police. He claims he heard a commotion coming from this apartment, then gunshots. That's when he called it in."

"So nobody knows nothing," Gomez said, shaking his head in disgust.

The crime scene investigation detectives had all but finished by the time Jack Mahoney arrived. He pulled Gomez aside and asked, "What have we got?" .

The detective shrugged. "A questionable self-defense shooting."

"Questionable?"

"It's all just too pat. Nobody saw nothing. Nobody saw this guy come into the building, nobody saw him force his way into the apartment. The woman claims she opens the door thinking it's a neighbor, and Scooter Cobb is standing there. Now, she just happens to have a shotgun lying on the hall table so when he attacks her she bangs off two shots, one of which nails him square in the middle of the chest. She does all of this while she's struggling to get loose from a guy who's three times her size. Pretty skillful for somebody who's supposedly never before used a shotgun—no?"

Mahoney, with a grin playing at the corner of his mouth, shrugged. "What about ballistics?" he asked. "You got anything there?"

"Not likely. I'm sure her prints are all over the shotgun, but the way that buckshot splattered, the lab guys are just gonna be guessing at the trajectory."

"I think she just might be telling the truth," Mahoney said. "Scooter Cobb's a mean old bastard. I wouldn't doubt he came here to kill her and the boy. There's an arrest warrant out for Cobb and enough evidence to prove he was the one who murdered the boy's daddy. Let me tell you, that was a brutal affair. About the worst I've ever seen."

"You think maybe the kid shot Cobb for revenge?"

Mahoney shrugged. "Anything's possible, I suppose."

"Hmmm..." Gomez raised an eyebrow. "You figure if I push harder on the woman or the boy, I might get at the truth?"

"I doubt it," Mahoney said. "I truly doubt it."

Of course, Gomez didn't give up quite that easily. For weeks on end he'd come knocking on Olivia's door with some other question he'd forgotten to ask. Two months after the shooting he gathered together a flimsy packet of evidence and presented it to the district attorney. "The kid did the shooting, I'm certain of it," he said, hoping to get the go ahead on an indictment.

"Are you kidding?" the district attorney asked. "In an election year you want me to indict some little kid on this kind of crappy evidence?" He accused Gomez of wasting the tax payers' money and told him it was time to move on.

Afterwards the question of whether Olivia was telling the truth slid into oblivion, and that was the end of that.

JACK MAHONEY

I've worked many a case during my twenty years on the force, but never one quite as loose-ended as the Doyle murders. My gut tells me the kid's story is true, but now that Scooter Cobb is dead we'll never know the absolute truth of what came about. One thing I can say for sure. There's a sizeable amount of grief attached to the Cobbs.

Sam left the force. He's running his daddy's diner now, but with that bad leg of his he's gotta sit more than stand. Emma, poor woman, sold the house and moved off to Connecticut to live with her sister. The Doyle place went for taxes. Benjamin was up to his ears in debt, so there wasn't really anything left to hold on to. I doubt the kid much cared. Neither he nor his grandma had any interest in coming back here, and I can't say that I blame them.

Olivia Doyle swore up and down she was the one who shot Scooter Cobb and did so because he was trying to break into her house. Gomez had his suspicions about the truth of her story but couldn't get anyone to say otherwise. He finally gave up trying. Me? I don't doubt she's covering for the boy, but listen, the kid's already gone through enough. And besides, Scooter Cobb probably got what he deserved.

Christine always says the Almighty doles out His own kind of justice, and you know what? I'm beginning to think she's right.

THIRTY-TWO YEARS LATER

E than Allen Doyle, who for the past three years has presided over Richmond County Family Court, is said to be the fairest Judge in all of Virginia. He is also the youngest ever appointed to the bench. Some claim it was the influence of his grandmother that gave him a uniquely strong character. Others believe he was simply born with a clarity of purpose. One thing is for certain: the youngsters who appear before him seldom walk away without a better understanding of life.

Once a year Judge Doyle's courtroom is closed. No cases are heard, no young boys admonished to watch their language, no children reset upon a pathway that's more straight and narrow. That day is always the eleventh of April, the anniversary of when his grandmother passed away. On that day Judge Doyle, his wife, Laura, and their two boys visit the cemetery and place a large bouquet of flowers beside the headstone that reads "Olivia Ann Doyle, Wife of Charles and Beloved Grandmother of Ethan Allen." On this, the fifth anniversary of her death, they do as they have always done.

Spring is late this year. Some of the streams are still frozen, and there are no crocuses poking their heads from beneath the soil. On this particular morning there is a bitter chill in the air and a wind that tears through overcoats like the pointy tip of an icicle. But Laura bundles the boys in warm parkas, and off they go.

Their first stop is the florist where, despite the fact that cut flowers are astronomically expensive this year, Judge Doyle buys a bouquet of twenty-seven long-stemmed red roses—one for each year that he and his grandmother shared.

The younger boy, Charles, was but a baby when she died, so he has no memory of his great-grandmother. Oliver, the elder of the two, barely remembers her. Their father, Ethan Allen, remembers her with more love than it seems possible for a heart to hold. "I surely do miss you, Grandma," he sighs as he bows his head before the grey headstone with an angel carved into the face of it.

"How come Daddy always says that?" Charles asks his mother.

She looks over at her husband and smiles. Ethan takes hold of the boy's hand and answers, "Because I do miss her. Your great-grandma was quite a woman."

Laura can tell by the upturned corners of Ethan's mouth that he's remembering the way it was. Soon he will, as he always does, launch into stories of the years they spent together—the boy and his grandmother, a woman who at one point claimed to have no use for children and then risked everything to protect him.

"I'm named after her," the eight-year-old Oliver boasts.

"So what?" Charles answers. "I'm named after Grandpa Charlie!"

"Big deal," Oliver taunts. "Grandma Olivia is the one Daddy loved most."

"Boys," Laura chides, and they stop bickering.

"You're right, Oliver," Ethan finally says. "I did love Grandma Olivia the most, but that was because I never knew Grandpa Charlie. Grandma did, and she said he was the finest man who ever walked the earth. She loved him until the day she died. A person has to be pretty special to warrant that kind of loving, don't you think?"

Charles gives a get-even grin.

"Daddy had a special secret with Grandma Olivia," says Oliver, needing to have the last word. "Right, Dad?"

"That's right, son. A very special secret."

"Tell us the secret," Charles whines.

"If I did that it wouldn't be a secret anymore, would it?" Ethan says. He squats beside the grey tombstone and traces his fingers along the etching of his grandmother's name.

How easily it all comes back to mind—his mama dead without ever once seeing New York City, his daddy beaten so viciously that he was no longer recognizable. Ethan Allen had stood by and let those things happen. What could he do he reasoned, he was just a kid. But then there was that fateful night. The night he finally found enough courage to protect a person he loved. Killing wasn't a thing to be proud of, but he was proud. He was proud of being able to set his fear aside and do what had to be done to save his grandma. He was proud enough to have shouted from rooftops his doing of such a deed. But Grandma Olivia saw it differently. She wanted to protect him as he had protected her. Only three people knew the truth of what happened that night. Two of them had died without telling, and if that was the way Grandma Olivia wanted it to be, he also would take the secret to his grave.

Ethan silently says the words to the Lord's Prayer; then he stands and turns to leave. In the misty grey of an April morning, with his wife walking alongside and his boys bounding several steps ahead, Ethan turns back and whispers, "I love you, Grandma."

"I love you too," Olivia answers, but of course the words came to him only as a thought. A remembrance of her having said those words countless times before. She said it at night when she tucked him into bed, mornings as she sent him off to school, the day he graduated high school, the day he graduated law school, the day he got married, when each of the boys was born. She'd said it a million times, maybe ten million. Little wonder the memory of her saying such a thing is so easy to call to mind.

HEAVEN

Olivia and Charlie Doyle linked hands as they watched Ethan Allen and his family leave the cemetery. *You can surely be proud of the way you raised that boy,* Charlie said without speaking the words. For in heaven words are unnecessary. Thoughts simply float from a person's heart and settle where intended.

I am, Olivia responded.

He's wrong, Charlie said. *Wrong in thinking only three of you knew what happened that night. After I was forced to leave the earth so suddenly, I began watching over you. I watched over you every minute of your life, including that night. I knew you were telling the truth when you told Detective Gomez you'd been the one to do the shooting.*

Olivia smiled the smile of angels. Not so much an upturning of lips, but a warm thought that floated across in the same manner as words.

Charlie knew the truth of what happened. He knew that Ethan Allen fired off the first shot then fainted dead away. Scooter Cobb had been hit in the side, hit hard enough to be stunned and fall over, but not hard enough to stay down. The man had barely hit the floor before he was pushing himself back up and coming at Ethan Allen. Olivia, who had tripped and fallen back onto the carpet, saw what was happening, scrambled across, grabbed hold of the shotgun, and fired the second barrel of the Browning square into Scooter Cobb's chest. She fired when he was less than five feet from the boy. When that shot hit, it ripped the man's chest open and cut through to his backbone. The second shot was the one that killed Scooter Cobb.

You never told the boy the truth of what happened that night, Charlie thought, directing the words to Olivia.

No, she answered, *I didn't. I knew he got far more joy from believing he'd saved my life than he could have ever gotten from knowing I'd saved his.*

A soft chuckle touched down in Olivia's heart, and she understood it came from Charlie. They kissed in the manner of angels, a touching of hearts rather than lips. Then they turned their eyes back to earth, to the Pancake Palace where the Doyle family was having breakfast.

Ethan Allen had just finished a cup of coffee, turned to the two boys, and said, "Did I ever tell you about the time your great-grandma…"

ACKNOWLEDGMENTS

For I know the plans I have for you declares The Lord…
Plans to prosper you and not to harm you,
plans to give you hope and a future.
Jeremiah 29-11

Writing a novel is never easy; writing a novel that explores both the good and bad in people offers an even greater challenge and I could not have done it alone. Every day I thank Our Heavenly Father for blessing me with the talent to do this and giving my heart the encouragement to go on. I hope you'll forgive me when my characters use profanity; it's part of who they are. Without exposure to the darker aspects of humankind, there is no barometer by which to measure the goodness, generosity and love we have all been gifted with.

I also want to thank the people who have contributed to the story development of this book. I am extremely grateful to Joanne Bliven for working with me to refine the language and characteristics of an underprivileged child. I thank my friend and fellow author Sunny Serafino for her wise advice and editorial guidance; and I thank Geri Conway for reading every word I write, always believing in me, being my sister and helping me to remember the sage advice of our Southern Mama. And, as always I thank the wonderful women of my book club—

for being avid readers, astute listeners, caring friends and an unending source of inspiration.

Lastly, I thank my husband Richard, for reasons too numerous to list; but most of all for loving me and being the best life partner a woman could ever wish for.

FROM THE AUTHOR

If you enjoyed reading this book, please post a review at your favorite on-line retailer and share your thoughts with other readers.

I'd love to hear from you. If you visit my website and sign up to receive my monthly newsletter, as a special thank you, you'll receive an e-book copy of "Stories" – A behind the scenes look at the inspiration behind each novel.

To sign up for the newsletter, visit:
http://betteleecrosby.com

The Books in the Wyattsville series include:

SPARE CHANGE
Book One in the Wyattsville Series

JUBILEE'S JOURNEY
Book Two in the Wyattsville Series

PASSING THROUGH PERFECT
Book Three in the Wyattsville Series

THE REGRETS OF CYRUS DODD
Book Four in the Wyattsville Series

BEYOND THE CAROUSEL
Book Five in the Wyattsville Series

ALSO BY THE AUTHOR

THE MEMORY HOUSE SERIES
Memory House

The Loft

What the Heart Remembers

Baby Girl

Silver Threads

THE SERENDIPITY SERIES
The Twelfth Child

Previously Loved Treasures

STAND ALONE STORIES
Cracks in the Sidewalk

What Matters Most

Wishing for Wonderful

Blueberry Hill, A Sister's Story

About the Author

AWARD-WINNING NOVELIST BETTE LEE CROSBY brings the wit and wisdom of her Southern Mama to works of fiction—the result is a delightful blend of humor, mystery and romance.

"Storytelling is in my blood," Crosby laughingly admits, "My mom was not a writer, but she was a captivating storyteller, so I find myself using bits and pieces of her voice in most everything I write."

Crosby's work was first recognized in 2006 when she received The National League of American Pen Women Award for a then unpublished manuscript. Since then, she has gone on to win numerous other awards, including The Reviewer's Choice Award, The Reader's Favorite Gold Medal, FPA President's Book Award Gold Medal and The Royal Palm Literary Award.

To learn more about Bette Lee Crosby, explore her other work, or read a sample from any of her books, visit her blog at:

http://betteleecrosby.com

32648718R00163

Made in the USA
Middletown, DE
06 January 2019